SKYROCKET

Books by *Eugenia Sheppard* and *Earl Blackwell*

SKYROCKET

CRYSTAL CLEAR

SKYROCKET
A Novel About Glamour and Power

Eugenia Sheppard
&
Earl Blackwell

DOUBLEDAY & COMPANY, INC.
GARDEN CITY, NEW YORK
1980

ISBN: 0-385-15695-2
Library of Congress Catalog Card Number 79–8012

To New York, the city that adopted a girl
from the Midwest and a boy from the South,
and helped them, as well as thousands
of others, launch their skyrockets.

PART ONE

CHAPTER ONE

"The helicopter is ready on the south lawn of the White House. Now the President is coming out of the door after saying good-bye to the White House staff. With him are Mrs. Nixon, who is managing a brave smile, and their daughters, Julie and Tricia, with their husbands, David Eisenhower and Edward Cox. A royal red carpet has been laid down all the way to the helicopter, and it is lined on both sides with an honor guard from the military services. Waiting for them at the end of the carpet is Gerald Ford with his wife, Betty."

All over the country millions were watching Schuyler Madison on UBC's special broadcast. They were listening to the voice they had grown to count on for truth, seasoned with sympathy, understanding and humor. United Broadcasting Company's evening-news program with Schuyler Madison had become one of the most popular television half hours in the country.

Madison continued, "Julie Eisenhower throws her arms around her father and kisses him. David Eisenhower and Gerald Ford are kissing Mrs. Nixon, and there's Betty Ford embracing the President. Now the President's party is climbing into the helicopter that will take them to Andrews Air Force base, where the big silver-and-blue plane awaits to fly them to California. . . . At the last moment, the President reaches out for the Vice President's hand, shakes it warmly, and then touches Mr. Ford's elbow with his left hand. It's like a football coach sending in a substitute."

A double screen showed the helicopter and a head shot of Madison as he spoke again: "The President is the last to board. He mounts the steps and, though his eyes have been filled with

tears many times this morning, he raises his hand in what seems
to be a gesture of victory."

Madison's face suddenly occupied the entire screen. He looked
directly into the camera and his usually pleasant face was sol-
emn: "And may I remind you, ladies and gentlemen, that this is
the first time in the history of our country that a President has
resigned."

As he finished his broadcast, Schuyler Madison picked up his
glasses and gathered his papers together. The red light flashed
off, which meant he was off camera. He pulled a handkerchief
from his pocket and began to mop his forehead. He turned to his
producer, Oliver Prince. "Poor Bastard. It needn't have happened
if he'd come out with the truth."

"You did a great job, Sky." Oliver Prince slapped him on the
back. "The boss and I were watching the other networks, too,
and we were on top as always."

"That's good." Sky looked pleased.

"They were all pretty lenient, but most of the country still
thinks he had it coming to him."

Sky's smile faded. "I pity the poor devil going home in that big
Air Force jet with his tail between his legs, and just two years
ago he was one of the world's great heroes when he stepped out
of that very same plane in China."

"Well, it's one President down, but another coming up." Oliver
Prince looked at his watch. "We've only an hour and a half before the Ford inauguration."

As he left the studio and made his way to the elevator that
would take him to his office, Schuyler Madison was stopped right
and left by editors, reporters, cameramen, secretaries, office boys
and receptionists congratulating him on his broadcast.

From the time he had come to UBC from California, where he
had had his own local news and feature program, he had been
liked and respected by the staff. The girls swooned over his good
looks, and the men found him a hard worker with a minimum of
star temperament.

His private office in the building, several floors above the studio, was a real hideaway. It was totally undecorated, except for
an oversize table desk. Suspended over the desk were three television sets so that while he worked he could easily watch what

the other networks were doing. The rest of the room was a clutter of books and papers and a couch on which he sometimes stretched out during the occasional marathon of broadcasts, such as Watergate had been recently. His secretary occupied an adjoining room and beyond were his editor and three assistants as well as a more formal office for interviews, decorated to look like the kind of setting the public might expect him to have.

He sat down at his desk and began looking through the wire copy that had been placed there, when his secretary came to the door. "Former Governor Harrison Kirby has been trying to reach you, Mr. Madison."

"That's a surprise. What the hell could he want?"

"He has called twice from Washington."

"I haven't seen Harrison Kirby since I was working for CBS Radio in Europe, and that was just after the war. He was the U.S. ambassador to France then."

"He said it was important."

"That's what everyone says, isn't it?"

She laughed. "Yes, I guess I hear it at least twenty-five times a day." She tore a piece of paper from her notepad and handed it to him. "Both *Time* and *Newsweek* called. They say it's important for them to have a statement from you about whether or not the top brass at United Broadcasting Company in any way influenced your point of view on the Nixon resignation. They must have it as soon as possible."

"They're getting a definite denial from me, of course." He turned to his typewriter. "I'll write what I want to say. You can tell them to send messengers, unless they want you to give it to them over the phone."

He had just written a few words on his typewriter when his secretary reappeared. "It's the Kirby call from Washington again, Mr. Madison."

He picked up the receiver, and Diana Kirby's familiar English voice came over the wire. "Sky, darling, how wonderful to hear your voice again. Not that I haven't been hearing it regularly and admiring your broadcasts, and especially this week."

"Thank you, Diana."

"Harrison has been trying to call you all morning. Now he has had to run off to a luncheon in the Senate dining room, and I said I would try to get through to you."

"I've been on camera most of the morning and just received his message."

"We realize how hectic life must be for you these days, but Harrison is coming up to New York on Monday and feels he must talk to you. He told me to ask if you could meet him for luncheon at 21."

"That's kind of him, Diana, but I have a hard-and-fast rule about not lunching out. I stay right here in the office. I've found it's the only quiet time possible for me, not only to think of the evening broadcast, but also to plan ahead."

"Of course, Sky, but this is not a social luncheon. It's terribly important, as you will see."

"I've never made an exception. Once you start, it becomes harder to say no."

"I care very much for you, Sky, and I would be the last to ask you to break your rule if I didn't believe that it was for your benefit." She paused and her voice became stronger. "Harrison has a wonderful idea that could change your whole life. Please see him."

"I will, of course, Diana."

"Then I'll tell him one-thirty at 21."

When he arrived at the restaurant the following Monday, he found Diana already ensconced at the No. 1 corner table on the second floor. She was busy with her little mirror and lipstick and as he approached the table, he could see that she was as eye-catching as ever, not the skinny, chic, contemporary type, but a woman who was all softness and curves. The red-gold hair that she was famous for was freshly arranged in the proper curves around her oval face with the fabulous pink-and-white English skin. She was wearing a linen dress in a mauve shade that had become her favorite since so many men had told her that it matched her violet eyes.

"What a surprise, Diana. I hadn't expected to see you here." He leaned across the table and took her hand.

"I know you didn't, but I finally managed to persuade Harrison to let me join you two. He'll be here in just a few minutes but I'm glad he's late. It will give us a moment to chat." She squeezed his hand. "It's so long since I've seen you, Sky, except, of course, on television."

"It has been rather a long time but you still look as beautiful as ever. How do you like living in Washington, Diana?"

"I love it. It's far different from my New York and London days but I find it fascinating, and especially with Harrison, who knows everyone."

"He must be an interesting man."

"He's extraordinary. He's served under four Presidents, you know, and still today has more energy than any man half his age. But let's talk about you, Sky. I'm truly thrilled at your great success."

She leaned forward and gave him the full benefit of the violet eyes under the long, dark lashes that always seemed to be full of warmth and concern.

"You haven't changed, Diana, and I see you still have that feminine trick of looking at me as if I were the most fascinating guy you've ever run into."

"Maybe you are, Sky. Those few gray hairs at your temples make you handsomer than ever, or is that just a smart touch of theatrical make-up?"

"No. No, it's real. I can assure you, Diana."

"You've always been extremely photogenic. I don't think you have one bad angle." She leaned forward and almost whispered. "I must confess, Sky darling, that sometimes when I'm watching your dear face on television my mind begins wandering. I keep thinking of your body and those delicious nights we spent together in London and on the Riviera." She sighed, "Oh, Sky, it seems a million years ago that we were lovers."

"It was a million years ago, Diana." Just then heads began turning toward the entrance of the room. Harrison Kirby, who was silver-haired, tall, slim, slightly stooped, and the very image of a successful diplomat, came into the room. He was guided quietly to their table by the *maître d'*.

Sky stood up quickly. "This really is a great honor, Governor Kirby."

"I hear from Diana that you spend most of your noon hours

working, instead of lunching out, and I thoroughly approve of that," said Harrison Kirby as he sat down beside Diana on the banquette.

"It's really a matter of necessity, sir."

"I hope you'll be glad to have broken your routine. I have wanted to talk with you for a long time, Mr. Madison, but shall we order luncheon first before we move on to more serious things? Will you have something to drink?"

"Thank you, no. Never in the daytime."

"For me, too." He signaled the waiter and they placed their order.

While they were eating, Harrison Kirby talked about his years in France where he had first met Diana. "I loved her the first moment I looked at her."

"How sweet of you, darling. I remember the evening. It was a dinner in the Élysée Palace."

"I could hardly believe that I wasn't dreaming and that she was real." Harrison Kirby went on, "Later we danced together and the next day had tea at her apartment. I knew instantly that I was in love with her, but there was nothing I could do about it. I was ambassador to France and married at the time."

He went on to discuss the part the media had played in what he called the Nixon tragedy. "It was the first time that television really proved its power. The Watergate story would never have swept the country, but would have remained a minor scandal discovered and developed by a single newspaper if it had not been for TV."

"Some critics have said we pushed too hard and then they did an about-face and found us too soft," Schuyler said.

It wasn't until they were drinking their coffee that Harrison Kirby came to the point of their meeting. "Now, Schuyler, you know that Nelson Rockefeller is to become our new Vice President, leaving the gubernatorial post empty. I have been in close contact with some of the most important members of our party and we have discussed many men as possibilities." He paused.

"I can see that it's next to impossible to replace Nelson Rockefeller."

"We have found only one man who, for many reasons, might be able to win, and that is why I came here today."

"I don't understand."

"We think that with the backing we can give you, you have a more than good chance of becoming the next governor of New York State."

Schuyler Madison set down his coffee cup and saw that his hand was trembling slightly. "Naturally, I'm flattered that you've thought of me, Governor Kirby, but I'm also stunned. I have absolutely no firsthand knowledge of politics."

"We realize that, but we believe that the country has turned against professional politicians and that you have many other assets that will compensate."

"I hardly know what to say."

"I can understand that. I want you to meet some of the other members of the party before you make up your mind, but there is not too much time to lose."

"I'm still in a state of shock."

"If I seem pressing, it's because I have followed your career closely. I like your wholesome, middle-western background, where you grew up, but I also know you were born in New York to one of the founding families of this state. I knew your grandfather, for whom you are named. He was a real gentleman of the old school."

"Thank you, sir. He died when I was just a little kid, perhaps four or five years old, but I remember him."

"How old are you, Schuyler?"

"I'm fifty-four."

"That's perfect."

"What do you mean, sir?"

"I mean that by 1984 you'll be a good age for the White House. The governorship is just the first stage in what the party has in mind for you, so you can see why it was imperative for me to talk to you personally today."

"The idea is almost too staggering to contemplate."

"You will adjust yourself to it little by little. In your present position you have complete awareness of world politics and far more than average knowledge of many other subjects. You also have a tremendous following across the country of people who already feel well acquainted with you."

Diana spoke up for the first time. "Harrison told me I mustn't interrupt, but Sky, don't you realize that you have all the women in the country batting their eyes at you, and the amazing thing is that you have the husbands on your side, too."

"Come, darling," broke in Harrison Kirby. "This is a serious discussion and has nothing to do with women batting their eyes." He turned to Sky, "The point is that you have proved yourself an intelligent man. Your present position has armed you with a great deal of power that would be especially advantageous to you in your initial campaign to become governor."

"You have thought of everything, haven't you?"

"I have tried to. I realize that it will be hard for you to give up your present position and to give up a certain amount of independence that it carries with it. I believe, though, that one must go on, and for you this is the ultimate challenge."

"I realize that very clearly."

"I don't expect an answer today, and you would be foolish to give it without due deliberation."

"I've changed my mind, Governor; I think I will have a scotch."

"Of course." Kirby beckoned for the waiter. "You seem to have the respect of the press, Madison, and I am sure we can count on the Bradshaw Green newspaper chain. Their flagship paper, the *Globe*, here in New York, is important for the first candidacy and the others across the country later on in the presidential race."

"Bradshaw Green was always my nemesis. For many reasons he hated my guts."

"Bradshaw Green was an unusual man who had tremendous power, but sometimes used it in strange ways."

"He had an uncontrollable temper. Diana, I'm sure you will agree to that."

She nodded, "Brad could be ferocious. I shudder to think of some of his scenes."

"He certainly managed to foul up my early life," Sky said.

"Diana and I discussed your situation, but that is long past history now and even if it weren't, I don't believe their opposition could stop you." Harrison Kirby signaled to the waiter to bring the check. "Now you must find time to consider what we have talked about today and visualize what may be in store for you. I don't expect an answer tomorrow. We are flying back to Washington this afternoon and I will call you later in the week to set a date for our next meeting."

"Whatever my decision is, I can't thank you enough, Governor, for your confidence in me," Schuyler said as they rose from the table.

Harrison Kirby smiled. "Yes, I am virtually guaranteeing your success and I am equally sure there will be no opposition from the Green papers."

Schuyler Madison was still in a state of shock. After he had kissed Diana good-bye, shaken Kirby's hand and watched their limousine pull away from 21, he walked back to UBC. In his office he buried himself in his work, and the luncheon soon took on the dimension of a dream.

He found himself enjoying every detail of his daily routine even more than usual—the conference with his editor and writers and even the tense hour that preceded the actual broadcast. When it was over he went back to the Carlyle, where he kept a small apartment, and ordered a light supper sent up. He undressed, took a shower, put on a robe, sat down in an easy chair and stretched out his long legs on an ottoman.

There was a pile of newspapers on the table beside him and when he idly picked up one of them it turned out to be the *Globe.* He leafed through it and then tossed it on the floor. He closed his eyes, and his mind flashed back to the luncheon and the decision he had to make.

Why the hell, he thought, does Bradshaw Green turn up as a threat in every crisis of my life? The bastard has been dead now for years but his image still hangs heavy over my head. He could remember the first time he ever saw him. It was the summer his mother and father took him to Europe and he was nine years old.

CHAPTER TWO

June 1928

At the age of nine, Schuyler Madison didn't like to miss anything. When he woke in the little stateroom next to the suite occupied by his parents, he could feel the motion of the boat and knew that the *Île de France* must really be out in midocean at last. Of course, the sailing the evening before had been exciting, what with his father arguing with the bootlegger who had managed to deliver a case of champagne for their *bon voyage* party but had forgotten the gin.

Schuyler and his twelve-year-old cousin, Gage Hale, whose parents were also on board, had left the party when the champagne corks started popping, and had gone down to the main deck to watch the last stragglers arriving. Baskets of fruit and flowers were being delivered by the dozens. Western Union boys in their olive-gray uniforms and Postal Telegraph boys in their navy-blue outfits were holding stacks of telegrams. Photographers were yelling and jostling each other for the best spot to snap famous arrivals. One long black Pierce-Arrow with the chauffeur honking its horn, followed by another identical limousine, moved slowly through the crowd on the pier until it reached the foot of the gangplank. Out of the first one had stepped a man wearing a brown derby. He was smiling. "Say, that's got to be Al Smith," Schuyler had said to his cousin.

The governor was followed by a large man wearing a black homburg hat, and a small woman on whom the photographers converged, snapping the pretty face under a gauzy turban, from every possible angle.

To hear who they were, young Schuyler had snuggled closer to the woman standing next to him. She had a pad and pencil and seemed to know everyone. "There's the newspaper tycoon, Bradshaw Green, with the governor. And naturally, he's got his movie queen, Nora Hayes, with him, too. Look at her, she always wears her head wrapped up in something, and her face photographs like a million dollars. Who's that in the second car? Oh it's Green's little daughter with her governess. And that young woman with the glasses must be his secretary, and you can be sure his party have got the best staterooms on the ship."

Schuyler peered over the railing to watch the small girl in a short, starchy dress, white socks and Mary Jane slippers. She stepped out of the second car, slapped the hand of her governess who was trying to hold onto her and walked up the gangplank herself, looking neither right nor left.

"That little brat is going to be one of the richest girls in the world someday," Schuyler heard his neighbor say.

Soon after the two limousines arrived, the ship's gongs started ringing, the orchestra swung into the "Marseillaise" and the stewards began pushing through the crowd, yelling, "All ashore who are going ashore."

As the guests began to leave, more of the passengers came on deck and began waving to friends on the pier. It seemed to Schuyler that they would never leave the dock, but at last the gangplank was pulled up. Streams of confetti blew from the ship's deck to the pier, handkerchiefs waved as the *Île de France* slid out of its berth into the center of the Hudson, where it swung slowly around and headed for the Battery and the ocean beyond.

Schuyler had hardly slept the first night at sea. He jumped out of bed when the wall clock told him it was 7 A.M., and pushed back the curtains of his porthole. There was nothing in view but whitecaps for as far as he could see. He took a quick shower and couldn't wait to get into the new white linen knickers that his mother had bought for him just a few days before. He had two sweater sets with matching socks, and finally chose the blue-and-white one. Before any of the rest of their party, he wanted to make a personal inspection of the *Île de France*, find out where everything was and what the people looked like.

Walking carefully, because his mother's ears were highly

trained and could detect the turning off and on of a light switch, to say nothing of the gentlest opening and closing of a door, he left his stateroom.

Schuyler tiptoed past their door and was free at last. The corridor ahead of him seemed endless, but finally he reached a marble foyer, something like the one in their New York apartment house. Flights of wide steps led up or down, but he decided to go as high as he could for a starter.

A few minutes later he came out on the sun deck, where the French stewards were already setting up chairs. He walked past the shuffleboard games painted on the deck floor and went to the railing. All around him were miles of nothing but water, which made the *Île de France* suddenly seem small and helpless, although it had looked like a giant the day before. The sun was shining, but even on the sheltered afterdeck the wind was blowing. It was making the waves slap smartly against the ship and, as he leaned over the railing, there was a fine mist that he couldn't see but could feel moistening his cheeks.

A woman was coming along the deck toward him, and Schuyler saw that it was the movie star he had watched come aboard yesterday afternoon. This time her head was wrapped in a silk scarf that was blowing behind her. As she came closer, he saw that she looked exactly the way he had once seen her in a movie and had been carried away with her long eyelashes and a beauty mark next to her round mouth.

She was carrying a large canvas bag on one arm and just as she passed Schuyler a few large pieces of paper flew out of it. They fluttered to the deck and were sliding toward the sea as Schuyler rescued them just in time.

Nora Hayes was just settling into a deck chair in a shady, secluded spot when Schuyler caught up with her.

"I think these are yours, Miss Hayes, I saw them blow out of your bag."

"Good boy. You must be very quick on your feet."

"I thought you might need them." He gave her the ready smile that he had already discovered was an asset that had usually got him whatever he wanted.

She took off her dark glasses and smiled back at the towheaded boy with the big brown eyes. "What's your name?"

"It's Schuyler Madison, but most of the fellows at school call me Sky."

"That's a good name. How old are you, Sky?"

"I'm going on ten," he said.

"I see you are an early riser, just as I am," Nora Hayes said.

"I wanted to get up early to get acquainted with the boat."

"It's my Hollywood training that keeps me from sleeping late. Sometimes I have to be on the set at half past five in the morning."

"I haven't been to many movies, but during the Christmas holidays I saw you with Ronald Colman and you were wonderful."

"Thank you again, young man. Would you care for an apple?" She reached into her bag and handed him one. "I like apples, just as I like all natural foods."

As he took the apple, Sky realized suddenly that he was hungry. Nora Hayes was putting on her glasses and opening a book.

"Now, Sky," she said, "if you'll do me one more favor. Please go to the steward over there and ask him to have some hot beef bouillon brought up here to me as soon as possible. Eleven o'clock, when they serve it below, is a long way off."

"Of course I will, Miss Hayes, and it's been very nice meeting you." Sky hurried to the steward, who was setting out the equipment for the shuffleboard players, and gave him the message.

"Thanks, *mon petit,* she'll get it *tout de suite.* Nora Hayes has crossed with us before and she's a real nice lady, not stuck on herself like some of them are."

Sky ran downstairs and found his mother and father just ready to go to the dining room for breakfast. "There you are, Schuyler. I was worried when you weren't in your stateroom, but your father told me not to be foolish. Please knock at your aunt and uncle's door, and tell them to meet us in the dining room, will you, dear?"

Most of the *Île de France* passengers apparently had settled for trays in their staterooms, for the main dining room was quite empty.

"You see, Sam, I was right. No one is here. My brother, Ed, has always detested the idea of eating in bed and Addie goes along with anything he says, but after this I'm not coming down in the morning." Alice Madison was quite determined. "Let them eat down here and Schuyler can join them if he wants to," she said.

Alice Madison was used to having her own way. She had an indulgent father and as a girl in Fort Wayne she was pretty enough and rich enough to become thoroughly spoiled. When she came to New York just after World War I as a middle-western heiress she was yearning to become a painter. Instead she met good-looking Schuyler Andrew Madison at a gallery opening. He was still in his officer's uniform and hadn't started his Wall Street career. They eloped three months later. Since she had married into one of Manhattan's founding families Alice began to concentrate on always doing the right thing, which meant living, behaving and thinking identically with the group she identified as the right people. Luckily, since she was still pretty and rich, her easygoing husband chose to regard it as a feminine quirk.

Alice's only brother, Edward, with whom she had shared their inheritance, had chosen to stay in Fort Wayne and had no desire to leave a place where he was popular and respected in the business community, belonged to the best clubs, and could travel whenever he felt like it. He and his wife, Addie, had known each other since their school days. He was the boss of their home, though Addie was the only woman he had ever had in his life, and he adored her.

When the Hales arrived, Addie was carrying the passenger list that had just been delivered to their stateroom. "It's exciting," she bubbled. "You won't believe how many famous people are on board."

While the food was being ordered she was still skimming through the pages. "Bradshaw Green, the publisher, is one of the passengers and naturally Nora Hayes is with him."

"We saw them arrive last night, didn't we, Gage?" beamed Sky, who was sitting next to his cousin.

"Yes, and Governor Al Smith brought him right up to the gangplank in his car. We knew him by the brown derby."

"Bradshaw Green is a remarkable success story," Gage's father said. "His grandfather, Innis Green, started his career in a shoe factory in Indianapolis. I remember our dad speaking about it, don't you, Alice?"

"Yes, of course," Alice nodded.

"Now his grandson, Bradshaw Green, owns thirty-seven newspapers. He is a tyrant in politics. There's nothing he wouldn't do to get his own way."

"There's one time he didn't get it," Sam Madison interrupted. "He was doing his damnedest to get into the Knickerbocker Club. It was the year I was president and the board saw to it that he didn't make it."

"He sure wields his power. No wonder Al Smith is courting him for the coming presidential election."

"And Nora Hayes is courting him, too," Addie said. "Well, she'd better mind her *p*'s and *q*'s on board this ship. They say he once pushed a man overboard for flirting with Gaby De Lyn, who was his girl of the moment."

"It's Nora Hayes I'm interested in," went on Aunt Addie. "I just hope she comes to dinner some night wearing a fabulous dress and a lot of jewelry."

"Oh my dear, I'm afraid you may be disappointed. Most of the really famous people dine in the privacy of their suite and may occasionally invite a friend to join them," Alice Madison told her sister-in-law.

"But Miss Hayes is such a nice, friendly lady. I'm sure she won't hide away. She gave me this," and Sky held up the big red apple for all of them to see.

"I must say you do get around, Sky," said his father. "How did she happen to give you an apple?"

"We met on the deck this morning. She's an early riser, because it's a Hollywood habit, she said." Sky tried to speak nonchalantly but he had already decided he would keep the apple as long as possible as a memento of his meeting with a Hollywood star. As he ate his bacon and eggs with the crisp croissant, he made up his mind that she wouldn't be the last.

Before the end of their breakfast, Addie had gleefully discovered that novelist Elinor Glyn was a fellow passenger. "I just adore her books, especially *Three Weeks*, where they slept on a bed of roses."

"Oh come now, Addie," Alice Madison said.

Also on board, Addie reported, were Jeanne Eagels, who had just been appearing in *Her Cardboard Lover*, and there were

Grace Moore and Georges Carpentier, the French prizefighter. When she reached the z's she cried out, "And guess what? Florenz Ziegfeld is on board with Billie Burke and their daughter, Patricia. I just can't believe it."

"Of course, living in New York, we are used to well-known people," Alice Madison said.

"Well, here's a funny name—Mrs. Stuyvesant Fish."

"She's very, very social, my dear."

"Well, Ed and I have one distinction, at least. We're the only passengers from Fort Wayne, Indiana."

"I don't wonder," Alice said. "I've never understood why you insist on living out there so far away from everything that counts."

"We like Fort Wayne."

"Just think what a marvelous life Sam and I have managed for ourselves in New York and with the minimum of stress and strain." She turned to her brother. "People don't have to sweat like Horatio Alger heroes these days. It's all done with the stock market. I've given Sam every cent of my inheritance to invest, and Ed, you should do the same."

"That's what I'm always telling him, but all you have to do is look at Ed to see that he's overcautious, and Gage is just like him. Always hanging back."

Gage looked up from his orange juice. "What do you mean, Mother?"

"Well, you are three years older than Schuyler, and he's out before breakfast meeting movie stars."

"Come on, Gage, down below there's a real swimming pool and a gym," said Sky. "They have movies, if you'd rather, but we've got to check on the times. Where shall we start? Just say."

"I say Ping-Pong for a start."

On the way to the Ping-Pong tables, which were set up in an enclosed area just off the main deck, they passed the bar, which was already crowded with men.

Gage was a good, steady player and he easily won the first set from Sky, who liked to try erratic slam shots that often failed and kept Gage running from one side of the table to the other trying to retrieve the ball.

"How about letting me have a look at your friend, Nora Hayes?" Gage suggested finally.

By this time Sky had discovered the elevator and they took it to the sun deck, where Nora Hayes was still ensconced in her deck chair. She was immersed in the papers that Sky had retrieved for her and didn't look up as they passed.

"What a pair of legs," said Gage when they were a safe distance away. "No wonder old man Bradshaw Green is crazy about her."

"Maybe I'll have a chance to introduce you sometime before we land," said Sky, who never liked to push his luck.

They went below, checked on the time of the next movie, and found that just after luncheon one of Nora Hayes' films, *Wild Orchids*, would be shown in her honor. They decided to kill time by a warm-up in the gym and a cool-off in the pool.

"No swimming without a reservation, boys," said the steward when they arrived at the dressing rooms.

Gage was turning away disappointed but Sky said quietly, "Of course, sir, but my father did make a reservation for us to swim every day. He's Schuyler Andrew Madison from New York and his suite number is 218 on the A deck."

"All right, young man. We have a crowd here, but I'll slip you in this time, but tomorrow if you want to swim at a busy time like this, better bring me a note from your dad."

"You've got a lot of guts, Sky," Gage said when they reached the dressing room.

"This is the life. I like it fine. Don't you?" Sky said.

"It's exciting but I liked it just as well last summer when you visited us out in Indiana and we went camping by the lake. Remember?"

"It was fun," agreed Sky, who was starting to undress and put on the bathing trunks and a top laid out in the dressing room. Secretly, he remembered the camping trip as a not unpleasant but somewhat lonely experience.

He remembered sleeping next to Gage in a small pup tent and going skinny dipping in the lake each morning before cooking their breakfast over a camp fire. Sky also remembered how they pretended to each other that they knew all about sex, even to one evening playing with one another.

"I like to do everything outdoors. I don't think I could stand being cooped up in New York," Gage said.

"I'm not cooped up there. It's wonderful. I wouldn't want to be anywhere else"—Sky hesitated a moment—"except, maybe, Hollywood."

Sky reached for his trunks and noticed Gage staring down at him. For a moment he was embarrassed and then pleased when Gage said, "My, yours has grown a lot in one year, Sky. You are already bigger than I am."

"Come on, Gage, I'll race you to the pool." Sky ran ahead of his cousin and dived into the water. "Gee, it feels good." He started swimming down toward the other end of the pool, using the Australian crawl, which Gage's father had taught them last summer.

Already Sky felt at home on the ship, and during the next few days he and Gage continued exploring. They managed to get into tourist class, where all the passengers seemed much younger and livelier than they did on the upper decks. They went through the shops, never missed a movie, sat solemnly looking at the tea dances that took place between the movies and dinner.

Suddenly it was the last night aboard and time for the captain's gala. His mother and Aunt Addie were up early to keep their appointments on the beauty salon's crowded calendar. When Sky went into his parents' stateroom, he could see that a half-dozen dresses were laid out on his mother's bed and she was asking his father to decide which one to wear.

"You know, Sam, the dress you bought me in Paris last summer has more style, but the Hattie Carnegie is brand new and maybe more becoming. What do you think?"

"You've worn the French dress quite a lot, Alice. Put on the Carnegie. You'll be happier in it."

When he came into his parents' suite that night, he saw that his father had made the right choice. His mother had never looked prettier. Her short blond hair was parted on one side and swooped down to her eyebrows on the other side, with the ends slightly flipped up. Her pale green dress hung from her shoulders with the hem cut into deep points that showed her pretty knees and legs between them when she moved.

It was his father, though, whom he admired most. He had a

way of always looking elegant without making any fuss about it. "Dad, how old must I be before I have my first dinner jacket?" he asked his father, while looking down at his own navy-blue jacket and white linen knee-length shorts.

"I'm afraid it will be all of eight years, son, when you are graduating from high school and getting ready to go to college, but I hope my tailor will still be around to make it for you."

When the Hales arrived at the suite, Sam Madison opened the bottle of champagne that had been cooling in a bucket of ice. While they were enjoying it, Sky and Gage retired to a corner, but all the while they were talking, Sky couldn't help noticing that Aunt Addie's dress was too tight around the top and too bouncy over the hips, that Uncle Ed's dinner jacket didn't fit the way his father's did and that even Gage's jacket was too broad at the shoulders and his shirt and collar didn't fit his neck.

Uncle Ed seemed to be enjoying his champagne. Sky heard him say, "I've decided you may be right, Addie. I like this life and yesterday when Sam and I were talking I gave him an order to invest some of our capital."

"Hooray," Addie shouted. "Someday, Alice, we may be joining you in New York."

When the champagne was finished, the entire family progressed to the big dining salon, which was filling rapidly. They merged with the crowd that was just entering the room, and Sky was carried away with the scent of the different perfumes and the glitter of necklaces and the jingling of the bracelets on the ladies' wrists.

"Everybody looks so rich and glamorous. It's just the way Elinor Glyn describes them in her novels," sighed Aunt Addie as they sat down.

Their table was quite close to the captain's. Sky saw that it was still vacant and was sure any minute Nora Hayes would arrive to sit in the place of honor at the captain's right.

Sky's heart began to beat faster the moment he saw Nora Hayes appear at the top of the stairs on the arm of Bradshaw Green. They paused for a moment while everyone in the room turned to stare at them, then walked slowly down the stairs. She was wearing a white dress that stopped at her knees in front and swooped to the floor behind. Around her neck was a string of diamonds, and diamonds also glittered in her ears as she turned her head. He found himself counting laboriously, "I'm nine and maybe she's twenty-five, but ten years from now I'll be nineteen with a dinner jacket, and she'll only be thirty-five."

His father cut into his reverie. "What are you mooning about, Schuyler? I want you to pay attention to the gentleman who's just coming in to sit beside Nora Hayes at the captain's table. He's today's most famous art dealer, Lord Duveen. I only wish I had enough money to invest in some of his collection."

"Are paintings very expensive?" Sky asked.

"Yes, son, the good ones are, but if you can afford to hold them for a while, the returns can be enormous. When we reach Paris, I'm planning to buy you a painting that you can hang in your room and watch accumulate in value."

"Thanks, Dad. I'd like that and I'd like to go around to the galleries with you when you choose it, if you'll let me."

"Fair enough, son. We'll shop together."

"Do you still do any painting, Alice?" Ed Hale asked his sister. "You had a lot of talent when you were growing up."

"I just haven't had time, but I plan to start again soon," she said.

After dinner, they moved on to the ballroom, which was decorated with French and American flags and had little bowls of red, white and blue carnations in the center of tables arranged along the walls. An orchestra was playing the latest hit that Sky, who had already made a point of memorizing the lyrics to the popular song he had heard so many times on the radio, recognized as "I Can't Give You Anything but Love, Baby."

"Oh I love that tune. Let's dance, Sam," cried his mother.

"Anything but the Charleston. I'm getting too old for that," mumbled his father.

Just then Gage called across the table, "Gee whiz, look around, Sky. Your friend from Hollywood seems to be hunting for you."

Sky swung around and saw that Nora Hayes was headed straight for the table. He stood up, feeling his knees wobble as she called out, "Hello, Sky."

He broke into a big smile, and then managed to say, "These are my parents, my aunt and uncle, and my cousin, Gage."

"Your son saved my life the other morning and I can't tell you how grateful I am," Nora Hayes said, addressing his parents after she had smiled and nodded at the rest of the party.

"We're glad to hear that he was helpful," his father said.

"Not just helpful, but an absolute angel. He rescued some papers that blew out of my bag. They were about to blow overboard, and they just happened to be the script of my first talking picture, which I start to work on the day I get back to Hollywood."

"That will make the film even more fascinating to us when it opens. Won't you sit down with us?" his father said.

"Thank you, Mr. Madison, but I really came to ask a favor. Could we borrow Sky for a short time?" She put her hand on Sky's shoulder. "He told me that he is nine and we have Mr. Green's little daughter, who is six, at our table. She is totally bored with us, and I thought it might make the evening bearable for her if she had someone her own age to talk to."

As Sky got up from the table and crossed the ballroom floor with Nora Hayes he was in a state of utter bliss. If only he could sit and talk to her instead of some stupid little six-year-old.

Tho littlo Groon girl was sitting noxt to hor governess, who got up to make room for Sky. He remembered seeing them come on board the evening of the sailing. Before he sat down, Nora Hayes took Sky around to meet Bradshaw Green.

"Brad, this is young Schuyler Madison, whom everybody calls Sky."

The publisher set down his drink and held out his hand. "Glad to meet you. Any relation to Sam Madison of Wall Street?"

"He's my father. His name is Schuyler Andrew Madison, and his initials, S.A.M., make everyone call him Sam."

"I know him. He's a big shot in that high-hat Knickerbocker Club." He looked across the ballroom and waved a casual hand at Sky's father, who returned the greeting.

"Glad you've joined our party, young man," went on Bradshaw Green. "This is my daughter, Indiana."

"Hello, Indiana," he said, sitting down beside her.

While he was talking to her father, she stared fixedly at the table and all he could see was a mop of black curls, but now as she raised her head her dark blue eyes seemed to look straight through him. Finally she spoke, "I don't like boys."

He began to laugh. "That's tough on me because there's not much I can do about being one."

"Do you like girls?" she asked.

"Yes, I like them a lot, though I don't know any of them very well. I go to a boys' school, so I just see them at parties and the dancing class my mother makes me go to."

"You're lucky. I wish I could go to that class. I'm stuck with my governess, Miss Prune Face, who was sitting here before you came."

"But why can't you?"

"My father likes for me to stay at home. He says he has lots of enemies and he's afraid some of them will kidnap me."

"Is your name really Indiana?"

"Everybody asks me that. I wish I could change it."

"Oh I'm sorry," Sky tried to apologize.

"If you really want to know, I'll tell you now and get it over with. My great, great, I don't know how many greats back grandmother was the first white baby born in Indiana. So my father had the bright idea of naming me after her. I hate my name."

"I like it. It's got personality and it's not like everybody else's."

A waiter was placing a plate of chocolate ice cream in front of them. "Here's hoping you like chocolate," Indiana said, and for the next few minutes they were quiet.

The orchestra had been playing a lot of Gershwin and Irving Berlin tunes but Sky held back from asking Indiana to dance. He didn't want to get stuck on the floor with a kindergarten kid who probably couldn't keep time to the music. Anyway it would be humiliating, especially in front of Nora Hayes.

When the music changed to "Indiana Moon," he felt obliged to say, "This is your tune, I guess. Would you care to dance?"

She frowned. "I'll try anything once."

They went out on the floor, but she had no idea what to do. "Put your left hand on my arm, give me your right hand, relax and let me lead," Sky said.

For a minute they awkwardly hopped around the floor. "This is dumb. I don't like it," Indiana finally said.

After they sat down, she asked, "Where do you live?"

"In New York, at 910 Fifth Avenue. It's at the corner of Seventy-second Street."

"We live in New York, too. Our town house is at Eighty-second Street and Fifth Avenue, but our real home is in Westchester."

After they talked for a few minutes the orchestra broke into the Charleston. At dancing school the Charleston was taboo, but Sky and his friends had been practicing diligently. He felt that it was completely safe to ask Indiana if she wanted to do the Charleston, since he knew she wouldn't have a clue.

He was astounded when she jumped up, crying, "Do I ever Charleston! Come on, let's cut a rug. I heard that on the radio but I have no idea what it means."

With her skinny arms and long legs flying and the short skirt of her dress flipping out above the knees, she looked almost cute, though he hated to admit it.

"You don't know how to dance, but where did you ever learn the Charleston?" he asked.

"In the kitchen, of course. That's where I learn lots of things. The upstairs maid started teaching me. The butler is pretty good at it, too, but the chauffeur is a real whiz. I tell them upstairs that I'm going down to look for a cookie but I really go to Charleston. They'd have a fit."

When they returned to the table he could see that Nora Hayes was smiling in their direction and clapping her hands.

"It must be wonderful for you to have a lovely person like Miss Hayes around," Sky said. "I'm sure she could persuade your father to get you into a dancing class, if you really want it."

"Oh her. She's just one of Daddy's girls. Old Miss Prune Face says she's buttering up Daddy so that he'll back her new talking film, but his secretary, Miss Peacock, says she doesn't think he's going to do it."

Sky was so appalled at hearing his idol attacked that he turned away. He then saw that the party seemed to be breaking up. Both Nora Hayes and Bradshaw Green were standing and she was reaching for her beaded evening bag.

"Well, I guess it's good-bye, Indiana." He hardly looked at her in his haste to reach Nora Hayes to bid her good night, but before he left, he heard Indiana say, "Good-bye, and I still hate boys."

Across the room his family table was breaking up, too. "What was she like?" Gage asked.

"A real horror. She hasn't a good thing to say about anything or anybody."

"I danced with Patricia Ziegfeld but she's older and seemed terribly sophisticated. The girls at home in Fort Wayne seem more sincere."

When he reached his stateroom, Sky packed his clothes but it was hours before he could go to sleep. Scenes from the past few days on the boat kept passing through his mind as if they were part of a movie, and especially the morning meeting with Nora Hayes.

The sound of the ship's engines, which he had grown accustomed to, was missing, and everything seemed deathly still when he woke the next morning. For a moment he couldn't remember where he was, then he heard the rustling in the passageway and the bumping of the luggage that was already being taken out, and realized they must be at Cherbourg.

He didn't see Nora Hayes again, and he guessed that the Bradshaw Green party had left ahead of the crowd and probably had been spirited away in more black limousines.

Over breakfast, his father said, "Well, son, we're in France and we will soon be on the boat train to Paris. You'll be amused at the quaint European trains."

"What's Paris like, Dad?"

"It's the most beautiful city in the world, son."

"Will we be able to look for my painting today?"

"No, but maybe tomorrow."

CHAPTER THREE

June 1940

Schuyler Madison was getting ready to leave Princeton. He had already said good-bye to his roommate, Chuck Fuller, packed his evening clothes and suits that he would wear in New York, where he hoped to get a job, and wanted to live.

"I'll have to be quick, too," he thought, rolling up sweaters and stuffing them into one of three bulging old suitcases. He had decided he couldn't afford even one cheap new one at this time.

After he had finished with his clothes, he left his bedroom and went into the living room of the little suite in Holder Hall that Gage had passed on to him when he graduated three years before. He had passionately hated the overstuffed furniture that was cast off from Aunt Addie, but now that he was leaving them he felt a sudden sentimental fondness for the oversized chairs and the formidable sofa with the shiny mahogany frame. He had some wonderful times in the room during the past three years, especially playing bridge and working on the Triangle Club shows. Aunt Addie had told him to sell the furniture and keep the money. He needed it, but he hoped the secondhand dealer who had bought it wouldn't come to take it away while he was still there.

Sky went to the dormer window and stood for a minute looking out at the familiar Princeton scene. From open windows all around him came laughter and chatter of families and friends who had come for the commencement festivities. Aunt Addie was the only member of his family who had come and he was pleased that he had put her on the train early that morning for her return trip to Fort Wayne. He was glad to be alone. The actual commencement exercises were just a formality, he felt, and now that the whole experience was over, he was eager to get on to something else.

He sat down at his desk and began going through the incredible rubble that had accumulated during the four years. It was like living them over again. He tore up all the letters but decided to keep the theater programs of all the plays and musicals he had seen in New York, where he had gone virtually every weekend, usually taking an early-morning train on Saturday so he could catch a matinee as well as an evening performance.

As he leafed through the programs, he paused to look at Helen Hayes' photo on the cover of *Victoria Regina*. Then there was Gertrude Lawrence in *Lady in the Dark*, *Life with Father*, Ethel Merman in *Du Barry Was a Lady*, Katharine Cornell and Laurence Olivier in *No Time for Comedy*, *Keep Off the Grass*, *Star and Garter*, Tallulah Bankhead in *Antony and Cleopatra*, and Constance Collier in *Aries Is Rising*. Both flops and hits, but he had managed to see them all. The names and the programs might be useful, he thought, since he had made up his mind to become a part of the theatrical world.

Every time he was mentioned in *The Daily Princetonian* he had cut out the story, and he was surprised to find how many clippings there were. There was the time he was asked to join the Ivy Club, Princeton's most exclusive eating club and, after that, his total involvement with the Triangle Club—first as one of the chorus, the next year playing one of the leads and the last year writing and directing one of its most successful shows, which he called *Roll Out the Barrel*. It had received rave reviews, not only in Princeton, but also when they went on tour around the country in Pittsburgh, St. Louis and Chicago, they were written up by critics on the major newspapers.

He kept the reviews, but threw away the invitations to the parties that filled the weekends wherever they went. Not that the parties weren't fun, not only for the Princeton troupe but also for the local girls who were swept off their feet by a line of some sixty extra stags to cut in on them. He hesitated for a minute over a photograph of Kitty Parks of Pittsburgh, who had written to him several times, but finally tossed it after the invitations.

"I can't bother. I'm going to be too busy," he thought. The last clipping in the pile was a recent story on the senior class, "Sky Madison Named Most Likely to Succeed."

Under the clippings was a copy of *Theater Arts* magazine, with his first byline article, titled, "Do We Need a Federal Theater?" and a class paper titled "Power."

He looked at his watch. Time was passing and he was in no mood to miss his train to New York. Almost overnight Princeton had become a part of his past, and New York was ahead, bright and shining.

He went to the wall, took down the framed sketch that was hanging over the desk. He wrapped it carefully in tissue paper and put it into the piece of hand luggage next to his portable typewriter, which he was carrying.

The sketch was one of the gifts his father had promised him on their trip to Paris, but it had happened by chance. They had spent what Sky recalled as a wonderful day together, going from one gallery to another. Both were fascinated by a Spanish painter named Picasso, but his father was surprised at the price and hesitated for a moment. While the sale was being concluded, Picasso had come in. Sky remembered how he looked and how he smiled when the dealer told him the painting was going to the small boy. Picasso broke into a wide grin, patted Sky's shoulder and said, "The boy in the painting is my son Paulo, who is about the same age as you." He asked for some drawing paper and while they watched him, he sat down, made the crayon sketch, signed it, and handed it to Sky.

When they had returned to New York, both the small painting of Paulo and the sketch were hung in Sky's room, but not for long. He could still remember every detail of the late-October afternoon when he returned from school. He had gone into the kitchen to get a cookie. The butler and cook had turned the radio on and were talking about a crash on Wall Street but stopped quickly when they saw him.

That night he had dinner alone but he had seen his father's face and later heard his mother screaming over and over again, "I can't believe it. How could you have possibly done this to me?"

From that day his whole life had begun falling apart. Daytimes at school were the same but in the evening his father was too harassed to talk to him, and his mother was either weeping or had taken a sedative and gone to bed. There was no longer a car or a chauffeur. The butler and maid had left and there was only Ida, the cook, who was always complaining that the grocery bills hadn't been paid.

He would never forget their last Christmas together. They were packing to move to a smaller apartment that his mother constantly referred to as a tenement. Sky had already been told that he would have to go to public school starting in January, and he had accepted it stoically. Besides, the same thing was happening to many of his friends. When his mother had heard that her jewelry was being taken away from her, though, her screams were so piercing that his father had to call a doctor for an opiate to quiet her.

The paintings in the apartment had disappeared one by one but his painting and sketch had remained. His father had said, "Your small Picasso was bought and paid for as a gift to you, son. I'm giving you the bill of sale and putting it in a safety deposit box in the same bank where I started a small account for you the day you were born." He had given Sky the passbook for the savings account.

One evening just before New Year's his father had come home looking more troubled than usual. Sky, who had been reading a book in his bedroom, had come out to greet him and saw him pour a glass of his favorite scotch, drink it even without the usual ice and then pour another.

He was still wearing his overcoat and, at sight of Sky he had said, "Glad to see you, son. It's a nice clear evening and I've decided to take a little walk. If I'm late getting back, tell your mother not to worry. I'll be all right."

Sky had followed him to the door. His father kissed him and he never saw him again.

When Sam Madison didn't return for dinner, Sky wasn't worried and Alice Madison, who had ordered a tray in her bedroom, didn't even notice, but the next day the horror had begun. His father had not come home. His mother was hysterical again and the cook called the police, who came in asking all kinds of questions until Ida threatened to leave. Long days of suspense followed, and it was a week before Sam Madison's body was found washed up on a shore of the East River. He must have fallen into the water after drinking all that scotch, Sky had tried to tell himself at the time. Some of the newspapers called it a sudden heart attack while one suggested suicide. That was the one Ida tried to hide from him.

Aunt Addie and Uncle Ed had come quickly from Fort Wayne and had packed his belongings along with his paintings, and Aunt Addie had taken him back to Indiana, leaving Uncle Ed to cope with the details. His mother seemed to be lost in a kind of mental fog, and Sky felt she hardly knew who he was when very sweetly and politely she said good-bye. After a week Uncle Ed returned to Fort Wayne without her. He had put her in a private sanitarium for mental treatment.

In Fort Wayne with the Hales, Sky soon adjusted to the change and slowly regained his enthusiasm for everything. A whole group of young people less conscious of money and prestige than those he had grown up with, was ready to welcome the towheaded boy from New York, who had already lived a dramatic life.

He thought constantly of his mother and asked Uncle Ed about her, but Uncle Ed always shook his head negatively. The reports weren't good, he said, but he would take Sky to see her next summer.

He kept his promise, but afterward Sky was almost sorry they had gone. She didn't recognize either of them and she had changed so that they scarcely recognized her. Sky was stunned six months later when a message arrived that she had died in the clinic. He had a terrible feeling of emptiness and grieved for his mother, but as time passed he was able to remember her again as gay and pretty, always ready to go anywhere and wearing ridiculous hats that amused his father.

The next fall he was ready for the eighth grade, and Aunt Addie had decided to send him to Culver Military Academy, where Gage was already in attendance. It was going to be a financial hardship since they were suffering during the Depression along with everyone else, but Aunt Addie was determined and Uncle Ed agreed.

Culver was a new experience. It meant wearing a uniform, living in a barracks, making beds, cleaning corners, shining brass, and going to bed early but at the time it had seemed safe and secure.

When he was ready to follow Gage to Princeton, Uncle Ed, who had been in ill health for several years, died suddenly, leaving Aunt Addie financially insecure. "There's just no way I can afford Princeton for you at this time," she had said and Sky had interrupted her with, "Aunt Addie, what about selling my painting?"

"I don't know about such things but that might do it."

The next day Sky and Gage were on a train to Chicago. Though they had got what they considered a pretty good price at the time, fifteen thousand dollars, the money for the painting had just about seen Sky through four years of Princeton with only a few dollars to spare. He felt his father would have been happy to know that he had provided him with four happy years at college.

Much as he liked Fort Wayne, Sky had never become a full-fledged Hoosier, in spite of the affection Aunt Addie and Uncle Ed had given him. As he took a last look at his college rooms he felt that Holder Hall had been the only real home he had had since his parents died.

"Oh well, I guess I've got plenty of homes ahead of me," he thought as he closed the bags, took a last look and ran downstairs to get the waiting taxi driver to come help him carry them.

At the little station in Princeton, he caught what had always looked to him like a toy train, which took him to Princeton Junction. It wasn't until he was on board the New York train and settled down in his seat with some New York papers and the weekly *Variety* that he began fully to realize his situation. He was twenty-one years old, had actually graduated from Princeton, and was now on the way to New York to start a life of his own.

It had to be in the theater, he thought, first doing anything they'll give me, then on to acting, writing and producing. He opened *Variety* to see what was being planned for the new season, pulled out a little memo pad and began making notes. "I'll go see George Abbott and Guthrie McClintic, and certainly Josh Logan, who's a fellow alumnus," he said to himself. "Maybe I can get something in the summer theater, though I suppose it's too late."

At Penn Station, he checked his bags and went to a pay telephone to place two calls. The first one, to Sally Middleton, was unsuccessful, but the second one, to Gage at the New York *Globe,* where he was working, received a hearty response.

"Hi there. I'm glad you're sprung at last from our good old alma mater. I wanted to be there for the ceremony with Mom, but this damn job at the paper keeps me working six days a week."

"You don't happen to be free for lunch today?" Sky asked.

"Sure thing. Come on up to Bleeck's on West Fortieth Street, just off Seventh Avenue. It's not far. The shingle outside says 'Artists and Writers.'"

"Great, I'll be there in five minutes."

"You caught me in time, I was just going down there for lunch."

When Sky pushed open the door and went into the restaurant, he looked around for Gage. The front room was long and narrow, and the bar almost completely filled it except for a table and chair in the front window. The crowd around the bar was two deep with men who, to Sky, all looked important. He edged in and could see that a free lunch of cheese and crackers had been laid out on the counter at the far end. He was starving, but felt he should wait for Gage.

"What'll it be?" asked the bartender, who was pink-cheeked, round and looked friendly.

"A whiskey sour."

"Scotch or rye?"

"Scotch, please."

"New on the paper?"

"Oh no. I'm meeting my cousin, Gage Hale, who works on the *Globe.*"

At this moment Gage came through the door and suggested they move on to the restaurant that was beyond the bar. "Henry, just send me a gag to the table," he said.

"Gage, what the hell is a gag?" Sky asked, feeling very much a naïve outsider as they sat down at a corner table.

"It's just a Bourbon old fashioned without the fruit but with the bitters. Somebody invented the name because it took too long to describe what he wanted. It's the kind of thing to have when you come in here."

While they were eating their luncheon of sauerbraten and red cabbage, a specialty of the place, Gage asked, "Well, now that you are free, what are you going to do about it?"

"I don't know. For the moment I'm out of luck. I was counting on shacking up with Sally Middleton the way I did last summer when we were both at the Cape in summer stock. She has a neat apartment on Fifty-fifth Street, where I've spent a lot of weekends, but when I called her today a strange guy answered the phone and said she was on the road and that he was there on a sublet."

"My hours at the *Globe* are from late afternoon until eight in the morning. If you like, you can sleep on the sofa bed in my living room until you get something better."

"Great guns, Gage, that sounds terrific. I'll certainly take you up on it."

"It will be good to have company."

"Say, what does all this night work do to your sex life?"

"The night work is good because I'm headed in the right direction, toward the managerial part of the paper. And my sex life is great, at least it is every other Tuesday."

"For chrissake. What do you mean, every other Tuesday?"

"I have a steady date every other Tuesday. She's a nurse, and that's the only time she can take off."

"Gad, I'll have to help you broaden your list. I'm sorry Sally's not around. She would have a lot of friends, but I guess I'll be meeting plenty of babes in the kind of job I'm headed for."

"Broadway, I suppose?"

"Yes, something to do with the theater. I think I've wanted it as long as I can remember, but I'm ready to take almost anything."

"I saw you in the last Triangle show, Sky, and I must say I was impressed, but I guess like any career, it will be a tough struggle to start. How are you fixed for money?"

"I've just about spent the fifteen thousand we got for the Picasso. You know I've never been extravagant, but I didn't stint when it came to living well and dressing well in college. I'll have to hustle now for I only have a few hundred left." He picked up his coffee cup, "So you like your job?"

"Yes, a lot. I've just been promoted to be an assistant night editor."

"Do you like Bradshaw Green? What's he like?"

"I haven't met the old man yet."

"Well, he's always fascinated me. At Princeton we had to do a class paper on 'power.' Some of the fellows chose Hitler, F.D.R., Churchill and Howard Hughes, but I chose Bradshaw Green."

"He must have made a good subject."

"That's for sure. What a hell of a career he has had and unbelievable power."

"People say he pushed Dobbs Hall, the film director, off the *Mauritania* for flirting with his girlfriend."

"Yes, and he's supposed to have been involved in the assassination of President McKinley, too."

"Everyone is scared to death of him at the paper." Gage turned around, "Speaking of power, there's someone standing at the bar who holds Broadway in the palm of his hand, Richard Maney."

"Good God, where? He's New York's top-ranking press agent."

"He's the one, just taking off his glasses. I'll introduce you as we go out."

Gage paid the bill and they started back through the bar. Richard Maney, a stocky man with blond hair streaked with gray, pale blue eyes and a perpetual smile, was leaning on the bar eating cheese and crackers and talking to the bartender. Gage hailed him with, "Hi, Dick. How's Broadway?"

"Couldn't be better."

"This is my cousin, Schuyler Madison. He just got out of Princeton and is headed for a career on Broadway."

"Oh those ivy-covered walls," said Dick Maney, waving his arm dramatically. "You were one of the Triangle boys, no doubt."

The pale blue eyes were uncommunicative, but Sky could see they were taking in every detail, from his haircut to the navy blazer that he probably shouldn't have afforded.

"I guess I have to own up to writing the last show and playing the lead in it," Sky said.

"Believe it or not, I saw it and it was a good one," Maney said. "Staying with your cousin?"

"Yes, I am."

"If I think of anything, I'll give him a ring."

"Thank you, sir," Sky beamed.

"Say, *The Little Foxes* is going on tour in another month or so and they are looking around for someone to replace the weak nephew." He took a long look at Sky. "I'm afraid you're too tall and strong, but if you want to take a chance, call Herman Shumlin's office and say I told you to."

Sky went back to Penn Station for his bags and took a taxi to Gage's apartment on East Fifty-third Street. Afterward he walked around the neighborhood, exploring the grocery stores and drug stores and where the best hamburger-type restaurants were. He decided to walk up Fifth Avenue to Seventy-second Street. He passed 910 Fifth Avenue and it was just as he remembered it, with the same canopy and the same doorman. He walked on quickly, feeling that it was no day for tearful recollections.

The next day he got a quick yes to an interview when he called the Shumlin office and used Richard Maney's name. As Sky opened the door of the office, his heart was beating fast as he thought of meeting a famous Broadway producer face to face. There was a brief wait and then the receptionist, who, he saw, was very much aware of him as she answered the telephone, finally said, "He'll see you now," and led him to the producer's private room.

"Maney says you've got talent but he's not sure you're the type for the part," Herman Shumlin said.

"I'd like very much to try."

"O.K. Here's a few pages of script. Read them over while I'm making a couple of calls, and then we'll see."

Sky remembered the part in the play, and he knew he was reading well and with the proper feeling. Herman Shumlin let him finish. "You read well and have a good voice—in fact, a very good voice." He shook his head, "But you may be too virile for the part. Miss Bankhead has complete cast approval. She will be here at three. Would you care to wait?"

"By all means, sir."

As he sat in the waiting room he was excited and a bit nervous at the thought of meeting the great Tallulah Bankhead.

At four-fifteen the office suddenly exploded with her entrance, and the room was immediately filled with the scent of her perfume.

"Hello, Gertie, darling," she called to the receptionist. "How's that sweet mother of yours?" She turned to look at Sky, and he gave her his best smile.

"Oh what beautiful teeth you have!"

He stood up. "Thank you, Miss Bankhead."

"Don't thank me, thank your mother and father." Then she turned to the receptionist. "Tell Herman I'm sorry to be late, but that damn sleeping pill didn't take effect until six this morning."

"I'm sure you can go right in. He's waiting for you."

It was another half hour before Sky was called into the private office and greeted by Miss Bankhead. "I've just been hearing about your reading. I like your name, Schuyler Madison. Do you play bridge?"

"Yes, I do."

"Do you like baseball, and if you do, what team do you root for?"

"The Giants, of course." He had read in many interviews that she was a Giant's fan.

"He's our boy, Herman," she cried. "That is, if Scott decides not to continue the tour with us."

"Mr. Madison," Herman Shumlin began, "we've learned in the past hour that Scott Meredith, who's now playing the part of Cal Hubbard, has reconsidered and may be willing to tour. If he should change his mind, we'll be in touch with you for another reading. Leave your name and phone number with Gertrude outside."

As he left the building, Sky was disappointed but not discouraged. It seemed miraculous that he had got far enough in two days even to meet Herman Shumlin and Tallulah Bankhead.

Sky spent the next day going from office to office. He stopped at the John Golden, Dwight Wiman, and Sam Harris offices without any success. He had a short interview at the Leland Harris office, one of the leading theatrical agents in the country, and spent over a half hour talking with Edith Van Clive in the

George Abbott office. She had nothing to offer but advice: "Decide between acting or writing, young man. Don't try to go in both directions at the same time."

When Gage came into the apartment at nine the next morning, Sky was having his second cup of coffee and reading the *Globe* and the *Times* want ads. After reporting his activities of the past three days to Gage, he said, "I'm a bit discouraged. Maybe I'd better look in another direction."

"I've got an idea," Gage said. "The World's Fair is on its second summer. This time without Grover Whalen and with banker Harvey Gibson in charge."

"Yes, I read about it."

"All the big exhibits are desperate for guides to take the celebrities around. They pay pretty well and it's not too boring. Besides, your mornings would be free for interviews."

"Where would I go to apply?"

"I'll call Bob Stoddard and tell him you're coming. He's with the General Motors exhibit, and if he hasn't anything, you'd better just make the rounds out there. I'll even do it right now." He picked up the telephone, reached Bob Stoddard and, in a few minutes, turned back to Sky. "He's not sure, but he thinks there may be an opening, so you'd better get out there before noon."

Sky took a subway to Flushing Meadows and the World's Fair. Soon after the opening last year, he and his roommate, Chuck Fuller, had explored the Fair thoroughly, so the trylon and perisphere, the sky ride, and Billy Rose's Aquacade were familiar to him. Fortunately Sky was able to remember the Futurama in the General Motors building, with the little cars that were like the Tunnel of Love in an amusement park in Indiana, as well as the clover-leaf road design that was predicted as the future solution for all traffic.

He had a long wait in Bob Stoddard's office. Actually, Bob Stoddard was so harassed that he had completely forgotten him, until his secretary reminded him.

"There's a kid outside who's been waiting for an hour or so. He says a friend of yours on the *Globe* made the appointment."

"Good God, now I remember."

He was about to tell her to have him come back at the same

time tomorrow, when she said, "He's good-looking. Very Ivy League and I think just what you've been looking for."

"Then show him in."

As soon as Sky came into his office, Stoddard knew that his secretary was right. He asked Sky a few routine questions, but hardly even listened to the answers. "All right," he said. "I'll take you on for the rest of the season. The Fair closes the end of October."

"Yes, sir, and what is the salary?"

"I'll pay you a hundred and ten a week. Your job will be taking some of the visiting VIPs through the building and the Futurama, I want you to start tomorrow so, even though you told me that you've seen it once, you'd better go through the whole place again to make sure. I'll phone outside and have someone give you a quick tour."

Sky was elated. Though he made notes during the tour that he could read over later, he was thinking all the while that he could afford to pay part of Gage's rent and telephone and still have enough left over to enjoy life moderately and continue to make contacts with the theatrical world.

At the newsstand on the subway-station platform, he stopped to buy an evening paper. A boy was just delivering a stack of *Life* magazines, and as he set them down on the counter, he saw there was a good-looking girl on the cover. He pulled out a dime and bought it just as his train was pulling in.

Jolting along in the subway car that was taking him back to Manhattan, Sky took a closer look at the *Life* cover. She was a beauty, but not the severe Hollywood type or like the dozens of pretty girls he had dated or danced with at college proms. The photograph showed only her head and bare shoulders. The animal magnetism of the heavy, dark curls tumbling over her bare shoulders, her bright, dark-blue eyes staring straight out of the page and her half-open mouth, as if she were about to laugh, came through to him clearly enough to make him wonder who she was. Not a young actress, he thought. She was too natural and unposed.

He read the name in small type. It was Indiana Green, a name that seemed vaguely familiar.

He followed the directions on the cover. "For further details, turn to page 19 for 'Debutantes,' a story by Myra Keller."

He turned the page to read, "The revival of the extravagant debutante party is just another symptom of the post-Depression boom that is sweeping the country. This year there are more debutantes than last. Most of them with well-known names in society are being introduced to their family's friends in lavish, private parties, rather than in a group, the less costly way to do it that has been prevalent over the past Depression years."

"Among all this year's debs," Myra Keller wrote, "Indiana Green has emerged as the girl of the year. Only child of Bradshaw Green, the newspaper tycoon, her coming-out party next fall is estimated to cost fifty thousand dollars."

Sky stopped reading and closed the magazine. He was remembering the *Île de France,* his parents, Bradshaw Green, Nora Hayes and the six-year-old girl he had to dance with. "That nasty brat," he said to himself. It had been a while since he had thought of Nora Hayes, and he decided to see if one of her movies was playing in New York.

CHAPTER FOUR

"I hate Walter Winchell, and I don't care what he says about me. We're going right on with the party, Daddy says." Propped up against a dozen lace-edged pillows in her canopied four-poster bed, Indiana Green was talking over the telephone to her best friend, Rosemary Baxter, whose family's country place was only a few miles away from theirs.

"Can you think of any possible reason, Rosemary, why Daddy shouldn't spend fifty thousand dollars on a debut party for me, if he feels like it? And he says he's been looking forward to it for years. Why, he even called up the Ritz-Carlton and reserved the ballroom before I was a year old." She paused to take a sip of milk from the glass on her tray. "Think of what it would do to the Ritz if he canceled now, and what it would mean to all those waiters and to the men who've been growing the orchids. Daddy had the party caterer order five thousand of them. People like Walter Winchell never think of things like that."

She was quiet for a minute. "I knew you'd feel the same way I do, and I think it's a shame your family has canceled your party. Personally, I don't give a damn that Finland has fallen. We're not involved with the war, and I'm determined to have my party. Besides, Daddy says he once turned down Winchell when he was looking for a job on the *Globe* and now Winchell is trying to get back at him. What did you say, Rosemary?"

Indiana finished her milk while she waited for Rosemary to answer. "Yes, I'm going to have a fitting on my dress. Why don't you come with me. We can have luncheon at Armando's afterward and stop at the World's Fair on the way back. Yes, I knew that my wanting another trip to the World's Fair would come as a shock, but I'll explain later."

Indiana pushed the white wicker breakfast tray to the foot of her bed, threw back the lace-edged sheet, and sprang out. She was ferociously hungry in the morning and the empty dishes that she left behind on her tray had held fresh orange juice, a bowl of peaches, a poached egg, a little platter of bacon and an English muffin drenched with butter and honey. She drank neither tea nor coffee. "I'm saving them for when I get older and need to be pepped up," she had once told a governess.

As she passed the big windows of her room, Indiana took a quick look outside. She never drew the draperies, because she liked everything to be bright and vivid around her when she woke and, goodness knows, there was no possibility, night or day, of anyone looking in.

Bradshaw Green's country estate was about the size of a national park and just as meticulously kept. The country was green and rolling, and in cooler weather she could sometimes see the herd of deer, some of which were tame enough to come to the door for food. Now the whole scene was veiled in the heat haze of a late-summer day, and she could smell the flowers in the cutting garden.

In her bathroom she took a quick shower and while she stood wrapped in a terry robe, she picked up the intercom, called the garage and asked to have her car checked, filled with gas and brought around.

While she dressed, she told herself that she must remind her father of his promise to redecorate her room. When she was a little girl, Bradshaw Green, carried away with sentiment at having a pretty young daughter, had suggested the story of Sleeping Beauty, and the decorator had complied literally. The rug had been specially woven with a scene from the fairy tale in the center. The walls and ceiling had been covered with a rambler-rose-patterned paper. The walls of her bathroom also told the story in pale pastels.

In the beginning, she had loved the room. It seemed to take her out of the real world and the loneliness of being an only child with just a governess and servants to talk to.

As she put on a short, dark cotton dress and tried out a new, bright-red lipstick, she thought to herself that she couldn't stand the room any longer. She hated its saccharine girlishness. "I want something clean and crisp, and modern."

Her car was waiting for her at the door. She had driven a car since she was fifteen, with the chauffeur sitting next to her, but once she turned sixteen she had her own Ford convertible that she always drove with the top folded down even if it was raining. But now that she had turned eighteen, her father had given her a pale cream-colored Continental. She loved driving, even if she was going nowhere special, but just exploring roads and looking at other places.

The iron entrance gates of the estate were already being opened for her when she arrived, but it was only because the house had called to say she was on her way. Getting into South Wind or even getting out of it was like coping with a prison, she often felt. The turreted little gatehouse was manned night and day by at least two armed men.

"Good morning." She waved to the young man who was doing guard duty. He waved back and called, "Enjoy yourself, Miss Green," as she drove away.

Rosemary Baxter was waiting on the steps of her parents' home. It was a traditional white clapboard house with a pillared façade, a total contrast to Bradshaw Green's South Wind that was something of an early 1900s monstrosity. Actually the clapboard house seemed just right, Indiana thought, for Rosemary, who was a blond china doll with a beautiful face that hardly ever registered emotion.

Indiana drove fast and they were soon on East Forty-ninth Street, where she parked the car directly in front of Hattie Carnegie's shop.

"Won't you get a ticket?"

"What if I do? Daddy will just send somebody to pay the fine, and they wouldn't dare take my license away."

They walked through the main floor, which was displaying beaded evening bags and lacy lingerie. "All that stuff is for older women," said Indiana as they climbed the stairs to the floor above.

At the top Indiana was greeted effusively by one of the salesgirls. "Oh Miss Green, I'm so glad you came today. Your dress is ready for a first fitting, and Miss Carnegie, herself, wants to make sure that it's just right. I'll tell her you're here."

The room was carpeted in pale sky blue, a shade that Hattie Carnegie was famous for liking. It was furnished with gilt sofas and little gilt ballroom chairs. At the far end was a curtained alcove, created for special customers, many of whom didn't want to be seen ordering expensive clothes these days. It was into the alcove that they were led.

In a few minutes Hattie Carnegie came in. She was small, blond, bright-eyed and brisk, and she was followed by a seamstress carrying Indiana's party gown over her arm.

"Naturally, I'm heartbroken that France has fallen. It's like a second home to me," Hattie Carnegie said as she greeted the two girls. "I dearly love the old place, but I'm glad that someone in this country is getting a chance to make your dress, my dear." Like all readers of society columns, Hattie Carnegie knew it had been ordered originally from Paris designer Pierre Balmain, and that she had won by default.

"I'm glad you're making the dress, Miss Carnegie, and it's nice that you don't think we should cancel the party."

"Of course I don't think you should. You're only eighteen once. Besides, I'm a businesswoman and not too easily swept by emotion."

"Come along, Rosie, I want you to see it," said Indiana as they started for the fitting room.

Once behind the velvet curtain of the fitting room, the seamstress suggested, "Perhaps you'd rather undress and put on the gown yourself. You can call me when you're ready."

"Oh don't bother. I'm not modest. I got over all that in boarding school." Indiana unbuttoned her dress, stepped out of it and stood revealed in a bra, garter belt, stockings and shoes.

"You girls don't wear any more than you have to, do you?" said Hattie Carnegie. "It seems to me that I read somewhere, Indiana, that you never wear hats."

"Oh that was the piece that came out about me in *Life*. I don't dislike hats, Miss Carnegie. They look marvelous on Rosie, as you can see, but they don't seem to suit my face." She stepped into the dress, and the seamstress pulled it up around her. It was made of white double satin. The strapless top was shaped and boned like a corset above a big, swirling skirt.

"It's nice. All shape and no decoration," Indiana turned and looked at herself from all angles in the mirrored wall.

"Of course we can add tiny straps, if you're nervous about the top falling down," the seamstress suggested.

"Oh no. I'm not a bit nervous, but there is one change I'd like to make, Miss Carnegie. I'd like to have the top cut quite a bit lower in the back, down almost to the waist to show a lot of skin. I want to look as if I were in a bubble bath with just my head, shoulders and bare back showing."

"You're quite right. It will be much more dramatic that way," Hattie Carnegie said, but as the two girls left, she turned to the seamstress, "That one is going to be a handful."

"I wish my mother would let me have a dress as bare as that," Rosemary said. "She's ready to faint even at the thought of my having a strapless." Armando, bowing and smiling, greeted them at the door and ushered them to the best corner table.

"Try to change her mind, Rosie, because I do think it's dynamite. You have no idea of the mail I've got since that picture of me came out on the *Life* cover. Hundreds and hundreds of letters, and mostly from men."

"Were some of them dirty?"

"Quite a few, and I thought they were funny but Daddy didn't. Now he has all my mail picked up. Miss Peacock, his secretary, goes through all of them and sends on just those she thinks are adorable. Have you ever?"

"She probably takes the bad ones home and gets an orgasm from reading them." Rosemary giggled.

"Orgasm?"

"Haven't you ever had an orgasm, Indiana?"

"How could I? I'm still a virgin." She felt defensive about admitting it. "Have you?"

"Well no, but it's not that I haven't tried, but I guess it's because making love in a car is too uncomfortable. Clyde and I are afraid to get into the back seat, because all the roads around Westchester are terribly well patrolled."

As they left Armando's and got into the car again, Rosemary

said, "Why do you want to stop at the World's Fair, or should I just ask who is the guy?"

"Well, it's the strangest thing. There's this boy at the General Motors building that takes you on tour through that Futurama thing. I guess I shouldn't call him a boy because he's just out of Princeton and is probably three or four years older than you or me." She stopped the car to pay the toll at the Triborough Bridge. "I have a thing for him, I don't know why. Most of the boys we know are jerks. They are either terribly conceited or so backward they fall over their own feet, but this one is different. I was so attracted to him that when we were going through the dark part of the Futurama I would have asked him to kiss me, if Daddy hadn't been in the car behind."

"Have you seen him since?"

"Yes, once. I went back to the Fair and said I was having a big coming-out party and I got his name and address and told him I was going to send him an invitation."

They left the car in a parking lot and walked into the G.M. building. As they opened the door Indiana said, "Promise not to bat your eyes at him, Rosie. I may hate him when I know him better, but I have dibs on him until I make up my mind."

"I promise."

They went to the information desk, and Indiana asked, "Is Mr. Schuyler Madison here, please?"

"I'm sorry, miss, but Mr. Madison is not on duty today. He has one day off a week, but he will be here tomorrow."

Indiana felt somewhat deflated as they drove home. Oh well, she thought, perhaps I was just in the mood and he isn't as attractive as I remembered. Anyway, the party is coming up and if he doesn't come, there'll be lots of others.

CHAPTER FIVE

It was the day of the party, and in his office Bradshaw Green was going over some of the last details. He was still sulking over his defeat in last week's presidential election, for which all his papers had vociferously backed Wendell Willkie.

"Do you still want Mrs. James Farley at your right for dinner tonight? I'm working on the seating," said Iris Peacock, his spinster secretary.

"Why not? I feel sorry for both of them." He banged his fist on the desk. "And after all he's done for that son-of-a-bitch in the White House I hear he's going to be replaced as Postmaster General by Frank Walker. Not that I have much sympathy for anyone who voted a third term for a liar, who promises everything and doesn't deliver." He looked up at Miss Peacock, "Mark my word, he has promised every mother and father to keep this nation out of war, but I'll wager anything we'll be deep in it within a year."

"And what about Miss Dorothy Darrow? I don't see her name on your guest list, and she's called three times this morning to ask what time she's to be picked up," said Miss Peacock, who was a fervent F.D.R. follower and sometimes had to pinch herself during Bradshaw Green's tirades.

"Miss Darrow is not invited tonight. My daughter especially asked me not to have her, and after all, this is her night."

"Shall I tell Miss Darrow that?" Iris Peacock was the only employee on the *Globe* who could say what she felt like to Bradshaw Green.

"No, get her on the telephone, please." After his first, "Hello, darling," there was a long silence and then Miss Peacock heard him say, "Why the hell are you making such a fuss over a kid's party? What if everybody is talking about it? I'm only going to be there for dinner with a few old friends whom you wouldn't enjoy anyway." He was quiet for a moment. "If you're feeling so damn tragic, why don't you go around to Cartier and tell Jules Glaenzer I said I wanted you to have something to make you happy."

After Bradshaw Green had forcefully hung up the receiver, Miss Peacock said, "There's a long cable from the orchid farm you recently bought in Hawaii. Shall I have one of the assistants answer it?"

"No, damn it, I want to keep that confidential, just between the two of us."

"I thought so." Iris Peacock had been handling all of Bradshaw Green's confidential activities for twenty-four years and often boasted she had a lifetime contract. It was said around the newsroom that if there were any bodies around, Miss Peacock certainly knew where they were buried.

There was great commotion in the Fifth Avenue town house that same day. Presents were being delivered and flowers were arriving by the carload.

"No, I don't want my hair brushed up on the top of my head, Carlos," said Indiana to the hair stylist who had come to arrange her hair. "I don't care how picturesque it would be. I want it to look just the way it always does, only better."

She had driven in the day before, hating to leave the country and gritting her teeth at the very sight of the town house, which she had always hated. "Hello, Morris," she said when the butler opened the door. The downstairs always seemed to her to have an ancient smell. "I wish you'd buy some kind of flower spray and try to make the place a little more exotic."

"Yes, Miss Indiana." He went to the elevator and pressed the button, but she had already started running up the marble staircase.

Since then she had been massaged, had a pedicure, a manicure, a facial and a special make-up that made her eyes look fascinating and very sophisticated, she hoped, as she looked into the magnifying mirror on her dressing table. The whole process reminded her of the grooming she used to watch the stable men give her father's horses when he was sending them off to show.

Carlos was still brushing her hair. "You have magnificent, healthy hair, Miss Green, but you also have a beautiful, long neck that all those curls hide. That's why so many of my ladies have decided to brush up. It's the new look."

"I'd rather be different. The lady who wrote the piece about me in *Life* said my hair was my most photogenic feature, so why should I change?"

Carlos said no more, but as he brushed each long lock he teased it a little and twisted the ends around his fingers. She felt that the effect was quite spectacular, so she pulled out her wallet and gave him a twenty-five-dollar tip.

It was half past seven and time for Philip Frelinghuysen and Timmy Phipps, the two boys she had asked to be her escorts, to arrive and take her to the dinner her father was giving beforehand in a special room at the Ritz-Carlton. She called for the maid to bring her dress.

"It's made just beautiful, Miss Indiana. It's as pretty inside as out," said the girl as she began fastening the tiny hooks of the corseted top. "Is it too tight?"

"No, Viola, but I guess you'll have to stay up to get me out of it. Better get some sleep now, because I'm going to stay out late, if I can arrange it."

The intercom telephone rang, and it was her father. "We're all ready and waiting, darling. Can you come down?"

"Right away, Daddy." She decided not to take the elevator, but to make a grand entrance down the red-carpeted stairs. Her father and the two boys were in the foyer and she could see by their faces that all the preparation that had gone on during the day had not been wasted.

"Darling, this is your night," said her father, kissing her. "Every bit of you is lovely, and where did you get those charming slippers? You know you have beautiful feet. They were the first thing I noticed the moment I was allowed to get a glimpse of you in the hospital."

"I'll bet I was a fright."

"You also had a fine crop of dark hair when you were born, just as you have now."

They got into the car and were on their way to the Ritz. "I can't believe this is happening at last, and I'm glad that horrid Walter Winchell wasn't able to scare Daddy from giving it," thought Indiana as they drew up at the hotel. The newspaper comment had drawn a big sidewalk audience. Photographers who hadn't been able to qualify for the party inside sprang forward feverishly and she was photographed with her father and then with Philip and Timmy who, she could see, were enjoying every minute of it.

At the Ritz, Bradshaw Green had engaged one table for himself and some of his friends, including Bess and James Farley, Linda and Cole Porter, who also originally came from Indiana, and Prince Serge Obolensky, who had been born a part of the last Russian Czar's court and had now become the current rave of New York society. Seated at a large table of their own were Indiana and her favorite friends, like Lucy Cochran of Boston, Rosemary Baxter and Esme O'Brian.

"You look darling, Rosie," Indiana said when along with the other girls they made a trip to the powder room after the dinner and before the dance. In the pink taffeta with cap sleeves that her mother had insisted upon, and her blond hair piled up in curls on top of her head, Rosemary looked more than ever as if she had just come out of a box from F. A. O. Schwarz, Indiana thought.

"You're the knockout, Indiana. None of the rest of us have a prayer tonight."

"Don't say things like that, silly. I've invited four boys for every girl, and they've all accepted. Daddy's secretary told me this morning. We're going to have the biggest stag line in history. You're all going to be rushed off your feet."

"How about your mystery guy from the World's Fair?"

"He accepted, too, but I'm so excited I don't know if I'm going to recognize him."

For Indiana's debut, the Ritz-Carlton ballroom had been turned into a tropical garden. Not only the main ballroom but also the Palm Court and Oval Room adjoining it had been reserved for the party and all of them were decorated in the same color scheme of white, yellow and gold.

The ballroom was outlined in palms, even behind the platform on which the Meyer David band was playing. Hundreds of white orchids attached to the palm leaves gave the effect of a jungle. Huge golden cornucopias in the four corners were full of trailing green moss, gilded leaves and more white orchids. Even the balconies at both ends of the room were wrapped in garlands of gold leaves that, decorated with orchids, dripped down almost to the floor.

Nobody has ever had such a glorious party, thought Indiana, as she watched the girls pull off orchids and tuck them into their hair or into the tops of their strapless dresses. Hers, she noticed with satisfaction, was the lowest-cut of all the strapless ones in the room.

"If you like orchids so much, I'll have a few dozen plants sent to you at the Waldorf tomorrow," she heard her father tell Bess Farley.

After Indiana had danced the first dance with her father, the evening became a blur. She could scarcely dance ten steps without a fresh face appearing over her partner's shoulder as he cut in. When she stopped dancing for a few minutes and went back to the head of the stairs, she was surrounded by boys and photographers. She was still standing there when the orchestra broke into a Charleston and half of the dancing couples left the floor.

"I hope you don't mind that I asked the orchestra to play this. I remember how much you like to Charleston," said a voice at her elbow.

She looked around, and just for a second couldn't think who he was. "Oh the World's Fair. I love to Charleston, but how could you possibly know?"

"Come on. Let's dance and I'll tell you later."

After they started dancing, most of the other couples gave up and stood around watching, and they had the floor to themselves. Both of them were laughing. Indiana was still clutching her orchids and the photographers were in a frenzy.

"Who is the boy?" Bradshaw Green was asking everyone in his group, but none of them seemed to know.

When the orchestra swung into another rhythm, Sky took her arm and guided her off the floor. "Now I'll tell you how I know you can Charleston like nobody's business."

"But I never danced with you before."

"Yes you have."

"But when and where?"

"When you were six years old and I was nine, and we were sailing to Europe on the *Île de France*."

"Good God. I remember that trip, but Daddy has taken me several times since. What was I like?"

"You were very negative, a real pain in the neck. You didn't like anything, especially boys."

She burst out laughing. "Well, I've changed my mind." She saw Philip and Timmy coming toward them and quickly said, "Keep cutting in on me, will you. I want to talk with you some more. And, if you're not too tired, stick around and maybe we can go somewhere when the party is over."

After that, she could only get a few feet with him when he cut in, but she managed to whisper, "You're the best dancer here tonight. I'd rather dance with you than anybody."

"You've got a good line, haven't you?"

When the orchestra began playing "Good Night, Sweetheart," Indiana realized the party was coming to an end. She saw that Schuyler Madison was still there, and with Philip and Timmy, went over to him. "Phil has to get up early tomorrow, but Timmy is still game. We're going to the Stork Club. Would you like to come with us?"

"Sounds like a lot of fun."

"I've got some good-byes to say, but we'll all meet at the car. It's right in front of the Forty-sixth Street door."

As Sky and Timmy went up the grand staircase together, Timmy said, "I dimly remember a kid in my kindergarten class named Sky Madison. Any possibility that it's you?"

"If the kindergarten was Town School, yes, and I had the same hunch about you."

The Stork Club was full, and everyone stared at Indiana as she breezed past the velvet rope with a wave of her white-orchid bouquet, and a captain led them to the only empty table. "I'm psychic. I felt this might happen, and I had someone call ahead."

When the waiter came with the menus, she asked, "What time is it, Timmy? Because if it's after three I'm going to order bacon, scrambled eggs and a big glass of milk."

"They were playing 'Three O'clock in the Morning' when we

came in, so it's got to be," said Timmy, looking at his watch. "As a matter of fact, it's quarter of four, and if you two don't mind, I'll take a quick drink and leave you. I've been up at dawn for the past three nights."

After he had left, Indiana turned to Sky. "I'm beginning to remember the *Île de France*. It was the trip we had with Nora Hayes along, wasn't it?"

Something about her tone made him ask, "Don't you like her? Yes, she was there." He felt as if she had suddenly thrown a glass of cold water at him.

"Oh I like her, all right. Daddy has had lots of movie-star girlfriends and, as a matter of fact, she's the nicest." She frowned. "I can't stand his present one, Dorothy Darrow."

He was slightly mollified. "You don't like movie stars?"

"I like them as movie stars but not as Daddy's girlfriends. They all try to mother me. I can't remember my own mother and I'm not interested in a substitute, especially when I know she is gooing over me just to show Daddy what a wonderful wife she would make.

"I'm sure Nora Hayes wouldn't be that insincere."

"Maybe not, but I've talked, talked, talked all night and I'm tired of talking. Let's just have one dance and not say a word."

They went to the dance floor but she was limp instead of springy, as she had been earlier. She leaned against him and he felt she would have liked to go to sleep in his arms.

When they returned to the table, the milk was there and so was Sherman Billingsley, who had brought a giant bottle of Sortilege perfume and congratulations. "Your father asked me to drop over, but I couldn't get away from here," he explained.

After he had left, Indiana gulped down her milk and asked Sky to order her another. "I feel better. What are you doing now, since the World's Fair has closed?"

"Nothing at the moment. I've had lots of interviews, and I'd like something to do with the theater."

She stopped eating her bacon and eggs and looked at him. "So that's why I felt you retreating from me emotionally when we were talking about movie stars. Well, you could be one, all right. You've got all the assets."

"Thanks. I wish some producer thought the same thing."

"Well, maybe we can do something. I'll think about it and Daddy knows a lot of people. Where do you live?"

"I'm sharing an apartment with my cousin, Gage Hale. He works for your dad on the *Globe*."

"Do you like newspapers?"

"Of course. Doesn't everybody?"

"I don't know, but I do especially. I like every part of them, and I like to hear the sound of the presses rolling. When I was a tiny girl, I used to beg Daddy to take me to the *Globe* in the evening when they start printing the paper. It used to put me to sleep and I still think the sound of all those printed words coming to life is thrilling."

While she was talking, Sky had been suffering agonies at the thought of the check that was soon going to confront him. He had a little more than ten dollars in his pocket. There was always a way out of everything, he had already discovered. His best course would be to go directly to Sherman Billingsley, give his name and explain that he had gone to the party without his wallet but would come back in the morning with what he was afraid would be, to him, a colossal amount.

Better get it over as soon as possible. "The check, please."

The waiter smiled. "There is no check, sir. You and Miss Green are Mr. Billingsley's guests."

He felt a wild surge of relief and wished he had asked earlier, so he could have enjoyed the bacon and eggs more. "We'd better go, I guess," he said as he handed the waiter five dollars.

"I suppose so, but I hate to have it end. Did you ever read Rupert Brooke's poem *Day That I Loved?*"

As they drove uptown, they could see that the sky behind the buildings on the East River was becoming lighter. She snuggled close to him and said, "After you leave me, the car will take you home."

He put his arm around her and pulled her even closer. "You must be dead tired."

"No, I'm still keyed up. I'm beginning to wonder what the papers will say. They'll be delivering the morning ones soon, and I may stay up."

When the car drew up in front of the town house, they stepped out and went up the steps to an iron grillwork door that protected the real front door a few feet farther back, and he thought he could see the shadow of a butler in the background. "Shall I ring the bell?"

"Aren't you going to kiss me good night?"

He laughed. "I like to do my own asking," but he put his arms around her and kissed her lips. He was startled. She pressed against him and her body felt wonderfully warm and alive as she moved in his arms. Though he hadn't meant to, he went on kissing her until he heard someone starting to open the door.

He released her quickly. "It's been a wonderful evening, Indiana."

The butler was now opening the grillwork door, but she still stood there, looking at him. "I love you, Sky. Call me tomorrow." She went in and the two doors closed.

CHAPTER SIX

It was past noon when Indiana woke and rang for her tray. After saying good night to Sky, she had felt she was floating instead of walking upstairs, and when she reached her room she had managed to unhook her dress and step out of it. When Viola appeared Indiana had said she didn't need her. She had flopped into bed just as she was with her make-up still on. How divine to go to sleep happy, she had thought as her head touched the pillow.

She had left her bedroom door half open and now Viola came in, all smiles and with the tray and all the papers tucked under her arm. "Wait till you see, Miss Indiana. In the *Journal-American,* you and and that young Mr. Madison look like a couple of movie stars doing that dance."

"Let me see, quick." She seized the paper and without a glance at the headlines she went through it until she came to the photograph. It was spread across six columns along with other photographs of the party and showed them against a background of orchids.

"Bring me a fresh white terry robe, Viola." She had them made to order by the dozen and used them like bath towels, an idea she had picked up in Paris.

"You need to order more robes. The laundress is terribly hard on these things," said Viola as she brought the robe, but Indiana didn't answer her. She was concentrating on the photograph of Sky. He does look like a movie star, she thought.

This time Walter Winchell ignored the party, but all the society pages, which had been suffering from a dearth of lavish entertaining, went wild. The New York *Times'* story started on a somber note with, "Though this country is walking in the shadow of what may be a second World War, there was no sign of worry or suspense in the Ritz-Carlton ballroom last night," and though it stressed the price of the Hawaiian orchids and the buffet, it ended by describing Indiana as the most glamorous debutante New York had seen since Barbara Hutton. The *Times* showed three pictures, and the *Herald Tribune* four. She and her father made the front page of both the *Sun* and the *World-Telegram*, and the *Daily News* filled two pages with photographs. She noticed that Sky appeared in most of them.

When Viola picked up her breakfast tray, Indiana decided to call Rosemary, who still seemed half asleep. "Guess what, Rosie? I'm in love."

"You don't have to tell me. I saw it happening last night, but you've been in the early stages since you met him at the Futurama. Who is he?"

"As I told you, his name is Schuyler Madison, but who he is, I don't know and I don't care. I'd be crazy about him even if he were a German spy."

Though she didn't say so, Indiana knew by this time that her father would have found out about Sky. She had seen her father watching them last night. She was sure that the first call he had made this morning was to the *Globe* morgue, a miniature library stacked with personal histories in newspaper clippings that required a staff of three to keep up to date.

Each time the telephone rang and she picked up the receiver she could feel her heart beginning to beat wildly, but it was always a friend thanking her for the party, a photographer, an agent who asked if she wanted to get into the movies or just a rude voice that said, "Lady, I'd like to lay you."

She was still thinking of Sky and willing him to call her when she heard the elevator going down and guessed by the sound of the servants' voices that her father was on his way home or had just arrived.

She ran down the stairs and he was already in the library and pouring himself a drink. "Well, my darling, your party got a fine press in spite of the adverse propaganda. You should be a very happy girl this evening."

"Oh I am happy, very happy, Daddy. I've been reading all the stories."

"I thought the photograph of you dancing the Charleston in your ball gown was especially catchy and I wish the *Globe* had been on its toes enough to use it." He put down his drink. "By the way, that young fellow you were dancing with is the son of Sam Madison, a member of old New York society. I always had a feeling he kept me out of the Knickerbocker Club. But he got his, he was wiped out in the Wall Street crash and found drowned in the East River a few months later."

"How dreadful."

"I understand the boy was brought up in Indiana by an aunt and uncle, and that he's just out of Princeton. We must see more of him."

"Whatever you say, Daddy." Indiana was trying to hide her delight. "I was thinking of having a house party Thanksgiving weekend in the country, if you're not having one there yourself."

"It wouldn't matter if I were, but I have to fly to the West Coast on business the end of next week and I was worrying about leaving you alone." Actually he had promised Dorothy Darrow that he would take her to Hollywood for a screen test as an appeasement for not including her in the party.

There was still no telephone call from Sky but by this time she had convinced herself that he hadn't been able to reach her. She had never given him the number. She fell asleep confident that he would call tomorrow. Anyway, she had the Thanksgiving weekend to offer now.

The next afternoon, when she still hadn't heard from Sky, she decided to visit the *Globe* to take a look at that cousin of his.

The newspaper's city room, where the writing and editing went on, occupied almost one entire floor of the *Globe* building. The center was filled with typewriter desks and chairs, and the most prominent spot was occupied by an enormous round table littered with papers. Around the edge of the room were open cubicles occupied by the department heads and their secretaries, who were separated by a railing from the reporters. Though it was too early for the rush of writing and editing to begin, copy boys were beginning to deliver communications to the various desks, and the whole place was filled with the busy sound of typewriters, voices and telephones.

As Indiana walked through, bareheaded and with her handbag hanging from straps over her shoulder, she knew that heads were turning and that typewriters had stopped clicking. She waved her hand at some of the reporters and stopped at the sports editor's desk, which was inside a railed enclosure. She and her father had had him in their box many times at football and baseball games.

"How are you, Harvey?"

"Fine, and I know you are. Seems to me I've seen a picture of you somewhere lately."

"You're kidding, but I don't mind."

"Why should you? A little publicity never hurt anybody. Today you're the most famous girl in town, and I bet you've had all kinds of offers, good and bad."

"You're right, Harvey," she laughed. "By the way, which one of the reporters is Gage Hale?"

Harvey stood up. "He comes in late and sits at that big, round table with the copy editors. There he is, the one wearing the green eyeshade and already copy editing somebody's story." Just then Gage got up and she could see that he was nice-looking, tall and skinny, with sandy hair.

She looked around the city room. "Haven't you got any girl reporters or editors?"

"Well, we have Karen Bert, who edits the crossword puzzles, and Florabelle Finley, the fashion editor, but why ask me? I don't do the hiring and firing."

"It was just a passing thought. I suppose I've got to get along home," she said turning and waving good-bye.

Indiana was still willing Sky to call her and when she reached home, she found that he had. "Mr. Madison called twice and would like to have you return the call. He left his number," the butler said, handing her a slip of paper.

As she rushed upstairs she felt such a violent surge of relief that, for a minute, she thought she was going to faint. She had to sit on the edge of her bed for a few minutes before she could dial the number. She made up her mind to be cool and indifferent, but she melted instantly at the sound of his voice.

"Wow, Indiana, that was some publicity. Gage finally got me your number but your line was always busy."

She laughed. "I know."

"I've had quite a few calls myself, since I've just made the new phone book, and something may come of one of them."

"I hope it does and, if it happens, I can get a story about you in the *Globe*."

"You mean something like 'Princeton Graduate Charlestons into Fame'?"

"That's not bad. Sure you don't want a job on the paper? That would be easy."

"Too easy. If I'm going to write it's got to be for the stage or the movies, Indi."

"I've never had a nickname. I rather like Indi."

"Saying Indiana takes quite a long time, and I don't have any time to waste. I really called to tell you it was a great evening and I want to see you again soon."

"Like when?"

"What about going to a movie with me Monday night?"

"I'd adore it, and by the way I'm having a house party over Thanksgiving weekend at the house in the country. Can you come?"

"Oh I'd love to but I would feel like a heel breaking a date I made only this morning to go hunting with my cousin, Gage. He has the weekend off and I'd hate to disappoint him. He's always been like an older brother to me."

"Hunting. Why, there's no better place than where we live in Westchester. Tell your cousin, Gage, to come along. We'll have fun and I'll get someone, perhaps Rosemary, to be his date."

"Great. I'm sure he would like that, and besides I'm anxious for him to meet you. He's heard so much about you from me, and read the tons of publicity. He already thinks you are special."

A few flakes of snow were falling but melting on the sidewalk when Bradshaw Green's limousine picked up Sky and Gage at their apartment at four o'clock on the Wednesday afternoon before Thanksgiving. Gage had brought his rifle, though he didn't expect to use it, and Sky was carrying a package of record albums they had bought for Indiana.

He had expected to find her in the car but, instead, Iris Peacock was tucked away in a corner of the back seat.

"Miss Green has gone ahead," she said. "She drove her own car so she could have it up there for the weekend. I'm Mr. Green's personal secretary. Since he's in California he wanted me to be out there to see that everything runs smoothly."

By the time they reached South Wind, the casual flakes had turned into heavy snow. The car was moving slowly since the road was slippery and the chauffeur could see only about six feet ahead. "Oh I do hope Miss Green is safe," Iris Peacock said. Up until that point she had been as quiet as a mouse but both Sky and Gage were aware that she was listening and observing all the time.

Indiana met them at the door. "You may be here for a long time," she cried. "The radio is predicting the biggest snowstorm in years."

Her eyes were sparkling and Sky knew that she liked the idea. "Indi, this is my cousin, Gage."

"Gage, I've heard so much about you, and not just from Sky but also from the fellows at the paper. I feel I already know you."

Gage was flushed with pleasure, and from that moment on was under her spell.

Like many Victorian mansions, South Wind had a baronial hallway with an enormous fireplace in which huge logs were burning. There was a staircase at the far end with a landing halfway between each floor.

"I'll take you through the whole place sometime," said Indiana. "We have everything but a ghost."

She led the way and they followed her, with the butler and a maid bringing their suitcases.

"I know where I belong," said Miss Peacock, who went off to the room she always occupied when Bradshaw Green brought her out for a weekend of work.

Indiana put Gage and Sky on opposite sides of the gallery that looked down on the master staircase. "I've given you both tower rooms," she said without mentioning that Sky's was quite near to hers. "When you've been unpacked, bring your bathing suits and come down."

"I thought Sky must be kidding when he told me to bring one along," Gage said, laughing.

"Well, if you didn't bring one, believe me, I've got lots of extras."

When they came downstairs, Indiana led them from one room to another. Sky saw that her father had been an inveterate collector with more greed than taste. A room lined with shelves of fine Chinese porcelain was followed by another of carvings from medieval churches that he felt were neither valuable nor very interesting. Corner niches in the dining room were full of Meissen china, but the hallway outside had early African carvings displayed on a long, narrow table. Some of them were extraordinary, he felt, but they were completely lost in the reasonless mixture.

Indiana laughed. "I'm going to open a museum someday." She had quickly caught and understood Sky's expression, accustomed as she was to guests who were ecstatic over everything, or at least pretended to be.

Whenever he felt like it, Bradshaw Green had built contemporary additions to his home. When Indiana finally opened a door at the end of what seemed to be an interminably long hall, stretched before them was an Olympic-size swimming pool. It was surrounded by white tile, white wicker furniture, palms in pots, and on one wall was hanging a large faded green canoe. Painted on one side was the word "Kuckee."

"What does 'Kuckee' mean?" Sky asked.

"Oh I don't know. It's something from Daddy's childhood. Let's have a swim before dinner." She pointed to the dressing rooms and in a few minutes all three of them were in the water, which was heated just enough to be pleasant.

"This is really the life," Gage said when they had climbed out and were sitting around the pool. Sky thought that he had never seen Gage so outgoing and so full of enthusiasm.

Indiana got up and turned on the lights that her father had once ordered installed all around the eaves of the house to make it a spectacular party setting. They showed the snow still falling thickly and the snowbanks building up on the outside of the long, double-glass windows. "My best friend, Rosemary Baxter, lives only ten miles from here. I invited her for the weekend, but the way things are, she'll be lucky if she makes it in time for Thanksgiving dinner. Tonight we can watch a movie in the projection room. I brought along at least ten films for us to choose from, or if you don't like that, we can play gin rummy."

"I'm for the movie," Sky said quickly. "Any more surprises for us, Indi?"

"Not many, but we'll explore the whole house tomorrow."

The next morning Sky decided to get acquainted with the kitchen instead of having breakfast served in his room. He went into the big, raftered room and found the cook and two maids waiting for the upstairs bells to ring. After he had told them what he wanted, he wandered idly around. There was a restaurant-size stove, besides two smaller ones, as well as three refrigerators and a lineup of deep-freeze bins. He counted thirty different brands of tea on one shelf of a cabinet and as many European mustards on the shelf below.

"You're interested in food?" asked the cook, beaming at him.

"I don't know much about it, but the dinner last night was great."

"Thank you, Mr. Madison. We all know who you are, because we saw your picture in the papers, dancing with Miss Indiana."

After Sky had breakfast in a small dining room somewhere off the kitchen, he went into the library. One side was tall windows, but the three others were lined with bookshelves and, like a public library, had a ladder on a track that could be pushed around wherever you wanted it. To his joy he found that one section was devoted to Hollywood, so he chose several books and took them over to the big table in the center of the room.

He was deep in early Hollywood when he heard footsteps and Miss Iris Peacock came in. He hadn't paid much attention to her the night before, but now he saw that she was quite a nice-looking woman, probably in her late forties but still sandy-haired, tall, well-built and dressed in expensive country clothes.

"Good morning," she said. "I see you're a morning person, too."

"Not usually, but the sight of the sun on all the snow got me up early. Can I be of help?"

She had gone to a shelf that was full of garden books. "No

thank you. I know my way around here pretty well. There's a book on Hawaii here that I need for some research I'm doing for Mr. Green."

"You've been working for him a long time, haven't you, Miss Peacock? Longer than anyone else?"

"Oh no. Tiger came before me."

"Who in the world is Tiger?"

"His name is Charles Tigar, spelled with an *a*, but we always call him The Tiger at the office."

"What is his job?"

"He's assistant to the publisher. The Tiger has been with Mr. Green since his first paper in Buffalo."

"When was that?"

"At the turn of the century. About 1899 or 1901. I forget exactly."

"Then when did you start to work for him, Miss Peacock?"

"Mr. Green hired me in 1916, when he was running for governor, to work on his campaign."

"I didn't know he had ever run for office."

"He has always wanted to be successful in politics but has never been able to manage it. Mr. Green is a difficult man and a bit overpowering, perhaps, to appeal to the voting public."

That's one way of describing it, thought Sky, as Miss Peacock went on. Her face was impassive but he saw that the pale-blue eyes were very keen.

"In 1920, when Ohio Governor James Cox was the Democratic candidate for President, Mr. Green had expected to be his running mate, but at the end, without any warning, Mr. Cox switched to Franklin D. Roosevelt. I've always thought that's why Mr. Green hates the President so intensely."

She took off her glasses and looked at him intently. "This violent hatred seems to me to be almost sacrilegious. I firmly believe that F.D.R. is a gift of God to this country."

Sky had no desire to start a political argument, so he decided to change the subject. "So you were with Mr. Green long before Indiana was born?"

"Oh yes, long before. He has doted on her from the first minute he saw her. I don't think I'm wrong in saying that Indiana is the only person her father cares for deeply, except himself, of course."

"So you knew Indiana's mother, too?"

"Of course. In a way she looked very much like Indiana, but everything about her was softer and gentler, if you know what I mean."

"Yes, I can imagine."

"She was the winner of the beauty contest that one of his small papers was conducting. It was the kind of thing that the girls had to send in photographs. Her photograph won the prize and when she came to get it, Mr. Green fell for her, head over heels." She paused and looked out into space. "He was past forty and still unmarried, and I think he thought it was time to get married and produce an heir."

"Too bad she died so young."

"She was just barely twenty." She shook her head. "Knowing Mr. Green as I do, I had never thought it would last, but I was surprised when it happened."

"Oh was there an accident?"

Miss Peacock took out her glasses and opened her book on Hawaii. "I really must get on with my work. Yes, I believe so, but I don't know what the problem was. It was all very sudden."

Sky went back to his Hollywood book, but in a few minutes, he asked, "Have you been to Hawaii, Miss Peacock?"

"Not yet, but I may be going soon."

"I suppose you travel quite a lot."

"Mr. Green takes me on most of his trips and has never failed to take me to Europe with him."

"In this book, I was just looking at a photograph of Gaby De Lyn at her Malibu house." Sky held up the book for her to see, "Was she really that beautiful?"

"Yes, she was pretty, but not in a way you would consider very attractive today. I must say she had beautiful skin but she looked milk-fed and had too big a bust. She came out of the Follies and was among Mr. Green's first girls. He even built a film studio for her."

"So you knew Dobbs Hall, the film director, too?"

Miss Peacock's face seemed to tighten and her eyes returned to her book. "I may have. There were so many people."

Just then Indiana came to the door. "Sky, I've been hunting everywhere for you. What are you doing, moping around in the library on a day like this?"

He closed his book and stood up. "Good morning, Miss Beautiful."

"The world outside is absolutely gorgeous. Get on your warm clothes. We've got a sleigh and one of the stable men is going to drive us over to get Rosemary and bring her back."

Sky was glad to get out into the sunshine and feel the freezing air on his cheeks and Indiana's warm hand in his under the fur lap robe.

Gage turned around from the front seat, where he was sitting beside the driver. "Who was the little woman who came running out with the fur robe, Indiana? This morning it was quite spooky. I woke up and she was standing by my bed. I said good morning. She answered, smiled at me, and went out."

"She shouldn't have done that, but there's nothing I can do about Pinkie. She's been in the family for ages."

"She brought a little bouquet of flowers and put them in my wash basin," Sky said.

"That was cute of her. Her mother worked for my grandfather, and Pinkie has been with the family ever since. If you look at her carefully, you'll see that she's at least part Indian. Her full name is Pink Blossom."

"She's a friendly spook at least," Gage said.

"Oh yes. She adores me and she likes to have young people around. Daddy usually has politicians or movie stars or both, and they work the staff to death."

The driver shook the reins, and the sleigh bells jingled as the sleigh sped along the road.

"I feel like somebody on a Christmas card," Gage said.

Days passed quickly and the weekend was half over. So far Indiana hadn't managed to have more than ten minutes alone with Sky. Gage was a dear, but totally insensitive to the vibrations that were going on between his cousin and her. If he saw them starting to walk away, he always hurried to join them.

If it wasn't Gage, it was Miss Peacock, who came in with a book and sat down in a far corner, looking totally absorbed but drinking in every word. Indiana was positive that Miss Peacock had checked on the sleeping arrangements and registered the fact that she had put Sky in a seldom-used bedroom near hers. Not that Iris Peacock would report to her father and try to make trouble. She was too smart for that. Though it sometimes irritated Indiana, she had a certain respect for both Miss Peacock's insatiable curiosity and her computer-type mind, which seemed to file away facts and situations for future reference.

She must outwit both Gage and Miss Peacock, and she thought she could. "I'll have a party," she decided. She picked up the telephone and began calling. By now, the roads had been cleared for driving, and everyone she called was tired of staying home. When she talked to Rosemary, she said, "Darling you've made the most terrific hit with Gage. He's crazy about you." Rosemary seemed gratified and Indiana felt that she would keep him occupied all evening.

Next Indiana called the cook on her intercom. "Maria, I've got twenty coming for dinner and I want two round tables instead of that long one Daddy likes. Please work out a menu and call me later and in the meantime put lots of Daddy's best champagne on ice. The butler will remember what year."

After dinner, they would have a movie, and she chose one that both she and Sky had seen. He's so Hollywood-crazy that I wouldn't have a prayer of getting him away from a new movie, she thought. Now that she had made her plans, she would let the chips fall, and if they didn't work out, she would think up some other scheme for Sunday. All day Saturday she made no special effort to be with Sky. She felt that he seemed a little surprised, which was good, and that Miss Peacock, for the time being, appeared to lose interest in their relationship.

Everything was going just as she planned. There was a long cocktail hour, and it was past eleven when dinner was over. Some of the couples left and others straggled into the projection room for the film. "You'll love it," she said, "but don't be surprised if I fade away before the end, because I've already seen it twice," she told them.

She slipped into a rear seat next to Sky. After what seemed like an eternity but was only about twenty minutes, she leaned over and brushed her lips across his ear. "Let's get out of here. We haven't talked all weekend."

"Good idea. Where shall we go?"

"To my sitting room upstairs. I'll slip out first and you follow me in about ten minutes. I'll leave the door half open, so you won't get the wrong room."

She took off her dress and put on the pair of white satin pajamas that her father had just brought back from one of his trips. Her bed had already been turned down and her nightgown laid out, so no maid would be coming in, she noticed with satisfaction.

When Sky tapped lightly on the door and came in, she was lying on a chaise longue beside the fireplace in the sitting room and, apparently, looking through a book.

He sat down beside her on the chaise. "What are you reading?" He glanced at the book. "Oh it's Duveen's. Are you interested in art?"

"I've been thinking about it ever since you told me about the painting you had to sell to put yourself through college. What was it like?"

He flipped through the book, and then suddenly stopped and pulled out his wallet. "Here's a small photograph of it. I hate to think how much more it's worth now."

She sat up and put her arms around his neck. "I'm going to start collecting. Will you help me, darling?"

"Of course I will." Her pajama jacket had fallen open as she sat up, leaving her breasts bare. She lay back against her pillows, the book slid to the floor and he leaned over, gently fondling her breasts and kissing them. The rush of warmth through her whole body was a sensation she had never known before and she blissfully closed her eyes.

"You're beautiful, Indi, but I have no business fooling around with you this way."

She opened her eyes, put her arms around him, and pulled him closer. "Kiss me some more, Sky. I want you to touch me anywhere you feel like it. Is it really just fooling around?"

"Of course not. I'm mad for you. Any man would be, but I'm not a very permanent person at the moment."

She stood up and the white satin pants fell to the floor. She was far more beautiful nude than in anything he had ever seen.

Still sitting on the chaise, Sky began taking off his shirt and tie, and she watched him eagerly as he undressed. "Oh, Sky, I do want you to make love to me, more than anything I've ever wanted in my life. Sometimes when I've been sitting beside you, I've felt I would die if you didn't."

After he had taken off the rest of his clothes, he pulled Indiana to her feet and they stood locked in each other's arms.

"Oh please, Sky. I want to be closer and closer," she said. It was the most overpowering emotion she had ever felt in her life.

"We'll go to your bedroom."

She clung to him. "I don't think I can move."

He half carried her to the bed, and she lay down and held out her arms. He sat beside her for a minute, running his hands over her body and feeling its response.

"Please lie down beside me, darling."

In a moment he was making violent love to her. She had expected it to hurt, as some of her friends had reported, but it didn't. Instead, it was the most marvelous happiness and relaxation she had ever known.

They lay quietly for a minute, and then Indiana got up and went into her bathroom. When she came back and got into bed again, she said, "I'm not a virgin anymore, Sky. I'm not a virgin anymore."

"Are you sorry?" He turned and put his arms around her.

"No, just happy." She was quiet for a minute. "Have you made love to many girls before?"

"Not many, and nobody as sweet as you."

He thought of the first time. It was when he was sixteen and still at military school. Gage had taken him to a whorehouse in Chicago, and he had gone off into a room with one of the girls. It took what seemed like a half hour for him to take off his sword, remove his sash, untie his puttees and the rest of his uniform. By that time it was too late and the girl demanded ten dollars.

"Stay with me tonight, Sky," Indiana was saying. "Nobody else is in this corridor and you can get back to your room easily in the morning."

When he came back from the bathroom, she had put fresh sheets on the bed and was lying under the covers, still nude. "I want to feel you whenever I turn over," she said.

It was early in the morning when Sky woke. Indiana was

sound asleep, so he slid out of bed and went into the sitting room, where he had left his clothes. He put on his shorts, and holding the rest of his clothes in his hand, he tiptoed back to his own room.

He had just got into bed and started to close his eyes when the door opened and the woman Indiana had called Pinkie came into the room.

He sat up in bed. "Good morning, Pinkie."

"You know my name already." She gave him a broad, somewhat toothless smile. She walked to the window. "Many years ago, I forget how many, there used to be a lake out there, with swans on it," she said, pointing.

She's crazy, Sky thought. "Well, there's no sign of a lake now."

"I know. Mr. Bradshaw had it covered up after she died."

"Who do you mean by 'she'?"

"Miss Indiana's mother. This was her room and she liked to look out at the lake, but she was here only two years before she died."

"She must have been very pretty."

"Yes, so pretty. Like they say in the kitchen, a little Irish colleen. That was her first name, Colleen. Mr. Bradshaw was always jealous of anybody that looked at her. I heard them arguing a lot, and she crying the night before she was drown." Shaking her head, Pinkie left the room as suddenly and unexpectedly as she had come.

When Indiana woke the next morning, she reached out instinctively, hoping to find Sky still in bed beside her. Even though he was no longer there she felt completely happy. She stretched luxuriously, living over every blissful moment of the past night, and closed her eyes again in complete contentment.

The sun streaming through her windows finally reached her face with its warmth and she sat up lazily. It was the same room she had always known, with the same idiotic wallpaper and her childhood books on the shelves, but she had become a different person, she felt. She got up and went into the sitting room to pick up her white satin pajamas that were still lying on the floor beside the chaise longue. The pajamas were a reminder of the enchanted evening she would never forget and she hugged them lovingly.

Suddenly she was in a hurry to see Sky again. She rushed to her closet, pulled on a pair of pants and a warm sweater. As she brushed her hair and faced her smiling image in the mirror, she thought, isn't it wonderful. I'll never be lonely again.

Their last day at South Wind passed quickly. Gage had taken his rifle, and Sky had gone with him walking through the woods to look for game, but either the game was too wary or they didn't try hard enough, because they came back with nothing.

Indiana had been wondering all afternoon and through supper whether Sky would come to her room. They all went upstairs early to pack and, as she undressed, she waited hopefully for the knock on her door.

She was just giving up hope when he came, and she flew into his arms. "Couldn't make it earlier. Gage came in to talk about some story the *Globe* is hot on, but even if you had gone to sleep, I was going to barge right in and wake you up."

She began prancing happily around the room.

"Come here a minute and sit down. I love every part of you, but there was so much to look at last night that I've just got around to noticing that your feet and ankles are something special."

"Don't tell me you have a foot fetish like Daddy? Do you know the night of my debut he didn't talk about anything but my feet."

"No, darling, I didn't. But I think I'm developing a fetish for you."

"I like that."

"Then let's go to bed. Who knows when we'll have such a marvelous chance again?"

CHAPTER SEVEN

"Where's the butler? I'm not used to doing menial things like this," Gage said laughing as he and Sky dragged their suitcases up three flights of steps to their apartment on Monday morning. He picked up the mail on the floor as he went in, and threw it on a table.

"It's hard to come down to earth, isn't it?" Sky said. "Believe me, I sure hated to leave." He went to the little kitchenette to make some coffee and as he looked around at their cramped quarters, he thought they were about the size of the closet in Indiana's bedroom. It had been hard to say good-bye. She had held his hand all the way in and when he kissed her and said, "I'll call you later," she had looked at him as if they were parting forever.

The coffee was ready and he took a cup to Gage, who was in his bedroom. "You and Miss Peacock seemed to be hitting it off pretty well. You were taking the *Globe* apart all through the drive into town."

"She's an interesting woman and I've always heard that she has tremendous influence with the boss. She can be very helpful to me if she cares."

"I wish I had a benevolent friend in my life," Sky said.

"You don't need one. It looks as if you have Indiana right in the palm of your hand."

"Think so? Anyway I don't want any part of her father's newspaper."

Sky went back to the living room and started going through the mail. He wasn't expecting anything and was startled to find two telegrams and a letter. He tore open one of the telegrams first and saw that it came from Leland Harris, then read the message: "Call me at my New York office. Important message." The second telegram was also from Harris. "The *Look* cover has created interest with director Lesley Ruggles. Can you fly to Hollywood to test for role in his new college film? Call my New York office at once."

"Good God, Gage. Come in here. This telegram says I'm on a *Look* cover and I'm to go to Hollywood for a screen test."

Gage rushed in and read the two telegrams. "I'm going to run down and get the magazine right away."

"Thanks, and here's a letter, too, which seems to be from somebody else." He sat down and calmly opened it.

When Gage came back, Sky was sitting in a chair, gulping his coffee. "You won't believe this, but the David Selznick office wants to see me too. It's from his New York headquarters and signed by someone named Kay Brown."

Gage handed him the magazine, and picked up the telegrams and the letter. "I always knew you were going to make it, Sky, but I never thought it would happen as fast as this."

Sky seized the magazine. The cover showed him with Indiana doing the Charleston, but this time it was in color, and the photographer had shot it from a slightly different angle, focusing a little more on Sky's smile than her laughter. Wait until Indiana hears what's happened, he thought. He was tempted to call her, but decided to telephone the Leland Harris office first.

The Harris office seemed to know exactly what it was all about. "I'm his assistant. If it's possible, why don't you run over here this afternoon and talk to us," said a woman's voice.

Though everyone had been pleasant on his first visit there, this time his reception was warm and friendly and he felt he had suddenly taken the first step into their world. Harris was not in New York but his assistant said, "We all loved the cover and Lesley Ruggles is especially keen on you testing for a part in his new college film. They're going to start shooting the picture early next year, so to save time they've decided to have the test made here in New York on Friday morning, if you can manage it. Robert Ross will direct it."

"Luckily, I'm available."

He was so elated when he left the office that he felt he couldn't wait to get home, he had to tell someone right away. He went to a telephone booth and called Indiana.

"Hold onto your chair, darling. I've had a couple of fascinating nibbles from Hollywood."

"Who nibbled and for what?"

He told her the whole story and though she repeated "how wonderful" several times, already he knew her well enough to know that she was disappointed that he might be leaving soon.

"It's all due to you, Indi. If you hadn't invited me to your party and if you hadn't been Charlestoning since you were a baby, there would have been no cover picture and no Hollywood offers. Can we have dinner tonight and celebrate?"

Sky would have been less keyed up about the screen test Friday if he hadn't called the Selznick office and found they might have something for him in January.

He was happy that Robert Ross was going to direct the test. He had followed Ross's theater career, knew he was Margalo Gilmore's husband and felt reasonably at home with him when they met.

Robert Ross gave him the script. "Read it over while I check the lighting. It's a very simple scene. I want you to open the door. You come in with your books under your arm and set them down on the table over there," he pointed. "Suddenly you see that this young woman is in the room and you register surprise, and then go into the dialogue."

Sky felt that this was not just routine for Robert Ross. He was being very careful. He changed the lighting and reshot the scene several times.

When Sky left the studio he felt that everything had gone well. Robert Ross said, "Nice meeting you, Schuyler. I feel you've got a future in films and I wish you luck."

The next week was agony. He could think of nothing else, and it was hard not to call the Harris office. After a few days, he finally gave in and dialed the number. Mr. Harris's secretary, Kate Malley, came on the line and said, "No news yet. We'll be in touch with you the minute we hear."

At least the answer hadn't been no, but were they just letting him down easily? he began to wonder after the rest of the week had passed. He started walking casually along Madison Avenue in the vicinity of Sixtieth Street, hoping to meet someone from the Harris office. In spite of his resolution not to make a nuisance of himself, he finally turned into the building and went into the penthouse office. "Nothing yet, Mr. Madison. We did send the test out to Hollywood by plane as they requested, but sometimes they're slow about making up their minds."

Now he was sure that Lesley Ruggles had already forgotten the whole thing and that his test was lying forgotten in someone's drawer. He was chagrined that he had been so childish as to tell everyone he knew about the test, and to believe that anything would ever come of it.

He was sitting moodily in the apartment the next morning reading the papers when the telephone rang and Miss Malley's voice said, "Well, good news, Mr. Madison. Hollywood has just telephoned. They like the test very much. Can you find time this afternoon to come into the office and talk about a contract?"

Sky could never recall how he answered. When he hung up the receiver, he got up and walked back and forth in the little living room, not knowing whether to laugh or cry. His whole future seemed to be unrolling before him, as if it were a script that he had written himself.

"Mr. Harris will see you personally," Miss Malley said as she led Sky to the private office that afternoon.

Leland Harris was talking over one of the telephones on his large desk when Sky came in, and Harris went right on talking but motioned for him to sit down. Harris wasn't at all what he had expected of Hollywood's most famous agent. He was a handsome man, with close-cropped hair, somber eyes and a romantic, dedicated look. He finished the telephone conversation, and with exactly the same tone he had been using, said to Sky, "You've got the part. I think I may be able to get you a term contract with the studio. They're developing a young company of actors and you're the type they want. If I can get you seven years, they'll start you at five hundred dollars a week, with yearly options escalating to five thousand dollars a week by the seventh year."

Sky's head was swimming. He could hardly conceive of making so much money so quickly. "Whatever you say, Mr. Harris."

"All right. We'll call you back when we finish negotiations and have the contract ready for you to sign. You'll have to be in Hollywood within a month."

When he reached the apartment, Gage was just getting up and fixing a light meal for himself before going to the paper. "Gage, you're never going to believe this, and I'm not sure I do either." He gave Gage a word-for-word replay of the whole scene.

"God, how great! Wait until Fort Wayne hears about this. Mom says everybody is talking about the *Look* cover. They sold out every copy of the magazine the second day it appeared on the stands. They couldn't get over you dancing with Bradshaw Green's daughter."

"Bradshaw Green's daughter is a dream girl." He sat down and dialed Indiana's private number. "Thank goodness you're having dinner with me tonight. I've got the greatest news."

"You're going to Hollywood?"

"Yes, I got the part. You're going to be pleased when you hear everything."

He had known that she wouldn't receive the news with undiluted joy, but he was glad she seemed cheerful when he picked her up at the Fifth Avenue house. "I never face anything sad until I have to," she said.

"It's not sad, Indi. You've known all along how much I want a career."

"I suppose I have, and I'm happy for you, Sky. When do you leave?" She looked as if she were going to cry. "At least you'll come to the country for Christmas, and promise right now that when you go that I can see you off."

"I'd love that, darling."

From then on, they had dinner together every night, either at his favorite hamburger place or at the Fifth Avenue house, where he had begun to feel quite at home. Bradshaw Green was never in evidence. "You know sometimes I go for weeks without running into Daddy. We just don't keep the same hours."

Sometimes Sky and Indiana even met in the afternoon to go to a gallery or see a movie. They talked constantly about his plans and how soon they could manage to see each other again. "Maybe you can come out there around Easter. By that time I ought to be pretty well established and have made some friends."

"Yes, I'll come then, but I'll write you regularly and talk to you a lot over the telephone."

"I'm sure I'm going to like Hollywood, and so will you. You know, darling, this is only a beginning for me. I'm not going to stick with acting. I want to go on to writing and directing."

"I know and of course you will."

On Friday, December 20, a long telegram arrived from Leland Harris. "Term contract with Olympia Studios has been arranged on exactly the terms we discussed. Have initialed it for you, and you can sign formally when you arrive. You are expected to report at the studio January 2."

Thanksgiving weekend in the country had been perfect and Sky had been looking forward to spending Christmas there. When he and Indiana drove through the gates of South Wind on Christmas Eve, they could see, even from a distance, that the house was outlined in a blaze of lights.

"Daddy must be here. He said he was going to be somewhere else, but I guess he's changed his mind or else she changed it for him."

As they drove up in front of the house, Bradshaw Green and a woman in a long mink coat were just going in the door.

"It's Dorothy Darrow. I'm surprised at Daddy. He knows I can't endure her. The minute I look at her, I begin feeling like a cat with its hair being rubbed the wrong way."

"Well, I'll keep smoothing it the right way," said Sky, who was determined to have as happy a Christmas as possible. As he went upstairs to his room he noticed that the house had been professionally decorated with pine branches, several different varieties of holly, and an occasional red bow. There was no tree in sight and he guessed the Green family life had never been constant or warm enough to support such an institution.

When Sky came downstairs for dinner he found Bradshaw Green sitting quietly in the library and smoking a cigar. "Good evening, Schuyler. Glad to have this chance to see you again."

"So am I, sir."

"I knew your father. He was a fine man, and I heard your mother came from Indiana."

"Yes, sir. Fort Wayne. My aunt still lives there and I grew up in their home after my parents died."

"Finest state in the country. True blue. The heart of America. My father and grandfather lived there, and that's why I named my daughter Indiana. I've always had a hankering for continuity."

"It's different, but somehow it seems to suit her."

Sky suddenly smelled perfume, and turned to see Dorothy Darrow come in. She was blond, rather pretty and pushing thirty, he guessed, but was dressed like a girl of sixteen, in a knee-length dress. Her short hair was swooped across her forehead and held back at one side with a small pale-blue bow, and she was wearing open plastic shoes with spiked heels.

Bradshaw Green put down his cigar. "Take off those goddamn whore shoes, Dottie," he ordered. "Those spike heels don't suit you and they certainly don't go with that 'Bo Peep' dress."

"Oh dear. They're such fun to wear." Her smile faded.

"Bring them here, Dottie."

She pattered across the room in her stocking feet and gave him the shoes. He threw them in the fire and pressed a bell beside him on the arm of his chair. "Pardon this little interlude, Schuyler. Miss Darrow has exceptionally beautiful feet and ankles, but she seems to have no idea how to show them off." The maid appeared, "Please go upstairs and bring down Miss Darrow's white satin pumps."

Dorothy Darrow was holding out her feet for Sky to inspect. He looked obediently at the pink toes that were clearly visible under the sheer stockings, but thought to himself that Indiana's feet and legs were much more gracefully molded.

At the same moment, Bradshaw Green said, "Of course, my daughter has the most beautiful feet I've ever seen. She inherited them from her mother."

"Feet! Feet! I get so bored with constant talk of feet," Dorothy Darrow shouted as the maid returned with the white satin pumps.

Indiana swept into the room, and Sky could see at once that she was angry. Her eyes were burning, and her hair was more tumultuous than usual. She was wearing a long silk dress with a shirtwaist top and no jewelry.

"What an interesting dress, dear. Whose is it?" Dorothy Darrow asked.

"It's mine but if you mean who designed it, he's a young American who works for Hattie Carnegie. I think his name is Norman Norell."

"I do still love the French look, don't you? And what are we going to do now that Paris has fallen?"

Indiana shrugged her shoulders and went over to Sky.

"I guess the Americans will have their chance at last." Dorothy went on chattering.

Bradshaw Green stood up quickly. "Shall we go to dinner?" At the table, while Dorothy Darrow held forth on the subject of fashion, Sky had a chance to study Bradshaw Green. His head was impressive with plenty of hair streaked with gray, but he had a mouth that seldom relaxed into a real smile. His skin was puffy and mottled, and Sky remembered that Gage reported recently, "The boss is spending lots more time than he used to at the bar in Bleeck's."

"For God's sake, Dottie," Bradshaw Green finally said, "let's leave the fashions to the fashion magazines."

"Oh isn't he dreadful?" Dorothy Darrow said, turning toward Sky. She smiled and leaned toward him, managing to give him a full view of her breasts. "I hear you're going to Hollywood and have just signed a wonderful contract. Is it true what the columns say?"

He laughed. "Sometimes I think I've dreamed it, but I guess it's true."

"I hope to be going there about the same time. We'll both be strangers in the wild, woolly West, so we must see lots of each other." She batted her eyes. "What's your first part? Do you know?"

"I believe Lesley Ruggles wants me for a college film, but of course I don't know for sure until I get there."

"Oh that's the picture I want so much to be in. I thought it would be just right for my debut in films."

She looks as much like a college student as I look like Eleanor Roosevelt, Indiana thought to herself. She tried to interrupt the conversation but Dorothy Darrow persisted, "I have a feeling you're going to be a great, big star. And my feelings are usually right. You're so handsome and you have the most beautiful smile."

Sky could feel the color coming up in his face. "I saw you in *Babes in Arms* with Mitzi Green, Miss Darrow, and you were very good."

"Oh yes, Daddy Green liked me in that, too."

Indiana thought to herself, I think I'm going to vomit. She turned to her father and said, "Sky has a cousin working on the *Globe*, Daddy."

"Yes, Gage Hale. He's out in Fort Wayne taking a week's vacation with his mother," Sky volunteered.

"Ever have any newspaper aspirations yourself?" Bradshaw Green asked.

"Not really, sir. I've done some writing and I enjoy it, but there's always been a connection with the theater."

"I doubt that you're going to like Hollywood as much as you think you are. It wouldn't surprise me a bit if you are right back here by this time next year."

While he was talking with Sky he had been observing him with approval. Miss Peacock had given him a favorable report but he had wanted to be sure she was right. Now he saw for himself that Sky had all the right assets—and old New York family name combined with an Indiana background; good looks and assurance without being brassy. In one of his rare reverent moments he thanked God for providing him with the perfect son-in-law at just the perfect time. He's intelligent with plenty of guts and could easily step into my shoes someday as head of all the papers, once he gets this damn Hollywood bug out of his mind.

After dinner he suggested running a movie, but Indiana said quickly, "Thank you, Daddy, but Rosemary is expecting us," and they went out.

It was after midnight when they returned. "Our first Christmas together, Indi," he said as he kissed her outside before they opened the door.

As they tiptoed through the hallway and started up the stairs, they could hear Dorothy Darrow sobbing and moaning, Bradshaw Green shouting and the crash of glasses breaking. "Daddy always throws them into the fireplace when he's very angry. He's frightening when he's mad, but it will serve her right if he throws her Christmas present into the fire after the glasses."

"What is it? Do you know?"

"Rubies, I guess. She craves them."

"When do you want me to give you your rubies, darling? Right now or tomorrow morning?"

"Oh let's have our Christmas now."

He went to his bureau drawer and took out a small velvet box. Inside was a delicate bracelet of gold links with a small gold heart charm dangling from it.

"Oh Sky, I do love it. Put it on my wrist and I'll never take it off."

" 'Never' is a long time, Indi."

"I know, but I truly mean it. Now I'm going to get your present, at least part of it."

She came back in a few minutes, wrapped in her terry-cloth robe and carrying a suitcase. "This is one of six. I couldn't carry them all but I got you all kinds and sizes of luggage from Mark Cross. I couldn't stand the thought of you arriving in Hollywood with those terrible things you brought here for Thanksgiving."

"Thanks to you, darling, I'll look like a millionaire in California."

"We have so few nights, Sky. Let's make love."

"Darling, I feel uneasy in this house with your father and that woman here. It wouldn't be right."

"All right. Then let's go back to New York tomorrow right after lunch."

Since Gage was in Fort Wayne, they spent most of the next week in Sky's apartment. "It's not exactly what you're used to," he said the first night, "and I suppose there isn't a chance you can scramble an egg or make coffee?"

"Not a chance, but I plan to learn. I'm going to learn lots of things while you're away."

"I'm glad. I'll be learning a lot, too."

She began helping him with his packing. He had decided to take all of his possessions with him, and as he transferred them to his new luggage he showed her old Triangle photographs and let her read some of the Princeton clippings. She seemed to be fascinated with the Picasso sketch and asked him to show her again the snapshot of the painting he had sold to get himself through college.

"You must have hated to give it up."

"Oh well, it's over and done with now, and the result was certainly worthwhile."

They spent New Year's Eve at the Stork Club, and the next morning it was suddenly time to leave for the airport. As he handed the porter his luggage at La Guardia he turned to her. "I guess this is it," he said.

They stood looking at each other for a few minutes and then he bent down to kiss her. "I'm very happy with you, Indi. Happier than I've ever been in my life."

"That's the nicest thing you've ever said to me."

"I'll say lots more then when I call you from Hollywood in a few days."

"I'll always love you, Sky."

"I hope so," he said, and then he was gone.

CHAPTER EIGHT

It was Sky's first major flight. He had taken aviation at Princeton and had even made a few solo flights as far as Red Bank and back. Now sitting in his window seat with his seat belt fastened, he realized that compared with this his previous experience had been like playing with a toy. Once in the air he felt exhilarated. He and Gage had often talked about flying to Fort Wayne, but in the end it had seemed simpler to take a train. Now as they left the waterfront and the tall buildings behind, and began flying over the countryside, he knew that he would never travel any other way, if it were possible. It was a clear day and he was amused to watch the shadow of the plane flying across the ground below. He read for a while and then, for the fourth time since it had been delivered, he reread the latest telegram from Leland Harris. It read: "You will be met at the Los Angeles airport and driven to the Château Marmont, where we have made a reservation for you. Please report both to Olympia Studios and our office on January 2." He could hardly believe he was going to be in Hollywood that night, the first day of 1941.

They stopped to refuel at Chicago and then again at Denver, and it was early evening by West Coast time when they began their descent and he saw the lights of Los Angeles.

Everything happened just as the telegram had said. He had hardly left the plane when he heard his name called. He went to an information desk, where he found an affable-looking young man waiting.

"Schuyler Madison? I'm Chester Fields from the Harris office."

They shook hands. "Nice of you to meet me. I've never been to the West Coast before."

"You're never going to want to leave. I was born out here and I wouldn't want to live anywhere else."

When they reclaimed Sky's luggage, he was aware that his were the best-looking bags in the mass of luggage and he must remember to say so to Indi.

As a porter managed to wedge the six pieces into Fields' little car, Fields said, "Well, I can see that you're planning to be with us for quite a while, at least."

"As long as they let me." The air felt like early spring. He took off his topcoat and threw it into the back seat.

Three quarters of an hour later, he asked, "What part of the city is this, Chester?"

"Say, call me Ches, everyone does. Now we are on famous Sunset Boulevard."

Sky began to feel ridiculously happy and to ask what some of the buildings were.

Ches responded to his enthusiasm, "I can see you're not dead tired, so I'll go a little farther and show you Hollywood Boulevard, but it looks pretty tacky now with the Christmas decorations still up." Sky, though, was charmed by its picturesque tawdriness.

They turned back and drove to the Château Marmont. Ches pointed across the street. "That's the Garden of Allah. Alla Nazimova, the silent-screen star, lived there, and now it's a de luxe hotel where some of the big-timers stay."

"Oh yes, I remember. People like Scott Fitzgerald and Robert Benchley." Sky had read about them all.

Inside, the Château Marmont seemed quiet and pleasant, and before they parted, Ches said, "I'll be around tomorrow morning around nine-thirty. We've ordered a rental car for you. It's the only way you can get around out here. I'll take you over to pick it up, then you can follow me to Olympia Studios."

"Thanks a lot, Ches."

"Here's my home telephone number. Feel free to call me for anything you need."

Sky went to his room, took a few of his lighter-weight clothes from one of the bags and went to sleep. The next morning it took him all of five minutes to realize that he was not in New York on Gage's sofa bed but on a bed of his own in a Hollywood hotel.

He and Ches picked up the car. Sky followed him to Olympia Studios, which he noticed were near Paramount.

He went in expectantly, taking in every detail of the place in which he would soon be working. They seemed to be aware of his name at the main reception desk, welcomed him with a smile, and pointed out the direction to the Ruggles bungalow.

When he gave his name to a secretary, Lesley Ruggles' assistant came out smiling. "We're glad you've arrived safely, Schuyler Madison. We've been looking forward to seeing you. Unfortunately Mr. Ruggles is still in Palm Springs and won't be in his office until next Monday morning, but he left word with me that he wants to see you then."

"Of course. Did he specify the time?"

"I should think about 11:00 A.M."

"I'll be here. Thank you." Sky felt a little let down. He was eager to get to work and had hoped to start immediately. He was about to turn away when the assistant to Ruggles said, "Don't go yet. Fritz Reid, the publicity director of the studio, wants to meet you. I'll take you over to his bungalow."

Fritz Reid came out of his office full of enthusiasm. "You're really remarkably photogenic, Mr. Madison. I was impressed by your test. I'd like to set up a session with you in our portrait department. We'll need lots of ammunition for the publicity build-up we have outlined for you."

"Fine, Mr. Reid. I'm at the Château Marmont and since I just got here I haven't made any commitments yet."

"Then my secretary will call you in the morning and set a definite time."

Sky went back to his car, and Ches, who was parked just ahead of him, called, "Follow me closely or you'll get lost." When they reached the Harris office in Beverly Hills he asked, "Think you can find your way back to the Marmont, or do you still need help?"

"No thanks. I've got a pretty good sense of direction and I can always ask." At the Harris office, his contract was all ready for his signature and just signing it made him feel more confident and secure. The staff was aware that Lesley Ruggles was not in town, and Leland Harris's secretary said, "Actually this is a break for you. It gives you a few days to do nothing but orient yourself.

Why don't you take your car and buzz around wherever you feel like."

It made sense. As he went out, Sky told himself he was being overanxious. He got into the little convertible, put the top down and began driving along the streets, even going up one of the canyon roads, where some of the houses seemed to be cantilevered out over space. When he came down he decided to go back to Hollywood and take a closer look at Grauman's Chinese Theater. Corny as he knew everybody in the movie world would think he was, he wanted to inspect the footprints of Douglas Fairbanks, Mary Pickford, and Nora Hayes.

The next morning Fritz Reid's secretary called and made an appointment for him to come to the photography studio on Friday. "Bring a sport jacket, some sweaters and scarfs and anything else you can think of as especially collegiate."

Since Sky had the whole day free, he went to the desk clerk and asked, "Which way do I go to get to the Pacific Ocean?"

"As you go out the drive make a right turn and keep driving west. You can't miss it."

As Sky drove along he was aware of all the roads that twisted down from the hills and poured into Sunset Boulevard and thought to himself, "If I do stay here seven years, I'll probably know a lot of people who live up there."

It was about an hour when he reached the top of a winding road, and saw the Pacific Ocean in the distance. It was magnificent.

At the bottom of the hill he decided to turn left on the wide ocean road that had only a narrow strip of land between it and the water. When a big, white clapboard house loomed up on the right, he decided it must be Marion Davies' famous beach house. Later on he turned left and decided to take Washington Boulevard to try to get back to town.

About twenty minutes later, he was aware of a long stretch of white two-story buildings. He looked on top of a taller building and saw a billboard on which the lion's head that had prefaced so many of his favorite films was printed along with three words, *Metro Goldwyn Mayer*. He drove to the curb, stopped his car and looked at it for a few minutes, thinking of Greta Garbo, Joan

Crawford, Clark Gable, Spencer Tracy and many of his idols who worked there.

Oh, God, would I love making a picture in that studio, he thought.

When he reached the hotel again, there was a message and a telephone number. "Please call Cobina Wright." He dialed the number, and a woman's voice, very warm and quite low, said, "This is Cobina Wright. You won't know me, Schuyler, but your mother and father were friends of mine, and my husband and I lost our money in the Wall Street crash just as they did. I was delighted to read that you're out here to start a career in the movies."

"I hope so, Mrs. Wright, and thank you for calling me."

"I want to see you and I thought perhaps you might like to come to dinner on Saturday night."

"I'd be delighted to, Mrs. Wright."

"I should have asked if you have a car because if you haven't, one of us can pick you up."

"I have a car and I think I can find my way."

He took down the address, and she added, "I'm just above 'Pickfair.' I have a daughter, Cobina Wright, Jr., just about your age, and quite a few of her friends will be here."

I guess I'd better get an engagement pad and something for telephone numbers, he thought.

When Friday morning came, he was happy to be on his way to Olympia Studios again. He had felt he was taking a step in the right direction when he had packed part of his college wardrobe. Fritz Reid seemed pleased with what he had brought, and the portrait photographer kept him over four hours while he made all kinds of shots.

Before he left the studio, word came down from the executive office that B. B. Balzer, the president of Olympia Pictures, wanted to see him Monday morning at ten. That would be an hour before he met Lesley Ruggles. It was going to be a momentous day, Sky thought.

As he drove up Summit Drive to Cobina Wright's party Saturday night, he knew he must be near her house when he passed the big white wall that surrounded "Pickfair." Even without

"Pickfair," he could hardly have missed it, since music was coming out of the windows and the line of parked cars reached two blocks away.

When he went into the large drawing room, Cobina Wright hurried to greet him. "You don't look a bit like your father, but I recognized you immediately from your photographs." Mrs. Wright was a warm, attractive woman who spoke with a suggestion of a pout. "Schuyler, I especially want you to meet my daughter, Cobina, Jr. She came out in the same group with Brenda Frazier, but darling Brenda got all the publicity." She leaned over and almost whispered, "I'm going to tell you something, my daughter never will, that young Prince Philip of Greece is crazy about her. They met a few years ago when we were all in Venice."

Sky had already recognized Cobina, Jr., as the blond girl in white who was standing by the piano surrounded by a group of men. She was beautiful, he thought, but a much less vital person than her mother.

Word that he had walked off with a sure-fire part at Olympia had already filtered out, and everyone he met seemed interested and helpful. Robert Stack asked him if he liked tennis and then if he'd like to play the next afternoon. Gene Tierney and her husband, Oleg Cassini, invited him to a buffet supper the following week. He went home at midnight feeling he had just walked into the warmest, most hospitable group of people he had ever known.

After an early breakfast he kept looking at his watch wondering what would be the best time to call Indiana in New York. Finally at nine he placed the call, figuring she would just be getting up. "Guess what I'm getting ready to do, darling," he said when she answered.

"It's snowing again here. I'm afraid to leave the house. What are you going to do, darling?"

"Well, I have my tennis shorts on and I'm going to play tennis with Bob Stack." He went on to tell her about Cobina Wright's party and, though she kept saying "how wonderful," he knew she was depressed. It was impossible to infect someone else with your enthusiasm, especially if the person was three thousand miles away.

Monday morning he arrived on the dot of ten at Olympia and was shown directly to the president's office. B. B. Balzer was smoking a cigar, and for a minute reminded Sky of Bradshaw Green. On his desk was the *Look* magazine with the Charleston cover.

"Good morning, Mr. Balzer."

"Hello, Schuyler. Glad to have you with us. I've been reading the material the office has given me and looked at the photographs of you. The test you made in New York was splendid, and I must say that I think you have the makings of a major star."

"Thank you, Mr. Balzer. That's very encouraging to hear."

"Our plan is to start you in a few collegiate films and capitalize on your youth for, say, a couple of years. Then we'll move you on to more romantic roles, which I'm sure you could play well. We have hopes of making you a second Tyrone Power. He's been making a fortune for Fox."

Sky laughed, "There's nothing I'd like better, Mr. Balzer, and I'll do my best."

Lesley Ruggles was equally enthusiastic. When Sky came into his office he held out his hand. "You're exactly what I had visualized for this part and, believe me, that seldom happens. Usually you just have to make do with what they finally give you."

"I'm sure I'm going to enjoy working with you."

"Yes, I think we'll get on. The working title of the film is *College Prom* and I think the name will stick. It sounds snappy."

"When do you expect to start?"

"Sometime next week. I've already alerted the wardrobe department, and my assistant will take you there to get measured for your clothes."

After the wardrobe department he was relayed to publicity, where the writer who had been assigned asked him for more information, if possible, to add to the press release that would be sent out to papers all across the country early next week. "The photographs taken Friday were all very good, and we think that a new face is going to add a great deal of interest to the picture," the writer said.

Sky left the studio so elated that he felt he had to drive around a little to make himself cool off. The rest of the week passed in a kind of happy daze. He swam, played tennis, and went to a few parties. Since he was all set for work next week, he felt he could indulge himself without feeling he was wasting time.

When the telephone rang early one morning, he was sure it was Olympia telling him when and where to report. It was Kate Malley's voice, though.

"I'm afraid you're going to be disappointed, Schuyler, but we've just had word from Olympia that you're not going to play the part in the Ruggles film after all."

It was such a sudden shock that he had to sit down. "But it was all settled, Miss Malley. They were all so enthusiastic and I was even measured for the clothes I was going to wear."

"We thought it was settled, too. We haven't the slightest clue as to what happened, and all I can tell you is that things like this often happen in Hollywood."

"Is there anything I can do about it?"

"Not a thing at the moment, but something will come along. You have a term contract and it may be that the studio decided to put you in a different kind of film. Anyway, we'll keep in touch with you, and don't hesitate to call us at any time."

He remained sitting on the edge of the bed for a few minutes analyzing every word of his interview with B. B. Balzer and Lesley Ruggles and wondering whether it was anything he had said or done that had changed their minds. "I suppose everything was just too easy and this is the kind of setback everybody has to take in his stride," he decided finally.

He went downstairs and across the street to Schwab's drugstore, which was always full of hopeful boys and girls from all over the country, drinking coffee and reading the Hollywood *Reporter* and *Daily Variety* and any other newspapers on the stand without charge. Last week he had been full of sympathy for them but now he was back in their league. Not quite, though. What am I so down about? he reasoned. I'm getting five hundred dollars a week no matter what happens, and, Miss Malley says, something even better may turn up. But he hated to think of the days of uncertainty and idleness that were ahead.

It was two days before he could brace himself to call Indiana and tell her what had happened. As he expected, she reacted violently. "I can't believe it. The fools. They must be out of their minds. Oh I miss you, Sky."

"I miss you too, darling, but don't worry. Something will turn up, and it may be that the studio has better plans for me. That's what they seem to think at the Harris office." He paused, "Yes, dear, they're still being very solicitous at Olympia and giving me quite the star treatment."

After he hung up he went across the street to Schwab's drugstore for a sandwich and Coke, and picked up the Hollywood *Reporter* on the way to the counter. A front-page story immediately caught his eye. "*College Prom* Called Off," it was headlined. He went on reading that Lesley Ruggles had left Olympia Studios in a huff after an argument with studio heads. When questioned, B. B. Balzer commented, "We regret losing Ruggles but hope to get *College Prom* rescheduled with another director soon." So that's it, Sky thought.

Though he had regained his self-confidence, Sky was still glad when Cobina Wright called him that night and asked him to a fancy dress party that Rex St. Cyr was giving at Ciro's. "He is new out here and asked me to do the guest list for him and I said I would," she had said.

"It sounds like fun."

"It will be. You'll see everybody in Hollywood and that will be good for you."

Sky decided to call the studio to ask to borrow a costume, and the reply was enthusiastic. "Of course, Mr. Madison. Come in and be fitted for anything you want. B. B. Balzer will be happy to know that you are circulating. Partygoing brings publicity that will help build your image." Sky chose something that Fred Astaire had once worn in a film. It was a Bavarian costume with a white shirt, green suede shorts to the knee, embroidered jacket, and long green wool socks. They were delivered to him by the studio on the afternoon of the party.

It was the first time he had seen top Hollywood at a mass gathering and he was sure it didn't happen often, except at the Oscar presentations. They had all turned out, partly because of the mystery host whom most of them had never seen, and because with a war looming, nobody else was in the mood for such lavish entertaining.

He looked around and could hardly believe his eyes. All the stars he had read about and idolized during his young moviegoing days were right there, and before the evening was over he would have talked to many of them. There was Dorothy Lamour, and Sonja Henie talking to Tyrone Power, and Ginger Rogers looking like a dream.

Just then Nora Hayes came in. She was wearing what he supposed was a Cleopatra costume with a jeweled band around her head and a long sheer robe over a jeweled bra and long skirt. She was alone for a moment and he went over to her.

"I'm Schuyler Madison, Miss Hayes, and I don't expect you to know me. I just wanted to tell you how lovely you look."

She smiled. "Of course I know you, Schuyler, whom almost everybody calls Sky, you once told me."

"How nice you are."

"I don't think you quite realize, Sky, how much publicity you have had recently, and that more people than you think are looking at you tonight and recognizing you, but of course you and I date back to our trip on the *Île*."

"I was madly in love with you."

"I hope you still are." She smiled. "I remember you dancing with the little Green girl. When I saw on the *Look* cover that you're still dancing with her, I was quite touched." She smiled at him, "Has she become as pretty as she is in her photographs?"

He had thought from the beginning that Nora Hayes was a sensitive, romantic woman and now he knew he was right. "Yes, but Indiana's more than that. She's a real beauty."

Nora Hayes took his arm and said, "I know from the columns what you are doing here, but let's go off in a corner for a few minutes so I can hear all about it."

He decided to tell her the whole story, and when he finished she said, "How disappointing, but Hollywood is famous for sudden changes. Maybe I can be helpful. Rosalind Russell is about to start a new picture and they're shopping around for a fresh face." She stood up. "Roz is here tonight and I'll take you over and introduce you."

On their way around the room, Nora Hayes stopped to introduce him to Louella Parsons, who was wearing a big hat and was dressed as Lillian Russell. She beamed, and said with her midwestern twang, "I had the exclusive story of you signing with Olympia, and I hope to have many more exclusives about you."

He thanked her and they went on to the table where Rosalind Russell, wearing a country cotton dress and a big straw hat pinned to the back of her head, was sitting with Frederick Brisson, Janet Gaynor, and Janet's husband, Adrian, the MGM designer.

Nora Hayes introduced Sky, and Roz said, "Sit down and join the guessing game. We're all trying to spot him. None of us have ever seen him, so the one who guesses right is going to get some kind of prize. We haven't decided what."

"Who do you mean?" Nora Hayes asked.

"Our host," Rosalind Russell continued. "All we know is that he's said to have married two filthy-rich Texas ladies, not at the same time, of course, who died quickly and conveniently."

"You forgot the best part, Roz," Freddy Brisson interrupted. "Each one was sweet enough to leave him millions."

Sometime later, Sky, who was talking to Adrian, overheard Nora telling Roz that Lesley Ruggles had apparently had a last-minute change of mind about doing *College Prom* and the film had been postponed.

He saw Roz studying him and thought, "What I wouldn't give to work with her."

She leaned across the table, smiling, "I hear your name is Sky and that you're available. Jack Conway, my director, happens to be looking for someone who might be you."

"There's nothing I'd like better than working in a film with you, Miss Russell."

"Well, it's not exactly my film. It's Clark Gable's, and I play opposite him, but there's a dandy part of my kid brother that might be just up your alley."

"I'd sure like to take a crack at it."

She turned to her husband. "Then, Freddy, write down where we can reach him. Someone from MGM will get in touch with you soon, Sky."

CHAPTER NINE

According to his calendar, Sky had been in Hollywood exactly three months and two days. Most of the time he had been reasonably happy, even though nothing definite had materialized.

The studio had kept him busy doing publicity shots. He had been photographed with Carol Phillips, a new starlet, fishing off the pier at Malibu. He had pretended to play polo at the Riviera stables, and the studio's cameras had also followed him to the races at Santa Anita where, at their request, he took a new contract actress, Ruth Reynolds.

To be a single man in Hollywood, he had soon discovered, was anyone's dream. By this time he knew all the starlets. Most of them were newcomers who were eager to get around and anxious to be seen with him. Besides the movie girls, not only Cobina Wright but also many of her friends wanted to enlist him as an escort for their career-minded daughters.

He had more invitations than he could possibly cope with. He had developed a kind of stalling technique. Whatever the invitation was, he answered, "I'd love to but unfortunately I have an unconfirmed date that I'll have to check on. I'll let you know later." At the last minute, he chose the best invitation.

He looked at his watch and saw that it was time to keep his lunch date with Fritz Reid at the Olympia commissary. There was a line waiting but Fritz was standing at the door and beckoning to him to come in.

They had a small table in the section that was reserved for VIPs. He looked around him and saw Carole Lombard, whom he

knew had come from Fort Wayne. He remembered the house her
family had lived in on the North Side, quite near Aunt Addie's.
She had been his idol since Culver days. Turning, he saw Ginger
Rogers at another table lunching with her director, Brad Dexter.

Fritz waved his hand at Ginger, then turned to Sky. "You
know, Ginger has a new film coming up soon. It's a nonmusical
and I think there's a part in it that might be just right for you.
Speak to B. B. Balzer about it."

"It sounds great." Sky's eyes had wandered from Ginger to a
table of young people about his own age who were wearing cos-
tumes for an early-American Western. They were laughing and
talking and he envied their involvement in whatever film they
were making.

Fritz followed his gaze. "You're cut out for something better
than that. We're not giving you all this build-up with the press to
have you gallop around in some B movie."

"I'm aware of that, Fritz, and very appreciative."

"Well, it all helps. Be sure to get the April *Photoplay*. It has a
whole layout and story about you."

"Thanks. I've seen it, and it's great." He had already bought
two extra copies and mailed one to Aunt Addie and the other to
Indiana.

He considered sending Indi the interview Hedda Hopper had
done with him, but decided not to. Hedda had really bubbled
with enthusiasm when she talked with him, and had written:
"Schuyler Madison is the most sought-after young man for Hollywood dinners these nights. The hostesses are all fighting for him
and he may have to take on a secretary to keep the invitations
straight." That was only the beginning. She had gone on about
his old New York name and his looks. He had liked her and it
was all very nice, but he would have traded the praise willingly
for even a minor part in a film.

On their way out of the commissary, Fritz Reid made a point
of stopping by the Rogers table and introducing him to the star
and her director.

During the rest of the afternoon, Sky wandered around the
sound stages, as he often did, watching various directors at work
and observing their different techniques. He had made friends

with the film librarian, and often when one of the projection rooms was available, sat hour after hour in a battered leather chair running one film after another.

That evening Indiana telephoned that she was, at long last, coming to Hollywood, and had reserved a suite at the Beverly Wilshire for two weeks. She had said her father insisted she take the *Twentieth Century* to Chicago and then cross the rest of the country in the *Super Chief*. He had also wanted Miss Peacock to come with her but she had argued him into accepting Pinkie instead.

Indiana got off the train in Pasadena with her hair flying and her eyes shining. She rushed into Sky's arms. "Oh Sky. Is it really true?" She looked up at him. "I'm so happy."

He kissed her. "Well, don't cry about it then." He helped Pinkie off the train and when they reached his car, Indiana drew back and looked at him. "You're the same, darling, but you look a little older and more serious."

"I don't see how three months could do all that to me, but you forget. I've always had my serious moments and I've had quite a few of them out here."

"But you're having a wonderful time. I read Hedda Hopper's column."

"I was sure you would, but good times can get to be like too much dessert if you don't have something solid to do in the daytime." By now they were approaching the outskirts of Beverly Hills. "Say, darling, everybody out here wants to meet the debutante of the year. You'll find a bushel of invitations at your hotel."

"It's funny, but that seems such a long time ago. Do we have to go to all the parties?" she asked as they drove along in his car.

"No. I go because the studio wants me to be seen everywhere. People here entertain constantly. They're nice and I like them, but I have no obligations and we can pick and choose just a few."

To have Indiana with him was more wonderful than he remembered. Once she and Pinkie were settled in their enormous suite at the Beverly Wilshire, he said, "Where would you like to go for dinner tonight, darling?"

"I'm sure you've discovered some favorite hamburger joint."

"Come on now, Indi. I'm now at least a would-be movie star

and I was thinking of either Romanoff's, Chasen's or the Brown Derby."

"Oh I'd love to see the Brown Derby, I've heard so much about it, but I don't care about seeing movie stars. I just want to look at you."

They lunched in her suite and never stopped talking. When they arrived at the Brown Derby that evening, Sky was hailed by several people as they went through the restaurant to their booth.

Robert Stack came over to their table, and Sky could see that he was instantly intrigued with Indiana. "I'm with Ann Rutherford. Why don't you join us at the Cocoanut Grove later?"

"It's up to Indi. She's just off the *Chief* this morning."

"If I manage to keep my eyes open we'll come," Indiana said, but after he left she looked at Sky and laughed. "I couldn't be more wide awake, but what I really want is to go someplace where I can take off all my clothes and let you make love to me."

"I guess I was hoping you felt that way."

He took her to his little apartment at the Château Marmont and it was just as wonderful as it had been the night they first made love in her bedroom at South Wind. They were lying in each other's arms when she said suddenly, "As I came in, didn't I notice a kitchenette?"

"Are you hungry?"

"Of course not. I was just going to tell you that I'm learning to cook. I may never do it, but at least I'll be able to tell someone else how to."

"What a surprise."

"Well, this is a kind of corny school that I saw advertised in our paper, but I rather enjoy it. So far I've learned to make white sauce and soufflés. We don't get on to meat and vegetables for a couple of months."

"I'm looking forward to a soufflé, but what else are you doing that I don't know about?"

"Quite a lot. By now you know I don't crave letter writing. It takes so long, but then when you are talking over the phone anything serious begins to sound tedious and boring."

"Tell me the news."

"It's not really news, but Daddy has been bugging me for

years to get more education." She sat up in bed. "He wanted to get me into someplace like Vassar or Wellesley, but I told him I had really had it with female institutions. They are all right up to a certain point, but then they're silly. I can learn more French from Viola than I could learn from a course in college. I just want to learn the things that will help me in the kind of life I'll probably lead." She lay down again and snuggled close to him. "Do you think that's wrong?"

"It makes sense to me." He put his arm around her.

"I finally persuaded Daddy to let me take some courses at Barnard in political science. If I'm ever going to take any part in running the paper, I've got to be up on both politics and economics, and I do care about the paper."

"I know you do. You once told me you love to hear the presses run."

She was quiet for a while and he thought she had fallen asleep. "I'm afraid you'd better wake up, darling. This isn't South Wind, and Pinkie will be expecting you."

"Pinkie loves me and she knows I love you. She'll never tell Daddy a thing."

The two weeks seemed hardly to have begun when they were over and they were saying good-bye at the Pasadena station. While she had been with him he had been happy and as confident as she was about his film future, but as he drove back to Hollywood, alone, the restlessness and uneasiness he had sometimes felt before her visit came over him again. Without her the Château Marmont seemed unbelievably quiet and lonely.

He made up his mind that he would begin to push harder at the studio, instead of accepting everything with a smile. The next day at Olympia he was lucky enough to find Bradley Dexter in his office.

"Oh yes, Schuyler, I remember meeting you with Fritz at the commissary the other day. Then my secretary said you had asked for a script of Ginger's new film."

"I read it and liked it very much. Naturally I would like the part of Tom."

"I don't see why you wouldn't be good for it. You're the type we're looking for and you're already under contract here."

"Is there anything I can do about it?"

"Not now. I've already been interested enough to run your original test and I liked it. All you may need is B.B.'s yes when he gets back from New York, and I can't think why he wouldn't give it. By the way, Miss Rogers wants you, too."

"That's encouraging," he smiled and shook hands with Dexter.

In a happy mood, Sky decided to go downstairs to the commissary, where he could probably find some friends to join for lunch. Just inside the door he almost collided with Dorothy Darrow.

"Why, Sky, I've just been hoping and hoping to run into you, because I hadn't any idea where you were living. You don't know how many times I've thought of you since Christmas."

"What a surprise, Miss Darrow. I didn't know you were out here."

"I thought your little girlfriend might have told you, because it was Daddy Green who arranged everything for me."

"Very good, I'd say, but what are you doing, Miss Darrow?"

"Oh please call me Dorothy. Let's get a table and I'll tell you all about it."

"I'm afraid I'm meeting some friends, but I'll sit down for just a minute." As he followed her to a corner table he had to admit, much as he disliked her, that she had a cute figure, but he couldn't bear to look at the dress with the sailor collar and the bright red shoes.

"It's just so exciting out here," she said as she sat down. "I'm going to be in the new Ginger Rogers film."

"I think I'm getting a part in that, too."

"How divine. Then we'll be seeing a lot of each other. I can't think of anything nicer." She leaned over and gave his hand a light squeeze. "Of course, you've met B. B. Balzer by now. If I didn't care so much for Daddy Green I could certainly go all out for him."

Sky saw Fritz Reid coming in, and he stood up. "Here comes my luncheon date. I'm afraid I've got to leave."

"Oh you're lunching with my darling Fritz. He's doing such nice things for me. Give him my love, but just don't go off without telling me where you're staying or giving me your phone number."

"I'm at the Château Marmont."

"That's a coincidence. I'm right across the street at the Garden of Allah. Daddy Green got me a lovely bungalow there right next to George S. Kaufman."

"Sit down," said Fritz. "I saw you making your getaway from the Darrow dame. It's not easy."

"I met her once in New York."

"Well, so did B.B. evidently, because word has come down from his office to roll out the red carpet and handle her with kid gloves. She must have given him the works."

A few days later Sky called Balzer's office and found he was still in the East. The same afternoon Sky returned to his hotel and found a message from Jack Conway to call him at his office at MGM. "Hello, Mr. Madison," Conway said as he came on the phone, "Miss Russell remembered you, and she thinks you would fit the bill for a key part in our new mystery thriller. Would you ask your agent to send me any film available on you, and to check with Olympia to see if they are willing to loan you to us?"

"Yes, sir, I'll be glad to."

"And maybe you'll come out to the studio next week and we'll talk over the part."

As Sky hung up the telephone he was deliriously happy to know that two great stars like Ginger Rogers and Rosalind Russell had both said they wanted him. Perhaps he was getting somewhere at last.

He made up his mind not to be impatient this time. He knew from the trade papers that neither of the two films he was hoping for were quite ready for production, and while he waited, time was passing pleasantly with daily visits to the studio. By now he knew almost everyone on the lot and if he wasn't running an old movie he was reading scripts, both new and old ones. Once late in May, he called Bradley Dexter's office and was reassured by the director's secretary, "Why yes, Mr. Madison, your name is still penciled in for the part."

"Daddy has asked me to go to Hawaii with him," Indiana announced on the phone. "It's business and he's taking Miss Peacock. I think he was surprised when I said I'd go, but I only said it because I figured I could stop by and see you on the way back."

Then a few weeks later she called from Hawaii. "That Darrow woman has come out for a week with Daddy, and I refuse to stay. Miss Peacock and I are sailing tomorrow on the *Lurline*. She'll be with me, but we'll manage somehow, and anything is better than nothing, I figure."

Indiana was on deck, leaning over the railing and waving to him, as the large boat anchored. She rushed down the gangplank, followed more deliberately by Miss Peacock, and threw her arms around Sky, crushing the lei of white orchids thrown around the neck of her navy-blue suit.

"Don't worry. They wouldn't have lasted through the trip if I hadn't kept them in the refrigerator so you could see them." She took them off. "They're not the kind of things you get at the pier when you leave. They're fresh from Daddy's orchid farm. I'll tell you all about it later."

That night as they were lying in bed together at the Château Marmont, she said, "Sky, I'm desperately worried about you."

"Why on earth, darling, when I have two such wonderful possibilities, as I told you about?"

"It's not your Hollywood career I'm worried about. I always knew you'd be successful. It's the war that's scaring me, and the fear that you'll have to go."

"Isn't that a little farfetched?"

"I don't think so. Daddy thinks it will happen within six months."

"What reason does he give?"

"Sky, this is top secret, but I can't keep anything from you."

"Of course."

"Well, Daddy's orchid farm is not just a business for selling flowers. It's also a device for watching Japan. He thinks the Japs are going to strike this country unexpectedly on the West Coast, and it might even be here."

"It sounds like a spy thriller in the movies, darling."

"I know you've never heard me talk this seriously, but I'm learning all kinds of things these days, so please love me this way, too."

"I love you even more, if possible, but tell me more."

"Daddy's foreman at the orchid farm is one of the Japanese group that doesn't want war with this country and he has given Daddy lots of information."

"Why doesn't your father pass it on?"

"He has already written to F.D.R. and tried every way he can to get through to him, but it's no use. Roosevelt really wants the war, though he tells everyone he doesn't."

"How does Miss Peacock take all this?"

"Even she's beginning to change her mind about the President."

"If this should happen, your father will get a tremendous break on the story for his papers."

"Of course, but I do think he's concerned about the country. You've only seen his worst side."

Through the whole week, Miss Peacock went her own way, saying she had friends to catch up with in Los Angeles and leaving them completely alone. It was only the last day of the visit that she joined them for lunch at Perino's.

That evening, as they were ready to board the *Chief* in downtown Los Angeles, Miss Peacock said, "I'll go ahead and leave you two to say good-bye." She shook Sky's hand and he felt she was looking at him very intently. "I wish you the very best of luck in your career, Mr. Madison. If I can ever be of any assistance to you, please let me know."

"That was nice of her, wasn't it?" he said to Indiana after Miss Peacock left.

"Yes, she's a strange one. I know she hates Dorothy Darrow, and I think she likes us."

On his way back from the station, he stopped to buy some fresh orange juice at one of the large markets that was open all night. As he passed the display of fresh fruit, he thought of Indiana when he had once taken her to the Farmer's Market for lunch. She had been especially fascinated by the giant-size strawberries and had even wanted to take some back to New York with her.

"I see you're one of the night shoppers, too," said a familiar voice behind him.

He turned around to see Nora Hayes, who was pushing one of the market's little wire carriers and already had it half full. "Hello, Sky. I've been expecting you to call me."

"I guess I still felt it might be presumptuous, Miss Hayes."

"I think you are old enough to call me Nora now. I read in the columns this week that Indiana has been here."

"I just put her on the *Chief* half an hour ago."

"Then I expect you're going to feel lonely for a while."

"That's for sure."

"You must come have dinner with me sometime soon."

"I can't think of anything nicer."

"Then come tomorrow night. I'll expect you at eight." She gave him the address on Crescent Drive. "It's in Beverly Hills between Sunset and Santa Monica."

"I'll find it. And thanks."

When he reached the Château Marmont, he sat down at his portable typewriter and dashed off a letter to Indiana. Instead of dropping it at the hotel desk, he decided to take it to the post office himself and sent it air mail. "She'll be surprised to find it waiting for her when she gets home," he thought.

Nora Hayes lived in one of the older Beverly Hills houses. It was surrounded by a white picket fence and well-kept gardens and, inside, it was not the kind of stage setting in which many of the stars lived, but looked like a real home.

There were bowls of fresh-cut roses in every room, and the library, where he was waiting for her to come downstairs, looked as if it were actually used. The coffee table had a pile of magazines and books that he was just beginning to delve into when she arrived.

They had a glass of champagne in the library. "I never drink hard liquor and I have to confess right now that I'm something of a diet freak," she said, indicating the hors d'oeuvres tray of sliced carrots and celery hearts arranged on top of ice cubes.

"I guess that's the only way to keep a wonderful figure like yours."

"I've been that way from childhood. My mother would never allow me to eat sweet things. She told me that candy was something to play with, and her friends used to be fascinated when they came to see her and found me playing marbles with lemon drops."

Sky laughed. "Didn't your friends ever tell you the truth about candy?"

"They may have tried, but I don't remember. You should see the way Mother looks today. She gets up on ladders and paints her garage, drives her car and acts like a girl of twenty instead of one in her midsixties."

"She must have been on the right track to keeping healthy."

"Somehow I had the sense to believe she was right so I never smoked and I stayed with wine in those prohibition days when all my friends were drinking themselves to death."

They had a light, delicious dinner served on an open patio covered with vines and fragrant with the scent of jasmine from a nearby flower bed.

"Beyond the flowers I have the usual pool and tennis court. I've just had the court lighted so I can exercise at night. We can play sometime, if you like."

"Do you ever show any of your own films?"

"Of course, if I think anyone is really interested in the old relics."

"I've always been fascinated with the changes in both the writing and acting techniques that have gone on in the industry."

"So am I, Sky, but most people don't go below the surface of glamour, you know. I'd be glad to run some old films and discuss them with you."

"I'd also like to see one of your old scripts, if you've kept any."

"They're all in my library. So you're interested in writing, too?"

"Yes, I've done a bit, and I hope to do more."

"Then let's go back to the library. We'll get some out, and have our coffee there."

When they had settled down on one of the library couches, Nora said, "Before we get into film history, there's something I want to talk to you about, and it's really why I asked you here tonight."

Sky wondered what was coming, and Nora went on. "Lesley Ruggles is an old friend of mine. Of course, you know he dropped *College Prom* and left Olympia enraged that top brass had interfered with his casting."

"What do you mean?"

"Les was terribly enthusiastic about you and determined to have you in the leading part. He had built the whole story around you, and just as everything was ready to roll, B.B. refused to let you have the part." She put down her coffee cup. "Whatever happened, and do you know why?"

He was stunned. "I thought it was the other way around, and that I didn't get it because the whole film was dropped."

"Did you ever have any trouble with B.B.?"

"No, he was unbelievably nice and encouraging."

"When Les demanded a reason for not letting him have you, B.B. simply shrugged and said, 'orders,' whatever that may mean."

"I don't understand it."

"Have you ever thought of asking Bradshaw Green's help?"

"Of course not. Why should I?"

"I thought, of course, you knew that he's one of Olympia's major stockholders."

"No, I didn't."

"Perhaps you should."

"I'd rather make my own way."

It had been a pleasant evening, but the story about Lesley Ruggles had left Sky vaguely uneasy. The next day he decided to call the Harris office to inquire about the MGM film with Russell and Gable.

"We were just going to call you, Mr. Madison. Your studio has refused to loan you. Mr. Conway is quite annoyed with them, and Mr. Harris would like you to come to the office to talk to him."

That afternoon when he reached the office, he was taken immediately to Leland Harris, who was looking even more somber than he remembered.

"Sit down, Madison. I'm not one to mince words. You are in trouble."

"What do you mean, sir?"

"You know about them refusing to loan you to MGM? Now we've just got word that top brass at Olympia has said no to giving you the part in the Ginger Rogers film, and that James Ellison is going to play Tom."

"I don't understand what B. B. Balzer could have against me. So far the directors have seemed to like me."

"So does B.B. He knows a money-maker when he sees one, and he was ready at the beginning to push you. He's taking orders."

"Orders?" Sky looked perplexed. "From whom?"

"Bradshaw Green is one of the major stockholders. He has just got Dorothy Darrow a fat part after she had been turned down by two or three other directors."

"I've only met Mr. Green twice, but I never felt he was hostile to me. In fact, once he vaguely offered me a job."

"Well, maybe he wants you back in New York for that job, then, or maybe he's picked you for his future son-in-law. I've read that you've been seeing a lot of his daughter."

Sky opened his mouth, but no words came. Finally he managed to say, "What do you advise, Mr. Harris?"

"There's nothing more we can do for you until option time comes up on your contract. You'll be on salary with the studio until January 1 and, after that, your future doesn't look too black to me."

"Thank you, Mr. Harris." He got up and left the office, followed by Kate Malley. As he stood waiting for the elevator, she looked at him so compassionately that he thought she was going to cry.

He got into his car automatically and drove back to the hotel. The desk clerk handed him a postcard with Indiana's writing on it, and he guessed that Indiana had mailed it from Albuquerque when the train stopped there. When he reached his room, he dropped it into the wastebasket without reading it, and called Nora Hayes.

"I've had terrible news and I have to talk to someone. Could I see you soon?"

"Right now, if you like. I'm sitting under a tree in the patio, reading a delicious book."

As he drove to her house, he thought, "Nora was hinting this last night and I was too dumb to catch on." Suddenly he remembered that he had had the same sensation with Iris Peacock at the station. She had obviously known what was going on. "They plotted this from the beginning," he thought, "and they must have been laughing behind my back when I was so sure I was going to become somebody out here."

Nora was sitting in the shade with a pitcher of iced tea on the table beside her. "You look exhausted, poor dear. Sit down and cool off before you begin telling me your troubles. This tea will do you good. It has fresh mint in it."

"Thank you." He drank the tea slowly. "I'm beginning to feel human again." Then he told the whole story and Nora listened without interrupting.

When he had finished, she said, "I was afraid it was going to be this way, but when you say that you are filled with such rage and resentment against them that it frightens you, you surely don't believe that Indiana was involved."

"I don't want to, but I don't know. She seemed to understand, but I know she would have been happier if I had wanted to take a job in New York."

"It would have been rather abnormal if she hadn't felt that way, wouldn't it? Bradshaw Green is a strange, lonely character who fancies himself as a superdirector of other people's lives and he adores power."

"I'll have to make up my own mind, but things aren't very clear now."

She asked him to stay for dinner, but he said, "I'm dog tired, Nora, and not good company. Give me another chance soon."

He was grateful that Nora had defended Indiana, but at the moment, in his mind, Indiana had been tainted by the whole episode. I don't know what I'll do, but I do know I won't fall into his goddamn trap and marry his daughter, he thought.

The next morning Nora telephoned. "If you need a shoulder to lean on, come over here this afternoon. Bring your tennis clothes and take out some of your anger on the tennis balls."

Nora was a good enough player to make it fun, but after a few sets they dropped down on the green grass under one of her big trees.

"You have gorgeous legs, Nora, I kept watching them as you played."

"Actually, it was my legs that brought Bradshaw Green into my life. He said he spotted them in one of my early De Mille films."

"I kept thinking of Bradshaw Green all night. What a monster he is."

"A strange character but not all bad, and there's no way he can do you any permanent harm."

"He's taken a year out of my life, and it was a very important year."

"Of course. Twenty-one is a turning point for a man."

"I've cooled down a bit today, as you see, and I've decided to do exactly as my agent advised. I'm going to stay on and collect my salary, and then hope to start over again next year with a different studio."

"Don't grieve over the lost year, too much." She put her hand over his and let it stay there. She had patted him several times in a friendly way, but this time he felt the warmth of her fingers all through his body. He had looked on her as a friend, but suddenly he saw her as a beautiful woman who might be eager to have him as a lover.

He went on talking. "I want to get out of the hotel. I'd like to find a little shack on a beach somewhere. I'd like to save some money and maybe do some writing."

"Perhaps I can help you with that, too. I have a friend who has a little house on Topanga Beach. He uses it for weekends but might be willing to rent it to the right person. We'll call him after dinner and see if it's available."

"What a darling you are, Nora."

She took her hand away. "What do you say we have a swim? Afterward we can have dinner in our robes and then change back to our tennis clothes if we feel like it. I enjoy playing at night." She stood up. "You'll find swimming trunks in the pool house and I'll give you a robe later."

While he was changing into trunks, Sky made up his mind that he must have exaggerated the warmth of her hand over his, but now that the idea of making love to her had entered his mind, he was unable to think of anything else.

She was already in the water when he came out and dived in. She swam as gracefully as she played tennis. As she swam along beside him, he was violently aware of her body and though her suit showed a great deal of it, he longed to see more.

"I usually swim in the nude," she said. "The pool is completely secluded and it's much more relaxing that way."

"Why don't you then?"

"Some other time I will, but I started this way. I suppose I thought you might be shocked if I suddenly appeared with nothing on."

"Come over here."

She swam over to the shallow end where he was standing. "I'm not tall enough. My feet don't reach the bottom," she said.

He caught her and held her against him. "I'm crazy about you, Nora."

"Then kiss me, Sky. I like to be kissed when I'm wet."

He kissed her wet lips. "Let's get out of here."

She ran ahead of him to the pool house and went into her room. "I'll be with you in a minute," she called back.

He was just starting to take off his wet trunks when she came in without bothering to knock. She was wearing something white and flimsy that clung to her wet skin and she was smiling as she came toward him. He put his arms around her and he could feel her eager hands pulling off his trunks. "Darling, you might take cold in those things," she murmured.

He stepped out of them, and she let her white robe fall to the floor.

"Let's take a shower together, Sky. It would be a perfect way for us to get to know each other, don't you think?"

"I must be dreaming all this," Sky thought for a minute as he went into the stall shower and turned on the faucet, but as he stood under the stream of water with Nora's warm body close to him, he forgot everything but her.

She was a work of art, he thought. Her body was rounded but slim. It had been firmed with exercise, and constant massage had kept her skin satin smooth.

He took a bar of scented soap and began lathering her body.

"How delicious, Sky. Now take a nice, soft towel and dry me."

"I can't wait to dry you, Nora. I want you just this way."

He looked around and there was no couch in the dressing room. He threw a big bath towel on the floor and pushed her down on it. He kissed her wet body, and feeling it respond under his was the most sensuous experience he had ever had.

CHAPTER TEN

During the first week of July Sky left the Château Marmont and moved into the little house at Topanga Beach that belonged to Nora's friend. She had called him, as she promised, and he had agreed to rent it for six months.

It was exactly what Sky had wanted. It had a living room big enough to work in, an adequate kitchen, a small bedroom with an enormous oversized bed and a fabulous view of the Pacific.

Topanga Beach consisted of four or five small houses on the curve of the road halfway between Santa Monica and Malibu.

He had left the hotel with all his belongings and left no forwarding address, except Olympia, and he had told the studio that he was available to them at all times, but that his telephone number was not to be given to any outsiders, no matter who called.

He had made many friends during his first six months, but at the moment he didn't want their sympathy. To make the next six months count, he knew he had to be alone.

Nora was the exception. "Let's not make a big thing of this," she had said soon after they had become lovers. "I'm in no mood for a grand passion and I'm sure you aren't either."

He had agreed happily. They talked frequently and she had promised to come out to the beach to see him. She was skillful at making each time he made love to her as exciting as the first, and their relationship had already become an accepted thing to both of them.

On his first night at Topanga, there had been a knock on the door. A small man in an unironed shirt and dungarees came limping in.

"For God's sake, can you give me a cup of coffee? I've run out," he said, running his hand through his disheveled dark hair.

"Sure thing. Sit down. I've just made a pot."

"I'm Sidney Garson, your next-door neighbor, and you're about to save my life."

"Glad to help. You're the screenwriter, aren't you?"

"Off and on, but mostly off, recently. Good ideas are scarce. What do you do?"

"I'm more or less in transit. I have a contract with a film company, but there's nothing doing at the moment and I thought I'd like to try some writing."

"Ever done any?"

"A little bit, but I was still in college."

"Got any ideas?"

"Not yet, but I just got here and I'm expecting this place to inspire me."

"Well, here's to you. I think best in crowded places where there's lots of noise, but right now I can't afford them." Sky poured his neighbor a second cup of coffee and watched him gulp it down.

"As far as I'm concerned, this is a damn lonely place," Sidney Garson went on talking. "I came to Hollywood when the silents were ending and the talkies were beginning. It was a hell of an exciting place to be, and I did some pretty good things."

"I know your name very well."

"I took this dump next to you when my third wife left me. I hope she never finds me here. In case she does, I'm warning you. She's a sex maniac." He got up and left as suddenly as he had come.

Sky woke early. He walked for a while on the beach and then swam far out into the Pacific and back. There had been quite an undertow and he was tired when he returned. After he had made his breakfast he started to unpack his belongings. As he looked at the expensive luggage he felt a sudden twinge of remorse as he thought of Indiana. She would be bewildered at his silence in the beginning and then bitterly angry, he thought. In a few weeks he would write to her and tell her what her father had done and explain his own feelings. At the moment he wasn't quite sure what his feelings really were.

He arranged his typewriter and copy paper on a convenient table and then hung his Picasso sketch where he could look at it as he worked. It was a long time since he had been totally alone. In Fort Wayne he had been surrounded by the Hales, and at college there had always been someone around. Now with only the sound of the surf to break the silence, he began to think of his mother and father. He had been so young when they died that he had never really known them. He had no idea whether they had been happy together. Aunt Addie had told him repeatedly how ambitious his father had been for him, and what joy he had brought to them when he was born. His father's death he realized was still a mystery and he had never really wanted to find out whether he had taken his own life or lost it by accident.

A little introspection would be good for him, he thought. As the days passed he swam, and when Sidney hadn't consumed too much rye, he talked to him about the theater and old movies every night.

One day as he was going through some of his old Princeton papers, he came upon his essay on power that used Bradshaw Green as an example. He reread it quickly. How could I have been so kind to the goddamn bastard? If I'd only known then what I know now, it would be a hell of a lot different, he thought to himself. He started to put the paper away, but the idea struck him suddenly. Why don't I rewrite it? Even if it came to nothing, it could be a project and it would get me going at the typewriter.

He went out and walked on the beach, and the idea began to grow on him.

He knocked on Sidney's door. It was opened by a wispy little woman who looked anything but the voracious sex maniac Sidney had been describing.

"This is my wife, Marcia. She's just leaving again, but she has fixed some food. Stick around and have dinner with me."

After she left, Sidney complained, "She kept me up all night, the bitch. She wears me out."

Sky was glad that at least he was sober enough to hear his idea. Over the ham-and-cheese sandwiches Marcia had made, Sky started talking about power and Bradshaw Green.

"Power is a hell of a good subject," Sidney said. "The funny thing is that last year I toyed with the idea of tackling the subject myself. I was going to do the power of a criminal like John Dillinger." Sidney reached for another sandwich. "Hell, he used to get more headlines than the President. I even did some research on Dillinger's motivation, but the whole thing fizzled out. Bradshaw Green should be a juicier subject. He's always been something of a mystery man."

"I've met him and I've been in two of his homes."

"You're lucky. How are you planning to handle all this?"

"I don't know. The idea just came to me. I've got too much material for an article and I don't think I've got the time to do a book."

"Hell, fellow, you've got an idea here that will fascinate millions." He put down his sandwich. "It could be the film of the century if you've really got the stuff on him."

"I believe that he killed one man and was at least involved in the death of his wife. Also, he played some part in getting rid of President McKinley. On the credit side, he's a dyed-in-the-wool American, has spent his own dough to set up an espionage center in Hawaii because he distrusts the Japs."

"You know that for a fact?"

"Absolutely."

"I wonder how the old Hoosier began?"

"His father started the first paper in Buffalo with money from his granddad's shoe business, and Bradshaw Green always looks at women's feet first."

"That's an interesting quirk. Sounds like you've got enough material to start."

"Want to work on it with me? I'd thought of a movie but I've never done a film script and wouldn't know where to begin."

"I've been dying to get my teeth into something like this. Sure, let's work together. You'll have to do the research," he said as he rubbed his leg. "I can't get around very much with this bum knee, and the two of us can put it together."

When he went back to his house, Sky was too keyed up to go to sleep. He sat down at his desk and began making random notes of everything he could remember about Bradshaw Green, his clothes, his cars, his homes and the occasional comments dropped by Indiana, Iris Peacock and even Pinkie.

The first and easiest person to interview on the subject was, of course, Nora. So he called her bright and early the next morning. "When are you coming to the beach, Nora? I miss you and the water is wonderful."

"There must be telepathy between us. I was thinking of this afternoon."

"Wonderful."

"I'll bring a picnic supper and we can have it on the beach."

Nora's picnic supper included champagne, caviar, cold chicken and chocolate mousse, all contained in a metal thermos hamper and carried to the beach by her chauffeur. "I've brought everything, even the ice cubes and champagne glasses," she said.

The combination of a full moon and the lovely surf enchanted Nora as he knew it would. "Do we have to be proper and keep on our suits?"

"People do as they like around here. There aren't many of us and I don't think anyone is paying attention."

She was able to hold her own in the surf. When they came back and were sitting on their beach towels, she ran her lips slowly along his arm. "I love the taste of your skin with the salt water on it."

"Not now, Nora. That comes later. Inside I've got the biggest bed you ever saw, and I've been longing to get you in it."

"That's nice."

"Yes, but now I'm starving and I want to talk."

"Shall I dress for dinner?"

"No, I like you undressed. You look barbaric, especially with your tan and that gold chain around your neck."

As they devoured the picnic, he told her about the script he was about to start with Sidney Garson as his partner. "I need your help, darling Nora. I want you to tell me everything, bad and good, that you remember about Bradshaw Green."

She was quiet for a minute. "He's so full of contradictions. He's a merciless dictator, but when anyone passes judgment on him, he falls apart. He can give it but he can't take it." She turned and looked into his eyes. "Of course, you know, Sky, that if you go through with this you will become the public enemy of his vast empire and sever all connections with the Green family."

"That situation will have to take care of itself. I can't let it

influence what I'm doing. That bastard has done everything in
his power to keep me from the career I wanted. I feel positive
that I can very possibly do something worthwhile with this
idea." He reached for the champagne. "I have never had any intention of not becoming successful, Nora. I'm born under the
sign of Taurus, and am a very determined person."

"I'm beginning to believe that. Where shall we start?"

"When you met him."

"I was seventeen. We started very young in the silent days,
and I had come to New York for a personal appearance." She
went on talking as Sky poured the champagne in both glasses.
"When I reached my suite at the old Waldorf—it was down at
Thirty-fourth Street in those days—the rooms were filled with at
least three hundred roses. I remember how thrilled I was. I ran
around sniffing them and in one of the bowls I found a note attached to a long-stemmed American Beauty rose."

"From Bradshaw?"

"Yes, he asked me to have supper with him on the Ziegfeld
Roof." She paused to sip her champagne. "It was a magic evening. He told me he had fallen in love with me when he saw the
shot in the De Mille film that showed me in a bathtub. I was
completely hidden by the bubbles except for my head, and my
feet were sticking up at the other end of the tub in a very pert
way. The next day he sent me a diamond anklet, which I later
changed into a bracelet."

"So your affair began. How was he as a lover?"

"Nothing special, just routine sex. He spent more time fondling
my feet than anything else."

"Was he married then?"

"No. Our love affair went on for over a year. He was very generous and gave me unbelievable publicity in all his papers. He
was hardly ever unkind and when he had a tantrum I simply
treated him as if he were a bad child. Sometimes I even felt sorry
for him." She held out her glass for more champagne. "I remember one time when he was running for governor. The
Pulitzer papers had slapped him down with a stinging editorial
and when I came into his Fifth Avenue house that night, he was
sitting there with tears rolling down his face."

"That's hard to imagine."

"I spent the whole evening comforting him. A few months later he got married and I never heard from him again for six or seven years. Out of the blue he called me to go to Europe. That was the *Île de France* trip, when we first met."

"Did you know Dobbs Hall, and do you think Bradshaw Green pushed him overboard?"

"Yes, I knew both Gaby and Dobbs. She was a pretty little flirt and Dobbs had made a great impression on me when I first came to Hollywood because he drove a low-slung car that was painted robin's-egg blue. Dobbs was on cocaine and whether Brad threw him overboard or just gave him a shove that helped, nobody will ever know."

"Is Mrs. Hall still alive?"

"But of course. She has been living happily ever since from an income that comes from who knows where. Naturally people say Bradshaw Green."

"Do you think there's any chance of my seeing her?"

"I haven't run into her for years, but I can call her and try."

"Tell her I'm doing a magazine piece on early Hollywood and thought she might be able to help with details."

"That's a good idea. You know, she wasn't an actress, but she was something of a hostess in those days."

Mrs. Dobbs Hall would be delighted to see him and give him her recollections of what Hollywood was once like, Nora reported in a few days. He called her to make an appointment and drove to North Rossmore, where she was occupying a penthouse.

Valerie Hall was tall, erect and deeply tanned. "I'm just back from Arrowhead, where I've been sailing every day. I have a little house there, too, and I just love it. What do you want me to tell you about Hollywood back in those young, carefree days?"

"Anything you remember as especially interesting, Mrs. Hall." He pulled out a small notebook and took brief notes as she talked. Some of her chatter might end by being useful.

"It's been my good luck to see Hollywood change from a little country town—a beautiful town, really—into the world center of the film industry. We used to have orchards and orange groves. On Vine Street, they even grew grapes. The street got its name from the grapes."

He brought up the subject of her famous parties and she

started to describe one in particular that was given at the old Embassy Club and mentioned among the guests Bradshaw Green. It gave him a chance to say, "I understand Bradshaw Green was on board the ship when your husband fell from an upper deck and drowned, or is this too painful a subject to discuss?"

"That was a long time ago, so I don't mind about it. I was on board, too, but not on deck at the time." She smiled. "My husband was flirtatious by nature. He and Gaby de Lyn had been carrying on at the dinner table but it meant nothing, I can assure you. I wasn't even the slightest bothered." Her smile faded. "Afterward, the two men went on deck, and the next thing I knew I felt the ship slowing and heard footsteps running and general commotion."

"What do you think really happened?"

"How should I know? I fainted dead away when I heard the news. The only witness was Brad's secretary."

"Was that Iris Peacock?"

"Yes, she had gone on deck to bring Brad a radiogram. There was a hearing and she testified that my husband was high on drugs and that he climbed the railing and jumped, calling back that he was going to take a swim in the big pool."

"Did your husband take drugs?"

"Yes, sometimes. I guess we all thought it was the smart thing to do in those days."

Sky was about to close his notebook when a maid came in. "The San Francisco *Globe* is calling you, Mrs. Hall."

"Excuse me." She got up and picked up the extension. By straining his ears he was able to hear her say, "Thank you for returning my call. My monthly check hasn't arrived yet and it's most inconvenient." There was a pause. "Of course, I was sure there was some good reason. I'll expect it then by the end of the week."

She came back smiling, but Sky could see she was terminating the interview.

He stood up to go. "Are you a writer, Mrs. Hall?"

"Not really, but occasionally I write something for the Los Angeles and San Francisco *Globes*."

"How interesting. As one writer to another, what's your field?"

"The social life at Arrowhead," she said, smiling.

That night when Sidney and he went over the notes he had taken so far, Sky said, "We're never going to be able to prove anything. That son-of-a-bitch has paid off everybody."

"Courage, comrade. That's the way we want it. We produce the glamourous atmosphere and all the possible evidence on both sides."

"I get it. We leave it to the viewers to give the verdict."

"Sure, they'll be arguing about it for months. It's going to be sensational. I can tell you right now."

"Should I go on?"

"The next step would be to try to locate Bradshaw's wife's family."

"I know she was a beauty-contest winner."

"Then there must be something written about her on file somewhere," Sidney said.

In the Los Angeles library, Sky found that Bradshaw Green had married Colleen O'Connor, an eighteen-year-old winner of a newspaper-conducted beauty contest, on July 20, 1920. She came from Seattle and died three years later. Sidney had a friend in Seattle and they called him to look up the clips on the beauty contest. "Some Cinderella story," he said when he called back a few days afterward. "She was the daughter of Mr. and Mrs. James O'Conner. They lived on Myrtle Street and are still living there, according to the telephone book."

"Should I drive up?" Sky asked Sidney.

"Takes too long. We've got to get going soon on writing this soap opera. Better take the train."

The house on Myrtle Street was simple, but recently painted and pretty. Sky braced himself to see someone who would remind him painfully of Indiana, but the middle-aged woman who opened the door bore no resemblance. He told her he was working on a feature story about Bradshaw Green for a national magazine. "I happened to be on the West Coast, and thought I'd try to get some firsthand information about Mrs. Green."

"She was my younger sister and I adored her. That's all I can say." She started to close the door. "Why should anyone want to rake up an old tragedy after almost twenty years?"

"It was tragic for her to die so young," Sky said with all the sympathy he could muster.

"It isn't just that. It was a tragedy from the start. I remember Mama and Papa didn't want her to send her photograph to that silly newspaper contest, but she was a little spoiled and did it behind their backs. They didn't want her to marry Bradshaw Green, either. He was too old for her and she had dozens of nice young beaux right here, and none of them poor."

She was looking a little less formidable, Sky thought. "May I come in?"

She hesitated for a moment. "Well, just for a moment, then."

They went into a small living room. The shades were pulled down and it was so dark that Sky almost stumbled over a footstool. When she raised one of the shades he could see that most of the furniture was Middle West Victorian. There was an upright piano against one wall with several framed photographs on top.

Sky sat down on a small settee. "Do you happen to have a picture of your sister?"

She went to the piano and brought him a photograph in a frame that looked hand-painted. "This is the same picture that she sent off to the contest. You can see how pretty she was."

For a moment Sky thought he was looking at a photograph of Indiana. The big eyes were the same but with less fire in them, and her other features were a little more delicate. "I can see why she won the contest."

"Yes, she was beautiful, and she was determined to marry Bradshaw Green. Nothing and nobody could stop her."

"What was the reason for her death? The files in the Los Angeles paper don't have the information."

"We were told that she drowned, and that's all we'll ever know. I couldn't get there in time for the funeral, but I went to their country house as soon as I could to pick up her belongings and to look at the baby." She took the photograph from him and put it back on the piano. "The old Indian maid told me Colleen had dreadful bruises on her neck when they found her, but no one else saw them because the undertaker managed to cover them up."

"What could have happened?"

"If she was unhappy, she never admitted it, and her letters were always full of going to the opera to hear Caruso and having so many beautiful clothes." She shook her head. "Please don't ask to talk to my mother and father. I never had the heart to tell them about the bruises."

"I understand."

"When I asked Mr. Green about the bruises he flew into a rage and used such vile language that I walked away and hoped never to see him again. He sent me a valuable present later on and another to Mama and Papa, but we sent them all back."

Sidney was happy with the notes Sky brought back from Seattle. "It all adds up to a good story, but what's missing is the motivation. What the hell has made him the kind of bastard he is? Did you ever hear anything about his childhood?"

"Not a word." Then he remembered the absence of the Christmas tree at South Wind last year as well as any holiday spirit. It made him wonder what kind of childhood Bradshaw had had. He must not have been close to his family, but only Pinkie could have told him if he was right.

"Well, if we can't find out we'll have to fabricate and it shouldn't be hard."

Sky had not heard from the studio for a month and hadn't given them a thought, when out of the blue Fritz Reid called. "I want you to do me a big favor, Sky."

"Anything for you, Fritz."

"I need you to escort Dorothy Darrow to the opening of the new Carole Lombard film. It's a big premiere at Grauman's Chinese and there's publicity value in it for you both."

"Glad to oblige." He gritted his teeth. If it had only been anybody else, he thought.

"I'll send a limousine to the Garden of Allah to pick you up. Give yourself plenty of time. There'll be a mob."

After spending most of his time for weeks in swimming trunks or an old T-shirt and dungarees, it felt good again to put on evening clothes. The studio had done quite a lot for Dorothy Darrow in a short time. She was wearing a simple white dress, and with very little make-up, her hair reduced from brassy gold to pale blond, she actually looked quite young and fresh.

"Daddy Green just sent me this," she said, touching the little white ermine jacket she had thrown over her shoulders.

"I doubt that you will need it tonight."

"I know that, but it's so pretty. If any photographs are taken of me, I'd like to be seen wearing it."

There was an interminable line of cars ahead of them as they moved along Hollywood Boulevard toward the entrance to Grauman's Chinese. The bleachers that had been set up on both sides of the street were filled with people who clapped and cheered when one of the limousines held even a fairly well-known person.

He was fearful that he and Dorothy might be received with dead silence, or the disappointed, "That's nobody" he had heard on other occasions. To his relief they received mild but adequate applause. As they joined the line of couples moving slowly toward the door, they paused once for photographers.

Though the crowd was held back by ropes, Sky saw a girl duck under one of them and come rushing toward them.

Dorothy leaned across Sky, smiling, but the girl said, "Oh sir, could I have your autograph?"

His old enthusiasm for the movie world, which had cooled slightly after his recent disappointment, was coming back to him in full force. "Of course." He took her pen. "What's the name?"

"Just say, 'To Holly,' and I'm going to start a fan club for you someday."

"Thanks." He wrote, "Best Wishes, Holly," and signed his name. She took it and disappeared into the crowd.

They had just reached the door when a wild furor of yells and cheers broke out. Looking back over his shoulder he saw Clark Gable helping Carole Lombard out of their limousine.

"I guess they're just about the most popular couple in the world. Wouldn't you just give anything to be them?" sighed Dorothy Darrow, clinging to his arm as they went down the aisle to their seats.

After the film they went to Romanoff's for a big party arranged by Olympia. It was a buffet supper and as they sat down at a small table with their plates, Dorothy said, "It's just a crime, Sky, that you didn't get that part in Ginger's film. You'd have been so much better than the fellow who did."

"I guess the producer didn't see it your way."

"Oh well, better luck next time, I always think. I'm just back from Hawaii, you know."

"I was admiring your tan."

"They didn't need me in the early part of the film, so I went out to see Daddy Green for a week. He can't talk about anything but war. When he gets hot on a subject he sometimes pursues it until it drives you crazy."

"Where did you two meet, Dottie?"

"Meet? Well, I've known him all my life."

"Really? How did that happen?"

"He was a dear, dear friend of my mother's and I called him Daddy Green and sat on his knee when I was a little girl."

"I had no idea. Who was your mother?"

"I thought everybody knew. They do at the studio. She was a Ziegfeld Follies girl named Gaby De Lyn."

"Good God. Gaby De Lyn."

"Yes, she was very beautiful. Daddy Green adored her. Sometimes he made scenes, of course, but he gave her everything she wanted up to the day of her death." Her voice changed. "She died during the flu epidemic of 1919. I'll never forget how he cried when he came to the funeral parlor."

"Where did your Darrow name come from?"

"Oh when I was very young I married a bandleader named Danny Darrow. I became the singer and traveled with the band. After I got a divorce, I went to New York and looked up Daddy Green."

"I'll bet you were a surprise."

"When he saw me grown up, he could hardly believe I was the little girl he had once brought a teddy bear to."

"So you've been together ever since?"

"Yes, I think he loves me, though not as much as he did my mother. She was a real beauty and really never had to work hard to succeed."

"He's not the easiest person in the world to get along with, is he?"

"Oh you're thinking about those spike-heeled shoes he threw in the fire. He's got a horrible temper, but he makes up with you right away and gives you loads of presents to make you forget. I've always felt kind of sorry for him."

"Sorry? Well, that's a new angle, Dottie."

"You see, I've known him longer than all the other girls he's had. They last through a couple of scenes and then they take their presents and run, but honestly, I kind of like him and I'd miss the excitement if we quit." She sipped at her drink. "He's always driving hard to get something but he never seems to get what he wants, if you know what I mean."

"What do you think he really wants?"

"I don't know and I'm not very good at analyzing, but I do know he had a rotten childhood. His mother didn't want to have him in the beginning. She and his father separated and he was brought up by his granddad."

"That's the one who started the Green fortune?"

"Yes, Daddy Green was always trying to please him, but he never seemed to succeed."

When they left Romanoff's, Dorothy said, "Don't you think it would be good for both our public images if we stopped at the Cocoanut Grove for a couple of dances?"

"Sorry, Dottie, but I've got a long drive ahead of me. It's not as if I were still at the Château Marmont."

"Oh if that's the problem, you could spend the night in my bungalow. I have two bedrooms and you'd be very comfortable." She took his arm. "We could talk some more. I just love to talk with you, Sky. You're so sympathetic."

"Sorry, Dottie, but I have to be up early to do some work."

"What kind of work can you do out there on the beach?"

"I'm starting to write a movie script with another guy and I'm quite keen on the idea."

"Then be sure to write a good part in it for me."

He smiled, "There might be quite a terrific one, in fact, made to order."

"You're such a darling." She kissed him as they got out of the limousine in front of the Garden of Allah.

I guess she would be a pretty good roll in the hay for somebody, but I'd better find out first whether Green has had her bungalow wired, he thought as he drove back to Topanga Beach.

He and Sidney began going over the notes and thinking over who the main characters in the script would be. "How are you on writing female dialogue?" Sidney asked.

"I've never tried."

"Well, I'm pretty good, but if we get stuck we can ask Marcia to come down. She'll talk about anything and we can type what she says and then rewrite it."

The morning after Labor Day Sky had another call from the studio. "We know you don't want to be disturbed, Mr. Madison, but we've had a long-distance call from a Mr. Hale, who says he's your cousin. He says it is urgent, and he wants you to call him at his New York apartment."

"Thank you. I have his number and I'll get in touch with him."

Sky had hoped that the silence from New York would continue a little while longer, but now that Gage had broken it, there would have to be a partial showdown, at least. Sky waited until he was sure it was time for Gage to be starting to get up and get ready to go to the office, and then put in a call to New York.

It was the first time he remembered hearing Gage actually angry. "Sky, what the hell are you doing with yourself out there? Nobody has had a call or a letter from you in nearly two months." Sky tried to say something, but Gage hurried on. "Indiana said she had a lovely letter from you after her last trip out there, and then nothing. She has sent special-delivery letters and tried to telephone but it's a dead end. She was crying yesterday when she got back from race week at Saratoga and found there wasn't any word, and Mother is just as upset."

"I'm sorry, Gage, but I've had unexpected complications out here. I couldn't explain and I can't now as you'll understand when we see each other and can talk."

"Well, I can't and don't understand now. If things have gone wrong with you, you have no right not to let the people who care the most for you in on your problems." He paused for a moment. "Where are you living and what are you doing?"

"I took a house on the beach for six months to save money and I'm working on a movie script with a fellow who's my next-door neighbor."

"I'm glad to hear it, but from back here it looks to us as if you're having one helluva good time. Your pictures are all over the slicks with a different girl each time. I read in somebody's column the other day that you and Nora Hayes were a romance or that she was robbing the cradle."

"She's one hell of a dame, Gage."

"Then, in that picture of you and Dorothy Darrow that we used in the *Globe* yesterday, you couldn't have looked happier. It was just about the last straw for poor Indiana."

"She's usually a smart girl. She should have known it was strictly studio orders."

"That's easy to say, Sky, but you can't expect a girl in love as much as she is to be logical." His voice became slightly softer. "I'm glad you're all right and I'll spread the word around, but please do me a favor: Please take the time to communicate." He hung up the receiver.

For a while after the New York call, Sky sat quietly in front of his typewriter. He had to admit to himself that with Nora as a playmate and Sidney as a partner in a new project, his martyrdom had not been too painful and might turn out to be a blessing in the end. In the meantime he must write to Indiana.

He made three starts and tore them up. Finally, he wrote: "Darling. Everything seemed so smooth and easy when you were here, but just a few days after you left something happened to shatter my hopes ot getting any kind of part in a film this year. When we meet again, I'll try to explain the situation and am sure you will understand. At the moment I am working every day on a movie script with a well-known screenwriter who happens to be my neighbor. As soon as I can see where my career is going and am reasonably sure of success I hope we can resume our relationship. That's all I can say now, except that I love you."

He knew Indi well enough to be sure that she would feel the letter was cold and evasive, but it was the best he could do. He wrote a second letter to Aunt Addie, drove to the Santa Monica post office and air-mailed them both. As he drove back to Topanga, he felt marvelously free.

CHAPTER ELEVEN

By mid-November, Sky and Sidney had almost finished the first draft of their script. In the beginning they had spent several weeks arguing over how to present the story. Sky felt it should begin with the death of a powerful tycoon, whom they named Endicott Spencer Brown. It should start with his stupendous funeral and follow with a playback of his life story.

"I've already used that one. Wish I'd saved it," Sidney said.

Finally they had decided to make it an unsolved mystery thriller. The powerful tycoon was to be indicted for the murder of his beautiful young wife twenty years after her death. All the evidence was to be given by women who had known him at different times of his life, and in each of the scenes he was to be shown through their eyes. In the end the guilty or not-guilty verdict was to be left for the spectators to decide.

"It's good and gutsy," said Marcia, who had been called in as a critic. "It can't help but be a hit with the women."

"Let's begin by listing the women who will testify," said Sidney when Marcia had left. "I can't think unless I type, so you start talking about each one and I'll get them on paper."

"Well, there are five women characters who will give evidence at the trial. We'll of course change their names, but they are: Iris Peacock, Valerie Hall, Pinkie, Isobel O'Connor and Dorothy Darrow."

"Tell me more about Iris Peacock."

"She's a prim spinster who never misses a trick. Don't forget she had been with Green only two years before the Dobbs Hall episode. There's never been any romance between them and I'll guarantee she'll be a stone wall on the witness stand."

"Who do you see playing that part?"

"I was thinking of Edna May Oliver. She's a hell of an actress."

"That she is. Now let's go on with the other women characters."

"Well, there's Valerie Hall, the widow of the film director. She's slick, suave and sophisticated, and knows what she's doing. Hidden fires, I think, but won't talk."

"What the hell, kid. They're all going to talk. We're not doing a reporting job but telling a story. There's got to be a surprise quirk, and after we start working we'll find it. And don't forget, we're not trying Green for the Hall 'accident,' in quotes, but for killing his beautiful wife, Colleen."

"That makes Colleen's sister, Isobel O'Connor, and Pinkie the most important parts."

"Right. Isobel is the tear jerker and the one we go to town on. We'll make her the younger sister instead of the older and as pretty as Colleen. When she goes back after the funeral, the old man even makes a pass at her."

"I don't like that."

"For God's sake, kid, quit being so literal. Do we want to make a blockbuster of a movie and a hell of a lot of money, or don't we?"

"I guess we do."

"The Indian squaw leaves me cold. Why can't she be a French maid who is getting herself laid in the boathouse and dimly sees the whole thing happening?"

"Because a French maid is trite, and the Indian squaw is unique."

As their work progressed, Sidney kept complaining, "We still don't have enough about Green's childhood. Can't you call up the squaw and pump her some more?"

"Not a chance, but I might try Darrow. She likes to talk about Daddykins."

"Then for God's sake, make a date with her. Sometimes a silly little detail that nobody thinks is important can be the crux of the story."

"All right. I'm willing to sacrifice myself."

When he telephoned her she suggested lunch at the commissary since she was still working. She had improved, he thought, looking even better than the last time they met. She was obviously copying Ginger Rogers now, looking more natural, and as if she had just come off a tennis court.

"You seem to be doing very well, Dottie," he said as they sat down at a table for two.

"I'm concentrating on it. There are so many angles, like I just realized how important the cameraman is. If he's not interested in you, he can kill you dead and vice versa. I hear Gregg Toland is a marvelous cameraman and I'm dying to meet him. You don't happen to know him, do you, Sky?"

"I've met him, but that's all." He beckoned to a waitress.

"Daddy Green keeps calling to know when the film will be finished. I tried to explain to him it takes weeks and sometimes months to complete a film. He ought to understand because he thinks of nothing but work himself."

After they had ordered, Sky said, "Doesn't Bradshaw Green ever take time off for some sport like golf or tennis?"

"You must be kidding, Sky. He never owned a golf club or touched a tennis racquet in his life."

"Well, he must like to swim, at least. I remember there's both an indoor and outdoor pool at South Wind."

"I suppose he can swim, but I've never seen him in either of them. I do know, though, that he does love the water. He likes the trips to Hawaii and Europe, and he had an artificial lake constructed once at South Wind, but the place has been covered over for years. Oh, look, there's Gregg Toland now." She turned and her eyes followed him as he left the commissary.

Sky waited a moment and then continued. "Did he ever have boats on the lake?"

"I don't know. I never saw one, but I do remember he once talked to me about a canoe trip he took with his grandfather down the Tippecanoe River in Indiana."

"What did he say?"

"He said it was the happiest time of his childhood." She shook her head. "I thought it was pathetic. How could any kid be all that happy paddling along in a canoe with an old man?"

"What was your happiest day, Dottie? Do you remember?"

"Give me a minute, but I think I know." She paused, then clasped her hands. "I know. It was the day I was confirmed. I loved wearing the little short veil, and I heard someone say to my mother, 'Gaby, that daughter is going to follow right in your footsteps.'" She looked at Sky. "What was yours?"

"Offhand, I would say it was my first day on an ocean liner, when my mother and father were taking me to Europe."

When he returned to Topanga Beach, he found Sidney despondent. "You know, kid, there are good days and bad days and this is sure Black Tuesday. I've tried coffee, Marcia and aspirin, and nothing works."

"Where is Marcia?"

"In my place, fixing us some food. I didn't remember how much I'd relied on her when I was doing my last job, until I started on this one."

"I got something out of Darrow that sounds like the kind of thing we can use." He told Sidney the story of the canoe trip. "The best part is that he has a canoe, probably the same one, rigged up on the wall of his indoor swimming pool at South Wind. It looked so incongruous that I kept asking questions about it when I was there last Thanksgiving but nobody seemed to know. All they could say was that it had been there for ages."

"What does it look like?"

"Just what any small canoe looks like. It has 'Kuckee' painted on the side."

"What the hell could that mean?"

"I couldn't make any sense out of it at the time. I have a feeling that my cousin may be going there again this year for Thanksgiving. I'm going to call and ask him."

Gage was eating his usual early supper. "Yes, Indiana has invited me and I understand her father may be around. I hope so. I still haven't met him."

"How is Indiana?"

"She seems fine."

"Give her my love, and do me a favor, please. It's important, and just between you and me. Ask Pinkie what the name 'Kuckee' means on that canoe in the indoor pool room, and call me back as soon as you can."

"Why on earth do you want to know that?"

"I know it sounds crazy but I need it for a little thing I'm writing. Don't forget."

As Sky put down the receiver, he was feeling genuine pain. He had managed to put Indi completely out of his mind, but as he talked with Gage he could see South Wind as it had been last year with the snow, the sleigh, Miss Peacock, Pinkie and, most of all, Indi, warm and eager as they lay in her four-poster bed.

"I'm tired, Sidney. I guess I need a swim before I go on working." He put on his trunks, went out to the beach and plunged into the surf.

Gage was on the Sunday-night shift at the *Globe* so he left South Wind early after the Thanksgiving weekend and called Sky before he went to the paper. "I found out what 'Kuckee' stands for, and we ought to be ashamed of ourselves for not guessing."

"Why?"

"Pinkie says the canoe was named for Lake Maxinkuckee at Culver. I remember now that the Green family had a big place on the shore, and Pinkie says that Bradshaw spent a couple of summers there with his grandfather. The whole name was too long for the canoe, so they shortened it to 'Kuckee.'"

"Was Indiana's father there for the weekend?"

"Off and on. I met him and we had a nice long talk. He was asking me about my own childhood in Indiana. Most of the time, though, he was talking about the war in Europe."

"Do you believe we'll get involved?" Sky asked.

"Hell, no."

"Thanks for calling back with the information, Gage. I thought I'd send Aunt Addie some California oranges for Christmas. Would you like some, too?"

"You bet."

Sidney shouted, "Great," when Sky relayed the meaning of "Kuckee" later that evening. "That's the key to his childhood."

Up to that time, Marcia had come out every Saturday to spend the night with Sidney, and Sky had gone into town for a movie or more often to spend the night with Nora. Time was running short since Sky's six-month lease would be up soon, so they decided to tighten their schedule and work weekends, too.

In the beginning, they had yelled frequently at each other and one or the other left in a huff, but returned a half hour later after a swim. After they set a deadline, though, they had worked much more quietly and reasonably together.

Saturday night, December 6, they wrote the last words of the script, though it would take several weeks of tedious revisions before they could submit it. It was early Sunday morning before Sidney typed the last words and looked at his watch. "It's almost 3 A.M. What have you got around here to drink?"

Sky opened the refrigerator. "Nora brought me a bottle of Russian vodka the last time she arrived with caviar." He opened the bottle and poured two drinks.

"Here's to my coauthor, whom I've wanted to kill sometime every day since we started work on this opus," Sidney said as he raised his glass.

"I'll make the same toast to you on the second round."

It was almost four o'clock when Sidney went home singing and Sky fell into bed. He slept until noon and as he started to make his coffee he saw that Sidney was just going out to swim. "When you get out, come on over here and I'll give you something to eat."

They were just sitting down to scrambled eggs and toast when they heard Sidney's telephone ringing. "Don't worry, if she doesn't get me there, she'll call me over here." When Sky's telephone started ringing, Sidney said, "I told you so." He got up, took the receiver and turned back to Sky, still holding it in his hand. "She just said, 'For God's sake turn on the radio,' and then she hung up."

For the next few hours they sat mesmerized in front of the radio. In the beginning the details of the Pearl Harbor bombing were scant, then the actual facts started to pour in. Three hundred sixty Japanese planes had attacked Hickam and Wheeler fields and the U. S. Pacific Fleet anchored at Pearl Harbor. The battleship *Arizona* had been totally destroyed and the battleships *Oklahoma, Nevada, California* and *West Virginia* had been severely damaged. Two thousand officers and men were reported killed among Navy and Marine personnel, and approximately another thousand were wounded.

"Goddamn those sneaky Japs." Sky finally broke the silence. Sidney sat motionless, never uttering a word as they turned from one station to another for more news. "What about some more coffee?" Sky volunteered.

"That dulcet voice of F.D.R. lulled the whole country into a sense of security," Sidney said, finally snapping back to life. "Like a lot of people, I never thought we'd get into this mess."

"It sure changes things in a hurry. Yesterday I knew exactly where I was heading, and now I'm going somewhere else."

"What do you mean?"

"What do you think I mean? I'm going to enlist as soon as I can. I made up my mind five minutes after we turned on the radio. You know I went to a military prep school and I took aviation at Princeton. I should be able to qualify for a commission right away."

"You're a quick thinker, all right. I guess I envy you your chance and I'd do the same if I were your age." He flexed his muscles. "Although I'm a healthy forty-six, with my game leg they'll never take me."

Sky reached for the telephone. Since Gage was on the night shift, he would have been in the newsroom of the *Globe* when the story first broke, but the circuits to New York were all busy.

"You know, Sidney, we've got to hand it to old Bradshaw Green. I'll bet his papers were all prepared and out on the streets an hour ahead of the others. He's been predicting this very thing for a long time, almost to the exact date. He had some kind of espionage thing going in Hawaii hidden by an orchid farm. His daughter told me so in confidence last June."

"He's a genius. There's no doubt about it."

As Sky handed him his coffee, he said, "I guess we'll have to go over the whole thing and soften it up a little."

"Let's do more about the orchid farm."

"The secretary character can bring that into focus."

"Say, kid, I'm all for your signing up, but I wish you'd stick around for a little while to help do the revisions. This war is going to be a long pull, I'm afraid, and a few weeks won't matter one way or another."

"Okay, that's fair enough. We'll both begin thinking it over and get started right away."

When the telephone rang it was Nora. "Sky, darling, you must get away from that beach house immediately. My guest room is waiting for you and I truly need you. The whole West Coast is in danger and we may be bombed any minute."

"I don't think so, Nora. Now that they've involved us, with this surprise attack, I don't think the Japs have the strength to move in on the mainland."

"Everyone says they will. Please come."

"I promise to come in and see you next week, but I'm so involved in this damn script that I feel an obligation to finish it before I get into the war."

"You're not going to enlist?" She sounded frantic. "Do take your time, Sky, and think it over."

Hers was the first of a succession of calls. Cobina Wright also offered him a home. "Dear Sky, we haven't seen much of you recently, but I thought of you the first thing this morning when I heard the news. People are saying that Jap submarines have been sighted off Santa Barbara, and I suppose you know that a total blackout has been declared."

While Sky had been talking, Sidney had gone out on the beach. "I guess we're going to be alone in our glory here," he said as he came back. "They're all packing and beginning to load their cars. Do you think we're crazy?"

"No, I think the whole West Coast is in a state of hysteria. How's Marcia taking it?"

"Not too well. The first time I talked to her she was screaming and crying and begging me to come into town, but I said no and there was no use for her to argue."

"I heard your phone ringing just now."

"Yeah, it was Marcia again. She now says she would rather die with me than without, so it may be that she'll come. She likes candlelight, says it makes her feel sexy. God help me, but at least she can cook our meals."

By the next morning all the little houses on Topanga Beach had been closed and shuttered, except theirs. "There's nothing like having the whole western edge of the country for a private beach, is there?" Sidney said, when they went out for a swim before getting down to work. The only sign of life as far as they could see was a stray cat and the tin bucket and pail that one of their neighbors' children had left behind.

Marcia had arrived late the night before. She had stopped at a food market and was loaded with all kinds of food packages.

"You must have bought out the place," Sidney said.

"People were buying like crazy. There was almost no sugar left and I managed to get the last five-pound bag."

"You know I never eat sugar on anything."

"Oh well, I've got it anyway, and maybe Sky likes it."

Sidney decreed that they would have all their meals in his house and do their work at Sky's. "That will keep her out of our hair most of the time. We can leave our papers in a mess on your table and not have to clear it off for food."

Later that day Sky was able to get through to Gage. "The whole editorial staff here is eating humble pie. We thought the boss was crazy. He was around here all last week ordering editorials. Some of them were already in type and so was our headline 'JAPS STRIKE.'"

"I suppose the *Globe* was way ahead of the others on the newsstands?"

"Sure, since all we had to do was write the main story."

"That must have pleased him."

"I haven't seen him, but I'll bet it did. The radio stations have all mentioned what they call the *Globe* scoop. How are things out there?"

Sky told him he was planning to finish the script he had been working on. "After that I'm going to get into the Air Corps as fast as I can. I'll keep in touch."

"By the way, Indiana called to ask if I had heard from you. With all the talk about the West Coast in danger she seemed concerned about you."

It pleased Sky to hear it but he said, "Tell her when I know what I'm doing I'll write and tell her."

Their script at last had a working title. They had decided to call it *The Power and the Glory: A Portrait of a Man*, and it filled 308 typed pages. "We've got too much talk in it," Sidney said. "It's more like a play than a movie and it's too long for a play. Each of the women's parts has to be cut a little. The action of the camera should take the place of a lot of the dialogue."

Cutting was much more difficult than the writing had been,

Sky soon discovered. When Sidney ran a pencil through one of Sky's favorite phrases, he would scream with rage.

"Sorry, kid, but it's gotta go. What we need is action."

They decided to call off their work for Christmas afternoon only, so two days before, Sidney sent Marcia into the city to buy a turkey. "And I mean turkey, not a chicken, a capon, or a duck, all of which you have sometimes tried to substitute. I don't care how many markets you have to go to. I don't expect to see you back here without a genuine turkey that weighs at least twenty pounds."

The windows of Sidney's house were covered with a double layer of blankets, in accordance with the Coast Guard instructions of complete blackout, and they ate Marcia's turkey dinner by candlelight. "I do adore candles, but with all these blankets I think this place is stifling, don't you?" Marcia said. "We should have had a Christmas picnic on the sand."

"Stupid, don't you know that the light of a single match is a clue for dropping a bomb?" Sidney said.

"Let's let Marcia read our script and get her reaction," Sky suggested.

"Good idea. I've always said she represents the general public."

While they washed the dishes, Marcia curled up in a corner beside a kerosene lamp and began reading the script. "It's terrific," she called to them in the kitchen. "Endicott Spencer Brown is absolutely fascinating and I love the way you make me change my mind from one page to another about whether he's guilty or not. Is he really supposed to be Bradshaw Green, and won't he sue you for saying he killed his wife?"

"We never say so. We just show different incidents as those women saw them," Sidney said as he rinsed a plate and handed it to Sky to dry. "We've changed all names and places to escape libel."

"That's pretty clever of you. I think it will be a great big success, and I just love the funny woman who keeps calling him Daddykins."

"She's the only comic relief," Sidney smiled at Sky. "I had a feeling the public would go for her, and we'd better build up that part." He handed Sky another plate. "Wouldn't it be great if we could get Darrow to play herself?"

"You must be kidding, Sidney."

"I guess you're right. If she so much as thought of it, Daddy-kins might take her on a boat ride and come back without her."

By New Year's Day they had eaten turkey sandwiches, cold turkey, creamed turkey, turkey soup and turkey hash, and their last meal had been curried turkey.

"Marcia, have you no mercy? I will never mention the name of this species of fowl again, to say nothing of never wanting to taste it again," Sidney said.

"You told me to get a twenty-pound turkey and, so help me, you're going to eat every goddamn bit of it."

"She may sound tough but she knows that I know that she secretly adores me," Sidney said when Marcia had retreated to the kitchen.

Sky had called his landlord for a month's extension to his lease and was assured he could have it for as long as he wanted. Beach houses were considered to be neither salable nor rentable these days.

By the end of the first week in January they felt they were getting near the end of their work. They were arguing whether to let the Iris Peacock character have a lover in her past, when Hedda Hopper called. "What's this I hear, Sky? Have you really been living in seclusion at Topanga Beach because you are writing a sensational movie script with Sidney Garson? He's a great writer."

"Sidney and I have been working on one, Hedda, but it's not nearly finished and it may come to nothing."

"I doubt it, especially if it's about the inside life of Bradshaw Green, as I hear it is. Is that true, too?"

"It's the portrait of a tycoon, and I suppose some people may relate it to Bradshaw Green, but of course the character is completely fictitious."

"Well, I can hardly wait to see it. He's a fascinating man and I've always been madly curious about him. Have you shown it to an agent?"

"It's not finished, as I said. How did you happen to hear about it?"

"How can I remember? Somebody was talking about it at dinner last night, and I wondered why you had gone into retreat." She laughed. "I had an idea it was a hot love affair."

"Just a love affair with work, Hedda," he said as he hung up. Turning to Sidney, who had been listening to the conversation from across their work table, he asked, "Who could have possibly told her? I certainly haven't mentioned Bradshaw Green's name to anyone."

"I have just one thought." Sidney went to the door and shouted, "Come over here, Marcia." A few minutes later, when she stuck her head in the door, he asked, "Did you talk to anyone about our script?"

"You didn't tell me not to, but I didn't say a word to anyone, except to my next-door neighbor, Lee Anderson, who didn't perk up her ears until I mentioned the Bradshaw Green angle."

"You are a pain in the ass, Marcia, and you'd better get out of here before I wring your neck, the way somebody's wrung that turkey's."

"Oh come on, Sidney, you know the publicity will be good for both of you. Now I've got to go start dinner."

By the end of the following week they had finished the revisions and were beginning to talk about where they should take the finished script.

"I can take it to the Harris office," Sky said. "They've been very friendly to me from the beginning."

"Yes, but I've got a literary agent. He's handled all my stuff, and he's uncanny about knowing who's going to like it."

"Fine with me. I think you're right, but since Harris is handling me, I'll have to check in to see if that's all right."

Sky began sorting through his possessions. He threw away most of the college clippings that had seemed so precious to him less than two years ago and now seemed relegated to things that had happened too long ago to matter. He packed the small Picasso sketch carefully and put it in one of the suitcases he had decided to ask Nora to keep while he was away. "Good old Picasso may have to get me started again when I get back, if we haven't sold the script by that time," he thought aloud.

He would ask Nora to keep his typewriter, too, but before he closed the case that night he sat down at his work table to write three letters. Aunt Addie's was short and so was the one to Gage, but he took a lot of time with Indiana's. He felt that the telepathy that had gone on between Indi and him had been cut off sharply.

Finally he began to write.

"Dearest Indi, if I could only see you, I feel it would be so easy to explain everything that has happened to me here, but now that won't be possible. I am going into Los Angeles tomorrow to enlist in the Air Corps."

The letter continued. "I hope this will come as a surprise to you, that the career I had hoped for in Hollywood was deliberately ruined by your father. After being accepted for three good parts in major films and then turned down at the last moment, I was finally told point blank by my agency that I should not expect to work in films as long as I was under contract to Olympia. As a major stockholder in the studio your father had given orders to that effect. It was surmised that he wanted me back in New York, where my future would be brighter and more beautiful. You can imagine my total disillusionment after I had started with such eagerness and high hopes. I have never believed that you had any part of this maneuvering, but, knowing me as you do, I'm sure you realize I could never submit to becoming a puppet.

"The script that my friend and I have been writing may have been started in a mood of retaliation. As you undoubtedly read in Hedda Hopper's column, the main character is a tycoon that may suggest your father. It may never be produced but it has helped pass six months that would have been worse than hell without something to occupy my time.

"With who knows how long a period of military life ahead of me, there's nothing more I can say, is there? Except that I'll go on thinking about you, no matter what happens." Then he signed it.

Next morning when he drove into Beverly Hills to the Harris office, Leland Harris sent out word he wanted to talk with him personally. He was greeted warmly and Sky explained that, as soon as he left his office, he was going to enlist.

They talked about *The Power and the Glory* film script, and Harris said, "Garson's right. He has an established reputation for being a good storyteller and an excellent technician. His agent can represent your property with our blessings."

"I think what we've done with the script is interesting and off-beat."

"I don't doubt it. I read the Hedda Hopper column, but I've got to warn you, Sky. You're playing with dynamite. Bradshaw Green carries a lot of weight in the whole film industry. He has unpublicized investments in some of the other film companies."

"Probably we'll never manage to sell it, then, but right now it doesn't seem to matter."

Leland Harris held out his hand. "I guess not. You've got time and talent. Come back to see us when the war's over and we'll try to start your career all over again."

At the Army enlistment office in downtown Los Angeles, Sky filled out reams of paper with age, parents, place of birth, schooling and state of health. They stamped the date "January 17, 1942" on the top and told him he would be eligible for an immediate commission and to report for assignment three days later.

Before getting into his car to drive back to the beach he picked up a paper. The headline across the front page read, "Carole Lombard Dies in Plane Crash." The story continued with, "The wife of Clark Gable was killed instantly when a TWA DC-3 crashed into a mountain thirteen minutes after leaving Las Vegas. She was returning from a war-bond tour."

The news seemed to him like an extra paragraph added to the finale of his own Hollywood chapter.

PART TWO

PART TWO

CHAPTER TWELVE

May 1946

It was the day before Indiana's wedding. Her bedroom in the Fifth Avenue house was in a state of utter confusion. Pauline, her personal maid, had already brought in three suitcases and was beginning to pack the clothes she would wear on her wedding trip.

"How many bathing suits will you need, Miss Indiana?"

"Oh, half a dozen, I guess. I suppose it will be warm in Bermuda, but I really don't care. Pack anything you think I'll need for the two weeks we'll be there."

"Yes, Miss Indiana." How can she be so indifferent, Pauline wondered. "Did you see your veil? It arrived early this morning. I've hung it next to your dress."

Her wedding dress had come from Sophie at Saks the night before. Made of pure white satin, it was hanging on a temporary rack, brought in because the train was too long for the closet. It's very regal. All I need is a coronet to look as if I were being crowned Queen, Indiana thought as she stepped around it on her way out.

The rest of the house was in as great confusion as her own room. The main floor had been totally redecorated, a process her father had started five months before, when she told him she was engaged. The dark satins and velvets she had hated since childhood had been replaced by lighter, brighter silks, but she still disliked the rigidity of the furniture and the uncomfortable way in which it was arranged. It will be all right for the wedding reception following the ceremony in St. Bartholomew's, but thank goodness we're not going to live here, she thought. The new apartment her father had given her farther down Fifth Avenue would be ready, with her clothes moved into it, when they returned from Bermuda.

In the drawing room Miss Peacock was inspecting the placement of the trees in tubs that were being brought in, and another work crew was taking out the furniture that would go to storage and return two days later, after the wedding reception. Without it, the room was beautiful, Indiana thought as she came in.

She was turning away when Miss Peacock called. "You're not going out, are you, Indiana?"

Indiana was pulling on her gloves, but she stopped as she saw Miss Peacock coming across the room toward her. "Yes, I am. I thought I'd go down to my office for a while."

"On the day before your wedding? I should think you'd want to stay around here with all the excitement that's going on." She's certainly a cool one, Miss Peacock thought. Any other girl would be out of her mind with joy.

"Is there any special excitement that I haven't heard about?" Indiana asked.

Miss Peacock smiled. "Well, even your father is taking most of the day off, and it's the first time as far back as I can remember." She followed Indiana back to the foyer where at least two dozen gifts had just arrived; one on top was wrapped in gold paper and tied with gold ribbon and tinkling little metal bells.

Indiana had opened almost none of the gifts herself. There were too many for her to cope with. The listing of each as well as the notes of thanks were being handled by two extra secretaries as meticulously as if it were a matter of state diplomacy rather than a wedding. She knew that she had written her signature once and that a skillful copyist had already reproduced it in at least four hundred letters, but when she looked at the presents arranged on trestles in one of the main-floor rooms, so special friends could admire them, she had no feeling that they had anything to do with her life.

"Mrs. Hale has just checked into the St. Regis. Your father reserved a suite for her there," said Miss Peacock. "Mrs. Hale says she's very tired and wants to rest before she sees you at dinner tonight."

"Please tell her to come early so she can see the presents. But after this evening I want the room closed, and no one at the reception tomorrow is to be permitted in there."

They went into a small office off the foyer where a table had been set up for a special secretary to take care of letters and telegrams. A fresh bundle had just come in.

While the two of them talked, Indiana wandered over to Miss Peacock's desk, where she found a little pile of letters and cables from Europe. She picked them up. "Why on earth weren't these sent right up to me? This one is from Philip Harlow in London. I'm so fond of him and I couldn't understand why he hadn't written." She looked closely at the envelope. "This letter is dated three weeks ago. Has all my mail been held up at your desk, Miss Peacock?"

"Of course not, Miss Indiana. But you know your father has always wanted me to screen your mail because of cranks and he also asked me to take out your bills so that he can pay them immediately."

"Not that it matters now, but I think I should always have known what I've been spending. I'll take the rest of these with me, anyway." She picked them up and started to put them into a paper shopping bag that was lying on the desk.

"Oh no, you have too much to do today," protested Miss Peacock, reaching out her hand for the bag.

The trouble is that I don't have enough to do, thought Indiana as she got into her car. So many people are in on the act that I don't feel as if it were my wedding at all. She drove down Fifth Avenue and turned into Central Park, where the white fruit trees were just beginning to bloom.

At the *Globe* her secretary jumped up from her typewriter when she saw her. "Oh Miss Green. None of us thought you'd be coming in today. We were even surprised to see Mr. Hale. But none of us expected to see the bride-to-be. We all thought you'd be completely carried away!"

"I am carried away, but who do you mean by 'we all'?"

"The girls who get together sometimes in the ladies' room. They all think that Gage Hale is terribly attractive and terribly nice."

She smiled. "Yes, he's both and I'm terribly lucky."

She went into her own office and closed the door. Once at her desk she picked up the paper's late edition and sat staring at the headlines.

She was in a sudden panic, and she felt her heart beating so violently that she thought her secretary must hear it on the other side of the door. Five months ago, to marry Gage Hale had seemed the best solution to her life, and it might still be all right if she could get through the romantic preliminaries. When she had said yes, she had seen their life together as a kind of effort-less companionship, with the *Globe* as a bond in common. They might even eventually make a success of running it together. Now she saw herself having to play an emotional part that she didn't feel. She was fond of Gage but had no desire to be closer to him mentally, emotionally or physically than she was right now. He was a good lover but Sky was the only man she had ever really responded to or ever would. What shall I do? Can I possibly get out of this nightmare? she wondered.

For a while after Sky's letter from Hollywood she had been happy in the belief that he knew she was innocent of what her father had done, and as he said, that they would get together again someday. As soon as she could get his address from Gage, she had written to him, and the next day she had gone to her fa-ther's office in the *Globe*.

"I know I have no appointment, but I want to see Daddy," she had stated firmly to Iris Peacock.

"It's one of his busiest days, Miss Indiana."

"I'll wait." As she sat going through the paper for the second time that morning, she wondered if she should tell her father that she knew all about what he had done to keep Sky from suc-cess in Hollywood, and that she didn't blame him for writing a detrimental movie script, but she decided not to say anything that might prevent a future reconciliation.

Half an hour later she was ushered into Bradshaw Green's big office. He was sitting behind an old-fashioned oak desk that, at the moment, was littered with papers except for a small bust of Teddy Roosevelt, a signed photograph of Al Smith and an inex-pensive clock that had to be replaced frequently since tossing it across the room to express his anger had become a habit. Loom-ing up from the table top behind his desk was a bronze owl three feet high. It was the owl that his grandfather had ordered photographed and used on the masthead of his first newspaper. It had been used on all the Green newspapers ever since.

"Well, daughter, don't you think our home is the best place for a business talk? I'm afraid, though, I haven't spent much time there recently." When he heard she was outside, he was sure she had come to accuse him of ending her association with Schuyler Madison, which he would explain to her was all for the best. He would not tell her, though, that he had not only successfully prevented the young fool's movie script from ever being produced but also had made sure that no future communications from him would ever reach her.

"I'm here because it's serious business, Daddy. I want a job."

"A job. What the hell for? Don't I pay all your bills, and give you an allowance besides?"

"Of course you do, but I want to work. I've had it with girls' schools but if you think I'm uneducated I'll take some night classes at Columbia or NYU."

"What kind of a job do you have in mind?"

"I want to work on the paper, of course. I've loved it since I was a little girl, and since you've been telling me that the *Globe* will be mine someday, I'd like to know a little more about it."

"That's impossible. The staff wouldn't accept it. They'd feel they had to give you special treatment."

"Oh come now, Daddy. You know your word is law around here, and I've never heard that you're exactly timid about saying so."

"What do you think you can do?"

"It's very simple. I want to be a copy girl."

"A copy girl?" he shouted.

"Yes, the boys you usually take on to start at the bottom are all being drafted and I heard from Harvey that one girl has already been hired."

"In the First World War all the young girls got together to make bandages or else they knitted sweaters for their boy-friends."

"Things are different this time. Women are going to break into a lot of jobs that have always been held by men. Just wait and see."

Bradshaw Green frowned as he picked up his telephone and

asked George Campbell, the managing editor, to come to his office. Indiana felt she had won her battle, so she sat quietly while her father went back to the newspaper he had been reading.

When George Campbell came in Green said, "My daughter, Indiana, here wants to work on the paper as a copy girl. I don't meddle with hiring the newsroom staff, so I'm tossing the whole business to you."

The managing editor smiled at Indiana. "I don't see why she shouldn't if she's willing to work hard for the twenty-five dollars a week the job pays."

He turned back to Bradshaw Green.

"It may cause a little excitement at first, but it won't last long."

"Oh thank you, Mr. Campbell. When can I start?" broke in Indiana.

"Right away, if you want. You can go upstairs to personnel and register for your Social Security number."

"I'll be here tomorrow. What time?"

"Around eleven-thirty. You're allowed time out for lunch but you'll have to work out the schedule with the other copy kids so that you aren't all away at the same time. If we need you, you may have to stay as late as eight o'clock when the first edition of the paper goes to press."

"Are you planning to hire many girls, George?" Bradshaw Green asked, "And does Tigar approve?"

"I believe so but most of the girls who've applied are obviously less interested in work than being part of a room full of men."

The next morning, after Indiana had gone through personnel, she was told to go to Charles Tigar's office. Damn it, Tigar hasn't enough to do, so he has to mess around in everybody else's business, she thought as she took the elevator to go upstairs.

In Tigar's outer office, she was told to wait until he finished an important long-distance telephone call. Though she sat quietly in a chair pretending to look at today's headlines on the front page of the *Globe*, she was inwardly seething. I don't really think he can stop me from getting this job, but he's going to throw his weight around by trying. As she turned the pages of the paper without reading a word, she thought, I've never understood what Daddy sees in him. I've never liked him and he knows it. One

day when she was four and had come running into the library
where Tigar was arguing with her father and seeming to her to
be threatening him, she had picked up his hand and had bitten it
as hard as she could. She could still hear him yelling, "What a little bitch of a daughter you have, Brad." At the time she didn't
know what the words meant, but had learned later.

A buzzer sounded and the secretary said, "You can go in now,
Miss Green."

He was sitting smoking a pipe, and everything in the office
seemed to her to be redolent of tobacco. "Sit down, Indiana," he
said, motioning her to the chair. A skinny little man, his face had
fallen into heavy wrinkles, and he had a perpetual smile that, as
far as Indiana was concerned, failed to camouflage his hard eyes.

She sat down. "You wanted to see me, Tigar?"

He put down his pipe. "How foolish of you, Indiana, to want
to play working girl."

"I don't intend to play. I want to work now, and I think I'll
probably want to work the rest of my life."

"I have no objection to your working, but not here. It has always been our policy not to employ members of the family."

She smiled back at him. "Didn't I hear somewhere that rules
are only made so they can be broken?"

"That may be elsewhere, but not here."

"I love newspapers, even the smell of the print, and I intend to
work for one someday. It seems only fair to me to ask for some
training here."

"If your father has given his consent I suppose there is no way
I can actually stop this foolishness, but I warn you, I'm going to
talk to him again, and I'll check carefully on the reactions of the
rest of the staff."

She stood up. "Thank you, Tigar, I'm sure you will." He knows
he can't stop me, she thought, as she went out and closed the
door. I despise him and if I ever get the chance I'll get even with
him.

On her way out, Indiana walked through the newsroom and
took a quick look at the copy girl who was already working. Indiana wanted to see what she looked like and what she was wearing. She realized that obviously her own suit and high-heeled
pumps wouldn't do.

As she put on a T-shirt, pleated skirt, and saddle shoes the next morning, she felt happy for the first time in months. Sky was off in a new world but now she was, too. She took a Fifth Avenue bus, rode to Fortieth Street, and walked west to the paper. I'm going to play this straight, she thought. It would be ludicrous for a twenty-five-dollar-a-week copy girl to arrive in a chauffeured limousine.

"I haven't the faintest idea what I'm doing," confessed Indiana to the other copy girl, a honey-colored blonde named Francie.

"I've only been here a week." Francie was smiling and seemed ready to help. "But it's easy after the first day. Each of the important fellows has a bell on his desk and when he rings it, whichever of us is nearer runs to find out what he wants."

"How do I know who the important ones are?"

"You'll soon find out and you'll be carrying copy down to the composing room, where they set up type, and you'll be taking memos from the managing editor all over the building."

To Indiana the clang of the bells seemed to come from all directions at the same time, and when it came time to leave she was more tired than she had ever been in her life. She dragged herself home the first night at seven-thirty, where she soaked her aching feet in warm water.

"You'll get used to it," Francie had told her, and she did. The newsroom was a little like a school auditorium, full of workers involved in the same project. Everyone seemed to know all there was to be known about everyone else, and the gossiping was unrestrained but usually funny. In the first few weeks Indiana learned that the handsome drama critic and the equally photogenic fashion editor were living together while they waited for his divorce to become final. The crossword-puzzle editor had already had five husbands, and her eyes were now on one of the editorial writers. One of the night editors, Edgar Hill, had made a bet with himself that he was going to lay all the women on the paper. He kept a notebook and crossed them off one by one. "He hasn't got around to me yet," said Francie, who provided most of the gossip, and was having her own little flirt with the national advertising manager.

Indiana had most of her luncheons in the *Globe* cafeteria. As she took her tray and walked along the long counter, usually choosing a peach or pear filled with cottage cheese and set on a lettuce leaf, she often thought of Rosemary, who would be meeting someone at Marguery or the Japanese Gardens of the Ritz.

"I don't see why you want to get yourself involved in the grimy kind of work you're doing," Rosemary had said the last time they had met, at a Sunday buffet supper in the country. "Why don't you just relax and have a good time?"

"I am having a good time." She felt that Rosemary was actually jealous of her because she had managed to escape from the narrow, inbred little circle in which they had grown up.

One night as she was passing the cubicle occupied by the sports editor, Harvey Griggs, she heard him call out, "Hi there, Indiana, want to do a favor for me?" He was waving a pair of tickets in his hand.

"Glad to, if I can."

"Then trot over to Madison Square Garden tonight, will you, and tell me if the toy poodle, the Welsh terrier or whatever wins the big prize in the Westminster Kennel Club Show."

He handed her the tickets.

"Just give me a few paragraphs about it tomorrow. I'll send a photographer along."

Indiana felt very professional as, for the first time, she flashed her press pass. An Italian greyhound was finally named dog of the year. She had just closed her notebook and was leaving the Garden absorbed in what she was going to write, when she felt a hand on her arm.

"So you're a dog lover, are you?" asked Edgar Hill.

"Not specially. I was just asked to cover the story. Are you?"

"No. Somebody gave me a ticket and I had nothing better to do. How about supper somewhere?"

"Fine. It just happens that I'm hungry."

They took a taxi to the Pen and Pencil. As they ate their steaks and baked potatoes, they talked and laughed and she decided that he couldn't be as bad as Francie had painted him. "I've always heard that the Pen and Pencil was a favorite hangout for newspaper people and now I can see why," she said as they were leaving.

"How would you like to see what a bachelor newspaperman's apartment looks like?"

Now here it comes, she thought. "Not tonight. It's too late and I'm tired."

"It won't take a minute. I have some things that I think will interest you."

"Give me a rain check, Edgar." She was determined he wouldn't cross her off the list on their first date.

A day later the picture of the winning dog appeared, but Indiana's story was not with it. "Was the little thing I wrote as bad as all that?" she asked Harvey Griggs.

"It was O.K., Indiana. Edgar Hill was making up the page that night and for some reason decided to throw it out."

She realized with amusement that Edgar disliked being rejected and was demonstrating his power.

After that both she and Francie began getting more assignments and running fewer errands. Francie had a real flair for writing, Indiana realized, and she wasn't surprised when Francie was promoted to become a real reporter.

A short time later, the managing editor, George Campbell, sent for her. "Indiana, I think you've served your time running copy. You've done a damn good job during the past year, and to tell you the truth I never thought you'd stick it out."

"I love this newspaper, every inch of it."

"All the editors like you but I'm going to put you in a new department that's being created. I'm going to call it women's features."

"I'm stunned and thrilled, Mr. Campbell. Recently I've noticed that other papers, especially the Chicago *Daily News*, are catering to women readers with better pictures and stories."

"I realize that. You'll be assistant to the editor. It will give you an opportunity to meet many of today's personalities and to absorb their ideas."

Her friendship with Gage had begun almost immediately after she started her new job. It was partly because he was one of the younger editors but mostly because she felt still close to Sky when she was with him. Often he talked about something they had done together when they lived in Fort Wayne, or even mentioned a note that either he or his mother had received.

During the first year of the war, Gage had made the gesture of enlisting, but had been turned down because of his poor eyesight. When he came back from the registration office, he had called Indiana in her office and asked her to come to Bleeck's to have luncheon with him. "I can't lie to you and say I'm sorry, because I want to go on with my work here." Shortly thereafter he became day city editor.

It was Gage who had introduced Indiana to Bleeck's, where she pre-empted the table in the front window, and often entertained school friends, who got a kick out of a brush with the newspaper world and new friends from the booming fashion industry that was just a stone's throw away on Seventh Avenue. No matter who was with her, Gage was always welcome to join the party and it had soon become an established thing for the two of them to report their daily progress to each other.

One morning Gage sent Indiana to a civic luncheon at which Mayor LaGuardia had put on the hat of a lady on the dais as he rose to predict the rise of American fashion. Indiana had reported the event but Tigar refused to let her have a by-line.

It was a few days later that Gage reported, "The editorial writers are all talking about those low-neck white blouses you wear, Indiana." He smiled. "I like them but they complain they can't concentrate and keep looking at you instead. I wrote and told Sky about it and I know he'll get a big kick."

If Sky was amused or pleased, Indiana never knew. As the months went by, she began to wonder more and more bitterly why he never wrote. Every now and then Gage had remembered to say, "Sky says to tell you to write and answer his last letter." She always wrote but no answers ever came. Gage had explained that mail delivery from North Africa, where Sky was stationed, was chancy. Indiana had blind faith that anyone she loved so much must love her just as much in return.

As soon as the war was over, she began to feel exuberant. She bought new clothes, though the fabric shortages were still keeping them short and skimpy. Every day she dressed carefully because Sky would come unexpectedly, she felt sure. There would be a knock on her office door and he would be standing there smiling. For weeks she jumped to answer every ring of the telephone, tore open telegrams with trembling fingers and looked up expectantly when she heard someone come into the outer office.

One day early in November Gage had said, "I doubt if Sky gets home for Christmas as we hoped he would."

"Oh really. Why not?" She tried to hide her eagerness.

"Well, he's had a bit of financial luck. It seems he and his friend have finally sold an option on that script they started in Hollywood before the war."

"How nice for him." She tried to force a smile.

"I guess they stand to make quite a lot of money, and he may stay over there and enjoy life for a while."

"Please tell him I'm happy about his success." Indiana felt as if a piece of ice were melting down her back.

"Why don't you write and tell him yourself?"

"Probably because he has never written to me."

"But that's impossible. He often writes about letters he has sent that you've never answered."

"He's not telling the truth, Gage. I wrote often for a while, but he never answered so I stopped." She turned away her head because she had felt her eyes filling with tears.

That night, as she lay in bed, she had faced the fact that Sky was never coming back to her. She had thought of him constantly for the past five years. After carefully calculating the time difference when she got up each morning she would think that he had just finished lunch. When she left work in the evening she would wonder whether he was already in bed or was still at some nightclub in Cairo with a beautiful girl.

It had all been a dream, and now she had to stop dreaming. She would soon be twenty-four. Most of her school friends were married, but she was alone and lonely.

Not that it would be hard to find a husband. Among the possibilities were Timmy Phipps, but he would want me to give up working, greet him wearing a lace-trimmed satin negligee every afternoon when he got home from work. Philip Harlow is really a dear with a good sense of humor, but I'd have to live in London.

Gage is the best bet, she decided. He understands me and won't make too many demands, and will let me go on with my work.

Since most of their meetings so far had taken place in the *Globe* or its vicinity, she decided to enlarge the scope and see how it worked. When she had dialed Gage and asked him to go

with her to the Broadway opening of *State of the Union,* he had
replied that he had made a tentative dinner date but was sure he
could put it off. She remembered from Sky that Gage was carrying on a lackadaisical affair with a nurse named Buzzie, but Indiana also knew that an invitation from her would be a kind of
royal command to Gage.

She and Gage had gone to the opening and then to El Morocco. She had watched with interest as he responded to the sophisticated atmosphere of the place.

"I used to think El Morocco was for Daddy's friends and older
people, but I guess I've grown up to it," she said as they sat on
the zebra-striped banquette behind what was obviously the best
table in the room. "This is really Daddy's table, and we're his
guests, so let's have some champagne."

Later, coming from the dance floor, they had stopped at other
tables and she had seen quickly that Gage was acceptable to the
men and actually pounced on by the girls who, she knew, were
always avid for a new face on the scene. He's good-looking when
he isn't nervous and concentrated on his work, and he's really
sweet, she had thought.

When he took her home, instead of the impersonal kind of kiss
that usually ended their meetings, she had pulled his face down
to hers and kissed him deliberately and warmly on the lips. She
could feel his startled response and found herself enjoying it, so
she kissed him again.

That evening had been the beginning of a totally different
relationship with Gage. They stopped talking about Sky and she
was quickly aware that Gage, who was a dogged fighter in his
own way, had made up his mind to marry his cousin's girl if he
could.

For a while it had been pleasant and satisfying to feel herself
being loved. Gage was always at her service, and he accepted her
moods and whims without reservations.

It was months before they first slept together, and she had had
to negotiate the whole happening. Gage came to South Wind for
the weekend, and they had both looked forward to long days of
riding through the trails in the woods, or else playing tennis. Saturday, though, had turned out to be damp and gray. As they sat
in the library talking about everything, their childhoods, their

friends, the newspaper and their likes and dislikes, the rain had been beating on the tall casement windows until Indiana had begun to feel that it was building a wall around them that separated them from the rest of the world.

After dinner that night she had flopped down on a sofa and stretched out with some cushions behind her head. Gage had pulled up a chair beside her and was talking for what seemed to her an interminable time about something that didn't interest her.

"For goodness' sake, Gage. I don't want to hear another word about Harry Truman. Do you love me?"

He got up and sat down beside her. "Indiana, you must be crazy. Of course I do."

"I feel like talking about love."

"What can I say? Any man in his right senses couldn't help loving you." He sat down on the edge of the couch and bent down to kiss her.

"Then kiss me harder. It's a wonderful, romantic night. It makes me feel like Wuthering Heights."

"I've wanted to make love to you, darling, but I've been afraid to spoil our wonderful friendship that has been growing so naturally."

He put his hand into the neckline of her dress and began caressing her, but his fingers had felt cold. She turned restlessly, feeling a desperate desire for contact with a man, almost any man, at this point. "Let's go upstairs, Gage."

"Shall I come to your room, Indiana?"

"No, I'll come to yours."

As she took off her clothes in her bedroom and put on a silk robe, she had thought to herself, I'll never have another man in this bed of mine, because it belongs to Sky and me.

When she came into Gage's room, he was wearing a terry robe and smoking a cigarette. He's nervous, she thought. She took off her own robe and sat down beside him. "If you love me as you say you do, prove it, Gage."

As she drifted off to sleep later, she felt satisfied and happy. He's the perfect Sir Lancelot and very predictable. Tomorrow he'll ask me to marry him, she thought.

Sunday morning the rain was still beating at the windows and she was still lying in bed with the Sunday paper scattered over the sheets, when Gage knocked at the door and came in. "I'm not asking if but when you'll marry me, Indiana."

She had laughed. "I'm not sure if I will, at all. I'll have to think about it for a while." They had spent the whole day and night together and by the time they left South Wind Monday morning, Indiana had begun to believe that their marriage would work.

When she told her father that she had virtually decided to marry Gage Hale, Bradshaw was enchanted with the news. "I've had my eye on that young fellow for a long time, and I've been hoping you'd have some good sense to like him. He comes from good middle-western stock, Indiana, just like your own family does. He'll make a good husband and he's right for whatever top jobs come along in the paper."

"But I'm not saying yes, Daddy. I've just said maybe."

"That's right, take your time and be sure—but Hale's a good man. He needs more spunk and maybe you can give it to him."

Two weeks later, Bradshaw Green announced the engagement of his daughter, Indiana, to Gage Hale, and the wedding date was set for May. Addie Hale had been in ecstasies over the news, but had called Indiana from Fort Wayne to lament the date.

"I will be so happy to have you as my daughter, darling, but shouldn't the wedding be sometime in June? I know it's a silly old superstition, but they say the month of May is unlucky for brides, and June is heaven-sent. That's the reason everyone gets married in June."

"We're going to change things and make May the lucky month," Indiana had said.

Now as she sat at her office desk with the wedding only a little more than twenty-four hours ahead of her, she wished that she had insisted on June. She would have had another month to make sure she could carry out what she had started. Both her father and Gage had urged May because they sensed that she was unsure, and might change her mind and go off on another tangent.

She wondered what would happen if she called both her father and Gage right now and told them that she couldn't go through with the wedding. Her father had never refused anything. He would stand by her, send back the wedding presents and help her slip off somewhere until the excitement died away. With Gage it was different. It would kill his pride and destroy him and perhaps it would be better to go on with the marriage even if she had to get out of it later. For the first time she wondered about the girl Buzzie, whom he had been seeing regularly for years and wondered if she was feeling heartbroken about losing him as she had been heartbroken about losing Sky.

Just then her secretary opened the door. "Miss Green, the hairdresser is at your home, ready to do your hair for the rehearsal dinner tonight."

"I'd almost forgotten. Tell him I'll be right there."

The next day, as she wandered about her bedroom in the Fifth Avenue house for the last time, everything seemed to be all right again. She and Gage cared for each other. They would have a good partnership and share a great deal of power together. She began to watch with real pleasure as the hairdresser brushed back her heavy, dark hair, fastened it high at the back of her head and curled the ends into long ringlets that hung to her shoulders. They would be hidden by the veil, but she liked the look.

Finally she was hooked into the dress and, before she picked up her bouquet, stood looking at herself in her full-length mirror.

"Oh Miss Indiana, I'm sure there never was such a beautiful bride," said Pauline, and Indiana could see there were tears in the girl's eyes. I look happy. I am happy and I'm going to be. I've got to be, she thought.

For the drive to St. Bartholomew's, her father rode in the front seat with the chauffeur, while the maid held her train in the back seat. As they approached the side entrance, into which she had expected to slip unobserved, she could see that the front steps were full of photographers and spectators, avidly watching the arrival of the ladies in their big hats and white gloves, and the men in striped trousers and cutaway coats.

Her four bridesmaids and Rosemary, who was her maid of honor, were already there. Dressed alike in white organdie over pale green, they were giving the finishing touches to each other's apple-green satin sashes. She saw that Addie Hale had just arrived, and while she was waiting to be shown to her seat, her mother-in-law-to-be was looking dubiously at the girls' big pale-green horsehair hats and even their bouquets of lilies of the valley, which were tied with pale-green ribbons. Oh dear, Indiana thought, wearing green is probably one of her superstitions, like not putting a hat on a bed, walking under a ladder or getting married in May.

After a few minutes she became aware that Gage's ushers had finished looping the white-satin ribbons from the back of one pew to another and were closing the outer door of the church. Pauline handed her the bouquet of white orchids she was to carry. They made her think for a minute of her debutante party, and she began to believe that it was a happy coincidence.

The music changed. As she put her arm into her father's and looked down the long aisle to the altar, she thought, this looks to me like the longest walk I'll ever take. She saw that her flowers were trembling and then the whole scene became a blur of flowered hats, white gloves and friendly smiles. She was aware of one or two people, whom she had deliberately not invited, beaming at her, and from the section reserved for the family there was Pinkie, who already had tears streaming down her face.

The ceremony seemed to take only a few minutes. She could hardly believe it was over when Gage kissed her and whispered, "You're beautiful, Mrs. Hale."

She felt a sudden rush of emotion for him, and when he took her hand she felt as if she were floating back down the aisle beside him. I've been alone so much in my life that to have a close companion is going to be wonderful, she thought.

Even the Fifth Avenue house filled with lights and flowers and all the smiling people seemed to have become warm and lovable. She had never seen her father look so relaxed and so elated. Even Miss Peacock looked less like a sphinx and more like a human being.

As she stood between her father and Gage, saying almost the same thing to each guest, Indiana caught occasional glimpses of herself in the mirrored wall across the room. Framed in the veil, her eyes were brilliant and her whole face looked soft and glowing. Anyone would think that I'm supremely happy, and maybe I am, and just have not had time to believe it yet, she thought.

Finally, the long receiving line was beginning to thin out. Bradshaw Green had been summoned to the telephone, and the bridesmaids had gone off to the buffet with the ushers. Indiana turned to Gage. "We still have that giant wedding cake to cut. It's monstrous. Are your hands steady?"

"Steadier than they were an hour ago. I'll go on to the dining room and make sure they bring me a good knife."

As she turned to follow him, Indiana saw that Gage's mother was coming toward her. She tossed her bouquet on a chair and put her arms around Addie Hale.

"What am I going to call you? You know, I never have called anyone 'Mother,' so I'm afraid the word would be hard for me to say. Shall I go on with 'Aunt Addie' or what?"

"Darling, I understand completely." She kissed her cheek. "I never thought I would know the happiness of having you for my daughter. I had always hoped, though, that you would be calling me 'Aunt Addie' when you married Sky."

"Sky?" She winced.

"Oh yes, Sky. I couldn't help thinking of him this afternoon when you came down the aisle looking so beautiful with the veil and the long train. I remember that first year he was out of Princeton he seemed to love you so much and was so happy when you were together."

"He only seemed to love me, I'm afraid. If it had been any-thing more, he would have written to me during the war."

"Not that it matters now, darling, but he did write to you. That I know, and he was surprised and hurt that you never replied."

"Not that it matters now, as you were saying, but no letters ever reached me, and it's hardly probable that all of them could have been lost. The mails aren't that bad."

Addie Hale was looking so bewildered that Indiana put her hand on her arm. "Let's go and cut the wedding cake," Indiana said, guiding her toward the long table.

Just as they reached Gage, the cake was brought in. It was four layers high and iced in white with garlands of pink roses. As she stood watching Gage cut a few of the first pieces neatly and precisely, Indiana's mind was racing back to what Aunt Addie had said. She seemed so sure, and if she was right, what could have happened?

"Try some of the cake, dearest. You're beginning to look pale," said Gage. He had turned over his job to one of the butlers, but passed her a plate with a slice of the cake on it.

"It's been such an exciting day that I'm beginning to feel a little tired. Can we get away soon, do you think?"

"Let's have some champagne together first. I feel the need of a little drink myself."

He motioned to a waiter, who opened a fresh bottle and filled two glasses. Gage raised his. "To my beautiful, wonderful wife, Indiana."

"I'll try to be wonderful. I truly will." Indiana started drinking her champagne and in a minute set her glass down empty. "I'd like another."

He laughed as he motioned to the butler. "Indiana, I've never seen you drink champagne so fast, but maybe it's just as well. We can't leave for another hour. It's only a quarter past five."

"Of course, you're right, especially since most people know we're spending the night in our new apartment and not taking the boat to Bermuda until tomorrow afternoon."

As they talked, Indiana was remembering the scene yesterday with Miss Peacock. She could see her long, thin fingers reaching out for the bag with the European messages. How ridiculous it had been for her not to realize that any kind of communication from Sky had been intercepted. How could she have sat by passively and let it happen?

When Gage turned away to speak to one of his ushers, Indiana looked around the room to find Miss Peacock. There was no sign of her, so she picked up her train and went into the drawing room. It was empty except for a couple on the sofa who were too engrossed with each other to notice the bride.

She must have gone back to Daddy's office, Indiana guessed as she crossed the hall and opened the door. Still wearing her navy-blue straw hat, and with her white gloves tossed on the desk beside her, Miss Peacock was sitting at her typewriter with her fingers flying over the keys. "My goodness, Mrs. Hale"—she emphasized the new name with a smile—"why aren't you out there enjoying your own wedding reception?"

"Because I want to be here. I have a question to ask you."

"What can I do for you?" She's angry. With all that hair and those big eyes, she looks like a lioness, thought Miss Peacock.

"I'm safely married now, so I'm going to ask you a question and I want an honest answer. Did you keep all Schuyler Madison's communications from Europe from reaching me?"

Miss Peacock hesitated for a moment. "Not because I wanted to. I had my orders."

"From Daddy, of course. How despicable. Were there many?"

She nodded. "Quite a few, especially at the beginning."

"How could you both have been so cruel, Miss Peacock?"

Her voice shook. "I have worked a long time for your father, as you know. He is a man who always completely finishes what he starts."

Indiana went back to the reception just long enough to retrieve her bouquet. "I'm going to throw it," she called to her bridesmaid and the other groups still drinking champagne and eating the watercress sandwiches.

She started climbing the stairs, looking back to see that her train spread over three steps behind her. Halfway up, she paused and held up the bouquet.

"Just a minute. This will make a marvelous shot, Mrs. Hale," called the photographer, who had been busy with his camera all afternoon.

Indiana waited just a minute before she tossed the orchids toward the dozens of pairs of arms that were reaching up to receive it. She saw that Rosemary jumped up and caught it just as she had often jumped for the basketball when they were playing in the school gym. Indiana climbed the rest of the way, her smile gone.

Pauline was waiting in her bedroom. She unpinned the veil and lifted it gently from Indiana's hair and began putting it into a carton with tissue paper between the folds. Indiana saw that a second box was ready for the dress.

"Madame will want to save these for her daughters to wear someday."

Indiana was trembling. "Take them out of here. I never want to see them again."

As soon as the maid left Indiana threw herself on the bed and buried her face in the pillow. The hatred she felt for her father was almost frightening. Tears rolled down her face and she sobbed uncontrollably.

Half an hour later there was a knock on her door and Pauline's voice said, "Can I help you, Miss Indiana? Everyone is asking for you downstairs."

Indiana stood up. "Tell them I'll be down in a few minutes." She went to her dressing room, washed her face and straightened her hair. As she started to put on fresh make-up she thought, there's nothing I can do now but go ahead and make as good a life for myself as I can.

Their new apartment was lighted and the staff she and Gage had employed was waiting in the foyer to greet them. There were fresh flowers in the drawing room, and as Indiana glanced in the library, she saw that the afternoon papers were laid out on the center table. "Let's sit down for a minute," she said, as she dropped down on a sofa.

"What a beautiful room you've made, Indiana."

"Yes, I think it turned out well." She looked at the paneled white walls, the light colors of the draperies outlining the long windows overlooking the park. It was everything that her father's Fifth Avenue mansion hadn't been.

They went upstairs and found that the beds in their adjoining rooms had already been turned down.

Indiana put her arms around Gage's neck and laid her face against his chest. "I've never been so tired. I need a good night's sleep. Tomorrow will be different. Anyway, it isn't as if we hadn't done this before."

"I understand, darling. After all, we have the rest of our lives together." He kissed her and went into his own room.

CHAPTER THIRTEEN

It was hard to believe there had ever been a war or that Paris had ever been occupied, Sky thought, as he looked around the big dining room at Maxim's with its stained-glass ceiling and the raised stage on which an orchestra was playing dance music. He still remembered quite clearly his first visit to Paris with his parents and even recalled that they had talked about taking him to Maxim's on their next trip when he would be a little older. That morning he had walked around the streets near Notre Dame trying to find the gallery where he and his father had bought the Picasso, but with no success.

After five years in uniform, it felt strange to be wearing civilian clothes, but he was glad that when they said good-bye to Cairo he and Philippe Lord, who had become his close friend during the war years in the desert, had stopped in Rome for a while to patronize a tailor.

He soon realized that the long table at which he was sitting was the focal point in the room. Albert, the rotund *maître d'* of Maxim's, was hovering around along with six waiters. The women on the dance floor in evening clothes and more jewels than he had ever seen never failed to stare as they danced past to the familiar American music that Sky knew by heart.

Their interest didn't surprise him at all, since his hostess was Lady Mendl. Philippe had sometimes mentioned her when they were still in Cairo. He had described her phenomenal success as the first great interior decorator. "She has made a million at least, and she's a marvelous hostess. She sometimes dyes her hair pale green and she's deep into yoga. She stands on her head at the least provocation, and once she came into a fancy dress party turning cartwheels," he had said.

When Philippe took him to her home at Versailles a few days before, he hadn't known what to expect, but it had been one of her quieter days, Philippe said afterward. When she came in from the garden she was snow white from her hair to her Chanel suit, and was so small and paper thin that she walked almost as if she was dancing. As she served tea and discussed the possibility of Philippe painting her portrait, Sky could see her studying him, too, with her restless, mischievous eyes.

During the war, Lady Mendl had retreated to Hollywood and had returned only recently to Le Petit Trianon, the historic French house in which Marie Antoinette and Louis XVI played farmers. As he looked at the beautifully proportioned rooms, the exquisite French furniture and the gardens, he could just catch a glimpse of the garden beyond the windows and he wondered how she had managed to wangle what was actually a part of the Palace of Versailles from the French Government.

She had caught him studying the scene and asked, "You like my French home?"

"It's the most beautiful place I've ever seen."

"I hear from Philippe that you've spent some time in Hollywood."

"Only a year, but it was an important one."

"It has its own charm, of course, but mostly outdoors. The open sky and the color of the light are magnificent, but I prefer living here."

"I can understand that."

"If you like my Trianon villa so much, you must come often. Where are you staying?"

"With Philippe."

"Lucky Philippe, with an apartment in both London and Paris." She had ended by asking them to dinner at Maxim's because, as she explained, her own home was not yet pulled together and in perfect running order. For Sky, it had been an especially propitious invitation. He had always longed to see Maxim's.

He looked up the length of the table to Lady Mendl, who

was sitting at the head. She was all in white again, with pearls around her neck and a huge diamond star dangling from them. He wondered if it was real, and was sure she enjoyed the thought that people were guessing.

When he came in she had said to him, "Dear boy, I've put you beside one of the great English beauties tonight. Diana Darby is the widow of one of England's war heroes."

He looked at the place card next to him just as Diana Darby, who had been dancing, settled into her place again. He stood up to adjust his chair. "I'm Schuyler Madison, Lady Darby."

She smiled. "You are an American, aren't you?"

"Yes, just out of the service."

She started to pick up her champagne glass as he turned to her. "I wonder if you'll drink a special toast with me, Lady Darby?"

"Of course. I'd be delighted." She picked up her wine glass and touched his. "To whom are we drinking?"

"I want to drink to the girl I thought loved me and to my cousin, whom she is marrying today instead of me." He glanced at his wristwatch. "As a matter of fact, it is five-fifteen in New York and at this moment Mr. and Mrs. Gage Hale are most likely cutting their wedding cake and drinking champagne, too."

She took a sip of her drink but set it down quickly. "Oh my dear. I'm so sorry." She put her hand over his.

Sky suddenly got the full impact of her red-gold hair and fabulous English skin. When he looked into the deep violet eyes under dark lashes he saw to his astonishment that there were real tears in them.

"It's not fatal and it's probably all for the best," he said. He realized that he had been longing desperately for someone's sympathy and he wished she would keep her hand on his. When she took it away, he said, "Let's dance, shall we?"

"What are your plans? Will you be here long?" she asked as they began dancing.

"No, I'm just spending a few days. Philippe and I were both with General Montgomery in North Africa for most of the war. We're good friends and I'm going on with him to London." She had a soft, very feminine body, and he was enjoying holding her in his arms.

"How fortunate. I live in London and perhaps we can see each other again."

"I thought it might be good for me to find something to do in Europe for a while. The language barrier in France is too great, so London seems the best bet."

"I think you are right not to rush back to America, especially under the circumstances you've just mentioned at the table. What did you do before the war?"

"I tried to be an actor and a writer but was not successful at either."

"You have an excellent voice, which is not true of most Americans. I'm sure you're going to be a great success in whatever you undertake." She looked up at him with such sympathy in her eyes that he felt genuinely touched and happier than he had been in a long time.

After dinner he took Diana Darby around the corner to the Crillon, where she was staying, then decided to walk across the Place de la Concorde and over the bridge to Philippe's small Left Bank apartment. It was almost an hour before he reached home, but Philippe was waiting up for him.

"You and Diana rather discovered each other tonight, didn't you, or was it just my imagination?"

"She's a beautiful woman. I've never met anyone quite like her."

"And probably you never will again. She's the one for whom those old-hat words *femme fatale* were coined."

"I'm not surprised."

"In case you're intrigued or just curious, I'll tell you all about her, but let's have a nightcap first." He poured two brandys and handed one to Sky. "I can tell you that she comes from a good English family, but not rich. She married Lord David Darby, who was good-looking, popular and had everything but money. He and his plane were shot down early in the war."

"What a pity, but I suppose she had dozens of men to help her."

"Yes, of course, but most of them are already legally attached, and any help they have given her hasn't made her exactly a favorite with the wives."

"They hate her, I suppose."

"Absolutely. Elsie Mendl is an independent thinker or Diana wouldn't have been at the dinner tonight."

"Does she have someone now?"

"I haven't the slightest idea. I did hear that she and Armando Maranini, the billionaire silk manufacturer, were very much in love last year."

"She told me she lives in London."

"It's a beautiful flat, with all signed French furniture and good paintings, but you'll see all that for yourself once we get to London."

"I may not see her again."

"It's a fairly safe bet that you will. Do me a favor and say that I still want to paint her just for the pleasure and no charge." He put his drink down. "Anyway, I would pay a fortune to paint her nude. They say that her body is as perfect as her face."

"I remember the last time you painted a beauty with no charge," said Sky as they both burst out laughing.

Later, as he undressed in the small guest suite that had once belonged to Philippe's French grandmother, Sky began to think how fortunate he had been to meet Philippe in Cairo.

In Los Angeles, after he had enlisted in the Army Air Force and spent the prescribed amount of time in a training camp, he was told his vision barred him from serving as an active pilot. So, undaunted, he applied for combat intelligence. After a three-month course in this branch of the service, he volunteered to go with a squadron of heavy bombers whose mission was to bomb Tokyo.

He found himself the waist gunner in a B-17 Flying Fortress that was suddenly grounded in India because the Japanese had taken the airport in China on which they were scheduled to land for refueling before setting out to bomb the Japanese capital. After three months in India, orders came from Washington to depart with all available fighting aircraft for Cairo. The British Eighth Army was, at that very moment, in full retreat across the desert.

The enemy was finally stopped at Alamein, and during the long, hot summer of 1942, the British and Americans did all they could to reinforce the Eighth Army.

After a long trek across the North African deserts the following winter, Sky's normal weight of 175 pounds had dropped to 135 and he was ordered back to Cairo for a rest.

Taking part in the social life of Cairo was part of his rehabilitation, and it was at one of the diplomatic parties that he had first met Philippe Lord, whom he learned was an established portrait painter from London. Though Sky had seen only a few things Philippe had had time to paint in Cairo, Sky could sense that Philippe had the kind of talent his father had taught him to admire.

At the time, Philippe's greatest ambition was to paint King Farouk's wife. Queen Fareda was said by those who had managed to see her to be the most beautiful woman in the world. Since the King was madly jealous and kept her totally secluded in his harem, there seemed to be little or no chance.

After a few drinks one night, Philippe had decided to write to King Farouk himself. In his letter he enclosed several photographs of his portraits. "What the hell, he'll probably throw it in the wastebasket," he predicted to Sky, "but it's worth a try."

To the surprise of both, an emissary from the King called on Philippe a few days later. The King had seen an exhibition of his paintings in Rome and would be delighted to have a portrait of the Queen. The stipulations were that it must be done during daytime hours and that they would never be alone.

The Queen was unbelievably beautiful, Philippe had reported enthusiastically to Sky. First he painted her on her throne wearing a royal robe and gold crown. She liked it so much that he was permitted to start a second, showing the Queen in her riding habit. He dreamed of doing a third, showing her as a chiffon-clad nymph running through the woods.

It was at about this time that he had conceived the idea of introducing Sky to the Queen, who had seemed eager to meet the painter's American friend.

A trusted servant was instructed to tap Sky on the shoulder at an appointed time and place. He was to follow the servant casually, and the route would lead to one of the Queen's rooms in the harem.

Everything went according to schedule, and when the door

opened and Sky entered the Queen's room, he could hardly believe his eyes. If Hollywood could only see this, he thought.

The Queen was half reclining against dozens of pale-green silk cushions on a rattan couch. She was as beautiful as Philippe had reported, with masses of dark hair and luscious red lips. Surrounding her were at least a dozen girls, almost as beautiful as she, all in chiffon tunics over pants and wafting peacock-feather fans to keep her cool.

"I have always wanted to meet an American," said Queen Fareda, smiling and holding out her hand for Sky to kiss.

She asked about Hollywood and listened avidly to his description of the parties, the restaurants and homes and what Nora Hayes, Tyrone Power and Joan Crawford really looked like in their private lives. When the Queen went on to discuss the progress of the war, Sky found that she was as intelligent and well-informed, if not better, than most of the women he talked to at diplomatic dinners. It seemed to him he had been with her no more than five minutes when the servant returned to tell him he must leave.

Philippe and he congratulated themselves that they had got away with the visit, but only a few days later a curt note from the palace canceled Philippe's future sittings with the Queen. Then almost immediately both their rooms were searched thoroughly, though they both had wondered what the searchers had expected to find. Soon afterward, the war had ended, and perhaps a good thing for both of them, they had left Cairo.

How fortunate I've been with my friendships, he thought as he got into bed. Each one has led to a new opportunity. He began to look forward to London.

CHAPTER FOURTEEN

Sky was happy to move on to London. He was feeling an increasing amount of pressure to establish himself in some kind of career. If nothing turned up in the next six weeks, he had made up his mind to go back to Hollywood and perhaps try another movie script with Sidney. It reminded Sky that their script *The Power and the Glory* had been shelved again and the option dropped. "Undoubtedly due to that bastard Bradshaw Green's interference," Sidney had written.

Philippe's London apartment consisted of a large studio with a skylight on the top floor, and the floor below had a small sitting room-dining room, kitchenette, and two bedrooms with a telephone in each. "My family, which consists of my widowed mother and two younger sisters, both married, all live in the country, but once in a while one of them comes down for shopping or the dentist," he explained. "It seems to me that they talk interminably and even though I can always retreat to my studio, I like to have a private wire when I feel like it."

"I won't stay long."

"Stay as long as you like. I'm used to you, and you don't bother me."

Philippe also had a daily char, who watched over the apartment when he was away, came every morning when he was there to cook a hearty English breakfast and clean the place before she left.

As Sky sat down the next morning at a table loaded with freshly baked muffins, orange marmalade and strawberries with heavy Devonshire cream, he asked, "Good God, do you eat like this every morning?"

"Always in England, and usually with bacon, but that's still being rationed." He reached for another muffin. "But I'm very adaptable, my boy. In Paris I can make do with coffee and croissants, but I'm more English than French at heart and I believe in stoking up thoroughly every morning to see me through the day, and especially now."

"Why now?"

"Because I'm going to have a little problem getting back into the hub of things."

"We Americans call it the rat race."

"Portrait painting is an art that flourishes in a leisure, somewhat self-satisfied society, and this country is far from being either of these now, and may never be again."

"I hadn't thought of that. Where would you go?"

Philippe reached for another muffin and the marmalade. "As I look around the world with a mercenary as well as artistic eye, I can only see two possibilities: your country and the Middle East, where everyone is more stinking rich than most people have realized yet."

"Now that you mention it, I think Hollywood might be a great spot for you, Philippe. The movie crowd is rich and full of both men and women who would go for a portrait by an English painter with a name." Sky poured himself another cup of tea. "Actually, if I don't find something here soon, I may go back there myself."

"Would you try films again?"

"I don't think so. I was just out of Princeton when I was there so consequently only considered for college parts but I don't feel that young anymore."

"I don't see you slaving away in the elegant obscurity of a bank or any other kind of desk job."

"God forbid."

"You're the kind of fellow who has to capitalize on personality. The theater in London is the best in the world."

"Yes, I know."

Philippe picked up a mountainous pile of mail and magazines, most of it addressed to members of his family, and began going through it. Sky decided to dress and go for a walk around London.

He had just finished shaving when Philippe called to him. "Here's a little package and a note. They've been hand-delivered for you, care of me."

Sky tore open the package that contained a paperbound book. It was *Present Indicative,* the autobiography of Noel Coward. The note read: "Dear Schuyler Madison, I just happened to see this little book. It reminded me of our conversation at Lady Mendl's dinner and I thought it might amuse you. Noel has made a success of both acting and writing." It was signed, "Diana Darby."

He held up the book for Philippe to see. "What a surprise. It's from Diana Darby. I supposed she would have forgotten the few words we said to each other."

"Diana seldom forgets anything."

"I must say it was very sweet of her. But how can I thank her? There's no address or telephone number on the note."

"She sent it here, and very possibly she even remembers that I am able to give you both."

"You're being sarcastic. You don't like Diana, do you?"

"Oh yes, I like and admire Diana. It's just that I am always mildly amused by the workings of the female mind."

"Is that why you've never married?"

"Not really. I genuinely like women in spite of my amusement and at this period of my life, going on forty, I'm quite in the mood to choose a female companion."

"Any special qualifications?"

"Only that she have elegant taste in providing my meals and not be given to jealous tantrums when I want to paint other ladies in the nude."

After Sky finished dressing he walked through the London streets, marveling at the destruction. Entire blocks had been wiped out, and it was evident that many who lived in them had been destroyed along with the buildings. The people he passed, though, looked cheerful, it was only the store windows that seemed dreary.

When he returned he found that Philippe had gone out, but had left Diana Darby's telephone number in plain sight on the top of his bureau. He decided it would be a good time for him to call and thank her for the book.

When her voice came on the wire she said, "Oh it's you, Schuyler. I have thought of you several times since Elsie's dinner in Paris and I sent you a little book, which I hoped would be at Philippe Lord's apartment when you arrived."

"It was wonderful of you. I don't think I've ever met such a thoughtful person, and I look forward to reading the book to-night."

"Though it has never happened to me, I can't imagine anything more bleak than arriving in a large city like London in search of a career, especially since it is hardly a boom city these days. I truly sympathize with you."

"Thank you. You seem to have a way of making me feel better about everything."

"I haven't begun to tell you yet all the nice news I have for you. The other night I was at the same dinner party here with Noel Coward. He's England's leading theatrical personality, you know."

"I know very well. I've been a fan of his forever."

"He's coming here for dinner next Tuesday night and I thought, if you were free, it might be an easy way for you to meet."

"It would be perfect, of course. I'd be delighted to come."

"Good. If it's convenient, why don't you arrive ten minutes or so early, and I can brief you on who the other guests will be."

It was fifteen minutes before the appointed hour when Sky reached Diana's flat, a word he had quickly discovered was the English equivalent of apartment. Not to be too early, he decided to walk around Eaton Square, which he thought must surely be the most elegant neighborhood in London. The leaves on the big trees in the center of the square were fresh and green and behind some of the wrought-iron fences that protected the buildings, the azaleas and spring bushes were in full bloom.

Diana's flat was just as he expected it to be. From a marble foyer, he was led into a library. It was furnished with big, soft sofas and chairs, covered with a white fabric that was printed in big, full-blown pink roses. Even though the long windows that faced the square were completely closed, the room seemed to be filled with the fresh scent of flowers.

When she came in she was wearing pale pink and carrying a

tiny gold-covered notebook and pencil. She tore a leaf out of the book and handed it to Sky. "Here is a list of our guests for dinner. I hope one of them will prove useful."

"That's nice of you, but whether or not, I know I'm going to enjoy it, Lady Darby."

"Perhaps it's time for us to be Diana and Sky, as I heard your friend Philippe call you. I didn't invite him this time because it's very small. I thought I would have other Americans for most of the ten. Noel is very fond of America. You'll see that Douglas Fairbanks, Jr., and his wife, Mary Lee, are coming, and the d'Erlangers. Edwina d'Erlanger's husband is a wealthy English banker, but she was born in Texas and grew up in your country; and then there's Janet and Edward R. Murrow, who are back in England on a visit."

"It's a very distinguished group."

"Keep the notes I've made for you on the English people, too. If you by any chance find something to do here, to know their background is a great help."

She thinks of everything, doesn't she, he said to himself during dinner. The table was beautiful, with low bowls of pink roses and many small candles, instead of the tall flowers and tapers he had seen hampering conversation at many parties he had attended. The food was delicious and everyone seemed to be happily seated.

Noel Coward was sitting on Diana's right and was keeping everyone near him amused. He wasn't handsome in the Barrymore sense, but his clipped voice, his gestures, the way he held his cigarette and the way he smiled gave an impression of an uniquely attractive man.

Before dinner he had chatted with Sky briefly about Hollywood. "I find it terribly tedious making movies," Coward had said. "You play a scene for the first time and the entire staff and crew go into convulsions. So then you do it another time for the sound, and then do it again because the lighting hasn't been quite right, or something's gone wrong, and by the time you get to the actual take, they're all going about yawning and looking away. That's why I prefer the stage."

Sky had seen many photographs of Edward R. Murrow and he recognized the heavy, dark eyebrows, the large eyes and the well-sculptured head as soon as he saw him, to say nothing of the mellow voice, which had become familiar to him over his radio in Cairo.

At the table he was seated between Janet Murrow and Mary Lee Fairbanks. Directly across from him was Edward R. Murrow, who had given him a friendly handshake and a quick over-all survey, but otherwise had paid no attention to him.

Mrs. Murrow was asking him about his experience in North Africa and he told her the story of the Egyptian Queen and she burst out laughing. "That's the most unique war story I've heard yet. My husband would adore it. He has a wonderful sense of humor and he would especially have liked your comment that Hollywood could have used the scene. You must tell him later."

"My years in Egypt weren't by any means all princesses and peacock feathers, Mrs. Murrow. There were many months of living in mud and sand with a minimum of food, but now that it's all over I tend to forget all that."

"Were you still in North Africa at the time of Rommel's final defeat?"

"Yes, I was just behind the firing line. I'll never forget the day. I was standing at the side of the highway with a fellow officer, both of us covered with mud, eating a bar of candy, when a car drove up. We quickly recognized General Eisenhower in the back seat, so we dropped the candy in the sand and went to the side of the car."

"That must have been a thrill."

"He was in a good mood when he got out, so he ordered a tent set up and invited us in for a feast. It's ironic in a war how different the same day can be for different men."

As they finished dinner and stood up, Mrs. Murrow said, "I see your name is Schuyler Madison. I can't tell you how much I've enjoyed talking to such a bright young American."

For coffee, which was served in tiny pink-and-white porcelain cups, they went into the drawing room. Though he had only become conscious of fine French furniture at Lady Mendl's home, he was sure all the pieces around him were pedigreed. He was studying a table desk when Diana came over to him.

"I see you like my most precious possession."

"I don't really know about French furniture, but this strikes me as good-looking."

"It should be. It was designed for Louis XVI and signed by the maker."

"I have a lot to learn."

"I can tell you all about furniture, at least." She put her hand over his, which was resting on the desk, and smiled at him as if they were sharing a special secret. "I think Noel quite approved of you."

She was probably just trying to be nice to me, it's her nature, he thought as he left Eaton Square. But at least it was a wonderful evening.

Sky decided to keep his suitcases still packed and ready to travel, but to stay on at least another week with Philippe in London. Together they made the rounds of some of the private art galleries, where the dealers were desperate and the bargains, he could see, were phenomenal.

Sky told Philippe about the Picasso painting that had put him through college, and the sketch he had left with Nora Hayes. "For God's sake, hang onto it, dear boy. The art boom in the next few years is going to be incredible and, if you can possibly afford it, pick up a few things here. They will be better than money in the bank."

Though his funds were running a bit low, he decided to invest in a small Dufy that appealed to him. Philippe was collecting Leger.

"I'm fascinated by his mechanical mind, probably because mine is so much the opposite," he said.

One morning a few days later, as they were having breakfast, Diana called him. "Darling, guess what has happened? Noel hasn't called for your telephone number as I thought he would, but Edward Murrow has. You must have charmed Janet at dinner, because he seems really interested. Do let me know what happens."

A few minutes later there was a call from Mr. Murrow, and an appointment was made for the next day for him to meet Howard K. Smith at the CBS London Bureau. Sky had never thought of radio as a career but when he stopped to think of it many successful careers had started that way. He liked the look of London, its Old World elegance, its politeness and the friendliness of the shopkeepers, and he was eager to stay on if he could find a job that would seem to be leading him somewhere.

Howard K. Smith's office was painted a drab gray and the desk behind which he was sitting was littered with papers. Murrow, seated close by, seemed to sense what was going on in Sky's mind and came straight to the point.

"Mr. Madison, this is Howard K. Smith, director of the London bureau of CBS. If I feel close to this bureau it's because I started it in 1937 and it was from here that I broadcast the Munich crisis, and the fall of Czechoslovakia and of course the London Blitz."

"Those must have been exciting times."

"They were, but I left to cover the war in the Pacific. I'm back for the first time since then on a purely social visit, and Mr. Smith is sitting in my chair."

Smith spoke up. "One of the young fellows on our news staff has been called back to the States. In fact, he has already gone, and we need someone as soon as possible. Mr. Murrow thought you might qualify."

"We had no time to talk to each other at Lady Darby's dinner the other night, Madison," Edward Murrow said. "But my wife thought you might fit into this job. She's a very perceptive woman."

"I'm very much interested. I'm at loose ends after leaving the service."

"Have you had any experience in radio?" Smith asked.

"Not in any behind-the-scenes way. When I was in Hollywood before the war I appeared on 'The Lux Radio Hour' with Nora Hayes. There was no problem. I'm not nervous."

Howard K. Smith continued, "Your work at first would not require any on-mike activity. You would be collecting news, putting it into organized, written form, to present to me."

Sky nodded. "I understand."

"I might discuss it with you if it were important, but more often I would make notes from it if I decided to use it. My staff and I have daily conferences."

"I'm sure I would like that."

"Mind you, I'm not looking for beautiful prose. I simply want the facts, presented accurately and with some organization."

"I believe I could do that. I've written several articles that were published and I co-authored a movie script."

"I don't mean that you would have no chance to broadcast. You seem to have a rather unusual voice. Have you done much about cultivating it?"

"It's not too different from the voice I was born with, but I've trained as much as possible. I was a stage-struck kid and wanted to be an actor."

"A successful broadcaster needs the same assets as an actor," commented Edward Murrow. "He has to feel for both the news and the people who are listening to it."

"I agree." And turning to Sky, "What I find interesting in your voice is its warm, sympathetic quality."

"I'm sure I would enjoy broadcasting."

"We will give you an audition," Howard K. Smith said, "and later, if things work out as well as I think they may, you will get a chance at the real thing."

"I'd like very much to work for you, Mr. Smith, and I think I understand what you want." He hesitated. "What will the salary be?"

"Not enough for you to become one of the high fliers in Lady Darby's set." He laughed, "But I'm sure that any unattached young man in the kind of job you're about to take will be inundated with invitations to dinners. We will pay you $150 a week in American dollars."

"That will be fine."

"I suppose you realize that it would be almost impossible for you to get a working permit here. The saving grace is that you will be employed by an American firm."

"I'm sure I can make out nicely."

"You'll find many friends, and very quickly, as soon as you start. Friends are a necessity for anyone in broadcasting, because they provide both information and admiration."

"I think I've already realized that."

Edward Murrow said, "I wonder if you've also realized that we are in on the birth of a new medium that will become the most powerful in the world. Television will reduce radio to a less important spot, and I predict it will outdistance the newspapers."

"Undoubtedly," Smith said.

Then turning to Sky, Murrow continued. "Madison, with your acting experience and a face that should be photogenic, you ought to be able to make the change and not fade into obscurity, as so many actors in silent movies did when sound was introduced."

"I hope I can justify both your and Mr. Smith's hopes for me. All I can say is that I'm eager to start. When will that be?"

"We'll clean up a desk for you tomorrow and you can come in the day after. I need help," Smith said as he left the room.

Sky suddenly realized that he had found a job and that the interview was over. He stood up to shake hands with Edward Murrow.

"When you came in I saw you looking around this room with some surprise," Murrow said. "Drab, isn't it, but I'm rather attached to it. I did all my broadcasts from here during the first years of the war. Our location had to be top secret for fear of bombing, and sometimes now I still forget that I can give this address quite freely."

Sky left the office happier than he had been since the day he opened the two telegrams and found out that Hollywood beckoned. He felt he must tell somebody, but when he reached the apartment he found that Philippe had closed the door to his studio and hung a "Don't Disturb" sign on it. Though he thought it was probably meant for the char, he hated to take a chance. Back in his own room he telephoned to Diana.

"Darling, how did it go?" she cried.

"I'm going to work for CBS, Diana. I start day after tomorrow."

"How wonderful. Tell me everything. I want to hear every word that you said and he said."

"It's all your doing, Diana. I think that Mr. Murrow has overencouraged me, but I'm longing to talk to you." He paused. "I'm sure that you're busy tonight, but I wish I could take you somewhere for dinner. Is there any chance?"

"My precious darling. Your happiness means a great deal to me. I have a dull date to go to the theater. I'm going to break it and we'll have dinner together at Les Ambassadeurs."

"You're wonderful. Shall I pick you up at about half-past eight?"

"Nine, please, dear. They know me very well at the club, so I'll call and ask them to give us a table in the corner, where we can talk."

I don't care if this evening costs me everything I have left in my bank account, thought Sky after they had been greeted by John Mills in the bar and Sky was following her to the corner table that was being held for them. She was wearing a pale beige dress that made her hair look redder and her skin even more delicate. Her rope of pearls looked luminous against her neck and along the deep-cut front of her dress.

He ordered a bottle of Dom Perignon and when the waiter filled their glasses, she said: "This time it's I who want to make the toast. To you, Sky, and to your new career."

He was beaming. "Since I owe it all to you, I hope to make you proud of me someday." He could hardly take his eyes off her bare shoulders and breasts, which were hidden only by a black lace ruffle.

"I am now, my sweet, but tell me absolutely everything he said."

While he talked her violet eyes never left his. Though she kept smiling, she seemed so moved that at one point he thought she was about to cry.

"What a wonderful human being you are, Diana. I suppose you've made someone unhappy tonight, but you've made me very happy by breaking your date."

"You've had some bad breaks and I thought someone should be with you to share this good one."

She continued to give him her undivided attention. When they danced he felt her responding even more completely than on the night they met. It was as if they were on a secluded island with no one but each other, instead of being part of the crowd in London's most popular night club.

As they were finishing dinner, she said, "Let's go back to my flat for coffee and some liqueur, if you feel like it. It will be very cozy and we can go on talking. I'm going away tomorrow and may not see you for a while. I don't know how long it will be."

He felt deflated. "Oh where are you going, or should I ask?"

"Of course you should, darling. I'd be hurt if you didn't care. I'm flying to Greece." She patted his hand. "A very old friend of mine has a yacht moored in Athens and we're going to cruise among the islands."

"I'll miss you very much, Diana."

"Of course you will, or at least I hope so. I'll be coming back soon, and then we'll have the glorious fun of being together again, just like tonight, and telling each other everything."

When they reached her flat, she said, "Come with me and choose what you want to drink." He followed her to a little cabinet in the pantry, off the dining room, and opened one of the cabinet doors. She looked at a row of bottles that were all sizes and shapes and filled with green, amber or red liqueurs. But instead of choosing one she turned around and smiled at him. "Do you really want a drink, my darling?" She put her arms around his neck and held up her face to be kissed. As he bent down to reach her mouth he could see that her eyes were closing and the long dark lashes were as appealing as her eyes themselves. He kissed them, too.

He could feel her quivering. "Diana, I want to hold you even tighter, but I'm afraid of crushing your pearls."

"Then let's take them off."

She took his hand and led him down a corridor to a large bedroom. It was all pale blue and white and exquisitely fragrant like the rest of the apartment. The big bed that seemed to have cloud banks of soft, white pillows, had already been turned down and he could see that the sheets were pale-blue silk.

She dropped the pearls into a big silver jewel box that had her monogram, along with a crest, on the lid. It was full of strands of colored beads that he supposed must be rubies and emeralds.

"What a collection of jewelry you have, Diana."

"Come here and let me show you. These are my favorites." She pulled out a three-strand of what looked to him like green glass, though he was sure the clasp was made of diamonds. "These are emerald beads, far more rare than the big stones you see in rings. They were bought for me from a rajah's collection."

"They are beautiful."

"Would you like me to put them on?"

He took the necklace from her hands and dropped it into the box again. "No. I want to see you without anything, not even a single bead."

She laughed. "I prefer that, too, my darling." She twisted her shoulders, and the dress dropped to the floor. To his astonishment she was wearing a miniature corset, which pushed her breasts so that they rested on the lace ruffles at the top.

"It's charming. You look like a romantic Victorian."

"Then pretend that you're a Victorian husband and unhook me so that I can breathe."

He unhooked the corset and held her beautiful body in his arms. "You were built to be loved, weren't you? When I first saw you I knew you were lovely, but you're a thousand times more so like this."

"Take down my hair, darling."

It had been piled up at the back of her head and he had to fumble for the pins that held it, but it soon fell in soft waves down her back and around her face.

She was shivering in his arms. "Are you cold?" he asked.

"No, no. It's only that I want you so much." She was fumbling, helping him to undress, and when he sat down on the edge of the bed she kneeled in front of him to take off his socks and shoes. "I've wanted you like this from the first minute I saw you, Sky," she said, looking up at him.

He was wearing GI issue underwear, left over from the war, and his erection popped through the fly.

"Heaven, Sky, you are tremendous and beautiful. I see there's no need for my old Chinese trick."

"What on earth do you mean?"

"Something I learned on a visit to China years ago. It's a way of stimulating my partner but I see that you need none of that," she said as she leaned forward and kissed him.

Hours later she turned sleepily on the blue silk sheets and whispered, "We'll do this lots of times, my darling. It will be our own private world."

He left the apartment early the next morning while she was still asleep. Whatever the butler thought, he displayed no emotion, and no surprise when he let him out the front door.

He went to bed and when he woke it was time for lunch. Philippe was working in his studio and the door was open. "You had a momentous day, and I gather a momentous evening yesterday," Philippe said as he greeted him.

"Yes, a memorable one, but tomorrow I turn into a serious type and, much as I've enjoyed staying with you, pal, I start looking for my own flat this afternoon."

It was three months later that Sky made his first broadcast on the CBS program. It happened by chance.

Howard K. Smith had decided to take a week's rest in the country and, though he kept in touch by telephone, had left the preparation of the newscast in charge of his first assistant, who would act as anchorman. Several were to participate, but since he was the most recent addition, Sky was not included.

The first assistant had just reported to Edward Murrow that the news was dull, when Sky dashed into the office. He had picked up from a newspaper column that Vivien Leigh was due to arrive in London from America by plane. Hoping for an interview, he went to the airport and when he found that the plane was nine hours late, with no reason divulged by Pan Am, he decided to wait for it to arrive.

As it turned out, her plane was more than ten hours late, but when Vivien Leigh finally stepped off the plane she looked as immaculate as always, in white gloves and a hair-do that looked fresh from a salon, but she had a frightening story to tell. She and Laurence Olivier had hardly left La Guardia when she looked out of the plane window and realized that one of the wings had caught fire. After her first scream there was turmoil on the plane. It turned back and made a crash landing in Connecticut. Miraculously, no one was injured; the passengers were driven to Hartford and later that evening were put aboard a relief Constellation Clipper for England.

Miss Leigh was still in shock and eager to talk, especially to a young man who said he had met her at Nora Hayes' home in Hollywood five years before.

Howard K. Smith's assistant telephoned Smith in the country. "It's the best story I've got. Shall we put him on with it?"

"He's got to start sometime. Tell him to organize the material for a two-minute talk, and plan to let him run over or be ready to fill in if he can't gauge the time right."

Sky was not nervous. He had been thrilled to see Vivien Leigh and meet Laurence Olivier. He delivered the account simply but with some excitement.

He knows how to pick the kind of details that the listeners lap up, thought Edward Murrow, as he listened from the country home of a friend.

"What did I tell you, dear," said Janet Murrow.

CHAPTER FIFTEEN

"I hate waiting. It drives me crazy." Indiana's fingers tapped nervously on the desk of the white-capped nurse. "Dr. Ward knows I'm a busy woman, and when I called him this morning he promised he would see me right away."

"I'm so sorry, Mrs. Hale. The doctor changed his whole schedule so he could be free to see you, but there was an emergency upstairs. A young lady in one of the apartments fell and injured herself on the stairs, and he had to help. Would you like to have a cup of tea while you wait?"

"Yes, that would be nice, but please try to reach him and tell him that I'm here."

The nurse left her desk and went into a little pantry. She turned on the burner under the tea kettle, plopped a tea bag into a cup and waited for the water to boil. She hadn't the slightest intention of disturbing the doctor. Just because she's rich, she thinks she's different. Let her wait like the rest of them, she thought.

A few minutes later she took the tea in to Indiana and set it down beside her with her sweetest smile. "Do you take cream or sugar, Mrs. Hale?"

"No, thank you. What did the doctor say?"

"He will be with you any minute now."

Indiana flipped through a pile of magazines, but they were all old, and she could see that many of the pages had been torn out. She looked at her watch. It was almost six o'clock. She reached over and turned the dial of the little radio on the nurse's desk. At least I'd better get the news while I wait, she thought.

Suddenly a familiar voice seemed to fill the room. "This is

Schuyler Madison in London. When Vivien Leigh and her husband, Laurence Olivier, arrived at the airport this afternoon she was wearing white gloves and not a hair out of place, but only she could have survived a harrowing experience with such style. . . ." Indiana stopped listening to the words and only wanted his voice to go on and on.

In a minute it was all over. She was trembling and she could feel tears rolling down her cheeks. She stood up, but the room seemed to be revolving in front of her. "Nurse, I think I'm going to faint."

The nurse took a bottle of smelling salts, came to her side and held it under her nose. "Don't be alarmed, Mrs. Hale. This is not unusual for a woman in your condition."

"How do you know what my condition is? That's what I'm here to find out."

At this moment the doctor came in the door.

Indiana stood up. "I'm all right. It was only momentary." She was still trembling, though, as she followed the doctor into his office and sat down across the desk from him.

"I think I'm pregnant."

"That seems quite natural, doesn't it, since you're young and healthy and recently married, but what makes you think so?"

"I've missed a couple of periods, but I've been busy at the paper and really didn't think anything of it until my breasts began to feel swollen and hard and the blue veins began to look prominent."

"I think there's no doubt that you're pregnant and I see no point in bothering you with a rabbit test. If you'll just slip off your dress, I can give you a quick examination."

The nurse helped her into a robe and as the doctor began to probe gently, he said, "I can still remember the day your mother came to me. I was just starting my practice and I was very proud to have Mrs. Bradshaw Green as a patient."

"What was she like, Dr. Ward?"

"She was a real beauty but very fragile, and you were a big baby. She had a hard time, but you are built quite differently and it should be easy for you."

"So I really am pregnant."

"Very much so. I should say well into your third month. You can expect your baby possibly as a Valentine gift next February."

"I suppose it always comes as a shock," said Indiana, after she had put on her clothes again and returned to the doctor's office. "Is there anything special I should do?"

"Just live naturally and come back to me next month. I've taken care of you over the years, Indiana, and I can promise you that, barring accidents, you have nothing to dread."

It was a warm evening and Indiana walked the few blocks to her apartment. Suddenly she felt like a different person. She was no longer herself alone, but carrying another person inside her body, who would always be part of her but an individual, too.

When she reached the apartment she went directly to her room and told the maid to bring her dinner on a tray. She was glad that Gage was working at the paper and probably wouldn't be home until midnight. She felt that she needed time to accustom herself to the new situation, but she would stay awake to tell him the news.

She put on a light robe, stretched out on her chaise and closed her eyes. She could still hear Sky's voice. It was as if an old scar had broken open and was bleeding all over again. If only I had got pregnant while I was sleeping with Sky, then Daddy would never have managed to separate us. It isn't that I don't love Gage. I do. I do love him and often think he's much too good for me. He will make a wonderful father.

Over her dinner, she decided that tomorrow she would go into her father's office. He's desperate for a grandson and I'm sure I'm going to have a boy. But I'll never let him maneuver my son the way he has maneuvered me and almost everyone else whose life has touched his intimately.

The day after she returned from her wedding trip, Indiana had gone to Bradshaw Green's office, where she found him enjoying a preluncheon drink from his own private bar.

"Darling, it's good to have you back again."

She sat down. "Daddy, let's get around to facts. I want to know from you whether you actually managed to keep Schuyler Madison from getting anything to do in Hollywood. I know that you kept all the letters and communications from Europe from reaching me, but I want to hear you admit it."

"Why do you come to me in such a mood, Indiana? You are a happily married woman, only because I knew what was best for you and saw to it that you didn't make a mistake."

"I guess you've got a God complex, Daddy, but don't try to play God with me anymore. I've had it."

"Indiana! I'm astonished."

"I can see that. Your face is turning red, but if you are planning to give me the same treatment everybody says you gave my mother, forget it. I'm a strong girl and I can make plenty of noise."

"I don't believe this. That you can be so tough."

"Only when necessary. I came in here today to tell you what's on my mind." She stood up. "On my twenty-first birthday you gave me a big block of stock in the *Globe*."

"Yes, and for your wedding present I gave you another big block. So what's it all about?"

"I know it was possibly for tax purposes, but altogether it amounts to 50 per cent and I intend to take advantage of it."

"What the hell do you mean?"

"Someday this paper will be mine, but in the meantime I intend to have something to say about it, especially before the *Globe* gets any farther behind the other New York papers."

"Am I expected to fire my staff?"

"Not at all. You're the publisher and editor in chief and I will be your associate. I want to be in on all the important conferences, including those with the business side of the paper. I've enjoyed working with the women's features, but I want to increase its space and scope. I plan to have the best-looking women's section in the country and instead of that syndicated supplement we run every Sunday we should have a small magazine of our own."

"Anything more?"

"Yes, I plan to hire a gossip columnist as good as the *Journal-American's* new Igor Cassini, if possible. The *Globe's* over-all makeup must be improved. It's becoming steadily duller and less interesting."

"I should think it would be more natural for you to demand this kind of power for your husband."

"Not at all. I want it for myself, and Gage agrees with me

completely. He'll continue in his editorial capacity, of course, and for quite a while I will confine myself to what might be called the paper's window dressing. God knows it needs it."

"I'm not going to take this from you, goddamn it." Bradshaw Green got up, seized the small bronze bust of Teddy Roosevelt from the top of his desk and threw it with all his might at Indiana.

She quickly stepped aside and it went crashing through the window. "You almost got me, Daddy, but maybe your aim is not as good as it used to be. I hope you didn't get someone down on the street. If you did there goes the *Globe* and all your millions."

Iris Peacock came rushing in. "What is it? I thought I heard a crash." She turned instantly pale as she saw the broken window.

"Daddy lost his temper again and threw Teddy Roosevelt at me."

"Oh Mr. Green, you must think of your blood pressure." Iris Peacock's voice was a bit stronger than usual.

"Blood pressure, hell. You had better send someone downstairs fast to see if anyone got hurt on Forty-first Street." Indiana's eyes were blazing. "I'll take care of him."

Maintaining her usual sphinxlike calm, Iris Peacock said, "I'll go myself, and also find someone to repair the window." She went out and closed the door.

They sat in silence until Iris Peacock returned ten minutes later with Teddy Roosevelt in her hand. She reported it had slightly damaged the roof of a taxi and that she had told the driver to have it repaired and to send the bill to her attention at the paper.

Indiana finally broke the tension. "It's lunchtime, Daddy. Why don't you go down to Bleeck's and try to get hold of yourself?"

"Perhaps I will." His voice sounded almost feeble.

"I'll be talking to some of the editors myself this afternoon."

"I'll have to first mention it to Tiger."

"You're damn right you will, and he's not going to like it. He's always stood for old-fashioned hard news instead of juicy by-line columns."

"Tiger's a good newspaper man."

"He may have been forty years ago. Just be sure that he understands that I'm assisting you in directing the overall policy of this paper from now on."

He glared at her but she continued, "If you don't, I have already consulted a lawyer on my rights, and the stink will rock New York."

"I can't believe that this is my little daughter talking to me this way."

"No matter what I think of you, I can't deny that I'm your daughter and that you've passed on some of your incredible drive to me."

A few days later Indiana had arrived at the *Globe* with an interior designer, whom she had selected to renovate an unused top floor of the building for her future quarters. It was to contain her own offices, a test kitchen for recipes, a small auditorium with a stage for fashion shows and speakers, and a miniature of the regular city room in which only women reporters would be working.

Indiana glanced at the little clock on the table beside her. It was at least an hour before she could expect Gage. She got up and found the leather shopping bag that she inevitably brought back full of homework. Reaching into it, she pulled out a slim, little book that had been sent to her at the office. It was called *River Boy* and on the flap she saw that it was the first work of a young southern boy, Lincoln LaPorte, who was in his early twenties. It was the story of a small boy, his family, his animals and his life outdoors. It was not the kind of thing that usually appealed to her but it was written with such simplicity and charm that she could hardly bear to put it down. Is it because I'm about to have a little boy of my own, she wondered. Anyway I must get him to write about children for the paper.

She heard Gage's footsteps coming along the hall and she called to him.

"Oh, Indiana. You waited up for me. How nice."

"Come over here and sit beside me. I'll move over." He was a fine-looking man, with a face that was gentle and studious and so frank and open that nobody could possibly dislike him, she thought as he crossed the room and sat down beside her. "Remember when somebody used to say to you, close your eyes, open your hand and I'll put something in it? I want you to do it now."

She put her hand in his and clasped it. "Darling, we're going to have a baby."

His eyes flew open and his glasses fell off as he leaned over to kiss her. "It's wonderful, but are you all right?"

"Of course I am. Girls don't fade away in childbirth the way they used to in the days of Charles Dickens."

The next minute Gage had put in a call to Fort Wayne. Though he woke Addie Hale from a sound sleep she was ecstatic at the news.

In the past few weeks Indiana and her father had only spoken warily to each other as they passed in the corridors or met in the elevator, but the next morning she breezed into his office to tell him the news. "He was elated at the idea of a grandson," she reported to Gage later.

"You mustn't set your heart on having a boy, Indiana."

"I'll send her back if she's a girl," but she was sure it wouldn't happen. She was confident that with her own determination she could create a boy.

Later in the afternoon she remembered the book Lincoln LaPorte had written and asked her secretary to call his publisher for his telephone number. It took two hours to trace him at the small West Side hotel where he was staying.

"I asked for Mr. LaPorte. Please call him to the phone," she said when a girl's high-pitched, childish voice came over the wire.

"This is Mr. LaPorte, or at least I've always believed."

"I've been reading your book and I like it very much. I'm Indiana Green of the *Globe* and I would like you to write something for me."

"What kind of thing?" asked the childish, high-pitched voice.

"I'd like to meet you and discuss the matter. Could you lunch with me at Bleeck's tomorrow?"

"Bleeck's? I never heard of it. I don't know where it is and I hate hunting. Can you make it the Colony? I eat all my meals there except when I go to the corner drugstore or Schrafft's."

"Then the Colony tomorrow at one o'clock."

"Can't you make it one-thirty? I like writing late at night and I just never get up that early."

When she arrived the next day punctually at one-thirty, he

wasn't sitting in the small foyer or the tufted banquettes in the restaurant, but Gene Cavalero, the owner and *maître d'*, assured her that he would straggle in soon.

When he came, he looked to her like a precocious child, with pale yellow hair falling over his forehead and pale blue eyes that were magnified by glasses. He hardly came up to her shoulders and when he spoke, the southern drawl was more pronounced than it had been over the telephone.

After they ordered luncheon, she said, "Your book was so beautiful that I thought you might be interested in writing an article of the same kind for our new Sunday supplement."

"You mean the kiddie stuff? I don't know about that. I have fantastically romantic memories of my childhood, but somehow I got them all out of my system in that book." He turned to face her. "You're about to have a kid of your own, I read in the paper today."

"How could it possibly be in the paper? I just found out myself."

"I don't usually give away my sources, but this time I'm willing to make an exception." He grinned, "I go to Schrafft's a lot for breakfast. I eat at the counter and I'm naturally friendly, and I always get to talking to the people on the stools next to me. I really look forward to my morning chitchat. If you're curious enough you can get some kind of tidbit out of almost everybody."

"But who told you about me?"

"She's quite nice. I don't know her name but she's an office nurse for some society gynecologist on Park Avenue. Yesterday she spilled the whole bio on you. I thought it was interesting, so I passed it on to Ghi Ghi Cassini, who's a friend of mine. A few hours later you called me. It was quite a coincidence."

"What else did she tell you?"

"Oh just the usual, all about your country place with the wild deer, and the debut among the orchids, all of which I already knew. When I was a senior in high school I even went so far as to tear off the magazine cover that showed you dancing with your handsome boyfriend. I kept it for quite a while. I thought it was cute."

He peered around. "Do you recognize the woman in the red

turban, who's sitting on the banquette at the far end of the room?"

"No, I don't know her."

"I'm surprised. It's Lily Audley. You'll soon be reading about her divorce."

"So tell me ahead of time."

"That's the power of gossip. Everyone always wants to know everything. Well, to satisfy your curiosity, the socially registered Mrs. Audley is getting a divorce because of a romance with Sebastian, her butler."

"How horrid. You mean to say she is having an affair with her own butler?"

"Not at all, dear, but her husband is."

"That's even worse."

"Oh I don't know. It's a new twist in affairs, at least, and I rather like it."

Their luncheon came, but Lincoln LaPorte continued to produce thumbnail sketches of the women in the room. "The thin, very black-and-white one in the corner is Mrs. Byron Foy of the Chrysler millions. She is probably luncheoning on a lettuce leaf to keep thin enough to wear all the Paris clothes she has just bought. . . . Over there to my far right is Gloria Vanderbilt. She's too young and beautiful to settle for living in Stamford with a man old enough to be her grandfather. Just wait and see."

"I don't seem to know anybody today but you know them all."

"See the woman who is just going out and is peering madly at us because she doesn't recognize you, and Gene gave you the best table in the room. I'm sure she's longing to know who you are. She has been nicknamed Death Dreary, though I believe the name is really Leary. She is what I call an instant personality who was created by the imagination of Maury Paul, the late columnist, in return for a favor that she did for him. Now she lunches here every day at the same table just inside the dining-room door. Silly people who believe everything they read stop to pay court to her on their way in and out and she carries on like a *grande dame.*"

"Do you really think that a columnist can create a person?"

"What do you think Winchell has done with Sherman Billingsley? May I call you Indiana? It's a direct, refreshing name and it quite goes with you."

She smiled. "Please do."

"Well, Indiana, to get back to the question you asked me, I believe the power of the personal column is just in the baby stage. The postwar boom is just beginning. Everybody is going to be filthy rich and nothing is going to titillate them like gossip, the worse the better. They are going to be like the wealthy old Romans, sitting in the arena and shaking with pleasurable excitement and even laughter as the lions devour the Christians."

"I enjoy reading Cassini, but I hadn't stopped to think why."

"I adore gossip, and I don't mind admitting it. It's no worse a vice than drinking or taking dope. I even pride myself on being something of an expert and I subscribe to the London papers like the *Daily Mail* and the *Express*."

"You do?"

"Yes, they dish it out superbly and the English take it lightly as if it were a dash of Tabasco added to the very bland white meals that they eat."

"Lincoln, I asked you to luncheon because I wanted you to write a whimsical little piece from your store of childhood memories, but I've changed my mind. How would you like to write the world's hottest daily gossip column for the *Globe?*"

"You flatter me, dear, but that word 'daily' has an ominous sound. I've never worked on schedule."

"To compete with your friend Cassini, it would have to be daily, I'm afraid."

"Of course, if the salary were princely enough and I had an adequate expense account, I might manage to pull myself together, but that father of yours is said to be a miserly old bastard, among other horrendous rumors."

"You seem to know everything, but apparently you don't know that I am in complete charge of the paper's lightweight features and for hiring the people who create them. I want a column from you and I am sure we can get together on the salary."

"I have some hot news items tucked away in my pocket right now, but I will save them for 'LaPorte Reports.'" He paused. "How do you like that for a title?"

"I like it."

"Good-bye, Igor. We are now competitors to the death."

"Come to my office tomorrow. I'll have a possible contract drawn up and you can bring your lawyer if you like."

"Just one more question, boss-lady-to-be. Can I be as mean as I like?"

"Of course. That's the point, isn't it? Just make sure you're not libelous."

After Lincoln LaPorte had signed his contract, Indiana went the rounds of all the paper's special editors and found them pleased and even excited. The news was sent out to possible advertisers as kind of a postscript to an earlier prospectus outlining her plans. The women's feature section had had several trial runs and was scheduled to make an appearance the middle of September, and now "LaPorte Reports" would be added to it. The new Sunday supplement wouldn't be launched until November but the advance response by local and national advertisers to both new developments had astonished even Bradshaw Green.

"LaPorte Reports" was an instant success. Indiana's telephone rang all morning, and she could hear her secretary saying, "Oh yes, I will certainly tell Mrs. Hale. She will be happy to know that you like it." Rosemary, whom she hadn't seen since her wedding, insisted on being put through to say, "Darling, I simply must meet that man. He is so cruel but in such a pretty way."

Indiana had been delighted with the column. Lincoln's simple, almost childlike style intensified the sting it contained.

She had to dial Lincoln's number several times before the line was free. "Help, help, Indiana. Every press agent in the world is already on my neck with stories about their clients."

"You'll have to get a kind of secretary-assistant to fend them off."

"I already have a great gal from Texas for an assistant but I need to also find an enigmatic Iris Peacock. I love the way she guards your father's office like a Great Dane."

"Even she is enjoying the column. I caught her laughing as she stood by the elevator reading it."

"Indiana, I'm longing to see you, and my generous expense account now permits me to invite you to Le Pavillon for lunch. Would next Wednesday suit?"

When she came in, Henri Soulé came bouncing toward her with a beaming smile on his round face. He led her to the first table on the left, where Lincoln was seated.

"I can't believe it, Indiana. From the nadir of unpopularity, where I always was, I have swung to the peak. Soulé has never even bothered to notice me before and today he assigned me to the No. 1 spot." He looked around, "The ladies have all been introducing themselves to me. The blonde over at the table near the bar, whose name is Vivienne Wooley something or other, and looks like a Viennese waltz even in the daytime, says she is your best friend and that I simply must come to a party she is giving somewhere in Connecticut. I told her I hate the country and am afraid of cows."

"Dear Vivienne, but don't let them rush you off your feet."

"Don't worry, darling, and of course I'm kidding about cows. I actually envy them. They look so contented standing in the pasture and licking a huge hunk of salt."

"What are you writing about tomorrow, Lincoln?"

"To begin with, I have a hot story from London about Lady Diana Darby and her romance with Schuyler Madison, the American who has become the fair-haired boy at CBS over there. Edward Murrow discovered him at one of Diana's inty little dinner parties."

"Who is Lady Diana Darby?"

He saw her face change. "Sorry, darling. I forgot that Schuyler Madison is the ex-boyfriend who does a mean Charleston."

"I haven't seen him for years. He's my husband's cousin, you know."

"Oh that little tidbit I didn't know. But don't let Diana worry you. It will be a brief interlude and he'll be all the better for it. She is kind to her men and pampers them while the romance is going on and there never seems to be any unpleasantness when she moves on."

"How does she manage it?"

"She needs money to keep her in eighteenth-century luxury but the Italian multimillionaire she has been concentrating on is generous but permanently attached. If she can only find an unattached multimillionaire she will make a good wife."

"You're kinder about her than most people."

"Women don't like her at all, and if you ever meet her, I am sure you will hate her on sight."

They spent an hour discussing the new format of the paper, with Lincoln making suggestions now and then. Over their coffee he said suddenly, "Now let's talk about you."

"About me. Why?"

"Where are you lunching tomorrow?" He leaned forward and put his elbows on the table.

"At Bleeck's probably. It's the easiest."

"That's what I hoped you'd say, because Bleeck's has got to go."

"Why must it go? I rather enjoy it."

"All right, occasionally then. But why should you, a young woman with so much potential power and glamour, be lunching at a midtown restaurant mostly full of minor reporters and dress manufacturers?" He looked at her with a critical eye. "And why should you be wearing nice but unexciting clothes instead of living up to the power position you already have?"

"What do you mean?" She looked startled.

"I mean it's just too bad that your very nice husband doesn't require you to keep seducing and charming him every minute, but wake up, girl. A whole new social era is beginning, whether it's in society, art, music, food, people or whatever and you can be a top number in it."

"I'm sure you're right, Lincoln. I've been too absorbed in the paper to look around everywhere else."

"You've got your own way with the old man, so cool it for a while. I'll give you until you've had this kid, but kid or no kid, you're going to Paris next summer to get some drop-dead clothes."

"That would be fun." Her eyes sparkled.

"Afterward, we'll do the Riviera, which is a perpetual spring of the most unmerciful gossip in the world. It wouldn't surprise me a bit if we ran into the old Charleston specialist there, but only time will tell. It will be good for both of us anyway."

When she left Lincoln, Indiana felt happier than she had in months. She was still smiling when she reached home. She saw that Gage was already in the library surrounded with newspapers, and after she had changed into a pair of black crepe evening pajamas, she joined him.

"Mix me a nice, strong daiquiri, will you, Gage?"

"Darling, do you think it's good for you in your condition? I thought you had decided not to take a drink until after the baby."

"Well, I've changed my mind. One cocktail won't hurt me and if you don't want to make it, I'll do it myself."

He got up, made the cocktail and brought it over to her.

"Don't look so disapproving. I had such fun at lunch today with only a tiny glass of wine."

"Where were you lunching? I looked around for you at Bleeck's."

"Lincoln took me to Le Pavillon. It's the restaurant Henri Soulé started when he decided not to go back to France after the World's Fair."

She sipped her drink, "I loved it and we must go there for dinner one night. The French food is wonderful and the walls are painted with the most charming scenes of the Riviera. The best part, though, was Lincoln. He's so entertaining."

"He's a great writer and an asset to the paper, but I'm surprised at your taking such a fancy to him."

"You sound so stuffy, Gage. Lincoln is going to give me all kinds of leads for stories. He knows all about everybody."

"I'm sure of that. All the fellows in the city room like his column."

Indiana took his hand and held it briefly. "You know, darling, if we keep going along this way, we're going to have the greatest newspaper in the country and have something colossal for our son to inherit."

The next morning as Indiana was taking her shower she noticed that her waistline was thickening. As she was drying herself with a towel, she felt for the first time the tiniest hint of a movement inside her body. Fascinating, she thought. It's an experience every woman should have.

On her way to the paper that morning she decided to stop at Maximilian Fur Salon on Fifty-seventh Street. Maximilian, himself, wasn't there but his sister, Madame Potok, who reminded her of a chirpy little robin, came rushing into the salon to greet her.

Indiana bent down and kissed her on the cheek. "Dear Madame Potok, I'm sure that, like everyone else, you know by this time that I'm having a baby. I want something lovely to wrap around me so that nobody will notice that I'm getting big and ungainly."

"What do you have in mind, Miss Indiana, another mink, perhaps? I know better than to suggest Persian lamb." Indiana shrugged as she continued. "I remember the first time your father brought you here for a coat."

"So do I." She laughed recalling the incident.

"He fancied a very curly brown lamb, but you always knew what you wanted. You stamped your foot and said, 'I won't wear lamb. I want pale-gray squirrel.'"

"I got it, too, as I recall. I was a spoiled brat and I still am. To tell you the truth, I think it's time for me to wear sable."

"We have the most beautiful natural Russian sable skins in the world. They're soft as silk and light as a feather. Actually, we are making a coat that is still in the workroom, but it is far enough along for you to try it on to see if you like it."

One of the girls from the workroom came in with the coat, handling it as reverently as if it were a diamond necklace. It was everything that Madame Potok had said. "I want it if you have enough extra skins for me to have a big, soft hat. I suppose the price is atrocious."

"The cost is fifteen thousand dollars, but it's an excellent investment. The price of sable is going up and next year a coat like this will cost twice as much. Besides, it is so simple and classical that you can wear it forever."

"Don't tell me fairy tales, Madame Potok. You know as well as I do that I'll be back here two years from now wanting something else." She took it off. "I'll take the coat."

"The coat you tried on is a special order but we will make you one just like it."

"That doesn't make me very happy. Who will be wearing the other?"

"You don't have to worry. She lives in California. She's an actress. Her name is Dorothy Darrow."

"Don't tell me she's in New York?"

"Oh yes. Her new film opened at the Music Hall last week."

"Of course, we ran an interview with her. I'll bet I know where the bill for her coat is going."

Madame Potok smiled, but didn't answer.

"Well, I'll take the coat anyway. Please see that it is ready before Thanksgiving and let me know when to come in for a fitting." She started to leave, then turned, "Send some extra skins right away, so I can take them to a milliner."

The weather turned cold during the second week of November and a long, freezing winter was predicted. On the first day with snow in the air, Indiana put on the sable coat and hat and went for luncheon at Le Pavillon, where she had become a steady customer and a special pet of Soulé. By this time she had gained ten pounds but her face had remained unchanged and with her new furs she still managed to feel glamourous.

She and Gage spent the Christmas holiday quietly at South Wind. Bradshaw Green spent most of the holiday in California but he was at South Wind for two days, working with Miss Peacock. Obviously he was happy about the progress of the paper and eager for the birth of his first grandchild.

When she returned to the city in January, Indiana continued to work every day in her office and at the composing room, where the type was set. The typographers liked her and she often stopped to chat with one of them or to look at her pages when the type lines were arranged in page-size forms and to suggest changes if she didn't like the look.

"Much as I really don't like her," the nurse from Dr. Ward's gynecologist office confessed to Lincoln over breakfast at Schrafft's, "she doesn't worry about anything, including her looks. The baby hasn't dropped yet, and it may not come before March." It was the same morning she gave him the scoop on Bobo Rockefeller's pregnancy.

It was a mild February and they continued to spend weekends in the country. After a pleasant Saturday of walking, talking and doing crossword puzzles at which Iris Peacock was adept, Bradshaw Green telephoned to say that he had been detained and was not going to join them and that he wanted Gage to come into the office at once. Miss Peacock, who had been waiting for him impatiently, was told she was not needed and to return the next morning with Indiana.

"I'm sure it concerns our editorial on Dewey," Gage said.

"Then I'd better come back with you, Mr. Hale. He may need me," Iris Peacock ventured.

"No, Miss Peacock. He explicitly said for you to stay with Indiana, and return in the morning," Gage replied.

When Indiana opened her eyes the next morning, the snow was falling like a thick white curtain beyond the window. She threw back the covers and as she gingerly got out of bed she had a strange feeling that something was happening in her body. There was no pain, so she took her shower.

Pinkie brought in the breakfast tray and stood watching her as she tried to eat. "Miss Indiana, I think you're having that baby right now."

"I don't think that's possible. I'm not having any pains, but perhaps you'd better call Carlos and tell him to get the car ready and please tell Miss Peacock to be ready too."

Pinkie went out and Indiana could hear her footsteps running down the corridor. Indiana threw her make-up and manicure set into a little bag and pulled on a sweater and skirt and her sable coat and hat. I might as well arrive at the hospital in style, she thought.

The snow was falling so thickly that the car proceeded at a snail's pace along the driveway.

Miss Peacock was sitting rigid in her corner of the car. She looked white and terrified.

"Don't worry, Miss Peacock. I haven't had a twinge yet and they say the first baby takes a long time to come. Anyway, I'm confident that if anybody can deliver a baby in a car, you can."

"Dear God, Miss Indiana. You know I'm a virgin and don't know anything about such things."

"You know about animals, don't you?"

"I once had a cat, but oh God, that was a horror. I hope I don't have to do that with you."

The road was like glass and the car was sliding a little from side to side.

Indiana leaned forward. "Take your time, Carlos. There's no need to be nervous."

When they reached the main road, the driving became easier, but every fifteen minutes, Miss Peacock inquired, "Are you in pain yet, Miss Indiana?"

"No, I'm all right. How are you, dear?"

"I've never known a day like this. I'm terrified to death."

It was two hours before they reached Doctor's Hospital. Carlos and Miss Peacock took Indiana's arms and helped her out of the car. Miss Peacock signed her in for the corner room that had been engaged long ago for her. "I'll stay with you, Miss Indiana. Don't worry."

As she undressed, Indiana felt slightly nauseous, but when the nurse asked if she was in labor, she said, "I don't think so, but I have a kind of nagging little ache in my stomach."

"Many women have false alarms, but we'll watch you closely."

The resident gynecologist came in a short while later and said the same thing, so Indiana decided to lie back and rest. Half an hour later she rang frantically for the nurse.

"What can I do for you, Mrs. Hale?" asked the nurse, coming in with a bright smile.

"Nurse, I tell you I am having this baby right now. I can feel it coming and if you don't get the doctor it's going to pop right here."

"You're just imagining." The nurse pulled back the bed covers and put them back quickly and rushed for the door. Indiana could feel the cart rumbling down the hall. She was lifted onto it. Afterward she remembered the bright lights of the delivery room, but a cone of anesthetic was put over her nose and she faded into unconsciousness.

When she woke and looked fuzzily at her clock she saw that only two hours had passed. Miss Peacock was sitting rigidly by the side of her bed.

"Oh dear, Miss Peacock. I'm so sorry to waste your time this way. It was a false alarm because I'm feeling all right again."

"Miss Indiana, your baby was born an hour ago and it's the most beautiful child I ever saw."

"I can't believe it. Where is Gage?"

"We telephoned to him immediately, but he was held up in traffic and is just looking at the baby now."

"What does he look like, Miss Peacock? Please tell me."

"I'm going to leave that to your husband."

Gage came into the room. He was flushed and smiling and he was followed by the nurse holding a bundle of pink blankets.

"Indiana, we have a fine, healthy daughter."

"A daughter. I don't believe it."

"Wait until you see her."

The nurse laid the bundle in Indiana's arms and turned back a corner of the blanket to show the baby's head. She had a curly fuzz of blond hair. Her eyes were wide open and, though Indiana had heard that babies saw nothing for several days, she seemed to be regarding her mother seriously with wide blue eyes.

"She came so easily that she's not red and angry-looking, like so many babies," said the nurse.

"I'm quite mad for her already, but what shall we call her instead of Gage Green Hale, as I had planned?" Indiana asked.

"Something that begins with *h*, perhaps," suggested Gage. "I've always liked alliteration."

"I can't think of any *h*'s. I don't much like Harriet or Hannah or Hilda."

Miss Peacock ventured, "I once read a novel that had a heroine named Heather and I've never forgotten it. It was so romantic. Besides, I tend to like names that are taken from the plant world."

"Heather Hale. I like it. Let's try it for a while, anyway," Indiana said.

The next day a bushel basket of flowers arrived with a card that read, "I hear you gave birth in a totally unchic, peasantlike way. Congratulations!" It was signed, "Lincoln."

Since there was a shortage of rooms in Doctor's Hospital, and Indiana was vociferous about her hatred of hospital routine, she and Heather were allowed to go home before Lincoln's flowers had faded.

CHAPTER SIXTEEN

It was a warm August afternoon in Cannes, and every table on the terrace of the Carlton Hotel was occupied except one. It was probably being held for Aly Khan and Rita if they weren't still pouting over their blowup at the Palm Beach Casino the night before, thought Lincoln LaPorte, who was sitting at the next table, and if it wasn't being held for Aly, it was sure to be for someone equally interesting.

A gentle breeze from the esplanade was fluttering the scalloped edges of the umbrellas that shaded the tables, and the sound of cocktailtime chatter rose above the noise of a few passing cars. He loved the French Riviera, and each of his summer visits with Indiana for the past four years had been more successful than the one before. Cannes, he decided as he sipped his drink and looked about at the mélange of people, had just about had it. The elegance of previous summers was disappearing, and now in 1951 too many tourists, who were nobodys, had discovered the Carlton terrace. He waved to Rosie Dolly sitting with her husband, Irving Netcher, and a group of Americans. She was deeply tanned and wearing pale green from turban to toes, including her emerald ring.

The new Paris fashions made the women look very pretty and feminine, and he could tell that most of them had been dressed by Dior or one of Dior's imitators. Thank God I persuaded Indiana to try Balenciaga this year, he thought. He understands her type and she's not going to look like everybody else in her new Paris dresses.

Just then he saw that the occupant of the next table was arriving. It was not Aly Khan after all, but Lady Diana Darby, who was being steered by the waiter to the most prominent table on the terrace. He got up and went over to her.

"Why, Lincoln! What a nice surprise." She held out her hand, and her violet eyes looked so warmly into his that, for a moment at least, he felt that he was the one person she had been longing to see.

"What are you doing here?" she asked.

"I'm doing what I always do, contemplating what's going on. If you're alone, Diana, why not come over to my table so we can talk about everybody together."

"I'd love to join you. Sky Madison and I have been here for the past week, but we're leaving in something of a hurry. He has just had an offer from UBC Television in California."

"Television? Is he leaving London for that?"

"He thinks it is a great opportunity."

"Are you going to the States with him?"

"Yes, but not to Hollywood. I've decided to go just as far as New York. Sky is upstairs packing now and we're having a farewell drink together."

"Don't let me interrupt a fond farewell," he said as they moved over to his table.

"It's a temporary farewell to the Riviera and not to each other." She sighed. "He'll fly off in a hurry but it takes a woman more time to tie up all the loose ends before she changes her way of life."

"Darling Diana, I hear that the loose ends have already been tied up in Milan." Lincoln motioned to a waiter and ordered two daiquiris.

"Oh aren't you naughty. You know everything. It's true that Armando Maranini's wife was threatening all kinds of things and that in his important position he simply couldn't afford a scandal, but we'll always be good friends."

"Of course. You have a talent for keeping your men friends."

"I like men, and I think I understand them. Sky is a wonderful friend, but just that. He has his own career to make."

He glanced around the hotel terrace. "Just from looking over this scene in the past half hour, I can't imagine you've made many new friends here."

"It is rather bad, isn't it? Sky and I had luncheon at Eden Roc the other day and it was virtually a snakepit."

"I've already been predicting in my column that the elegant crowd will move on to Cap Martin, Cap Ferrat and Monte Carlo. Indiana and I were at the lovely little port of St. Jean Cap Ferrat a few weeks ago, and I told her she should buy a villa there while the price is right. She's considering a beauty that once belonged to Isadora Duncan."

"She isn't here now?"

"No, she had to fly back because of some crisis on the newspaper."

"Is your Indiana as rich as everyone says?"

"I don't know what they say, but her father, Bradshaw Green, is one of the billionaires in America. I imagine he has already given Indiana plenty, since he gave his granddaughter a cool million in her own name the day she was born."

"Are there lots of other fascinating millionaires in New York, darling?"

"I'll have a list drawn up for you and I'll send it to your hotel the moment you arrive."

"I'll be at the Pierre. It will amuse me to read the list; however, I won't know any of them."

"I'll do better than a list. I'll give a little dinner for you to meet a few of them."

"How sweet of you, dear Lincoln."

"Not at all. You know, you should subscribe to *The Wall Street Journal*. That way you can find out who's making money and who's losing it. You can even find out when some of the wives die."

"Now you're being mean and teasing me." She laughed as she leaned over and patted his hand.

"Not at all. I think every girl should take her career seriously."

Just then he saw a young man come out on the terrace and speak to the *maître d'*, who motioned him toward their table. Feminine heads turned around as he passed, and without an introduction he knew that it was Schuyler Madison.

He stood up as Sky reached the table. "So you're the doll man," Lincoln said.

"He is a doll," cried Diana.

"No, I mean the fantastic collection of dolls he's sent to Heather Hale. Her room is overflowing with them, and she has a name for each."

"I'm glad to hear that. I've never met my cousin's little daughter but I've enjoyed sending her presents from the many countries I've visited and just this morning I managed to find a French peasant that I think she'll like."

"How dear of you, Sky. You're always so thoughtful. This is Lincoln LaPorte, the famous columnist."

"Hello! I've read many of your columns that have been sent to me or brought to me by friends from the States. I like your style. It can be quite brittle but always amusing."

"I'm glad we've finally met and I must say you're more devastating than I've always heard." Lincoln made a quick study of Sky from head to toe.

"Sky, darling, I was just telling Lincoln how disappointed you would be to learn that Indiana has been here and returned to New York only last week."

"Too bad. We're old friends. How is she?" Sky asked.

"She's been a sensation everywhere we went this summer. If you haven't seen her for a long time you may be in for something of a surprise when you do."

"I'm sure." It was a long time since he had thought of Indiana. Now he saw her in her bedroom at South Wind, looking at him with her big, wide-open eyes and waiting eagerly for him to make love.

Lincoln saw his smile fade and said quickly, "So you're going to Hollywood?"

"Yes, for the second time, but not for the same reason. I've been with CBS for the past five years in London. Now United Broadcasting Company has made me a tempting offer."

"I hear TV is at last getting into its stride," Lincoln said.

"I know it's going to be big. Besides, I'd rather work in my own country."

"You certainly have what it takes." Lincoln had been studying Sky's height, his blond hair and the smile that had already been commented on by British reviewers of TV programs.

"Just look at that car. Who do you suppose is inside?" cried Diana, who had lost interest in the conversation and gone back to studying the scene.

A liver-colored Rolls-Royce had just come to a stop at the Carlton's front entrance and a chauffeur in matching livery stepped out to open the door for its occupant.

As they watched a slim figure stepped out delicately and precisely, pausing on the steps as two photographers rushed toward her.

"Good God, Nora. Nora Hayes," cried Sky and Lincoln LaPorte simultaneously.

Sky rushed forward to welcome her as Lincoln expounded, "She's incredible, a bigger star today than in her silent days. She was idle for seventeen or eighteen years and then *The Lion Roars* puts her back on top again. She got an Oscar for it last spring and now I hear is turning down one movie offer after another."

"Oh yes, I've often heard Sky speak of Nora Hayes."

"Diana, dear, I think your friend Sky is something of a collector of live dolls, too." They both watched as Sky returned, leading Nora by the hand. All heads turned again to watch their progress across the terrace to their table.

Diana stood up to greet Nora. "Oh Miss Hayes. How wonderful to meet you. You've been my idol since I was a tiny little girl."

"Thank you, my dear. How beautiful you still are." She paused for a moment and smiled sweetly. "I remember getting a glimpse of you twenty years ago when De Mille was sending me around the world on unlimited expense accounts to make personal appearances. You haven't changed a bit since then. I suppose it's that foggy British weather of yours that keeps your skin so perfect." Nora pressed Diana's hand and sat down, leaving a space between them for Sky.

Lincoln signaled to the waiter again. He was feeling warm and happy as he realized that he was the spectator at what to him was a fascinating confrontation. "What will you have to drink, Miss Hayes? If I may abbreviate, lemonade or Vichy water with a touch of lime?"

"Oh aren't you clever to remember that I'm a health nut. Vichy, please. No wonder I adore your column. I never fail to read it in the Los Angeles *Globe*."

"You're making my life simpler, at least, just by being here. The French Riviera hasn't furnished me with many headline stories this season."

"I don't have any headlines to offer you. I came over in May for the Cannes festival and at one of the parties I met an interesting Austrian painter. He hates publicity, so please don't print this."

"Of course." He could hardly wait to get to his typewriter.

"We've had a wonderful summer together. I've been staying with my old friend Edward Molyneux in Biot, and my Austrian friend has a cottage close by." She threw up her hands, "But the telephones are impossible so I always drive over here to the Carlton to make my calls."

"Yes, the bilingual operators here are the best in France," Lincoln said. "And what did you say your painter friend's name is?"

Nora turned quickly to Sky. "Let me look at you, Sky. I haven't seen you since 1941. My God, that's ten years ago. I must say the years have certainly been good to you."

"And to you, too, Nora. I saw *The Lion Roars* in London, and your performance moved me deeply. I sent you a cable the night of the Academy Awards. Did you get it?"

"Yes, Sky, it's one of the few I treasured. Tell me about yourself. I know you've graduated from radio to TV."

"Yes, Nora. All the television news programs have adopted the old newsreels as a pattern, and as a result I've been with camera crews all over Europe getting material."

Nora and Sky went on talking, oblivious to the others, until Lincoln interrupted, "Do you have plans for another film in the near future, Nora?"

"No, not for the moment. Hollywood is changing rapidly," then turning to Sky, "You're not going to find it the same place, you know."

"Just how has it changed, Miss Hayes?" Lincoln asked.

"In every way. The last two years have been disastrous. In the past the big film companies owned their own theater chains and had to make a tremendous number of pictures to keep them going."

"Yes, I remember, it was at least fifty-two a year," Sky said.

"The government decided it was a monopoly," Nora went on, "and has forced the studios and theaters to be run as separate businesses. As a result the big studios started letting contract players go and firing writers and technicians right and left. It's been a panic. The marvelous world of Hollywood that Sky and I knew before the war has fallen apart and no longer exists."

"I had no idea it was so bad," Diana said.

"Most people don't and that's why I'm so glad that Sky has gone into television. It's all that anybody talks about in Hollywood today." Then turning to Sky, "I won't be home until at least mid-September. You must go straight to my house. I'll wire the butler that you're coming. They were all so fond of you that they'll be delighted. Plan to stay until you find out where you want to live."

"That would be great, Nora. I still have quite a few cartons of possessions in your garage. I'll go through them and get them out of your way."

"Don't hurry, darling. They've never been in my way. It's going to be wonderful to have you back."

Diana patted Sky's hand. "I'm so glad that Miss Hayes will be in Hollywood to mother you a wee bit."

"I'll do my best, my dear, but Sky's and my friendship is quite different. He's often been the stern father with me regarding some problem that had arisen."

When Nora Hayes said she must leave, Sky went with her to the telephone booth.

"Isn't she wonderful? How old do you think she really is?" Diana asked Lincoln as she watched them disappear into the hotel.

"Why didn't you ask her? It would have been a good way to cement the friendship I saw you two ladies building up." Lincoln hoped that Sky wouldn't take too long to say good-bye to Nora. He wanted to get back to his typewriter and get the encounter on paper.

It was Sunday morning when Indiana read the column. She had just come out of the pool at South Wind and sat down on one of the deck chairs to let her hair dry as she went through the papers. The column was written in Lincoln's best style and she laughed at the beginning: "Yesterday afternoon, two of the world's best-known *femmes fatales* were sparring lightly at each other across TV's handsome thirty-one-year-old Schuyler Madison as they sat at a table on the crowded terrace of the Carlton in Cannes."

When she finished the column, she took it over to Gage, who

was also deep in papers. "Here's something to cheer you up. It tells about Sky's new job, too. He's coming back to this country, but I suppose you knew."

"He wrote me that he was coming, but no details." Gage took the paper.

Heather had been squatting at her father's feet playing with one of her dolls but now she got up and trotted over to Indiana. She was a beautiful child, Indiana thought as she looked at the big, gray-blue eyes and the heavy blond hair that she could sit on. "You like that dolly, don't you, darling? It's a little Dutch girl. See the wooden shoes."

"Yes, I do like her, but not very much. I spank her all the time."

"Why on earth do you spank her?"

"Because she won't come alive and play with me, like the doll did in the story you read me."

"But that was just a story."

"Then why can't I have a sister or brother to play with?"

"I hope you will, darling, but not right now."

Indiana watched as Heather went back to Gage. She crawled into his lap and snuggled against him. She had always adored her father. If she had been a boy she probably would have responded to me in the same way, Indiana thought.

"You look a little down today, Gage. What's the problem?" Indiana asked.

Gage smiled as he put down the paper after reading about Sky. "I'm sure he's going to be a big success in TV."

"Yes, I expect he will."

"Of course, he doesn't worry and neither do you, Indiana. You're alike in so many ways and perhaps you should have got together. You both go straight ahead, and all the problems seem to fall away instead of crushing you, as they do some people."

"Why should you be afraid of anything crushing you, Gage? You have a pretty powerful job for a man who is only thirty-five."

"I don't know, darling. I'm an editor of an important paper, but I'm not an editor. Your father masterminds every part of the paper that you don't touch. He's behind every decision, however small, and nowadays he comes in to write all the important headlines."

"It's too bad, but just try to put up with it. Daddy can't go on forever, you know, and then it will be our responsibility."

"I have a feeling he has never trusted me since I made that foolish mistake three years ago."

"He'll get over it."

"I don't think so. I heard just recently from someone on the paper that my 'Dewey Wins' edition of the *Globe* has become a collector's item. People are willing to pay a lot of money for it."

"What of it? You made a mistake, and that's all, though I never have understood why you let it happen."

"Your father had brainwashed me into believing that Dewey was going to win in a landslide. I was so sure and so anxious to get our paper on the streets first."

"Well, you managed that, all right, but how you could have thought we'd have a Republican President when both Ohio and Indiana went Democratic early in the evening, I'll never know."

"Neither will your father. I tell you, Indiana, he almost killed me. He was shouting, and he came at me like a madman. If the window had been open he might have pushed me out. It was a nightmare and I keep waking up at night and reliving it."

"I know you do. Once I heard you calling out, 'don't, don't,' but by the time I got to your room you had gone back to sleep."

"Sometimes I've thought I should give up this paper entirely and get a job on a smaller paper in a smaller city. I've even attempted to consult a psychiatrist."

"Daddy has a horrible temper, but surely he wouldn't do you any physical harm. How are you getting along now?"

"Just so-so. You can see by the headlines that he is gung-ho for Senator Joseph McCarthy and his cross-country purge to spot communists in every kind of job. And Tiger goes right along with him."

"Don't mention Tiger's name. I've always detested him."

"Unfortunately, McCarthy has two strong points in his favor with your father: They both come from the Middle West and both seem to think in the same melodramatic way."

"I know. I hate the whole thing. I will talk to Daddy about you, but I can't touch McCarthy. We'll just have to be patient and sit it out, I guess."

"In the meantime, I think a little walk with my daughter to see her new pony will put me in a better mood." He stood up, set Heather down, and took her hand. "Want to come with us?"

"Not this way. I'm still wet, but I'll run upstairs to put on something dry. I'll catch up with you and Heather down at the stables." He really is terribly thin, she thought as she went into the house. I wonder if I should ask Daddy to transfer him to one of the West Coast papers until this whole thing blows over? If only Gage would be more aggressive and fight back.

It was soon Labor Day. Ever since her school days, Indiana felt that the first of September, and not January, was the beginning of a new year. Everyone came back refreshed from a holiday, and Gage, who had spent the last week of August with his mother, seemed much easier and happier.

When Lincoln returned from the Riviera, he had hardly set down his suitcase in his apartment before he was telephoning to Indiana. "I'm full of news, but most of it can wait. I came back on the plane with a friend of a friend of yours, and I just deposited her at her hotel."

"Who could that be?"

"Lady Diana Darby. After your friend Schuyler flew off to California, she clung to me like a limpet, whatever that may be."

"What's she like?"

"Oh very English, including skin and clothes. She's like a kind of sweet drink that can become habit-forming."

"I suppose I'll meet her."

"Naturally. I'm planning a dinner party just for that purpose, but she wants most of all to meet your father."

"That will never work. He's antisocial these days."

"Well, I'll give the dinner anyway, and I want you and Gage."

"Then you really like her?"

"Not necessarily, but her machinations amuse me and, as I told you, she's habit-forming."

It was well into October before the dinner party could be arranged. By this time Lincoln had persuaded Bradshaw Green to accept, since he had become curious about her from reading not only Lincoln's column but also Cholly Knickerbocker's and some of the others.

Lincoln had decided to have the party in his own home. He had taken a new apartment at 480 Park Avenue the previous spring. What with his salary and the outside benefits that came along with it, like an almost unlimited supply of liquor and press discounts almost everywhere, he had been able to afford it and decorate it with considerable taste.

He had a manservant who cooked for him and took care of his clothes, but for this special occasion he hired a caterer and staff. After he had finished briefing them the night of the party, he looked over the scene with real pleasure. It was obviously a man's apartment, with dark fabrics printed in the new geometric designs, and, after a rave notice in his column, he had been able to get a good price on some of the exciting new crystal and chrome furniture that the Italians were beginning to design. He was certain that none of his fourteen guests would have seen anything like it before.

Indiana would look smashing against the bare-white walls and the bold design of the furniture, he thought.

Diana arrived first with Chester Kendrick, a London friend. She looked totally and completely the great English lady in her pale-green chiffon, Lincoln thought. Not an ounce of style, but what a beauty. She was to have Bradshaw Green on one side of her at the table and Huntington Hartford on the other. Two millionaires are enough for one night, he had decided.

As always, he liked to mix different New York worlds. Each of them gets a kick out of talking to the other. He had smiled as he put Rosemary Baxter, now married to Andrew Hamilton, a successful stockbroker, next to Tennessee Williams.

Rosemary came in bubbling like the good champagne he had just handed to Diana for an apéritif. Lincoln had known that she was dying to meet the famous Lady Darby, and he had been glad to satisfy her curiosity. She had become one of his best sources for inside gossip in the city's most clannish, hard-to-penetrate social group, and repaying her was part of the game.

Rosemary's blondness was beginning to harden a little. She was dieting vigorously and seemed to him to be thin almost to emaciation, but she represented the typical chic New York woman, just as Diana represented London, he thought, as he watched the two of them talking.

Lincoln could always tell when a party was catching on and becoming a success. The social chatter became gradually a little louder and the voices rose a pitch higher. The evening had just reached that point when Indiana came in with her father. "Gage is stuck at the paper for a few minutes, but he'll make it in time for dinner," she said.

Indiana, in her black dress with her mass of dark hair and at least a half dozen strands of red and green beads around her neck, came as something of a surprise to Diana, Lincoln could readily see. He didn't know what she had expected, but certainly not so much self-confidence and vitality.

"Do come over and sit beside me for a minute," Diana said, beckoning to Indiana to join her on the sofa. "You know, I almost feel I know you, because Sky has talked to me so much about you."

"Oh really." Indiana tried to make her voice seem indifferent but inwardly she thought Diana was a bitch. "I haven't seen him for ten or eleven years, and he's more of a memory than a real person to me now."

"Oh but we must remedy that. You mustn't lose each other completely." Diana looked at her with such warmth and sympathy that Indiana felt herself warming to her slightly.

"And how beautiful and gypsylike your beads are on your black dress. They are rubies and emeralds, of course," Diana said.

"Most people don't recognize them because they don't glitter, and that's why I like them better than the civilized kind of stones that are cut and polished."

"I understand just what you mean. They have much more character than ordinary stones."

"Thank you. I never go overboard about jewelry, but my father gave these to me a few years ago for Christmas or my birthday, I forget which."

At dinner, since they were seated near Lincoln, Indiana could hear Diana Darby expounding at length to her father on his taste in choosing precious stones. After that Indiana lost track of the conversation when she turned to Tennessee Williams on her left. They began to discuss the movie version of *A Streetcar Named Desire*, which she had seen recently with Brando and Vivien Leigh. "I suppose you liked it best as a Broadway play," she said.

"Naturally, because I wrote it that way. When you write something it's like seeing your child murdered to have someone change it or tamper with it. I enjoyed the movie, but somehow it didn't seem to be mine at all."

"I understand that. Even with a no-matter story for a newspaper, it kills you when one of the editors chops off a line or two to make it fit."

"Did you ever dream of becoming an actress, Indiana, if you don't mind my calling you that?"

"Of course not. It's one state to another, isn't it, Tennessee? No, I never thought of the stage, but why do you ask?"

"Because most girls do, and because you would come across the footlights so well."

"I don't know if I would enjoy playing a character I didn't really feel for."

"I can see that. You project yourself so completely without any footlights that it would be too hard." He smiled. "Some of the best actresses I've known have such mobile faces and change so completely that I'm never sure what their real faces, their everyday faces, are like, or if they have any at all."

"I've heard that, but never read it. Would you consider doing a feature for our Sunday supplement? We could have it illustrated with sketches, and all the thousands of girls who want to go on the stage, or don't want to, would enjoy reading it."

Before the dinner was over she had persuaded Tennessee to write not one but two articles on the subject of qualifications for a stage or a movie career. It had been one of the better evenings, she had decided, as she and Gage settled themselves in the car with her father.

Bradshaw was vociferous on the subject of the evening. "Best goddamn dinner I've been to in a long time. Even the food was delicious. I didn't think that fellow had it in him."

"I saw that you were enjoying yourself, Daddy, with the guest of honor."

"That Diana Darby is a real lady, and not just a title. I didn't know they made them like that anymore. Where did she say she was staying?"

"At the Pierre, I believe she said."

"Then I intend to send her a roomful of flowers tomorrow."

CHAPTER SEVENTEEN

Sky was sitting in his office at the United Broadcasting Corporation. He couldn't think when he had felt as happy and relaxed as he did this afternoon. Though he could see that it was getting dark and a few lights had been turned on along Sunset Boulevard and Vine, he had no desire to move. It was wonderful just to be quiet and to feel his contentment seeping through his whole body.

His six months in Hollywood had been quite the opposite of his first frustrating year there and what seemed to him like a lifetime ago. For the first few weeks he had been grateful for the comfort of Nora's house. She was right that Hollywood had changed. Many of the friends and acquaintances he had made at the time now seemed to be bewildered and to be drifting aimlessly, hoping for a return of the old regime, which he realized would never happen. But Nora's house, her pool and her servants had remained completely the same.

Many times, and never more than this afternoon, he had been thankful that what he had longed for so passionately ten years ago had been denied him. If he had become the college-boy hero of the film fans he might be at loose ends right now instead of being well on the way to a far more successful and rewarding career.

He was deeply involved in television. He had grasped its potential from the minute he met Edward R. Murrow in London. Now Sky had the satisfaction of realizing that he was well into its American beginning.

After he left Nora's house, he had taken a small furnished apartment in Beverly Hills, just south of Wilshire, but so far had done nothing about trying to make a home out of it. UBC had been more or less trying him out, he realized. He had supervised the filming of newsreels here and there, made several newscasts and acquainted himself with the staff, always with the feeling that they liked his work.

Soon after he reached Hollywood, the coaxial cable linking the East and West coasts had been completed, making the transference of news much faster and more accurate. He was glad, though, that the UBC station in Hollywood was a small one, and most of its programs were still local. It gave him much more opportunity to understand all phases of the industry both on and off camera.

He watched as many programs as he could, trying not to miss any detail of both the production and the performer's technique. Murrow was his hero, but he felt more closely related to Charles Collingwood, whose easy, ad-lib style of delivering facts he decided to emulate when they gave him a chance.

Most of his first assignments were off camera, but they were all challenging and he was more than willing to wait for what he really wanted.

He started each morning by reading the trade papers, and one day he came on an item that he thought his studio could certainly profit from. On the East Coast Don Hewitt, a CBS staff member, had discovered a new way to visualize the news.

Up to that time, Sky had to admit to himself that many TV news programs just showed a man reading a script and then a silent photograph or film flashed on the screen. Hewitt had discovered that by using two projectors, the commentator and the photographs could appear on the screen at the same time.

It's so simple, but what a big step forward, Sky thought. It will lure thousands from poring over the newspaper headlines. He had been quick to sense the cold war that was in progress between the press and the TV screens.

The next day he went to the office of the studio head to discuss the new development and was given the go-ahead to try it on the six-o'clock local news program.

The news came over much more vividly. The newscaster, Paul Brady, was delighted and the studio brass were pleased enough to make Sky the news program's co-ordinating director.

He enjoyed the job. Sky had always had a visual mind that quickly turned words and situations into pictures, and he enjoyed working with Paul Brady and his staff and making each evening's program come off fresh and, if possible, entertaining.

Once Paul Brady was caught in a traffic jam and Sky, who knew each day's script by heart, filled in for the first five minutes. A couple of months later, when Paul's wife was rushed to the hospital for an emergency operation, Sky did the entire fifteen minutes. Facing the camera was no problem to him. After all, I'm a thwarted actor, he thought, as he folded his papers and left the set. A few days later the studio handed him his first sheaf of fan mail.

He had spent the week between Christmas and New Year's with Sidney and Marcia at the beach. At their Christmas dinner, Sky had asked once more if there was any possibility of any other studio's interest in their old script.

Sidney, who was about to carve the duck Marcia had roasted, flourished a knife in a gesture of hopelessness. "Dead duck," he had said. "No more chance of bringing it to life than of this fellow getting up and waddling out the door. Every time Marcia mentions the thing to me, I say the same thing: 'dead duck.'"

"Have you tried recently?"

"Sure thing. Everybody says the script is great. I had a nibble last year but good old Bradshaw Green got wind of it suddenly and it was mailed back with a brief note of regret." He cut off several pieces and put them on Sky's plate. "I wish I could do this to the bastard."

It was getting late. Sky reluctantly switched on the light in his office and was gathering up some papers for his briefcase when the telephone rang. It was Nora.

"How about saying 'Happy Birthday,' chum? I won't tell you how many years it is, but I feel like celebrating."

"How did I forget that today is March 27 and that you're an early Aries?"

"Since you're still in your office, I guess that you're available. How about getting into your car and driving over here. I haven't seen you in ages."

"I'll be right out. I have something of my own to celebrate."

"Tell me right now."

"Not a chance. Just have a good drink ready and waiting for me."

He stopped at a florist to pick up some white lilacs, which he knew she liked, and when he arrived at the house she was sitting expectantly in the library with a bottle of champagne already open. "They're lovely," she said as he handed her the flowers, "but let's have the news. You know how much I hate to wait for anything or anybody." She rang for the butler.

"It's just this. They're going to try me with my own ten-minute program following the regular newscast."

"Isn't that smart of them, but I'm not really surprised. Every time you've been on camera, you've been very special, and it's not just my own preference for you. I've heard the same thing from my friends." She handed the flowers to the butler, then turned back to Sky. "You have some of what Edward R. Murrow has of seeming to be deeply interested and enthusiastic about what you're saying."

"Perhaps some of him has rubbed off on me. I admire him very much."

"I think you'll be very successful."

"That remains to be seen. I realize they're still trying me out." They sat down and picked up the glasses the butler had just filled. "I start in May and I'll have the summer months and they tend to be dull. Lucky for me, though, that this summer I'll have both the Democratic and Republican conventions."

"What could be better? Your first broadcast will be terribly important. Have you decided yet whom you'll be interviewing or what you'll be talking about?"

"Yes, after they told me this afternoon, I sat in my office until it got dark and you called me." He hesitated. "What would you think of General Eisenhower?"

She laughed. "Not bad. You shoot high when you finally aim your gun, don't you, chum?"

"I suppose I do, but it would be foolish of me not to try for him. I first met him in North Africa when I was in the service and I ran into him several times in London when I was with CBS. He seemed to like me and the one newsreel I made with him in Paris when Truman sent him over to establish NATO. Either Eisenhower or one of his staff may remember me. At least it's a gamble."

The next morning he started trying. Since the date of the first broadcast was not as far away as it sounded, he mustn't lose any time. After several fruitless days of calling Denver, where a secretary said to try Washington, where a secretary referred him to the Waldorf, he was finally fortunate enough to reach one of the staff members he remembered meeting in Paris.

"Sure, I remember you, Sky Madison. We had a great old evening together, as I recall, and you're the guy who crashed the harem. The general always liked that story."

When Sky explained the situation, including the fact that it would be the first one-man broadcast in this country and the fact that it would take only fifteen minutes, Bob Endicott said, "The general might just be willing to do it. But he's not too happy on TV, you know. He's no wisecracker but with you he might be less nervous than with some commentators."

"Do you think it would work out with his schedule?"

"I know he expects to be in Denver around the first day of May, visiting his wife's family. All I can say is I'll do my best and let you know."

Almost three weeks passed with no word from General Eisenhower. Sky had promised himself not to be too disappointed if the answer was no. He had gone on lining up men in the political headlines for the following weeks and several of them had said that they could be moved forward to the earlier date if they were informed far enough ahead of time.

Before he made the shift, he decided to try a final call. He reached Bob Endicott at the Eisenhower headquarters in New York. "Howdy, Sky, I'm sorry I haven't got back to you but we've been rushed off our feet. Yes, the general thinks he can make it."

Sky's heart seemed to leap to his mouth. "That's great!"

"The general feels he needs a boost on the West Coast, and especially the movie colony, where they seem to be lapping up Adlai Stevenson's oratory. Of course, something may turn up at the last minute that he can't help."

"I understand."

"It's always better to have a second choice in the wings, but I'll be with him and give you as much advance notice as possible if anything goes wrong."

"Tell the general I couldn't be more pleased or grateful."

"You bet. See you in sunny California on May 3."

The UBC studio could hardly believe its own good luck when Sky informed them that, barring accidents, General Dwight D. Eisenhower was going to be his first guest on "Close-up," the name they had given the program.

The coming event was immediately advertised and, following the announcement, both the Los Angeles *Times* and *Examiner* sent reporters to interview Sky. They described him as a protégé of Edward R. Murrow, who was about to become a TV personality on his own, and both papers predicted success for the new program.

Sky, himself, tried not to build all his hopes on the general's arrival but, two days before the promised date, a confirming telegram from Bob Endicott arrived from Denver saying the general was in fine form and was looking forward to the new experience of a long interview on TV.

The studio sent a camera crew to the airport to meet the general's plane, and Sky went with them. There had been enough advance publicity to attract a medium-size crowd of spectators and camera crews from the other networks. NBC's head cameraman told Sky's No. 1 man that his studio was green with envy.

The plane landed on the runway and as it taxied toward the airport, Sky followed the landing stairway that was being rolled out, and stood at the foot. Bob Endicott came out first, followed by several other staff members, and finally the general emerged to the cheers and cries of the spectators.

Except that he was wearing civilian clothes, he hadn't changed much since the first time he had seen him in the desert, Sky thought. He looked hearty and healthy and had the big, friendly smile that was going to win him millions of votes, Sky thought as he stepped forward.

"Well, my boy, I remember your face, though it was pretty covered with mud the first time I saw it."

"Mud and all, it was the most welcome tea party I've ever been invited to," Sky said. He and Bob Endicott walked on either side of the general, keeping the crowd, all of whom wanted to touch the general or shake his hand, at a distance. Finally, they reached the limousine that was waiting for them, and the general sank into the back seat.

"The people genuinely love you, General," Sky said.

He smiled. "I appreciate it more than I can say, but I find it a great responsibility, too. That's why I have been reluctant even to be a candidate for nomination at the Republican Convention in July." His smile faded. "Dealing with armies seems to me to be child's play compared with running a nation."

"Be sure to say that on television this evening, General," Sky said.

UBC had engaged a suite at the Beverly Wilshire Hotel for the general and his party, and the studio executives had planned a small, private luncheon upstairs for the group. While they ate, Sky studied the general intently and made mental notes. He was far from being a flip, quick-on-the-uptake personality, but left to talk about something he liked, he would be amusing and natural. The warm smile would be dynamite on the screen, Sky was sure. Before he left he had decided to conduct the close-up on a much simpler and more personal basis than he had originally intended, and to keep the general smiling.

Sky was already made up and ready for the broadcast when the general arrived at the prescribed hour of seven o'clock, one hour ahead of the broadcast. "None of that, hell no," the general said, waving away the idea of a make-up man.

"Have it your way, General, but this is the way I feel. The whole world thinks of you as a suntanned, outdoor hero. Unfortunately, studio lighting hasn't been perfected yet, and instead of coming over the way you really look, you'll appear like a ghost on the screen."

"Have you got than pancake stuff on your face?"

"You can bet I have. I want to look healthy."

"All right, son. I guess I'm in your hands."

"I won't steer you wrong, and I'm sure you're going to be pleased with the broadcast and its results."

They had a few more minutes of conversation before the program started. Sky told him they would start talking about their first meeting, go on to the changes the general had found when he returned to this country and finish with his feeling about the possibility of becoming President. "Don't worry about the timing. I'll give you plenty of warning when there's a commercial and when we have to stop. You'll be surprised how quickly the time goes."

During the broadcast, Sky sat across the little table that separated them, smiling at the general, who smiled back frequently. He told about meeting Sky at the side of the road with mud on his face, chatted about the end of the war, said he still felt strange in civilian clothes and went on to his early reluctance to be a candidate at the Republican Convention.

When the program was over, the studio's telephones were flooded with calls, but Sky left all of his for his secretary and drove back to the hotel with the general's party.

"Good God, it's the best performance I've ever seen him give," Bob Endicott said. "He doesn't really like being on stage. He even accepts interviews as if they were medicine he has to take and he's quite hostile to radio."

At dinner General Eisenhower had suggested a game of poker, but soon after he finished his cup of coffee, he began yawning. Finally he stood up, saying, "Let's make it an early night, boys. Sky, I'll see you tomorrow before I take off."

"I'll be at the airport, General."

Bob Endicott accompanied the general to his room. When Endicott returned he ordered two scotch and sodas. "Now let's talk," he said, sitting down next to Sky. "First of all, let me tell you that the general likes and trusts you. He's sure to be nominated and if you could see your way clear to work with us on his presidential campaign, you could pretty well name your salary, within reason."

"I like him very much and think he's the man for the job, but I've been batting around here and there, and I can't afford any detours right now, financially or emotionally."

"I see what you mean."

"I'm deep into television and I intend to go right along with it. People are still underestimating its power, but it has already altered the course of the movies and will soon threaten the newspapers. This will be the first time it has been used in a presidential election, but mark my words, from now on it is going to make or break the candidate."

Bob Endicott put his drink down. "I hadn't thought about it

but, of course, it's true. So how do we use it? A New York advertising agency, Batten, Barton, Durstine and Osborn, is going to manage the campaign but I'd appreciate hearing your thinking. Ike isn't strong on speechmaking. When he reads the speeches that have been written for him, they sound that way."

"You'll have to capitalize on the warmth and emotion he engenders wherever he goes. Borrow some of the old movie techniques."

"How do you mean?"

"Well, since speechmaking isn't his forte, don't spend all that prime time you're going to pay a fortune for showing him on the platform turning page after page of what he's reading. Cut the speech short and give them lots of atmosphere."

"Illustrate."

"You have to have camera crews at different stations. You start with the general and Mamie arriving in a car. There's a lot of enthusiasm and they can hardly get through the crowd. Second shot: The general has entered the convention hall. People are falling over him, women thanking him for sending their sons back as he smiles and pushes along. Third shot shows Mamie entering her box with friends greeting her. The general reaches the platform and mounts the rostrum. Then there are random shots of the crowd while he is introduced, with close-ups of celebrities or beautiful young people already spotted. The general makes his speech but even the speech is broken by shots of Mamie clapping and crowd hysteria. Of course, his voice continues all through it. Get the point?"

"It sounds terrific."

"Any good TV outfit you engage should have plenty of other ideas, as long as you give them the original direction."

"I get the idea. It's great. How about at least joining us through the convention in Philadelphia and giving us moral support through that?"

"Fine, I'm sure I can arrange it. I'm all for the general and I think he's a sure winner."

"The Democrats will have Adlai Stevenson, who couldn't care less about television."

"Yes, I know. He's still living in the Victorian days of fancy words."

On the drive to the airport the next morning the general was in even better spirits than the day before. The accounts in the morning papers of both his visit and his TV appearance had been enthusiastic. "I may take to using that make-up you had them put on my face yesterday evening," he told Sky. "My wife's cousin called me this morning and said she had seen our performance and that I looked like a teen-ager."

"You certainly looked in top form, sir. I'll send Bob the number of the shade, and all you need is water and a little sponge to do it yourself."

After the plane had taken off, Sky spent the rest of the day going over the messages and returning the telephone calls. In the late afternoon his secretary appeared rather frantic. "A Mrs. Balzer has called at least eight times and won't leave a message. She's on the phone again. Won't you please take it?"

"Hello, this is Schuyler Madison."

"Surprise! Surprise, Sky. This is Dorothy Darrow Balzer."

"Oh I did hear somewhere that you had married the head of the studio, Dottie. Congratulations! And how are you?"

"Wonderful. B.B. and I saw you on television last night and you were great. B.B. even said, 'How did I let that fellow get away from me?'"

"Oh well, that's water over the dam."

"Damn is right. Daddy Green acted so outrageously about you, and he was so furious with me for marrying B.B., that he sold his stock in Olympia."

Sky promised to have dinner with them soon and went on with his work. Advance notices of "Close-up" had already brought a small amount of letters from politicians, press agents, writers and personal friends, all of whom had suggestions of people whose careers and opinions should be aired. He had engaged a second secretary to weed them out while his original secretary collected the background material on the guest he would select each week.

One fifteen-minute spot a week had sounded like a small stint, but he realized quickly that it was going to absorb almost all of his time.

During the next few weeks, he dipped fearlessly into the Red Channels situation by having as one of his guests actress Jean Muir, whose contract for an appearance on "The Aldrich Family" had been suddenly canceled. He considered that he might be fired, but evidently the "Close-up" ratings were too good to result in anything more than a mild caution.

When convention time came, he was glad to get away for a while. Since by this time Eisenhower's nomination was a foregone conclusion with Taft following closely behind, there was no tension in the proceedings. The nomination was made by two speakers, and Sky was sitting in the back of Mamie Eisenhower's box with Bob Endicott when an usher tapped Sky on the shoulder.

"They tell me you're Mr. Madison. You are wanted on the telephone in the manager's office. It's long distance and important."

It must be the studio in Hollywood calling him, Sky supposed, as he tiptoed out of the box as quickly as possible.

It was a woman's voice. "Darling, how are you?"

"Who is this?" He was startled.

"Diana, of course. Don't you recognize my voice?"

"I do now, but may I call you back in an hour? Eisenhower is just making his acceptance speech and I'm sitting in their box."

"Of course you may, but just listen to my news. I'm married."

"Good for you, but who is the lucky guy?"

"Bradshaw, darling."

"Bradshaw Green? You're joking, and if I'm not laughing it's because I know you're kidding."

"But I'm not joking. Bradshaw and I were married two hours ago in a judge's office. I thought you'd be happy for me."

"Diana, you must be out of your mind. Why didn't you talk to me before you did such a thing?"

"Probably because I remembered you had some silly kind of thing against him. I can tell you that whatever it is, you are quite wrong. He is a very fine man and he tells me that he has been lonely for years."

"He's more than thirty years older than you, Diana. How did it ever happen?"

"Remember I once told you about my old Chinese trick?" she giggled.

"Well, good luck, and take my advice: Don't make him angry. He can be a maniac." He banged down the receiver.

CHAPTER EIGHTEEN

In her office at the *Globe*, Indiana was watching the convention on the small television set beside her desk. From the start she had followed its every development. She had surrounded herself with sets, and the goings-on in Philadelphia were coming through bright and clear on all the networks.

Since her father had given her the amount of power she demanded, the *Globe* had assumed a different personality and had become the most talked-about of the city's newspapers. Though she was no feminist, as she always maintained, she believed in the rise of woman power. The columns, the layouts and features about career women who were beginning to appear in politics and big business had created a new audience and had made the *Globe* one of the most powerful papers in the country.

Indiana no longer dreaded the competition of other news-papers. She had stopped scanning them feverishly, and now she was becoming fascinated with TV. She never missed the start of a new series like "I Love Lucy" or the CBS experimental theater, not because she had become a fan, but because she sensed that the influence of this gargantuan medium might someday threaten the newspapers she loved.

The convention reporting was especially skillful, she thought, as she saw the crowd pressing against Eisenhower as he came into the convention hall. It's certainly a challenge to the *Globe* reporters covering it to make their copy interesting enough for those watching to want to read their stories, too.

Suddenly the picture switched to Mamie Eisenhower's box, and she caught a glimpse of Sky sitting in a far-back corner. "Oh," she cried involuntarily.

"Did you call me, Mrs. Hale?" asked her secretary, who was working in the next room with the door open between them.

"No. It was just a comment on the convention, which I was watching."

Indiana, herself, was startled at her sudden emotion. She felt that she had put her feeling for Sky as safely and thoroughly away as if it were in the bank vault like the jewelry her father had given her. I'm a happy woman, she had kept telling herself over the past few years, and in a way she knew it was true. Her life had flowed smoothly, without any turbulence that comes from passionate love. She had a devoted husband and a beautiful daughter, but most of her attention had been given over to creating the new *Globe*. Now here she was, trembling as if she were still a debutante and longing for his face to come back on the screen again.

Her secretary came to the door. "It's Mr. LaPorte calling. He says it's terribly important."

She picked up the receiver. "I'm just watching the convention, Lincoln."

"Forget it. It's a cold potato compared with the hot news I've got for you."

"What? Tell me."

"Hold onto your desk, darling. Your father and Diana Darby have just managed to get themselves married."

"I don't believe it."

"I've checked it and it's true. They took out a license and your daddy bribed somebody not to file it right away. They drove out to Connecticut and were married in some judge's office. They're at home in South Wind right this minute, waiting for congratulations."

"I still don't believe it. How could Daddy not tell me?"

"Diana doesn't believe in taking chances. You might have raised a row."

"I don't know what I would have done. I'm completely stunned."

"Igor Cassini is going all out with the story for the Hearst papers. Obviously, I feel like cutting my throat because I can't touch it."

Miss Peacock came to the door, looking flushed and excited.

"Your father wants to talk to you, Indiana. He has some wonderful news for you."

"I've just heard."

"I'm so happy for him. She's a real English lady, the kind you read about, and so gentle and sweet."

Indiana glared at her. "What line is he on?"

"You can pick up the call on No. 3."

Bradshaw Green's voice came booming over the wire, "Well, my little darling, I have a surprise for you that I hope will make you as happy as it has me. Just three hours ago by my watch, Lady Diana Darby consented to become Mrs. Bradshaw Green."

"Naturally, I'm surprised, but I hope you'll both be very happy."

She could hear Diana's voice in the background but couldn't distinguish the words as her father went on talking. "I'm sure you two will become good friends. She talks constantly about how much she admires you."

"I'm glad."

"Right now she's telling me that she's going to be Mrs. Bradshaw Innis Green. She likes my second name, which I hated when I was a kid. She says the initials spell BIG, and that's what I am."

"How clever of her." Shrewd would have been a better word, Indiana thought.

"Nobody has ever listened to me talk about my childhood before, but she enjoys every detail. We've had some marvelous evenings just sitting and talking."

"I'm happy for you, Daddy."

"Let me turn the phone over to Diana. She's longing to talk to you."

"Darling Indiana, we must become very close, so that we can both take care of this dear man," Diana said.

"Of course, I'm sure we will." At least I'll make every effort, she was thinking to herself, and make an effort to be polite.

"I hope you're not hurt that we didn't let you in on our little secret. We've known we were going to do it for several weeks, but I do hate any kind of publicity, especially in those nasty columns. We thought if we were married on the day of General Eisenhower's nomination all the reporters would be busy with something more important than we are."

"I think you have a perfect right to surprise us all, and I'm looking forward to hearing how it all happened."

"I told my dear husband that you would react just this way. Now tell me how soon you can come to visit us here."

The word "visit" struck Indiana unpleasantly. She had always thought of South Wind as her own place of refuge. She had played in every corner of it and loved its Victorian eccentricities, but probably her father hadn't had a chance to explain all this to Diana.

"Gage and I will come for the weekend," she promised.

When she finished talking to Diana, she went into her father's office, where Miss Peacock was already busy taking calls. "The notice of their marriage license is in today's papers, and all the reporters in New York are calling for details on Lady Diana. I referred them to Mr. LaPorte, who seems to know everything about everybody."

"Did you know this was going to happen, Miss Peacock?"

"All I know, dear, is that your father has been filling her hotel rooms with roses every day. I'd hate to think of how many pink roses he has ordered over the past few months."

"To say nothing of other gifts, I'll bet," Indiana couldn't resist saying.

"I didn't take it too seriously, though, because we have been through the same thing many times, as you know."

"I guess that's what surprises me."

"Lady Diana is quite different from any of the others. She is well-bred and, as his wife, can do a great deal to make your father's life attractive."

"I hope so. We'll see."

"I find her charming. When she heard it was my birthday recently, she gave me this little gift." Miss Peacock held out her wrist and showed Indiana a little bracelet of gold links.

The telephone rang, and as she heard Miss Peacock begin the routine, "Yes, isn't it exciting?" Indiana left the room and returned to her office.

Gage received the news as being good. "Maybe if he has something else in his life he'll be drinking less and not be so finicky about details on the paper."

"You've got to learn to stand up to him, Gage. Once Daddy realizes that someone is afraid of him, no matter whether it's a man or woman, he turns into a perfect horror. I learned that long ago."

When they turned into the gates at South Wind, Indiana instantly sensed a change. A truck was parked on one side of the gate house. It was filled with rhododendron and mountain laurel, and several gardeners were already hauling them in, under the direction of the chief maintenance man. Several cars were parked near the entrance steps, and as they got out of the car, the front door opened and two men came out carrying rolls of papers and shopping bags full of what looked to Indiana like fabric samples.

Diana, in a little mauve cotton dress, was still in the foyer. "Oh darlings," she cried as she rushed to hug and kiss Indiana and then Gage. "I'm just bursting with happiness. Brad has given me carte blanche to do over this dear old place. I knew you'd be happy, because he says you love it, too."

"How nice. That should keep you busy for quite a while," Indiana managed to say, but inwardly she was seething.

"Houses are my hobby, you know. This one in a way is very English and I fell in love with it the minute I saw it. We had an architect here two weeks ago, and we plan to make just a few architectural changes before we get on to the actual decorating. We moved your clothes to another suite, darling. I knew you wouldn't mind when you see the actual result."

"But I may mind, Diana. I've always loved my rooms just as they are."

"They won't really be different. We've just taken away one tiny closet, so Brad and I can have a glorious morning room in our suite. I'm sending for all my English furniture to make it cozy. I have some lovely pieces, and I'm planning to give you whatever you want for your own quarters."

"Where are we staying this weekend, Diana?" Indiana could hardly control her rage.

"You and Gage are quite welcome to your own rooms, dear, if you don't mind being wakened at dawn by workmen. Both of you look a little tired and I want you to feel that this is a place where you can rest completely."

When they reached the suite to which Indiana's clothes had

been moved, she rushed to the window and stood looking out. Gage came over and put his arm around her.

"How could Diana do such a thing to me, and how could Daddy allow it?" she asked.

"Come now, Indiana, you're not being quite fair. I'm sure she means well and in the end you may like the result."

Indiana turned back into the room. She felt a violent desire to smash something into the fireplace. She even picked up a crystal vase, but set it down quickly. I'm behaving just like Daddy, she thought. I've got to stop and make up my mind to take all this. "Let's put on our bathing suits, Gage, and cool off in the pool."

Once downstairs, Indiana rushed for the pool and dived in. Gage lingered on the edge, folding his towel neatly and laying his glasses on top of it. As she looked up at him she thought, he's so precise about all his possessions, but especially those glasses. After swimming several laps in the pool she began to feel better and more able to cope with the new situation.

When they came downstairs that evening, the main floor smelled deliciously sweet and fresh. Diana and Bradshaw were both in the seldom-used drawing room, which now had its big casement windows open, flowers on the tables, new cushions and a general look of being lived in.

"Don't you just love the scent of those candles?" Diana asked. "I ordered them lighted an hour ago and had them snuffed out when we came in, but the fragrance stays on for a long time."

It was an excellent dinner. The dining room was lighted only by candlelight, and Indiana saw that Diana had already thoroughly explored South Wind's china closet.

"Diana was very nice tonight," she said to Gage as they were undressing. "I have always taken for granted that South Wind was mine, but I'm not going to count on it anymore. I think we should have a place of our own, possibly on Long Island."

"You can't imagine how happy that makes me, Indiana. I've never felt like anything but a guest, and sometimes an unwelcome guest, at South Wind."

"Darling, you should have said so long ago. It will be fun looking, and we'll take Heather with us. It should probably be either Westbury or Oyster Bay."

"I think there's a good girls' school near Westbury and we can look into it for Heather when she starts to school this fall."

"I've thought a lot about Heather's education, Gage. I would like to put her into the same school I went to in Switzerland. She'll be protected, learn languages at an early age and get a good foundation for anything she wants to do in the future."

"It's O.K. with me, Indiana. All I want for my daughter is for her to turn out to be as perfect as her mother." He took her in his arms and turned out the light.

They were awakened early the next morning by the workmen. They were knocking down what had once been one of Indiana's closets. It was to become a shallow alcove that would hold a miniature stove and sink in Diana's new morning room.

Indiana threw on her robe and went to the window, but even the scene she had loved so much no longer looked the same.

She turned to Gage, who had already ordered his tray and was eating his breakfast. "Let's go home, Gage. I'm going to pack a few things and next week I'll send out one of the maids to get the rest. I'll come back occasionally when I have to, but that's it. I don't care if I ever see South Wind again.

"You don't really like Diana, do you, dear."

"I'm honestly glad Daddy seems happy, but as far as she's concerned she's too good to be true."

"I find her charming and very genuine. When you talk to her she listens as if she were really interested."

"I know, you men all adore her, but honestly I prefer people with a few faults. You can fight back at them and you always know just where you are with them."

"Try not to be difficult right now, Indiana. Your father was pleasant to me last night, just as he was when we were first married, and I'd like to keep it that way. It will make life easier if we stay for lunch."

"All right. I'm willing if it means that much to you."

On the drive home that afternoon Indiana found Gage more relaxed and happy than he had been in a long time. Diana had made a special effort to draw him out on the subject of a current dispute with the typographers' union and Indiana had admired her skill at seeming, at least, to be fascinated with something she could care less about.

CHAPTER NINETEEN

"Closeup" soon had one of the highest ratings of any program on the West Coast. Sky's interview with the presidential nominee was soon followed by other personalities in the news, like Christine Jorgensen, Clare Boothe Luce, and Rocky Marciano.

He had a full schedule and accepted only those dinners that came from close friends like Nora or that brought him into closer contact with men or women he wanted to observe closely and know better. Often after his newscast, he stopped by a quiet little restaurant, ate by himself and went back to his office to look over his mail and his calendar for the next day. It was so much easier to think without the sound of the telephone constantly ringing and his secretary telling most of those who were calling that he was unavailable at the time.

He was going through his mail in a leisurely way one evening when the all-night watchman called him. "There's a Mr. Sidney Garson down here, who says he's a friend of yours and wants to talk to you."

"Of course. Tell him to come right up, please."

Sidney came in and dropped into a chair in front of his desk. "My co-author of a still-unsold movie script called *The Power and the Glory,* among other things," Sky said as he saw that Sidney was looking more sallow than usual, and had dark circles under his eyes.

"More recently, I've been tagged as a communist spy. I'm on the Hollywood blacklist in a big way."

"What do you mean? How the hell could that happen?"

"The top brass in the studios will be afraid to speak to me, let alone buy anything I write."

"It's unbelievable, Sidney."

"As you know, my family were originally Russian. They changed their name from Garnovosky two generations ago, but I still have relatives in Moscow and Leningrad to whom I send Christmas cards with a few bills enclosed. That's my only crime, as far as I can find out, but that's enough."

"I've been shocked at all the blacklisting I've heard about, but this is the first time I've personally come in contact with it. How does Marcia take it?"

"Poor kid. She's sticking right by me. She had to go back to selling dresses."

"I'm sure there's nothing she hates worse than fashion talk and fuddy-duddy ladies."

"You're right, but she's great at the job. She talks like a blue streak, and the customers think she's kidding. She may get fired, though, if they find out that she's Mrs. Garnovosky."

"When did all this start, Sidney?"

"About six or seven months ago, I guess. They sent an FBI agent down to the house on the beach. He wanted to see my passport. Then he asked me for the name and the place of birth of both my mother and father. All I can think of is that there is somebody at the post office to keep an eye out for mail that goes to Russia."

"It's hard to believe that this kind of thing is going on in this country of ours."

"Well, it is and it's going to get worse if nobody does any more about it than just feel shocked."

"You're right, Sidney. I will have to think about it carefully, or I could do more harm than good."

"That's what I'd hoped you would say."

"Why didn't you mention any of this to me at Christmas?"

"Oh well, after the first episode with the passport, I thought it had all blown over. Then two months ago all hell broke out, and they started bothering my poor old dad in Iowa."

"Sidney, let's get out of here and go somewhere and have a drink. We can talk some more about it."

Later, as Sky lay in bed trying to go to sleep but thinking only about Sidney and Marcia, he knew, as Sidney had implied, that it was up to him to do something about it. His first idea was to fly to Washington to get some advice from Bob Endicott but finally decided, I have enough power right here on my "Close-up" program to start the ball rolling. I must do it in my own way without too much conflicting outside advice or it won't come through as real, he thought, as he finally dozed off to sleep.

The next morning he started making telephone calls to people whose servants, co-workers in offices or even friends had been blacklisted. There were even more of them than he had expected, but he decided to send out the staff that collected material for his newscast to do advance interviewing. He would finally zero in on one or two more cases besides Sidney's for a broadcast that would attack the whole business of tattling and spying that Senator Joseph McCarthy was pushing so violently.

Sky decided to give UBC no more advance notice than the week before, when he was required to give them the subject of his next broadcast. He had an alternative ready in case they objected to its title, but apparently "The Business of Blacklisting" created no furor in the offices of the top executives.

Nevertheless, when he started his broadcast it was the first time he had been even faintly nervous. He had decided to give a minimum of personal comment and to let the cases speak for themselves. He could tell even before the program was finished that the result had been dramatic.

Ivan Garson, an older and frailer edition of his son Sidney, stole the show when he said that he and his wife had been Iowa farmers all their lives. Then he continued, "How would you like it if you heard your son had lost his job and become a traitor because he sent a Christmas card and a few dollar bills to some old people in Russia whom he had never met?"

Sky expected some comment from the management before he left the studio, but none was forthcoming. "We're not fired yet," he told his staff when they met late the next morning for their daily conference.

It was several days later that he was called to the executive offices of United's West Coast studio. "Of course you've stirred up a hornet's nest, Madison, but somebody had to do it, and we're glad you took it on your own shoulders to be the one. It made it easier for us, too, that you didn't ask our permission."

"I'm glad you feel that way. What have the results actually been?"

"The response was tremendous, but pro and con, of course. About a third wanted you fired and over two thirds think we're tops in intelligent broadcasting."

"That's about the way I figured the percentages."

"We agree with the two thirds. The East Coast has Murrow speaking his mind and now we have you out here. Take it easy, though, and don't press too far."

Though the broadcast didn't bring Sidney any immediate work, at least he assumed the status of a hero to the friends and acquaintances who had seen the broadcast.

For his next step in campaigning against McCarthyism, Sky decided to shoot at the top, just as he had done when he managed to capture General Eisenhower. This was going to be harder, but he wanted McCarthy, himself.

By this time Sky had many friends in Washington, some of whom had managed to see "Close-up," and many others who had simply heard or read about it in the accounts carried by *Time* and *Newsweek*. All of them lauded Sky with all the fervor given to a new face, especially a personable one when it comes forcefully on the scene.

Sky was passed from one person, said to be close to McCarthy, to the next one, who was said to be even closer. Sky went along patiently, but it was several months later when he realized he was getting close to the big fish that he wanted. McCarthy was not coming to the West Coast, but he consented to appear on the program if he could meet Sky beforehand and hear what the introduction would be; and the broadcast would have to be from a Washington studio.

By this time it was beginning to be apparent that McCarthyism was losing ground, and McCarthy himself was eager to put his case before the public. Still, he had given few interviews in depth, and United was quick to give Sky the go-ahead.

When he arrived in Washington he found that the filming had to be put off twenty-four hours. Roy Cohn, McCarthy's aide, assured him there would be no further delay. The senator would see him for a few minutes in his office that afternoon, but he had been too desperately busy to finish or go over what he intended to say, with his lawyer.

Feeling a little let down, Sky decided to call Gage in New York. If he wasn't tied up with some crisis on the *Globe*, he might be able to fly down for dinner or for lunch the next day.

Gage had just reached his office when the call came. "Good God, Sky. It's great to hear from you. I've been reading about you and now I hear that you've got McCarthy. I suppose that's why you're in Washington."

"We were going to make the film today, but now it's tomorrow. I'm hung up here and I just got a wild idea that you might be willing to fly down and have dinner with me. It's been a hell of a long time since we've seen each other."

"I just might. It so happens I'm all alone this evening. Indiana is in Switzerland. She took Heather over there last week to put her in school."

"School? My God. I still think of her as a baby. I'll have to stop sending the dolls and switch to books."

"She isn't that grown up, but she's already had two years in preschool. Indiana has pronounced views on education and feels that the expensive schools she went to in this country were something of a flop. The only one she feels that contributed is the place we're sending Heather."

"That's good; then she'll grow up bilingual."

"That's about it."

"Come on down then, and we'll have dinner. We've got so much to catch up on."

"O.K." Then, after a slight pause, "Say, I think I'll bring our TV editor with me. She's a girl, thanks to Indiana. She can do an interview with you first, then fly back and I'll stay on for dinner and catch a later plane."

"Great. I'm at the Mayflower. Try to make it by six and I'll meet you in the cocktail lounge."

Gage and his TV editor, Marie Bory, arrived shortly before six, and Sky jumped up. After he and Gage had exchanged warm greetings, Sky turned to shake hands with Miss Bory.

"You don't know what a pleasure this is, Mr. Madison. Our

paper has been so pro-McCarthy, due to Mr. Green. I was thrilled that Mr. Hale decided to take this step."

As they sat down to order drinks, Sky said, "I hope it won't cause either of you any problems."

Marie Bory took out her notebook. "Oh I don't think so. I'll stick strictly to facts and not go overboard about what you did on the West Coast to stop the blacklistings." She opened her notebook. "Now, do tell me what gave you the original impetus. I have to hurry a little to catch my plane."

She questioned Sky, and they talked for around an hour. "I guess that will do," she said. "I'll call you here at the hotel tomorrow if I need more." She closed her notebook, dropped it into her big handbag, and left.

Sky ordered another drink for them. "Your TV editor makes me think that Bradshaw Green is as poisonous as ever. Is he?"

"Certainly as far as I'm concerned, he is. I made one bad booboo, I have to admit, and I swear he's never let me forget it. He sometimes acts like a maniac."

"That's what he is."

"Indiana tells me I must stand up to him and yell right back, but you know it's not my nature. You remember I never could stand arguments, and when he gets himself into a state I just get flustered."

"I thought Diana might have managed to calm him down."

"She has, but only a little, and not on the subject of politics. He dotes on McCarthy, as Marie told you."

"How do you find Diana?"

"She's always sweet and interested in what I have to say. I enjoy talking to her, but I'm afraid Indiana doesn't. She says it's like walking through slush."

Sky burst out laughing. "Indi is still Indi, I gather."

"Very much so. Her great love is the paper. Our marriage has been reasonably happy, though it's hard for Indiana to understand someone with less drive than she has, and I often think she still cares for you."

"Me?" Sky looked surprised.

"Yes, she often talks about you. Things should be better for us now. Since Diana has taken over South Wind and is busy enter-

taining all the visiting titles, either there for English-style weekends or at the Fifth Avenue house, Indiana decided we should
have a country place on Long Island."

"That's good, Gage. You'll enjoy that."

"It will be great to be completely out from under Bradshaw
Green's thumb."

"What will the new place be like? It must have been hard for
Indi to give up her beloved South Wind."

"When she makes up her mind she never seems to look back. I
don't think she has a sentimental bone in her body."

"Yes, I suppose you're right." But Sky wasn't sure he agreed.

"She adores the new place. It's a beautiful piece of land, high
on a cliff and overlooking the sound. We hired a very modern architect. Indiana wanted lots of glass walls and the whole thing
gives you a sense of living outdoors. That's what Heather likes
about it."

"It bothers me to think of that dear little thing being left alone
in Switzerland."

"That dear little thing is already a very independent charmer.
She was eager to go when we talked to her about it and I doubt
if she'll be any more homesick than Indiana was when Bradshaw
put her there. If she is, of course Indiana will fly right over and
bring her back."

"You are lucky, Gage."

"What do you mean? I've never thought so."

"I mean to be married and have a child. I've always wanted
one."

"Give yourself some more time."

He reached over and touched Gage's shoulder. "I hope you are
right. When do you and Indi move into your new home?"

"Almost any minute now. It's not completely furnished but we
can take our time about that. You must promise to visit us as
soon as you can."

"The next time I fly East, and it may be soon."

They talked about Fort Wayne, Aunt Addie's death when Sky
was on an assignment in Greece and didn't receive the news until
he returned to London a week later to find the cable. After that
they reminisced about schoolmates and girls they had laid while
serving as lifeguards at Lake Magoo during summer vacations.

Gage was smiling for the first time that evening but when he took off his glasses Sky could see that his eyes were tired, and his fingers were tapping nervously on the table.

"We didn't know what good times we were having, did we?" Gage said. "I keep thinking that things will be better for me after we get through this McCarthy era, but in the meantime I've been seeing a psychiatrist."

"What on earth for?"

"I thought he'd tell me whether I should go on bucking the big time or settle for a job at a smaller paper, as Indiana has sometimes suggested."

After Gage looked at his watch and left hurriedly, Sky thought, he's such a genuine friend, and my only link with the past. I must never lose touch with him again.

Next day the filming of the McCarthy interview went more perfectly than Sky had dared hope it would. His introduction was simple and factual, with no overtones of either praise or blame. The senator stated his own case, and the more violent and excited he became, the cooler Sky was in the questions he asked. When the senator had finished, Sky ended the fifteen minutes with, "You've just heard what Senator McCarthy has to say. He has created a great national controversy. It is now for all of you to decide whether this country will remain the sweet land of liberty, as the song goes, or become something else."

Back on the West Coast UBC refused to advertise the McCarthy "Close-up," but made no objection to Sky's paying for it out of his own salary. Since the station declined to accept the responsibility but made no effort to stop the broadcast, he decided to pay for advertisements in both Los Angeles and San Francisco papers.

If the blacklist program had produced a furor, the McCarthy interview created a frenzy. A large number of viewers had seen McCarthy in newspaper photographs, but had never heard him speak and understood only vaguely what his search for hidden communists was all about. To many of them McCarthy managed to demean himself by his own admission and without any assistance from Sky.

UBC's wires were blocked for the rest of the week after the broadcast, and Sky's own mail began to assume tremendous proportions and he realized without any word from the top executives that another coup had been scored. Among his own communications that interested him most was a wire asking him to get in touch with Edward Murrow, and another similar request from NBC.

As he leafed through the pro and the con news clippings that his secretary had laid on his desk, he found what he considered a fine and very provocative review of the broadcast in the New York *Times*, but not a word from Marie Bory of the *Globe*. Probably vetoed by Bradshaw Green, he decided.

He felt a sudden impulse to talk to Gage, and told his secretary to put in the call. It was about six o'clock in New York, when Gage would certainly be at his desk. He could hear her talking to the *Globe* operator. "An accident? What kind of accident? I can't understand you. It's Mr. Hale I want. Don't hang up, please. Wait just a minute."

Apparently the *Globe* operator did hang up, and he could hear her dialing again. He went to her door. "What's the matter? Can't you get through?"

"There seems to be some kind of trouble at the *Globe*. I could hear a woman screaming somewhere in the background. Now they're not answering."

"Keep on trying until you get them." He wondered if it was a bomb scare with one of Bradshaw Green's enemies involved.

Fifteen minutes later, his secretary called. "The operator is on the wire, but nobody is answering in Mr. Hale's office."

"Try Miss Iris Peacock's office."

"I can hear them buzzing, but there's no answer there, either."

"Then ask for Marie Bory's in the TV Department." In a moment he heard her voice. "Hello, Marie. What in the hell is going on at the *Globe* this afternoon? I'm trying to locate my cousin and your editor, Gage Hale."

"Oh Mr. Madison." Her voice sounded desolate.

"What's the matter?"

"It's just that I hate to be the one to tell you. Mr. Hale has had a terrible accident."

"He's badly hurt?"

"I'm afraid so."

"Try to tell me what has happened."

"We don't quite know. They say that he had a heart attack in Mr. Green's office."

"What?"

"No one was around to see what actually happened, but Mr. Hale had apparently staggered to the window for a breath of fresh air, lost his balance and had fallen to a roof three stories below."

"What you are telling me is that Gage Hale is dead?"

"We don't know for sure, but I'm afraid it's true. I'm sorry, Mr. Madison. We all liked him so much."

"Just one more question before you hang up, Marie: Was there any problem about your reviewing 'Close-up'?"

"I think there was. One of the secretaries told me that Mr. Green threw it in the wastebasket, but I'm sure there was no connection between that and the accident."

"Thank you. I'm taking the first possible plane to New York and I'd like to talk to you some more about your review when I arrive."

Sky told his secretary to check with all the airlines and get him on the next plane to New York. He called his staff, talked over the research necessary for his next two "Close-ups" and asked management to give him a substitute for his Friday-night newscast. He promised to be back in Los Angeles in time to deliver the Monday-night one.

It was Diana who went to meet Indiana on the plane she had wired she was taking from Europe. Wearing a new black broadtail coat and a black chiffon scarf around her red-gold hair, Diana's usually smiling face was set in a pattern of pain and sympathy. She had secured a special pass so that she and her chauffeur could drive across the field and pick up Indiana as she stepped off the plane and drive her directly home. An immigration officer was on hand to stamp her passport, and a second driver would claim her luggage and bring it after them.

As she emerged from the plane, Indiana saw Diana and the chauffeur waiting, and as she stepped off the landing stairway, she found herself enveloped in Diana's arms.

"Oh my darling. You can't imagine what your poor father and I have been through these past twenty-four hours. We are heartbroken." Tears were running down Diana's face and she was wiping them off with a little lace handkerchief.

"I've been through a nightmare, myself, Diana. I had to change planes three times. I'm desperately tired, and all I really know is that there has been an accident and that my husband is dead."

"Yes, dear."

"I still keep thinking that it can't be true."

"We must be calm, mustn't we, dear?" She took Indiana's elbow and guided her toward the car. "I have gone ahead and arranged everything so that you will suffer as little as possible. We knew that Gage would want it to be that way."

"But what really happened? That's what I have to know."

"All I can say, dear, is that Gage must have been much much more fragile than any of us realized. He and your daddy were talking over a review of some broadcast that was against McCarthy when Gage turned pale and seemed to be choking. Your daddy rushed for help and when he came back, Gage had apparently fainted or leaned out the window to get air, and toppled over the sill. It wasn't such a long drop because there was a roof, but there was nothing we could do."

"But Gage had a complete check-up recently. There was absolutely nothing wrong with his heart."

"These things often happen suddenly and inexplicably, darling."

Indiana was quiet for a moment. "Will I see Gage?"

"Oh no, darling. I don't like to tell you this, but he was too shattered. He wouldn't have wanted you to."

"But I feel I must."

"Why not discuss that tomorrow with your daddy, after you have had a few hours' sleep? We want you to be with us for a few days at the Fifth Avenue house."

"I think I'd rather be alone for a while."

"I've already picked up the things you'll need most, so do let us take care of you. It will be a perfectly beautiful service at St. Bartholomew's, with all-white flowers. We thought you would like that since you were married there."

"Oh God," said Indiana.

CHAPTER TWENTY

After the funeral, Sky had decided to walk up Park Avenue for a while. It reminded him of the day he arrived in New York from Princeton and had wandered about discovering the city for himself. Everything made him think of Gage.

When Diana had telegraphed the news to him in Hollywood, she had asked him to join the family group for the services, and the message had been quickly relayed to the Élysée Hotel in New York, where he was stopping.

As he entered the small room adjoining the altar of St. Bartholomew's, Diana had come toward him with both hands outstretched. She was all in black and her big violet eyes were swimming in tears. He had never seen her look more beautiful.

"Oh darling, it was so good of you to come all this way."

"Of course I came. Gage was not only my cousin but also my closest friend."

"You should have stayed with us instead of at the Élysée. Promise to do it the next time."

"I hardly think so, Diana." He knew that Bradshaw Green had seen him come in but had deliberately turned his back and started talking to someone else.

Indiana must have taken a sedative, Sky felt, as she was going through the scene like a spectator while Diana played the part of the grieving woman whose husband had been killed. Why am I saying "killed" and not "died"? he thought as he went across the room to Indiana.

"Oh, Sky, what a tragic way for us to meet again. I was just sitting here thinking about my little girl, Heather. She adored her father."

"I'm sure."

"They were very, very close and she cried for a long time last week when we flew off to Switzerland and she had to say good-bye to him at the airport."

Though she was pale and drawn, Sky could see that she was still young and beautiful, and not jaded or hardened by anything that had happened to her.

"I wish I could help in some way, Indi." He took both her hands in his. He saw the color come into her cheeks and, sud-denly she was just as he remembered her, with the big dark blue eyes searching his face.

Her hand was icy cold and her fingers curled desperately around his. "There's something I don't understand about this, Indi. I had dinner with Gage in Washington only several nights ago. He seemed a little tired but otherwise fine."

"I feel the same way. I don't accept it at all, but at the mo-ment I feel as if I were surrounded by a dense fog that I can't get through."

Her hand was warmer and he had felt her fingers relax. "I have to rush back to L.A. early tomorrow, Indi, but I'd like to call you in a few days after I have found out all I can, and then we can discuss the situation."

"Please do. Where are you staying?"

"At the Élysée, on Fifty-fourth Street."

Diana had come across the room to them and put her hand on Sky's arm. "The service is about to begin and your father would like to have you with him, Indiana, dear." As Indiana released Sky's hand and moved away, Diana had added, "Poor dear, she simply can't resign herself to what has happened."

"There is no resignation in Indiana's character, Diana, and I admire her for it. I must say there seems to me to be some very strange aspects to Gage's accident."

"Why don't we sit down at the service together, and leave Brad to take care of Indiana. He adores her."

"I think I'll take a seat by the door, Diana. I only have a short time in New York and I have lots of things to do."

After Sky had walked ten blocks along Park Avenue he turned and walked over to Lexington Avenue, where he had found a drugstore with a pay telephone. He called Marie Bory at the *Globe.*

"Oh Mr. Madison. I just this minute came back from the funeral. It was all so sad."

"Could you have a quick early dinner with me, Marie? I'd like to have your account of the accident before I fly back."

"Of course, Mr. Madison. I don't blame you."

He gave the name of a small East Side restaurant where they would be undisturbed, and met her there shortly after she finished work.

After he had ordered for them, he said, "Just start talking, Marie, and tell me what happened the day after your trip to Washington."

"I wrote the interview the next morning. Mr. Hale said he wanted to read it before it went through, so I sent it over to his office by a copy boy."

"Yes, go on."

"Later in the afternoon he called to say that he liked the story and suggested only a few word changes. I never saw him happier or more excited. He kept saying it was wonderful that someone at long last was going to put down McCarthy, and he was so proud that it was you."

Sky had been glad to hear that, and Marie had gone on. "My story was due to run the next day. Mr. Green got wind of it or maybe Mr. Hale told him. He was almost overconscientious, you know?"

Sky nodded as she continued. "It would probably have been better if he had just let it get through, because Mr. Green never read the whole paper."

"What then?"

"Mr. Green sent for him. Mr. Hale stopped at my desk and asked me if I had a carbon copy of the story. He looked all right but terribly nervous, and that's the last time I ever saw him."

"Did you hear anything?"

"The girls upstairs say there was a terrible rumpus in the office, and Mr. Green was shouting your name and using all the four-letter words, as he often did. Everything quieted down. Mr. Green went out to lunch and didn't come back until long after they discovered Mr. Hale."

"Was it Miss Peacock who found him?"

"Oh no, she wasn't around. It was one of the girls who went into the office. Those long windows were so wide open that she decided to close them, and then she saw the body."

"What do they say about it in the city room?"

"Some of the reporters think it was a heart attack and others believe Mr. Green harassed him so that he couldn't take it anymore."

"Any other guesses?"

"Everybody in the place knows about Mr. Green's temper and a few of them are whispering around that Mr. Green may have knocked him unconscious and walked off to lunch not bothering to make sure what happened."

She shook her head, "There's been a lot of talk."

"I thought so."

After Marie left, he stayed on and made a few more calls. Since he was quite sure no autopsy had been performed, he called Campbell's, where Gage's body had been taken, and had to put the power of both the *Globe* and UBC behind the questions he wanted answered.

"It's vital to me to find out whether Mr. Hale was wearing his glasses when his body was found."

"Just a minute." There was a long silence but he kept feeding coins into the telephone at the restaurant lounge.

Finally someone picked up the receiver again at the funeral parlor. "You were inquiring about Mr. Hale's glasses?"

"Yes."

"The empty case was found in his effects. The mortician says there's no doubt that he was not wearing his glasses at the time of the accident, otherwise splinters of glass would have been imbedded in his face."

After Sky left the restaurant he returned to his hotel and decided to call Iris Peacock and was pleased to find her listed in the telephone book.

"Miss Peacock, forgive me for disturbing you at home, but I was anxious to know about Mr. Hale's glasses. Do you know whether they were ever found?"

"Oh yes, Mr. Madison. I found them lying on the windowsill of

Mr. Green's office, as if Mr. Hale had stopped to put them there before the accident. He was always so precise, you remember."

"Thank you, Miss Peacock."

He turned from the phone and walked over to his traveling bag and took out the bottle of scotch he had brought along to help him get through the day. He poured a stiff drink, sat down and faced the fact that Gage had actually taken his own life. It was a well-known fact that anyone contemplating suicide always removed his glasses before jumping.

How, he wondered, could he have been so insensitive as not to realize that his cousin must have been close to the breaking point when they had dinner together in Washington only last week?

Gage had always been easily hurt, he remembered. When he first went to Fort Wayne, Gage had seemed like a wiser, older brother. He had been astonished when the teasing and rough talk that went on in the crowd of boys they played with rolled off his shoulders, but seemed to cut Gage to the quick.

Gage had become something of a star in the sandlot baseball team of the neighborhood boys, but his fun ended when they began calling him Four Eyes. Why he should have been wounded by the nickname when his teammates were known to each other as Fatso, Snake Hips and Runt, Sky had never understood, but Gage winced every time he heard his nickname. Soon he gave up baseball completely and began to play tennis. In those days Sky hadn't been analytical, but now he realized that Gage had never been able to take even the minor bumps that had come his way.

It was still early, but Sky was tired and had a plane to make first thing the next morning. He undressed and since he usually slept raw, slipped into bed and was just dozing off into a sound sleep when a knock on the door brought him back to consciousness.

What the hell, he wondered as he fumbled for a robe and went to the door.

Indiana was standing there. "I'm sorry, Sky, but I felt I had to talk to you before you left for California."

"I was only half asleep. Come in." He closed the door behind her. "These aren't exactly palatial quarters for entertaining, but luckily there are two chairs. Maybe you could use a drink. I'd like another myself."

"Yes, I need one." She took off the raincoat she was wearing over the black dress he had seen her in that morning, and sat down. She looked composed but still a little dazed, Sky thought.

"Luckily, I still have some ice, but the only thing I can offer you is scotch and water."

"Fine."

He went to the bathroom and came back with two glasses. "I think I can tell you one thing that you'll be relieved to hear."

"Please tell me."

"I have positive proof that Gage took his own life and that no one else is implicated."

"Thank God." She picked up her glass of scotch and drained it. "I knew that my father and Gage had had a shouting session earlier in the day and I was afraid to ask for details." She paused. "After all, he is my father."

"I said that no one was actually implicated, Indiana. Gage took off his glasses before he jumped and laid them on the window ledge, where Miss Peacock found them. That doesn't mean, though, that your father's tirade wasn't largely responsible."

"I suppose I have to share some of that responsibility. I've had some bad times, but I always manage to cope with them, myself. It's hard for me to understand someone who can't."

"I know what you mean." He filled her glass again.

"Gage had been going through psychoanalysis for years. He had mentioned wanting to kill himself several times. I thought it was just talk and his analyst told me that people who threaten suicide hardly ever go through with it."

"He loved you very much, Indi."

"I'm sorry that he did. I wasn't good for him. He could have had a happy life with another kind of girl and a less hectic job. He couldn't make last-minute decisions or anything that didn't go along with his beliefs."

"Yes, I suppose that's true."

"Once I even suggested that he switch to one of our smaller papers, where the pace was slower, but he wouldn't even listen."

"Would you have gone with him?"

She hesitated. "I don't know. I would have commuted, I suppose, but we didn't even discuss it."

"He was such a sweet fellow."

"I know, Sky, but sometimes sweetness is not enough."

"You never really loved him, did you?"

"Don't analyze me, please. At this point I don't know what I feel or ever felt." She put down her glass and stood up. "I guess I should go home and let you go back to sleep."

To his surprise, her eyes were moist.

"Why, Indi, I've never seen you cry."

"You never will. I don't believe in crying." She looked at him defiantly.

"Good girl. I'm glad you came and we had a chance for this little talk." He was always stimulated by her spirit and he went over and gently put his arms around her.

"Oh Sky." She raised her face and he kissed her. It was a long kiss and suddenly he could feel her hands untying the belt of his robe and beginning to feel him. It was such exquisite pleasure that he felt unable to move. Then the robe slipped off his shoulders.

"Shall I go home?"

"No, you little fool. You've managed to excite me again and I want you like nothing else in the world. Just take off that goddamn black dress."

She reached back and pulled the zipper. The dress fell to the floor and she stepped out of it, shedding her stockings and bra as fast as she could. In the few minutes before she reached the bed and he pulled her down on top of him, he had time to admire her strong, well-built body, which was such a good match for his.

"Do it harder, harder, much harder than you ever have before, Sky. I want to feel you all through my body." All the emotions of the day were melting into their mad desire for each other. Finally they fell asleep, but after what seemed to Sky only a few minutes he felt Indiana pressing against him and reviving him with her lips and fingers.

He had left a call for eight o'clock and when the bell rang, he sat up with a start, wondering where he was. He managed to answer the operator and then looked around to see if Indiana was still with him or whether her visit had been a macabre dream.

He knocked on the partly closed bathroom door, but she wasn't there. Besides the bed, the only signs of her visit were a damp towel and the black crepe dress, bought for the funeral, which she had stuffed into the bathroom wastebasket. She had slipped away sometime early in the morning, he figured, wearing her raincoat belted over stockings and a bra.

CHAPTER TWENTY-ONE

When Sky boarded his plane for Los Angeles that morning, his mind was in such a turmoil that he scarcely realized it when the plane was airborne. He had hoped that it would be half empty and he could have two seats by himself. He didn't even feel like saying a polite "Good morning" to a stranger, to say nothing of making polite conversation about the weather or politics.

He dropped into an aisle seat and noticed that a woman was occupying the window seat. Fortunately her face was turned away from him, so he opened his paper and hid behind the pages.

He stared at the headlines without reading them. His thoughts kept racing back to the nightmare of the past forty-eight hours. First, the news of Gage's death had come as a total shock, followed by the crowded church and the music. He hadn't been able to accept the fact that the words coming from the man in the pulpit related to his close friend and cousin or that the body under the blanket of white roses was actually Gage, but he was beginning to accept the truth now.

As he stared blindly at the photographs in his newspaper, he was filled with self-hatred at the recollection of Indiana's visit. He could still feel the touch of her lips and her eager fingers caressing him. She belonged to Gage, and how the hell could I have screwed her when his body was hardly cold? he kept thinking. I'm not sure that I ever want to see her again.

It wasn't until the stewardess stopped the bar cart beside him and asked, "Will you have a drink before luncheon, sir?" that he put down his paper and asked for a vodka and tonic.

"And will your wife have a drink, too?" The stewardess nodded at the woman in the window seat.

The laugh was so infectious that Sky looked at his seat companion for the first time as she ordered a ginger ale. She was young and fresh. Her big brown eyes were sparkling with amusement at the stewardess's gaffe, and when she laughed she showed a row of pretty, even white teeth.

She made no effort to continue the joke, but picked up her book and went on reading. Thankful for even a small diversion from his own thoughts, Sky noticed idly that she had a pleasant little profile with a nice little nose. The book in which she seemed to be totally absorbed was a medical treatise on the nervous system.

He went back to his newspaper and began reading it this time. His broadcast, usually the No. 1 interest, had been overlaid by his private life for the past few days and now he must hurry to make up for his neglect. When he finished the paper, he opened his briefcase, took out the copies of the latest newsmagazines and began skimming through them.

By the time his luncheon tray arrived, Sky had completely forgotten his neighbor until he heard her refuse coffee and ask the stewardess for tea. She must be one of the health nuts, he thought, recalling the title of the book she had been reading.

"I've been wondering if by any chance you're a medical student?" he asked, as he handed her the cup of tea.

She laughed again. "Oh no. My grandfather is a surgeon and a professor at UCLA, and I guess an interest in medicine runs in the family. I've often thought I'd like to be a pediatrician. I like working with children."

"Then why don't you go on with it?"

"My grandfather didn't advise it, and I listen to him. I think he's a great man."

"What is your grandfather's name?"

"He's Dr. Arnold MacIntosh."

"I've heard of him. Isn't he an advocate of the controversial new heart surgery?"

"Yes, he believes that it's not any more difficult or dangerous than many other kinds of operations and that once it is perfected, it will save many lives."

"I think I might like to meet your grandfather. How do I reach him outside of the university?"

"Do you have a heart condition yourself?"

"Fortunately, no, but I was thinking of the subject as a possible feature on TV."

"So you work in TV? I know my grandfather would be interested in any kind of exposé of heart surgery. Just a minute and I'll tell you where we live." She fumbled in her handbag for a notebook and pen.

"So you're a California girl?"

"No, not that I don't like it there, but my home state is Maine. I just spend a few weeks each year with my grandparents."

As he took the paper, he saw that it had been torn from a notepad. It had her name printed across the top. It was Holly Hastings. It quite suits her. She had a kind of Christmas giving quality, he thought, as he folded the paper and placed it into his wallet.

Sky was beginning to relax, and as soon as his tray was taken away he fell asleep. The stewardess's voice announcing that their plane had started its descent into Los Angeles International Airport wakened him. He stirred and started to collect his possessions, he saw that his neighbor was still immersed in her book and he was grateful that she hadn't been a talkative type.

When she finally closed her book and dropped it into a tote bag, Sky turned to her. "My name is Schuyler Madison and I have a weekly feature program on UBC. Maybe you'll be good enough to alert your grandfather that I'm going to call."

"You're Schuyler Madison?"

She burst out laughing so thoroughly that Sky felt himself smiling, too. "What's so damn funny about my name?"

"It's just that I've known you for a long time."

"I'm afraid you'll have to brief me on when and where."

"Naturally you wouldn't remember. I was about ten years old, and it was my first trip to the West Coast. I was standing in front of Grauman's Chinese. I ran up to you and asked you for your autograph as you were going into a movie opening with some pretty blonde."

"I have a vague recollection of a cute kid, and I remember well that I was flattered."

She was still laughing. "You don't know how funny it is. I even had one of those kiddie crushes on you and had a picture of you that I cut out of a magazine framed and on the table beside my bed."

She looked at him closely. "Here we are on a plane fifteen years later and I don't even recognize you."

"That was the first time anyone ever asked me for my autograph." He laughed. "If I'd had a few more fans in those days, it might have been helpful."

Sky stood up and moved into the aisle. She followed. Once in the Los Angeles airport, he soon lost Holly Hastings in the crowd. He was in a hurry to reach his office and in no mood to help anyone, even the first girl who had asked him for his autograph.

At his office the next morning, Sky told his secretary to call Mr. Garson. "Ask him if he can come by the office late this afternoon and have dinner with me."

"Yes, Mr. Madison. He called while you were in New York and wanted me to let him know when you returned."

When Sidney arrived at his UBC office that evening, Sky said, "I think I'm suffering from too much emotion and too little sleep. I figure I need a good dinner at Chasen's with you, and then a lot of sleep."

"I'm game for the dinner, but what have you got on your mind?"

"I think it's time for us to make a last try at getting *The Power and the Glory* before the public."

"Why not? It would be great on TV and with your present connection it should be a snap."

"Let's try."

"Great idea. Come on down to the beach this weekend and we can look over the script with the idea of subdividing it for a serial. But what has brought this on?"

At dinner, Sky told him the whole story of Gage's death, and as Sky talked, he began to feel more anger for Bradshaw Green.

"Do we add this on to the list of his sins?" Sidney asked.

"I think not. It's a little too personal with me. I think we stand on what we've already done."

That weekend at the beach, Sidney took the manuscript out of

his desk and they began to go over it. I'd completely forgotten
how good it is, Sky thought. It's more truth than melodrama, and
now that the craze for war stories is over, I think the public will
eat it up. "I'm sure we can sell it to UBC, but let's see how we
can carve it up into at least a four-part serial," he said.

The story was easy to subdivide into sections. They were
working along happily Sunday morning when Sky suddenly
swung around from his typewriter. "Damn it all. What an idiot I
am. We'll sell it as a movie and TV can have it later."

"Sky, you seem to forget that this script has been turned down
by every studio in town."

"O.K., Sid, but not since Bradshaw Green sold all his stock at
Olympia, and Dorothy Darrow became Mrs. B. B. Balzer."

"I follow your reasoning, my friend, but when did these miraculous changes come about?"

"I talked to her a short time ago, and she was suggesting that I
name my night for coming to dinner."

"Then name the night, but do you think it will work?"

"I do for the simple fact that both Dorothy and her mother
know the Bradshaw Green story backward. Besides, B.B. and I
always got on, though I didn't become one of his stars."

"If he still turns it down, I assume we'll go back to UBC with
it." Then, turning to Marcia, "But for God's sake, Marcia, don't
give up your job at the dress shop."

"Don't worry, Sid. I've long since stopped being a dreamer,"
she said, turning from the chicken salad she was making for their
luncheon.

"Marcia, you can make plans to buy out the shop if you want.
This time I smell money in the air," Sky said.

"I'd never buy out a dress shop. It's too chancey. All I want is
a regular cleaning girl. God, how I hate to scrub bathrooms."

The next week Sky called Dorothy Darrow and made a date to
have dinner with them. "We usually dress for dinner, but there'll
be just us this time, so don't bother," she said rather grandly.

The white-pillared entrance of the Balzer home was right on
one of the steep Bel Air roads, but behind it, B.B. had enough
acreage to play at being a farmer. While they waited for Dorothy
to come downstairs, he showed Sky his vegetable and flower gardens, for both of which he had installed irrigation.

"How do you like my new tea gown?" Dorothy wanted to know when she finally appeared. It was sheer and white with lots of ruffles and a little ruffle-edged train that rippled after her.

"It's very becoming to you, Dottie. I almost feel as if I've seen it before," Sky said.

"You have. Irene Dunne wore it in her last movie with Charles Boyer."

"Of course. I remember."

"I got it from the Wardrobe Department at the studio. I borrow a lot of my clothes from there."

Between exclaiming over their happiness and praising their fresh vegetables and fruit, Sky managed to introduce the subject of the movie script. "The main character is a ruthless newspaper tycoon."

"Someone like Bradshaw Green?" cried Dorothy.

"Somewhat, but of course not enough to be libelous."

"I simply adore it," Dorothy said when he had very briefly outlined the story. "It's Bradshaw Green, all right. He could be a horror but he could be pretty sweet, too."

"What do you mean, Dottie?" B. B. Balzer interrupted.

"Darling, I was just thinking of when I was a little girl. One Christmas when I was about three or four, he came in bringing me a doll as big as I was."

"Didn't he ever fight with your mother?" asked Sky.

"Oh sure. He used to yell and carry on, but my mother didn't pay any attention."

"How could she take it?"

Dorothy laughed. "She knew all the time he would send her something gorgeous the next day. Once I remember hearing her say, 'No more flowers. My florist is Cartier.'"

Later, as Sky started to leave, B.B. told him to send the script to the studio, but Sky couldn't tell whether he was genuinely interested or only wanted to please his new wife.

Sky had the script delivered the next day and decided to wait two weeks before he began needling Olympia for a reaction.

At the end of the two weeks, he made up his mind to ask B.B. for an answer, and if it was "no" to take the script to UBC. Almost instantly B.B.'s male secretary was on the wire and his voice sounded gloomy. "Mr. Balzer said he won't have an answer for at least another month. There are a lot of problems and he's not sure if the whole idea is feasible. He'll contact you when he's made a decision."

CHAPTER TWENTY-TWO

To assemble the perfect panel of medical experts on the subject of open-heart surgery was more difficult than Sky had thought it would be. Some of the doctors were away and others were unwilling to take one side or the other. It was two weeks since he had called on Dr. MacIntosh to discuss the group he had assembled.

When he called again Holly Hastings answered the telephone. "Sorry, my grandfather isn't at home, and I don't know where you can find him today."

"May I leave a message?"

"Of course, I'm just on my way to play tennis, but I'll leave it on his desk. He'll call you."

He had a sudden vision of her in a white dress with the scarf tied around her head and pretty, suntanned legs showing as she ran across the court. "Thanks. You must be quite a player. I remember you were just finishing a set when I came out to talk to your grandfather."

"Yes, I like it. Do you play?"

"When I have time, but that doesn't happen too often."

"Would you like to play here some afternoon?"

"Yes, I would."

"I need a partner for tomorrow afternoon, but I'm sure that's not giving you enough notice."

"I think I can arrange it, for at least two hours. I need exercise and some kind of relief from tension." It might even be killing two birds with one stone, since I may get a chance to talk to Dr. MacIntosh at the same time, he told himself.

The young couple Holly had invited turned out to be Joan and Peter Albert, just recently married and in Holly's age group, which Sky guessed must be the early twenties. Though he was ten years older, he was still the most expert player of the four. He and Holly won two quick sets and lost only two games in the third. He noticed that she had a good serve and a nice backhand stroke, but let him do most of the strenuous work, which he enjoyed. She's very feminine and damned pretty, he thought.

When the couple left, after making a date for a repeat match on their own court, Sky said, "You play very well, Holly. Want to try singles with me?"

She hesitated a minute before she said, "Yes, let's."

She put up a good fight, but he won the set easily. He would have liked to go on playing, but she left the court and dropped down on the grass under one of the big trees. "If you have enough energy, there's a little refrigerator over there in one of the dressing rooms. Why don't you get us some Coke or ginger ale and pour it over ice."

As he poured the drinks, he thought of the scene in Nora's poolhouse and how violently he had wanted her the first time he had made love to her there. Holly was as different from Nora as her ginger ale was from Nora's favorite Dom Perignon. He was smiling at himself as he looked out the dressing-room window and saw Holly sitting cross-legged on the grass like a little girl, with the sunshine and leaves making a pattern on her hair. She didn't attract him physically, but he was enjoying her wholesomeness. It reminded him of Fort Wayne and the nice girls he and Gage had sometimes taken to Saturday-night dances at the country club.

He handed her the glass and sat down beside her on the grass. "I like the way your hair swings with you, whether you're serving or volleying."

"Do you? I wear it this way because it makes life simpler." She ran her hand through her hair. "I can't stand beauty salons, and all that business of sitting under a drier and being combed out. I wash my own hair and let it dry in the sunshine."

It was soft and shiny, he saw, and as she smiled he noticed

again the small, even teeth, which were like a baby's. "You know you could become a crack player if you wanted to. Your form is perfect, but you never try for long shots."

"Don't I? I suppose it's instinctive. I can't remember it, but when I was a baby I had rheumatic fever." She frowned. "My family was terribly careful about everything I did, and I was kept out of all the rough sports like basketball. I hated it."

"You've grown up to be a lovely, healthy girl."

"Oh yes, I've outgrown whatever it was, though my grandfather is still babying me."

"I don't blame him. How old are you, Holly?"

"I'm almost twenty-five."

"You look almost eighteen, and you make me feel like a very old man."

"Come on, old man. I'll race you up the hill, where I can see Granddaddy is waiting for you." She sprang up and started running, and he followed her at a more leisurely pace.

The next week he and Holly played the return tennis match with Joan and Peter Albert, and once more Sky's mind went back to the peaceful relationships that had seemed so easy and so permanent in the Fort Wayne days.

The Alberts' small, charming house, part of which was cantilevered over the edge of one of the Beverly Hills canyons, had been photographed for *House and Garden* recently as an example of innovative contemporary architecture on a small scale. It included a model kitchen, from which Joan produced a dinner concocted from a *House and Garden* recipe. Though he felt a little like a character in a slick-magazine feature, Sky felt himself relaxing and losing some of the weariness that he had built around himself during the past year.

Playing tennis with Holly and her friends or just Holly, soon became a regular addition to his life. He often went to the MacIntosh home for two hours in the late afternoon, sometimes staying for supper if Holly had no other date. He realized that she was the therapy he needed, but he had no curiosity to know what she did when he wasn't around, or to make their relationship more personal.

They had a long, specially good singles one afternoon and as they sat on the grass drinking their ginger ale, Sky felt a warm surge of gratitude and affection. "Holly, if you're not doing anything special tonight, will you have dinner with me?"

"I'd like that."

"Then I'll go home and change and be back for you in an hour." He picked up his racquet. "I want to take you to a little French bistro in Santa Monica that I like. It's right close to the water."

Jay's at the beach was crowded that night, but the *maître d'* bustled forward to greet them when he recognized Sky. "Good evening. Mr. Madison. It's a pleasure to have you with us this evening. I've saved you this nice corner table overlooking the water."

"Thank you. That will be perfect, and I think we'll start with a bottle of Soave, nice and cold."

"I never miss your TV program, Mr. Madison. Sometimes I'm late getting to work on Thursday evenings but I always enjoy them so much."

"That's what I like to hear."

As they sat down, Holly said, "I see you're a well-known man."

"I'm well known here on the Pacific Coast, perhaps, but so far I haven't had any luck syndicating myself east of the Rockies." He looked up and smiled. "However, I hope to someday, and then I'll be better known and better paid."

"Sky, I've seen a lot of you lately, but we've talked about tennis mostly." Holly's eyes were shining. "I guess this is our first date."

Sky picked up his glass of wine. "Here's to our first date, and to lots more of them."

"I don't know about that, Sky."

"What do you mean?"

"You know I'm just a visitor, and I'll have to be going home next week. I've stayed much longer now than I expected."

"Don't say that, Holly. You've been so good for me." He leaned across the table and took her hand. "I met you just at a time when I needed to believe that someone could be good, happy and uncomplicated, and you're all those things."

"I'm not sure I am, but I'm glad I've been helpful."

"'Helpful' is too drab a word to express your qualities." He suddenly became serious. "I was confused and miserable and had to use a sleeping pill every night to get any rest, but since our tennis games started everything seems to have smoothed out."

"I'm glad." Holly looked as happy as a child with a birthday present.

"Now I fall asleep the minute my head touches the pillow and wake up in the morning feeling refreshed."

"You make me sound like some kind of new remedy. Maybe I should advertise myself and make a fortune."

"I'm only trying to tell you that I hate the thought of your going home."

"So do I in a way. I've enjoyed the tennis, too, but I love my home in Maine."

"What is it like?"

"It's a rambling, old-fashioned farmhouse on top of a hill that we've turned into an apple orchard. It slopes right down to the sea."

"It sounds ideal."

"Maybe you'll come to visit someday."

"Not for a while, I guess. I'm pretty much involved here, not only with my TV program, but also with an old movie script I wrote with a friend and have never been able to get produced."

"Why on earth couldn't you get it produced?"

"It's too long and tangled a story to tell you tonight, but sometime I will."

As they left the little bistro, Holly said, "You know, I've been coming to Los Angeles for years, but I've never been here in Santa Monica in the evening before."

"There are probably a lot of places you've never seen. Don't go back to Maine just now, Holly, and I'll give you the grand tour of the whole coastline." He turned the car off Sunset and it began climbing Laurel Canyon Road.

"What are you going to show me now?"

"Lookout Mountain. Don't tell me you've never seen it."

"This will be another first."

"Then you're in for a big surprise."

They came to the top of the mountain. Several cars were already parked on the plateau that had been cleared. Sky drove to the split-rail fence and turned off the car's motor. Spread out below them were the thousands of lights of Hollywood, Los Angeles and Santa Monica in the far distance.

"How beautiful," Holly exclaimed. "It's really magical."

"It's a fantastic sight but you can't help thinking of all the turmoil that's going on down there, and from here everything looks so quiet and peaceful."

"It's really as if you were looking down from heaven," she said.

"I thought you might like it. I used to drive up here by myself when I first came to Hollywood. I suppose I felt it gave me some kind of soothing perspective when I was discouraged, which was often in those days."

"Are you sorry that you didn't go on with your movie career?"

"At the time it was a bitter disappointment, but now I keep thanking God that it didn't work out, even though I'm still trying to make it to the big time."

"I wonder what problems the people in these other cars are working out, and whether this beautiful scene is helping them."

He glanced across the area at the quiet cars. "They may be making love. This is also a favorite spot for lovers."

"Then why are we just sitting here looking at the lights?"

"You're an adorable girl, Holly, and I've become very fond of you." He leaned over and kissed her and, to his surprise, her lips clung to his and he realized that she wanted more. He kissed her again and then started the car. "I'm going to miss you, Holly. Can't you arrange to stay a little longer?"

"Not really. My mother is in politics. She needs my help."

"Don't you have brothers or sisters who can do that?"

"Just a brother, but he's still at school; besides, I'm chairman of a Junior League benefit this year, which is only a few weeks off."

"I'm sure your grandparents will be lonely without you, too." He released one hand from the steering wheel and reached for hers.

"They realize I must go home." She held his hand with both of hers. "I've never stayed so long before and I think you have a little to do with that."

After he had delivered Holly at the MacIntosh home Sky began to think seriously about Holly for the first time. Her kiss had surprised him. I should have realized this was happening. She cares for me quite a lot, and if I were in the mood for marriage, it could be right. At the moment, though, I mustn't let myself get involved, he thought.

CHAPTER TWENTY-THREE

Sky drove Holly to the airport when she left for Maine a few days later. He gave her a tote bag with three just-published books. "Two of them are biographies, and I think you will like them."

"I'm sure I will."

"When you come back next summer, my friend Sidney and I may be in the midst of seeing our movie produced. It will be exciting."

"Will it be as much fun as our tennis?"

He laughed. "I'm going to miss those games, Holly."

The first call for the plane to Boston was coming over the loudspeaker and he bent down to kiss her good-bye. "Don't pick up your seatmate on the plane this time, Holly, dear."

She laughed. "What a nerve to make me believe I was the one who did the picking up." She turned away but he could see there were tears in her eyes. He stood and waved and then she was gone.

Sky drove back feeling slightly depressed and alone. He was totally free again, but suddenly the prospect looked a little bleak. When he reached Beverly Hills, he found himself driving slowly, looking at the houses and wondering what the lives of the people inside were like. The thought came to him that it might be pleasant if, instead of going to his office, he were going to a house. Holly would be around to open the door, looking at him the way she often did, as if he were the most marvelous most exciting person in the world, and their children would come running to greet him. He suddenly realized he had always wanted to be a father.

When he reached his office his secretary had gone home but Sidney was sitting in the anteroom. "Am I ever glad to see you, Sid. How about having dinner with me?"

"Good enough. I've been pacing up and down the beach waiting for a call."

"If there were any news, you'd have heard about it. The last word was ambivalent, but more discouraging than good. It's one of those 'I'll call you, don't call me' situations."

"Rough. I had real hopes this time. So what else has been keeping you busy?"

"A funny thing happened. I was coming back from my cousin's funeral in a damnable mood, and I met the most charming girl on the plane."

"A quick lay?"

"Not that kind of thing at all. She's rather quiet, not especially sexy but very sweet and easygoing."

"A good looker?"

"Not beautiful but cute and appealing. I've had a good time with her, playing tennis and drinking ginger ale."

"Girls like that are the most dangerous kind. They sneak up on you."

"It's the only time I've ever felt I might like to put down an anchor and get married."

"Don't let me talk you out of it. I make jokes all the time about Marcia, but I'd be lonely as hell without her."

"Oh well, there's no danger now. She's gone back home to Maine and won't come back again until next summer."

"For God's sake, then, concentrate on this script of ours. I read it over again the other night and I still think it could make us millions."

"Call me every day then, and bug me about it. As a start I'll call Dottie and take her to lunch."

Sky's secretary soon learned to expect Sidney's morning call and to say, "No word yet, but Mr. Madison is doing everything he can." She was in the midst of her little speech for the sixth time when Sky called to her from his office, "Tell him to hold on. Olympia is on my private line."

In a few minutes Sky went on the wire to Sidney. "Well, what

do you know? They want to see me at Olympia tomorrow morning."

"You mean to say it looks as if there is still interest there?" Sidney's voice sounded excited.

"You know damn well if there weren't, they would have just
sent us a chilly, no-dice note."

When Sky arrived at Olympia the next morning he found B.B.
in an agreeable mood. "Yes, I like the script. It's got a lot of suspense, and we haven't had many suspense movies lately."

"Then you think it has possibilities?"

"Just last year the U. S. Government made a long-overdue decision that films are part of the press. All the boards of censors
have finally phased out and there's a lot more freedom in producing off-beat stories than there used to be." Sky was hoping he'd
get to the point but B.B. went on talking. "On the other hand, I
don't have the freedom I used to have back in the forties, when I
was planning to make you a romantic young star overnight."

"How does it work then?"

"I'm trying to find you a producer, then Olympia will agree to
release the film."

"Have you a producer in mind?"

"Actually, I think I've already found one. Walter Cameron
read the script and he's enthusiastic. Thinks it can be a winner."

"Great."

"He says there won't be any trouble finding financing if we get
the right stars signed up. The backers always want the big names
for security."

"Any ones in mind?"

"Actually, Cameron has already been thinking about it, and he
would like to get Edward G. Robinson for the publisher."

"Terrific. Is there any chance?"

"Cameron has contacted his agent. It seems he may be available and is anxious to read the script. Dorothy read it last night
and is fascinated by it, and naturally she wants to play the part
of her mother, Gaby De Lyn."

"It would be very dramatic to have her as Gaby. I'd like to talk
to her someday about her mother."

"She would like that, too. Just the other night she told me the
whole story of her mother and Bradshaw Green."

Sky hurried back to his office to relay the good news to Sidney. That afternoon, as Sky sat at his desk thinking of Gage and Bradshaw Green, Sky realized that the production of the film was something he had to do for Gage's memory.

CHAPTER TWENTY-FOUR

Diana and Bradshaw Green were giving a dinner for the Duke and Duchess of Windsor. Bradshaw had made up his mind to take over the entire Le Pavillon restaurant, until Diana had said, "I don't think so, Brad. You have one of the most beautiful town houses on Fifth Avenue"—looking around the drawing room where they were sitting—"And you hardly ever use it except for entertaining business friends."

"What's so wrong about that?"

"They're so wrapped up in figures and percentages that they never look around. If they did, they wouldn't be able to tell whether they were sitting on a Louis XV or a Regency chair."

"I don't know if I could, either, my dear, but have it your own way." He squirmed in one of the French chairs that he had always found uncomfortable.

"The mood of the party should be very romantic and old-fashioned. I want it to be totally different from anything my dear former King and Wallis have been to in New York this year."

"I leave everything in your hands, my love."

"We will have lots of palms, and I want delicate food, but more courses than usual. There will be enchanting music in the background." Her eyes were shining as she imagined the scene.

"For a beautiful woman, you have an extraordinary talent for organization."

"Do you really think so? I only wish Indiana agreed with you. I often longed to have just a teeny-weeny chance to work with her on the women's section of the paper."

"For God's sake, Diana, leave the paper to my daughter. She

has loved it since she was a baby, and she has needed it more recently."

"Of course, Brad. Indiana has been wonderfully successful at starting a new life for herself over the past year. I admire her deeply, though I've never felt that she cared for me as much as I care for her."

"Indiana will be at the party, of course?"

"Naturally. I plan to have the Duke next to me, and Indiana on his other side. We'll have six round tables of ten in the dining room."

"I want to invite Tom Malone and his wife."

"Who, for heaven's sake, who are they?"

"He's important to me, besides being a good friend. The typographers' union is threatening to strike and he's one of the influential members."

"Of course, I remember him, darling. He's absolutely charming, but do you think he and his wife will feel happy in this group? They won't know anyone and it always hurts me to see people looking uncomfortable and unhappy."

"As of now, it's a must, Diana." He banged his fist on the table and looked at her sternly. "Of course, I know you'll be glad if they can't come."

"How can you say that, Brad? You know it's only that I care so much about my guests being congenial." She leaned over and patted his cheek.

The night of the dinner Indiana arrived with Colonel Serge Obolensky, whom Diana had chosen as her escort because he was an old friend of the Duke of Windsor. As she gave her white-silk cape to the maid, Indiana thought, I have to hand it to Diana for making this old barn of a house look like a home. The soft, pink glow of the lights seemed to bring out the patina of Diana's fine old French furniture, many of the pieces with museum quality. From the scented candles that had been burning all afternoon, the whole place was fragrant.

Diana, in black velvet with a deep, heart-shaped décolletage, seemed to fit perfectly into the scene.

The guests had all been asked to assemble before the Duke and Duchess, and when they arrived Indiana liked them both instantly. The Duke had a nice twinkle and the Duchess was more fragile-looking than she had expected. She was wearing a short evening dress that Indiana realized was the last word from Paris, and a sapphire necklace the same color as her eyes.

"What a beautiful home you have, Mr. Green," Indiana heard the Duchess say. "You know, homes are my hobby and I adore giving parties, making out the menus and choosing the china to use."

Indiana could see at once that her father had succumbed to the Duchess' much-talked-about spell. When Indiana reached her table she found herself seated beside the Duke and a man she didn't know. She had noticed him with his wife, looking rather lost among close friends of the Duke and Duchess like Edith Baker, Milton Holden and Susie Gardner, and names in the news like the young Senator John F. Kennedy and his wife, Jacqueline.

Since Indiana saw Diana leaning toward the Duke, with her diamond hairpins sparkling in the candlelight, she turned toward the stranger. "I'm your host's daughter, Indiana."

"I'm Tom Malone, a friend of his."

"My mother was Irish, you know. I like the Irish, and I always get along with them."

"That makes two of us. Actually, I kind of hoped I'd run into you here."

She smiled. "Really." She looked closely at him for the first time, and found his heavy, dark eyebrows and thick, graying hair attractive in a rugged kind of way.

"I sure do admire what you've done with that paper of yours and your dad's. My wife can't wait to get ahold of the *Globe* every morning."

"That's good. I've got a lot of talented people working for me."

"I don't know if you care, but you've got a lot of men cheering for you down in the basement, where they set the type and run the presses."

"I don't write anything, you know. I haven't any talent at all." Indiana liked the admiration in his eyes, and felt it was sincere.

"You sure do work hard, they say. I guess you get down there sometimes to make sure everything is the way you want it, and that's more than Brad Green does these days."

"I've always been fascinated with the actual putting together of a newspaper."

"So is my wife."

"Be sure I meet her when we get up from the table." At this point, she saw the Duke was turning toward her, and Diana was starting to talk with Laurence Brooke, the distinguished Canadian publisher who had recently purchased one of Bradshaw Green's U.S. magazines.

Indiana had expected the Duke to be reserved and formal. She was happy to find him quite the reverse, almost boyish-looking, with a beguiling smile and quick sense of humor.

"How does it feel to find yourself always at the top of any list of the world's best-dressed men? Is it a big bore or responsibility?" she asked.

He laughed. "I find it ridiculous. I've always been independent about what I wear. I've sometimes put unexpected things together and the first thing I know the odd combination has become a fad."

"Does the Duchess ever buy you a necktie that you absolutely detest?"

"She knows better than to buy me any ties at all. On the contrary, I'm always having my say about the dresses she wears."

"She has impeccable taste."

"Yes she does, but I like her in some colors more than others."

"She looks lovely this evening," Indiana glanced toward the Duchess, who seemed to be absorbed in talking to her father.

"She always looks lovely, but tonight's dress is one of my favorites. Blue is wonderful for her but never black. She's too small-boned to carry it off."

Before Diana claimed him again, Indiana and the Duke agreed on many subjects, including horses, dogs, and French cooking. When Indiana talked to the Duchess later, Indiana found her equally warm and very interested in the *Globe* and the attention being given to women on the paper.

After dinner, a little group of five musicians played Viennese waltzes. Serge Obolensky, who had been a dashing young man at the Czar's court and was still quite handsome, danced sedately with the Duchess and then swung Indiana around on the marble floor of the foyer.

"The Duchess is too tiny for me. I'm happier when I have a girl like you in my arms," he said. He was still something of a flirt, and ever since Gage's death had been one of Indiana's escorts.

Lincoln LaPorte was standing by a palm and watching the dancers with a sardonic smile. Indiana went over to him. "Are you enjoying the evening, Lincoln?"

"That Diana. And when I think it was I who introduced her to Bradshaw Green."

"What has she done to you?"

"In the first place, I naturally assumed this dinner was my exclusive story, and who should I see when I come in the door but that *World-Telegram* columnist, Joseph X. Dever. I don't know what the *X* stands for."

"Perhaps she told him to come but not to write."

"Of course he'll write. He'd be a fool not to. The guest list is pretty sensational, but guess who I was sitting next to? The only nobody in the place, a Mrs. Malone. While Joan Fontaine was giving Joe Dever enough of an earful for a week's columns, Mrs. Malone was confiding that she has an eight-year-old son who reads backward."

"I sat next to Tom Malone, but I liked him. He's a labor leader, I believe."

"Nothing is more boring to me than Labor with a capital *L*. And don't worry. I plan to get even with Diana somehow."

"I'm sure she'll manage to talk you out of it."

"Don't be too sure. Indiana, I would ask you to dance, but it isn't one of my talents. While I think of it, did you read the little tidbit about your father in Hedda Hopper's column this morning?"

"I didn't have time to read the *Daily News* today."

"It seems that your old friend Schuyler Madison and your father are at it again. Madison and some other fellow have written a blockbuster of a movie that Olympia is about to release. Naturally, it doesn't call him by name, but the hero is a certain publisher who does all kinds of uncouth things like pushing a fellow off the deck of an ocean liner and maybe strangling his wife."

"Strangling his wife?" Indiana looked puzzled.

"Not Diana, though I wouldn't mind if he did that right at this minute."

"What else did Hedda have to say?"

"The story was about two paragraphs in her column. She said everyone who has managed to see a preview says it's the film of the year and Edward G. Robinson will be up for an Oscar for his performance."

"This must be the script Sky was working on at least fifteen years ago when he was in Hollywood before the war."

"I guess nobody has told your father about it and he hasn't read Hedda yet."

As she turned away from Lincoln for a second, she saw Tom Malone coming toward her. She found herself admiring his powerful shoulders and his easy stride.

"Will you dance with me, Mrs. Hale?"

"Of course. I'd love to." She turned back to Lincoln. "Excuse me, dear."

Malone guided her toward the marble foyer where the music was playing. "I like to waltz."

"So do I."

He put his arm around her and they began to dance. As he held her close, Indiana felt herself responding to her partner. "You told me that you like to waltz, but not that you're a great dancer."

"We move to the same rhythm. I've watched you dancing all evening."

When the music stopped he led her to a corner of the drawing room that had been deserted by most of the guests. "Now sit here and let me find a waiter with two glasses of champagne."

"On the rocks, please. I like lots of ice."

"With champagne? That's a new one on me."

In a few minutes he came back with the two glasses, handed her one and sat down beside her. "You're not at all what I expected, Mrs. Hale."

"Call me Indiana, if you like. Even the pressmen in the composing room do."

"No wonder. It's a good name."

"How do you mean?"

"Well, it sounds solid and almost pioneer early American."

"I've often thought in some previous life I was a pioneer woman. I could have taken it."

"I can see that you still have that spirit in you, but underneath all the glamourous window dressing."

She smiled. "Honestly, I don't have time to be glamourous."

"That's what makes you so much more interesting than any woman in the room. I find you a warm, beautiful woman, Indiana."

"Most men don't."

"They are probably afraid of you. You have a lot of potential power behind you, but I'm a bold character who speaks his mind."

She laughed. "A real bastard, I've heard my father say."

"It's the pot calling the kettle black, but we respect each other."

"You do like Daddy, don't you?"

"We have our differences, but I admire his ruthlessness when it comes to getting what he wants. Are you like that?"

"I'm not sure." She suddenly thought of how tenaciously she had clung to the image of Sky and she wished with all her heart that he was sitting beside her this very minute.

"Thank God you inherited your beautiful Irish looks from your mother. Let's dance again."

In his arms on the dance floor she was aware of Tom Malone's strength again. I suppose most girls would like to go to bed with this man, she thought, but he doesn't turn me on, although I find him attractive.

When the music stopped she looked up and saw Diana glaring at her. "My stepmother is beckoning me. I'm afraid I must go."

"Too bad. There are so many things I'd like to talk to you about."

"It's been fun anyway, and I've enjoyed it."

He took her hand, "Indiana, don't think for a moment that you won't see me again."

It's probably just polite party talk, but I would like to see him again, she thought, as she turned to talk to Diana, who was frowning and shaking her head.

"Indiana, I'm sure somebody has told you about this absolutely scurrilous movie that our mutual friend, Sky, has perpetrated about your father."

"Yes, Lincoln did say something about it."

"We must put a stop to it immediately. Of course, Brad will sue him for all he's worth and the studio, too, but once the film is released, the harm will be done."

"Yes, I suppose it's like retractions. People are always complaining that they appear in tiny print and no one ever sees them."

"Oh dear. Brad's going to hear of this any minute now, and will be in the most dreadful rage."

"I'm sure you can cope with anything, Diana. It was a beautiful party."

"Thank you, dear."

"Certainly the most perfect one ever given in this house. Daddy should be in a wonderful mood." She turned, "Look at him now, laughing with Laurence Brooke."

"Oh yes. Isn't Larry Brooke a dear? I put him next to me at dinner and found him such an intelligent man, and so witty."

After the Windsors left, Serge Obolensky took Indiana home to the little penthouse into which she moved after Gage's death. She had rented the new house on Long Island, in which they had never lived, and sold the apartment her father had given her when they were married. Better start fresh, in an entirely new scene, she had thought.

It was a moderate-size Fifth Avenue apartment with all the main rooms facing the park. There was a small open terrace and in pleasant weather she spent her time there when she was at home.

The transition of living alone hadn't been too painful. She had retreated to Switzerland for a month following Gage's death to be near Heather, then returned to her work with more concentration than ever. Timmy Phipps, just over his second divorce, was the first to call for a date. Altogether it was not so different from the life she led before she was married, except for the number of people who were now interested in what she and the paper could do for them.

The morning after the party for the Duke and Duchess of

Windsor, Indiana woke feeling happy without quite knowing why. Every detail of the previous night seemed beautiful in retrospect and she laughed out loud when she thought of Diana's disapproving face, with the corners of her mouth turned down, while she watched her dancing with Tom Malone.

The sound of the telephone on her bedside table brought Indiana back to reality. It was Diana's voice. "We simply must do something to stop that dreadful film, Indiana."

"What can we do?"

"You will have to get in touch with Sky."

"I haven't talked with him since last year at the time of the funeral, and I certainly have no power to influence him even if I wanted to."

"But you must try, Indiana. You know Sky's and my friendship was just passing the time for both of us, but he has been very cool to me ever since I married Brad." She hesitated for a moment, "Of course there may be a wee bit of jealousy on his part that has brought this on, and this makes me completely helpless."

"I think the motives date back farther than that, Diana, so I suggest that you make the call."

"Oh dear. Then I'll have to go to California, I suppose. I'll call you later, darling," and hung up the receiver.

Indiana lay back against the pillows and thought of her last meeting with Sky in his hotel room. For a long time afterward she had expected to hear from him. Even in Switzerland she called home regularly to see if there had been any mail or messages fron California. After a month she had stopped hoping and faced the fact that perhaps her brazenness had been repulsive to him. Even now she fought a strong impulse to call him not to ask him to stop the film, which would be ridiculous, but to say she was glad it was going to be shown and that his writing effort had succeeded.

When the maid brought in her breakfast tray she said, "Miss Indiana, there are some flowers outside, but I don't think you're going to like them."

"Why not, Candida? Bring them in."

"They're very spiky, and didn't even come in a box."

Candida disappeared and returned in a few minutes carrying an armful of yellow gladiolus.

Even before she looked at the card Indiana was sure they had come from Tom Malone. She would send him a note of thanks and invite him and his wife for a drink. He could be a valuable asset someday in her dealings with the labor unions and, whether or not it was last night's champagne, she had liked him.

Before she left for the office that morning he called her. "I didn't think it was smart to call you at your office, but I want to see you again. When can you have lunch or dinner with me?"

"I can't say without looking at my calendar but I know I'm pretty much tied up now."

"Come on, Indiana. We had a good time dancing together last night. It's urgent for me to see you again, and I'm going to pester you until you set a date."

While he was talking she was thinking that it would be foolish for them to be seen together at a club or restaurant where they would be recognized. "If it's urgent, as you say, I do know that I planned to go to the Metropolitan Museum Thursday. We could meet for luncheon in the cafe."

"Sounds rather chilly, but I'm game."

"Then meet me at the door of the cafe at half-past twelve."

He was there when she arrived. As they picked up their trays and walked along the cafeteria counter, she was glad to see that the tables seemed to be filled with either elderly ladies or students.

They found a table to themselves, and began chattering about the weather and the newspaper headlines.

"You said you had something urgent to say to me, didn't you?" she said finally.

"I lied to you. I just had to see you. I haven't thought of anything else but you since the party."

"That's very flattering."

"To hell with flattery. All the time I was growing up in Jersey City, I dreamed about a certain kind of woman, and no matter how many girls I laid." He took out his pocket handkerchief and wiped his forehead. "Excuse me, I meant dated, I was still looking for that ideal woman."

"And then you met your wife."

"Let's leave her out of the picture. When I came into your father's house and saw you, it was like somebody had hit me with a ton of bricks."

"You've got quite a line, Tom."

"Don't kid me, Indiana."

"I'm not. Shall we go upstairs and look at the paintings?"

"I don't know hill or beans about art. I'm afraid you'll have to teach me."

"Why not?" She stood and picked up her bag.

"I don't even know what kind of flowers to send you. I'm sure they were all wrong."

"Don't be silly. I liked them very much, and I've changed my mind about seeing the paintings. Let's walk along Fifth Avenue for a while."

They walked down the steps of the museum and turned right. They were silent for a few minutes. Tom Malone was wondering what subjects would interest her. Finally he said, "What's your opinion of television, Indiana?"

"Unfortunately TV can cover spot news faster and better than we can. I think television is becoming more and more a threat to our newspapers."

"You're damn right. I keep telling that to my union."

"Then why do you fight us so hard?"

"Let's not go into all that but I promise you I'll try to do all I can."

She looked up. "This is where I live, so I guess we say good-bye."

"I'd like to see your apartment."

"Not this time, Tom, but soon."

"When is soon?"

She hesitated. "I'm having a few friends for cocktails Saturday at seven, and you can join us if you like."

"I'll be there," he said.

Going up in the elevator she thought, I don't have anyone coming for cocktails on Saturday and who on earth can I invite to meet this strange, uncouth man? Maybe I'd better see him alone.

CHAPTER TWENTY-FIVE

Sky was startled when he heard Diana's voice on the telephone. "Where are you, Diana?"

"My darling, I have the most wonderful surprise for you, or at least I hope you'll think it's wonderful. I'm right here at the Beverly Hills Hotel, and I was hoping you would want to take me to dinner."

"I'm sorry, but you didn't give me any warning and I have a business engagement tonight."

"Oh you men and your business engagements. I always know what that means."

"It means just what I said, Diana. Could you have luncheon with me at the Polo Lounge tomorrow instead?"

"That sounds lovely. I have so much to talk to you about. By the way, have you seen anything of Philippe Lord? I understand he's out here."

"Yes, of course. He's being lionized all over the place and painting every beauty in sight. He's staying at the Bel Air Hotel."

After he hung up he thought, she's probably just had time enough to read the Hedda Hopper column, and that old bastard has sent her out here to threaten me. Making the film had been tough. The shooting was held up several months while they waited for Edward G. Robinson. They had changed directors in midstream, and had to reshoot more than the usual number of scenes. Now it was finished and Sky was totally satisfied with the result. It was everything he had wanted it to be—eerie, suggestive rather than factual and certainly different from anything he had ever seen.

The next day he had almost forgotten how charming Diana

could be until she leaned across the table at the Polo Lounge to tell him how much she missed him every day of her life in New York. "We had such wonderful times together in London, didn't we, Sky?"

"Yes, we did. But you must be having a wonderful time with a new home and a new husband. I was reading this morning about your recent party for the Duke and Duchess."

"Yes, I'm happy, and knowing you as I do now, I'm sure that you haven't really written a libelous movie script about my dear Bradshaw."

"I must admit that the leading character is a giant publisher and was originally inspired by Bradshaw Green. When you write a script, though, the characters tend to take off and become personalities on their own. I no longer think of our hero as your husband."

"He's a powerful man, Sky, and can ruin you in any field of endeavor. I assure you that if he finds the slightest resemblance, he will sue you, damage your reputation and you will lose everything you might have made."

"Our lawyers believe that the case would be thrown out of court. Besides, if he claims the film is a self-portrait, he will be admitting that the story is factual, instead of being a suspense thriller."

"Then, Sky, dear, do me a favor. Please arrange for me a little private preview, so I can see for myself." She leaned over and patted his hand. "Then I can fly back with a happy heart and tell Brad that we have nothing to dread."

"Why should you dread anything?" He looked at her directly. "If your husband is willing to go to court to prove that he isn't the man in the film?"

"But I do so want the preview." She pouted.

"I'm sorry, Diana, but it's completely impossible. The studio decided no previews."

"Oh dear."

"Too many people like Louella, Jack Warner and Sam Goldwyn were asking for them, and we didn't want to give the story away. The film and the negative are now locked up in a vault at Olympia."

"I've made this long trip out here just because I was so sure you would help me."

"If you had called me I would have told you just what I've said now." He smiled at her, "Of course, I'm glad that you didn't, or we wouldn't be having luncheon together today."

The violet eyes were looking at him intently, and she patted his hand again. "You have managed to make me feel a little better, my dear. I shall tell Brad that we must get dressed up and go to the opening as if we had no connection with it, and more or less laugh it off."

"That's the spirit."

"When will the opening be?"

"Three weeks from now at the Rivoli in New York and the following week right here in Hollywood at Grauman's Chinese."

"You'll be coming to New York, of course, for the world premiere?"

"No. That very day I'm being married in Maine."

"Married, Sky? I simply can't believe it. Who is the girl?"

"Her name is Holly Hastings."

"What a pretty name, but that's not what I mean. Is she a movie star, a scriptwriter or just someone fearfully rich or maybe beautiful?"

"She's none of those things. She's just a sweet, attractive girl who makes me happy."

"One of those little brown wrens you read about, I suppose, who look demure but are terribly sexy in the boudoir."

"I don't think so, Diana, but you'll probably meet her someday and you can judge for yourself."

"You mean to say that you haven't been living together and that you don't know all about her by now? I never heard of anything so antediluvian. You of all people."

"I know all I need to know about her, Diana, and I think we have a good chance of a happy life together."

Diana leaned forward and the violet eyes looked intently into his. "Darling, you know from the moment I first met you I have wished and worked for your happiness. I want you to remember that if you are ever in need of anything, I will always be eager to help."

After he left Diana, Sky drove up Benedict Canyon to look at the little house snuggled into the hills that he had taken for himself and Holly. Outside, with its tiny garden, it somehow suggested the New England she was familiar with. Inside there was a big living room with a fireplace.

He already felt like a substantial husband and home owner as he opened the front door to find whether the workmen had finished the few structural changes he had suggested. One of the bedrooms was to be transformed into an office for him, and there was still a smaller one, which could be made into a nursery.

He was smiling to himself as he remembered Diana's surprised face, though he had to admit he had surprised himself by deciding to marry Holly. He had expected that the emptiness he felt when she left California would gradually disappear, but it hadn't. In fact, it had grown stronger. He had to satisfy his longing to hear her happy voice by telephoning more and more frequently. If she wasn't at home, he wondered uneasily where she was and he conjured up pictures of her dancing in the arms of some handsome young man and being fondled by him when he said good night.

Finally it was May and she still had no plans for coming back to California. She only laughed and said, "If you want to see me, why don't you come here? It's beautiful. The fruit trees are just beginning to bloom."

He managed to clear up his work a week ahead and telephoned to her that he was coming East and would include Maine in his trip. He asked her to make a reservation at the most convenient hotel.

When the small plane he had chartered in Boston touched down at the local airport in Ogunquit, Maine, Holly was waiting for him and when he saw her smiling, happy face framed in the swinging hair he instantly felt the warmth and reassurance that she always gave him.

"I can't believe you're here. Of course, you're staying with us. My brother is away at school and you can have his room."

Sky fitted easily into the pattern of the Hastings' family life. He liked the big breakfasts at the long table built to order of New England maple by a local carpenter and hand-finished and polished by the whole family. He enjoyed talking to Holly's mother, who was a writer now deep in local politics, and to her lawyer father. The whole setting seemed to have the peaceful permanence he had never found in his own life.

There was no tennis, but he and Holly walked or rode around the countryside, talking about everything but their own relationship.

"Is the ocean ice water and does anybody ever swim in it at this time of year?" he asked as they came out of the house and looked down through the water curling up on the rocky beach.

"My brother does at this time of year and I have occasionally when it's a warm day like this."

"I think I'll give it a try."

"If you will, then I will, too. Just give me a minute to put on my suit."

"O.K. I'll do the same."

When Holly returned she was wearing a one-piece maillot that followed every line of her pretty little figure.

"Don't you just love the combination of salt water and apple blossoms? It's a unique smell that you'll never find anyplace but here," she said as they started down the hill.

"Yes, I do love it, Holly, and I love you, too."

"Do you really mean it, or are you just saying it the way people say 'Good morning'?"

"I really mean it. I love you very much."

"When did you find out that you do?"

"I suppose I always knew it. You make me happy and I feel quite lonely without you."

"I'm glad, because I do, too."

They reached the water and Sky poked an experimental toe into the surf. "It's worse than ice water. I'll take a quick dip and be back in a minute." He plunged in, but when he turned around she was just behind him. "What a crazy girl you are. Let's get out of here."

Her teeth were chattering as they came out of the water and he put his arms around her. "You want to go wherever I go, don't you?"

"Of course I do." She picked up her towel and began drying herself vigorously.

"I meant what I said coming down the hill. I came here to ask you to marry me. Will you, Holly?"

She dropped the towel and threw her arms around him. "I thought you would never ask me. I love you, Sky. My insides turn upside down when I think of you."

He held her close and whispered, "I love you, Holly."

After a moment she broke the embrace and looked up at him. "I don't think I'm very sexy. I'm not nearly as sophisticated as some of your friends, but I'd like to lie right down under one of those apple trees and have you hold me in your arms and make love to me."

"None of that, my girl. I don't want you to have pneumonia and, besides, I want the whole thing to be old-fashioned and traditional."

He picked up her towel and put it around her shoulders. "I'll come back in September. I want to be married in the little church you took me to yesterday, and I want you to wear a white dress and carry a prayer book."

"Do you even want a big cake with the miniature bride and groom on top?"

"Yes."

"And lots of children?"

"Yes, darling." He kissed her but it was still with more tenderness than passion.

Sky was remembering this scene as he entered the new bedroom they would soon occupy. He smiled as he looked at the big king-size bed that had just been delivered.

CHAPTER TWENTY-SIX

Diana had planned to return immediately to New York but she found many European friends at the Beverly Hills Hotel. It was the first time since she had become Mrs. Bradshaw Innes Green that she had traveled alone. It was intoxicating to entertain friends instead of being entertained, to sign restaurant checks without even looking at the total.

Before leaving for New York she decided to call Indiana, and had apparently awakened her from a sound sleep. "Darling, I just had to tell you. Everything is all right with the film, but wait till you hear this. Sky is getting married instead of coming to New York for the opening." She paused. "What, dear?" Another pause, "No, I don't know her name but she's a Miss Nobody. What? I didn't hear you. It just seems to be one of those moonlight-and-roses affairs. I'm sorry I awakened you, dear. I keep forgetting the change of time. Good night. I'm returning to New York tomorrow."

She still expected to arrive at the Fifth Avenue house before her husband, who had gone to South America on a week's business trip, but he had taken an earlier plane and was pacing up and down the library when she came in.

"Where the hell have you been, and why didn't you tell me you were going to California?"

"Darling, I wanted to surprise you. It was a love journey entirely for your sake. I flew out to California to ask Schuyler Madison not to ruin himself financially by letting that new picture be released."

"That was a damn-fool thing to do. That son-of-a-bitch has been after me for years."

"Of course, he couldn't do anything at this point, but he assures me that the only resemblance between you and the character in the film is that you're both newspaper publishers."

"I'm going to sue the ass off him."

"I told him that, but I think we should ignore the whole thing, Brad. I have already taken four seats to the opening and have invited Louise and Larry Brooke to go with us."

"Nothing will drag me to that goddamn opening."

For the next two weeks, the coming of *The Power and the Glory* was widely advertised, and the general excitement was amplified by cocktail gossip that kept speculating whether or not Bradshaw Green would come to the premiere of another publisher's life story. Up to the last minute Diana had been sure she could persuade Bradshaw to go with her, but when she came downstairs that evening, wrapped in a white ermine coat that almost swept the floor, he was still in a business suit and dictating to Miss Peacock in his office.

"I'm so disappointed, darling. Won't you still reconsider? These things never start on time and I'll be glad to wait while you change."

"Not a chance. Why the hell don't you take off that coat and stay here with me?"

"You know that I would, darling, but I feel that it's absolutely essential to be present. I want to be photographed and seen by everyone."

Diana had invited the Brookes because she found them attractive and because she knew they were avid to become a part of the New York social scene. She stopped for them at their apartment at the Carlyle, and as they drove on to the theater she studied them even more closely than she had at the dinner party. Louise Brooke was a handsome, wholesome blonde, probably natural, Diana decided, who looked well enough in evening clothes, but would look even more gorgeous all in white on a tennis court. He would look gorgeous anywhere. Though Laurence Brooke couldn't be more than forty-five, she guessed, his wavy hair was silvery, still streaked with dark, and his eyes were remarkable under very heavy dark brows.

"So your husband finally decided not to come," Louise Brooke said.

"Yes, he's unduly sensitive because the main character is a publisher."

"I don't blame him," Laurence Brooke said. "I don't expect to like the picture myself, but to see it is a must. If it's too hard on the publishing world, though, I may leave and arrange to meet you two ladies later at 21, where I've reserved a table."

Louise Brooke gave one of her hearty laughs. "Men are so sensitive. If I were a publisher, my curiosity would be so great I'd sit through the picture no matter what."

Broadway was jammed with cars going to the Rivoli, and theirs moved slowly along the street. Finally, several blocks ahead they could catch a glimpse of the searchlights, and the crowd held back by the mounted police trying to keep order. They could hear the roar of excitement as each car unloaded its passengers.

Diana's arrival created more furor than that of several well-known actors.

"Just one more, Mrs. Green," shouted the photographers. The flashbulbs kept popping and the cameras clicking as Diana and her party progressed slowly into the theater. A dark, thin little girl with a notebook and pencil managed to wedge her way between two cameramen and catch Diana by the elbow.

"Mrs. Green, is it true that this film is about your husband?"

Diana gave her a special smile. "Of course not, my dear. If it were, I certainly wouldn't be here tonight."

It was after one o'clock when Diana returned to the Fifth Avenue house, but Bradshaw Green was in their upstairs sitting room. He had put a silk dressing gown over his pajamas and was watching the late news on TV.

"Well, what do you have to say? The goddamn critics are raving about this monstrosity." He paced up and down, flicking his cigar ashes in all directions.

"Oh darling, wait till you hear."

"I've just called the *Globe*. Our reviewer says it's the picture of the year. I told them the piece had to be rewritten or I was going to fire the damn critic. I may, anyway."

"How foolish, Brad. The film was fascinating. Everyone was raving about it, even at 21, where we stopped for a bite to eat.

No one I talked to mentioned any connection with you. I assure you."

"Goddamn it."

"Dearest, Laurence Brooke is the owner of many newspapers in Canada and he liked it immensely. I'm going to ring for them to bring up the early editions of the morning papers. They were just being delivered by one of the errand boys of the paper when I came in, and you'll see how foolish you are being." She was pressing the bell when she heard a crash and turned around. An agate ashtray that she valued especially was lying splintered on the hearth.

"How did you ever manage that, Brad? You must be nervous."

She started picking up the splinters. "I tell you that you have nothing to worry about. This film is the story of a perfectly dreadful man who pushes another man overboard on an ocean steamship and probably drowns his wife, though you're never quite sure. You have to make your own judgment about everything, and that's the charm of the picture."

Bradshaw Green got to his foot. "Throw the papers in the fire along with your damn ashtray. You're a fool. I thought you were an intelligent woman when I married you, and a real beauty, but I should have known better when I first looked at your ankles." He went into his bedroom, slamming the door behind him.

When his breakfast tray was brought up the next morning, both the *Times* and the *Daily News* along with the *Globe* were folded on it. He had slept restlessly, so he reached for a glass of water and a Bufferin, which he always kept on his bedside table.

He opened the New York *Times* first and read the film critic's review, which called *The Power and the Glory* a masterpiece of story, cast and production. The best thing that had come along in years. The *Daily News* was also a rave. He felt himself trembling with rage as he unfolded the *Globe* and looked for the review. His instruction had not been obeyed, though he could tell that a few minor criticisms had been introduced, probably to placate him. When he reached his office that day, he would not only fire the film critic, but also the night managing editor, who had been stupid enough not to obey his orders.

He called Miss Peacock and told her not to expect him at the paper until around half-past one or two.

"But you have several appointments this morning, Mr. Green."

"Never mind. I have something else I want to attend to."

"Anything I can help you with?"

"You're a damn curious woman, and the answer is no." He started to hang up and then shouted, "Tell my daughter to be in my office at two o'clock. I want to talk to her and call Nizer. I want my lawyer there, too."

Diana was sleeping when he left the house. He told the chauffeur to drive down through the park and come out at Seventh Avenue. When they reached the Park Sheraton he knocked on the window and said to the chauffeur, "Let me out here. I need a little exercise and I'll walk the rest of the way to the office."

The film had become an obsession with him. He could think of nothing else. The idea of going to the late-morning show, buying a ticket, slipping into the theater and seeing it alone had come to him during the night.

He had managed to get into the theater unnoticed and took a seat in the back row. As he waited for the film to begin he felt Diana was perhaps right and that he had exaggerated its importance.

The opening of the film showed a courtroom scene, with publishing tycoon Endicott Spencer Brown sitting beside his lawyer as the trial began. When Green realized that the charge against the publisher was for strangling his young wife and placing her body in a private lake, he suddenly felt himself nauseous and hurried to the men's room. A few minutes later he returned just as a prim secretary was put on the witness stand. He suddenly felt himself suffocating with rage and got up and left the theater.

Miss Peacock had just come back from an early luncheon when he came in. "Dear me, Mr. Green, you're looking tired. You must have been up very late last night after I left."

"I don't feel too well. I walked a few blocks and I guess I'm not as young as I used to be. Bring me a glass of ice cubes and a double jigger of Bourbon."

She brought them quickly and found him sitting in his desk chair with his necktie off. He had tossed it on the floor and was trying to unbutton his collar.

"I seem to have some trouble breathing. Perhaps you'd better open the window a little."

"It's anything but a pleasant day, and I'm afraid you may take a cold." Miss Peacock looked anxious.

"Do as I told you, for God's sake. I'm choking." His face had turned red and he was gasping.

Miss Peacock was frightened. She opened the window, rushed to her telephone and tried the resident nurse, and when she couldn't reach her, called Indiana's secretary. "Tell Mrs. Hale to come to her father's office as quickly as she can."

A moment later when Indiana came running in, Miss Peacock was pale and trembling. They went into the office together.

Bradshaw Green had evidently tried to get closer to the window. He had upset his chair and fallen on the floor, where he was lying with his eyes closed. He was still gasping for breath.

"Get the nurse. If you can't find her get somebody else. I'll stay here," Indiana said.

She turned back to her father and kneeled down beside him. "Just keep breathing, Daddy. We'll have someone here in a minute."

He half opened his eyes and she knew he had recognized her. His breathing seemed to be growing more and more difficult. Suddenly it stopped. For a moment, she thought he must be better, but as she watched him his face seemed to change and settle into a mold. She knew that he was dead, and she got up and rushed to the door. Miss Peacock and the nurse were just coming in.

"My father has just died," Indiana said.

"It's not possible. I'm sure everything is going to be all right," said Miss Peacock as the nurse went into Bradshaw Green's office, closing the door behind her.

Miss Peacock and Indiana stood looking at each other and it was Miss Peacock who broke the silence. "He was very eager to talk to you today. He said he had something important to tell you, and for you to be in his office at two."

Indiana looked at her watch, "It's five minutes to two," she said as the nurse came back.

"Mr. Green is dead," she announced.

Indiana left the task of informing Diana to Miss Peacock.

Tears were rolling down Indiana's cheeks as she went back to her own office to cancel her appointments and pick up her coat.

As she rang for the elevator, she thought, Why did he want to talk with me this afternoon? We haven't talked much lately. Was it about Sky, to say something about Diana or to discuss something that was going on with the *Globe?* She would always wonder.

Though she heard the sound of the elevator as it stopped at the floor below, she felt a sudden longing to go back to her office again. Once inside, she sat down at her desk, took off her hat and buried her face in her hands. This building and everything in it is mine now, all mine, she thought. I've always wanted it. Now that it has happened, I feel suddenly a little afraid, or do I really? What will it be like to occupy his office instead of this one? She suddenly felt a warm sense of excitement, like an athlete before an important game. She took a Kleenex from the box on her desk and wiped away the tears that were still on her cheeks. The first thing I intend to do is to fire Tiger.

PART THREE

CHAPTER TWENTY-SEVEN

It was four days after Sky's luncheon at 21 with Diana and Harrison Kirby, and no further word had come from them yet. Whenever he had a free moment, Sky had found himself nursing rather warmly the thought of becoming a governor, though he would have found it too extraordinary and farfetched a week ago. The thought of going farther was still too fantastic even for consideration.

He could see that up to now his career was somewhat similar to Ronald Reagan's. He knew that Reagan had been brought to Hollywood by a man who was struck by his voice as he announced the sports news for a small, middle-western radio station. Though he was more successful than Sky had been, Reagan had not become the great star he had hoped to be and before being drafted into politics he had toured the country making laudatory speeches for the General Electric products.

Sky had ordered the Reagan file to be sent up to him from the UBC library and he stretched out on his office couch during one of his rare free periods. I suppose I would be labeled as a conservative if I were to go into this thing, but commenting on the news is different from standing on a fixed platform. I have always been free to observe both sides of any question.

He got up and paced around the office for a few minutes. If Holly were still with me, she would tell me to go ahead. She would make me feel certain I could put it over and that it would be a wonderful adventure for us both. He picked up the framed photograph on his desk. It was of Holly, bright-eyed and smiling, as she almost always had been.

As a joke Holly often said he should become President of the

United States. He always replied that the only reason he would consider it would be to give her a spot in history along with Dolly Madison as Holly Madison.

He and Holly had had 4½ happy years together. She was loving and undemanding and fitted easily into his life. They lived very simply in the small house he had taken for them. While Sky was at the studio she continued her tennis or worked in their miniature garden. A cook prepared their dinners, since Holly's grandfather had warned Sky not to let Holly overtire herself.

He had been surprised at her eagerness to make love. "Am I any good in bed?" she asked him a few weeks after their wedding. "I know there are all kinds of tricks that some girls know, and I often wonder if I'm boring."

"You're fresh and you like it, and that's all I want in a girl," he had told her.

Sometimes it seemed impossible that Holly, who had such a love of life, had died so easily. They had celebrated their fourth anniversary with a small dinner, and after the guests had gone, Holly had fainted in his arms.

The next morning she seemed perfectly well but Sky called her grandfather to say he was concerned. That afternoon Dr. MacIntosh had called him at the studio to tell him that he felt Holly should be hospitalized for a few days. "I'm not entirely happy with her condition," he had said.

Holly had taken it all very lightly, even the dictum that to be a strong person, she should have a new valve in her heart. She had come home for a few months before the operation and they had enjoyed each other more than ever. When he had driven her back to the hospital, she threw her arms around him and kissed him. "Grandfather is fussy and overprotective, but I trust him. I'm going to be a big, strong girl, have lots of children, and live until I'm ninety." The operation was never performed, for Holly had died in her sleep that night.

Sky had closed the house, put it on the market and gone to live at a hotel. His loneliness was something that none of his friends could heal, and it seemed to him unbelievably fortunate when six months later he received an offer from UBC to work in New York.

He set down the photograph and came back to the present with a start when his secretary knocked and came into the room.

"I just got back from lunch. You've been so quiet, Mr. Madison, that I wasn't really sure you were here."

"Just doing a little research."

"Mrs. Kirby just called you from Washington. I was about to leave the message on your desk, but I can get her right back for you. She said she would be home for another hour."

"Please do."

Diana's soft British voice sounded excited. "Sky, darling, how are you?"

"I've spent the afternoon thinking, just as I promised."

"I'm so glad, and I'm sure you're going to end by seeing things our way. Pay no attention at all to the snide little item in Lincoln LaPorte's column today."

"I'm afraid I never read it. I seldom see his column."

"I have to admit that I do. Sometimes it's amusing, but not this time. Have you really been playing around in Soho, darling?"

"I've been there three or four times and not for many years."

"It doesn't sound like you, but shall I read it?"

"I suppose so, if it's something I should know."

"It's one of those blind items, in which a columnist can be irresponsible. Here it is: 'What TV personality, who gives the impression of being Mr. Goody Goody, was seen lunching with one of the Washington big wheels the other day, now has political ambitions? Do you suppose he means to take his little Soho playmate with him when he moves to the White House?' Does that make any sense to you, Sky?"

"Yes, I understand it. It's past history and it has no significance in my life. It's a long story, but I'll be glad to tell you all about it when I see you next."

"Harrison and I hope that you will come to us for the Labor Day weekend. That's really why I was calling you now."

"You mean come to Washington?"

"Oh no, darling, nothing so difficult. We're going to be at South Wind and I'd like so much to have you see all that I've done to it."

"I somehow thought that you had sold it."

"It has so much personality that I couldn't bear to give it up. Bradshaw left me the Fifth Avenue house, too, but for tax purposes I gave it to the British Alliance, and it's now a museum."

"May I come in time for luncheon on Sunday and leave early Monday morning so that I can be in my office by ten-thirty?"

"Of course you may. Harrison will be so happy."

"I need to talk to him again."

"After our luncheon the other day, he became twice as enthusiastic about having you as our candidate. We'll send a car for you. Where are you staying in New York?"

"I have a small apartment at the Carlyle."

"Good. We'll have our driver, Randall, pick you up there at ten-thirty Sunday morning. Then you will be at South Wind in time for a swim before lunch. He'll also return you to the city Monday morning any time you wish."

As soon as they stopped talking, Sky called his secretary. "Do we have a copy of today's *Globe* outside?"

"Oh yes, Mr. Madison."

She brought him the paper, and he read the paragraph that had a prominent place in "LaPorte Reports." He wondered if Indiana had passed along the story to Lincoln but discarded that immediately. He was sure the little episode had been forgotten and wondered how in the hell LaPorte could have unearthed it.

When Sky had first arrived in New York to become anchorman on UBC's evening-news broadcast, he was looking forward to plunging immediately into his new situation, but suddenly found himself with time on his hands. After meeting with all the top brass of the network and going over the format of the half-hour news program with his new producer, Oliver Prince, and the four writers assigned to him, he learned the show wouldn't go on the air for another three weeks.

After his first disappointment he was rather glad for the delay. I've always wanted to get better acquainted with New York, but I've never had enough time. Since everything will probably be hectic as hell once I get going, he thought, I might as well take a week off, relax and do some wandering around.

Just to walk the streets of Manhattan after lethargic California was an exciting experience. Though he still felt as if he were in transit, he had found himself responding quickly to the faster pace, the heightened sense of competition and the hostile faces of the crowds.

He spent a part of each day at the UBC building, meeting the other personalities, getting accustomed to the location of the various rooms, and talking with the men who were to make up his own team. Occasionally he had a drink or dinner with one of the men at the Élysée, where he was staying, but he made no effort to contact old friends. That could come later, after he settled into his new routine, he had felt.

On his nights alone, he made a point of choosing a different location each time, strolling along and going into a new restaurant that looked interesting. If I kept a notebook, I could have dashed off a *Lonely Man's Guide to New York,* he thought.

When he was free during the day, he visited a museum from a list he had made. The memory of his day at the Louvre with his father had remained quite clear in his mind, and as he grew up he had hoped to become successful enough to start collecting paintings. Now it was too late. The impressionists, at least, were priced for millionaires only and he had no feeling for pop or abstract.

As he wandered through the Museum of Modern Art and studied the Picassos, he wondered what had happened to his own. He knew that Picasso had painted his son at least twice, but perhaps neither one was museum quality. He was curious enough about the fate of his own to inquire at several galleries, but though the dealers knew of the paintings, none of those he spoke to had ever handled them.

Along about the second week, Sky discovered lower Manhattan. He became intrigued with Soho and the architecture of the old cast-iron buildings, many of which had been converted into galleries for the new artists. The atmosphere seemed younger and livelier. The narrow streets were full of freakishly fascinating shops, and to his surprise there were several top-flight restaurants.

The youth revolution was in full swing and the sidewalks were full of boys and girls wearing old shirts and jeans and sometimes indistinguishable as to sex, except that the girls' hair was usually a little longer. They're a new breed, he had thought. I remember when it was a big deal to make out with a girl in the back seat of a car, and now I suppose these kids are all living together.

After dinner one evening at an Italian restaurant, he had decided to walk along Houston Street until he could find a taxi. A crowd of boys and girls brushed past him. They were laughing and shouting at each other, and Sky realized they were high on whatever they were taking. When they turned into a side street he was curious enough to follow them to see where they were going.

It was a warehouse with an almost invisible sign, The Hawk Eye, at the ground-floor door. He opened the door and went inside. Upstairs, rock music from tapes was going full blast, so he climbed a flight of steps and went in.

The big room was two stories high and the crowd that filled the dance floor looked like extras in a Fellini movie. He joined a small group around the edge of the dance floor to watch a girl in a bridal veil and a white-lace dress with nothing on underneath. When she and her partner passed him on the way out, she said, "Hi there" so cordially that he had answered, "Congratulations. Just married?"

"Oh no. We just renew ourselves here every six months or so, but don't write about it if you're a reporter. I'm a public-school teacher and it wouldn't sound good."

He went back to watching the dancers. Now girls in white robes were passing trays of marshmallows that he supposed were sprinkled with LSD. The dance floor was being filled with a manufactured mist that made the scene more eerie than ever. He had been watching the tall black boy, who was a fantastic dancer, and his partner, a slim little blonde. He could see only their heads now, rising above the clouds, but as they passed him, she broke away and came toward him out of the mist.

"What are you doing here all by yourself, handsome? Come dance with me and have some fun."

"What made you leave your partner? He's a great dancer and I'm not on to this kind of music and don't know the steps."

She tugged at his hand and pulled him toward the dance floor. "There aren't any steps, stupid. You just let the beat flow through your body and then you do whatever you feel like doing."

Though Sky felt like a fool, he managed to follow some of her gyrations as she maneuvered him into a dark corner. "You're okay, but this isn't what I feel like doing," she said. "I want to go to bed with you and have you fuck me." She raised her face and he could see that the big gray-blue eyes were overly bright and glazed.

"I guess I'm not used to hearing language like that from a pretty little girl like you."

"I'm not a little girl. I'm twenty-four."

"I don't buy that."

"I'm really nineteen."

"That's more like it."

Her hand was reaching for the fly of his pants and he pushed it away. "What's your name, Miss Blue Eyes?"

"It's Tania Thomas."

"All right, Tania. Let's go over to the bar and I'll buy you a drink before I duck out of here." They started to walk toward the bar. "Before I leave, I'll find that black fellow of yours to make sure you get home safely."

"You really are Mr. Square, aren't you?"

"Of course, you must have spotted that the minute you saw me." They sat down on bar stools, and he looked at her more closely than he had before. Her heavy blond hair was held back by an Alice in Wonderland band that showed off her delicate little nose and small Cupid's-bow lips. With her jeans she was wearing a sheer, lace-trimmed blouse, under which beautiful little breasts and nipples were visible. "Before I order you a drink, tell me what you're high on. Is it speed, LSD or whatever?"

"How do you know I'm on a high?"

"By your eyes mostly, and the fact that you're talking like a tart in a whorehouse."

"I've been through marijuana, and I don't like LSD, but I get a real kick out of cocaine."

He ordered a scotch on the rocks for himself and white wine for her, which she had asked for. "You're a little fool, but your whole generation is out of line," he said.

She sipped her drink meekly. "Are you going to reform me?"

"Not a chance. I have better things to occupy my time."

"Too bad, because it really might work if a handsome guy like you cared enough for me."

"I'm sure you can find plenty of willing helpers if you try. Do you live alone down here?"

"Yes, I rent a loft. I want to paint, and I'm taking lessons."

He felt his first real spark of interest. "That's great. Does your family help?"

"Since you're not interested, why this questionnaire?"

"Just fatherly instinct."

"Well, my father died a long time ago. My mother is deep in her career, and I ran away from home. That's the story."

"I hope it all works out the way you want it, and I wish you the best of luck, Tania."

"And if there's ever anything I can do to help you without involving me, I'll be happy to do it. That's what you were thinking, wasn't it?"

"Right now I'm going to do something for you by finding your friend to take you home."

"He left long ago." She looked at him smugly. "I told him to. I wanted to be with you."

"Then I'll find a cab for you and send you home." They left The Hawk Eye and walked toward Houston Street. She was very quiet but when he hailed the cab she took hold of his arm. "Just ride with me to my place, I don't feel too well."

He followed her into the cab and she leaned limply against him. Since Holly had died he had had almost no close contact with women. The smell of her long, blond hair on his shoulder was very pleasing and after a while her hand stole between his legs and began caressing him.

When they reached her address, she said, "The loft is upstairs. You will come up with me, won't you? I hate to go in alone."

He found himself paying off the cab and going upstairs with her. The key was under the mat. She opened the door and they went in.

It was a large loft, decorated with considerable taste, he saw quickly. The living section was full of plants and there were paintings on the walls. Beyond that he could see a bedroom and a kitchen.

"I'll make us a cup of coffee," she said.

"No thanks. I have an early appointment."

"What a square you really are." She put her arms around his waist and pressed herself against him, moving gently from side to side. She leaned back and pulled down the zipper of his trousers and felt his rigid erection. "What a fraud you are. You want me as much as I want you."

He seized her by the shoulders and shook her until the band slipped from her hair and the long strands fell over her face. "All right, you little bitch. I'll fuck you until you yell for help. If that's what you're looking for, I'm going to give it to you."

She unbuttoned her blouse and let her jeans fall to the floor. He could see that she wasn't faking and that her body was ready for love. "Is there a bed in the house or do you want it right here?"

He had never made love with hatred before, and he hardly knew whether the hatred was for her or himself. He was rougher with her than he had ever been with a girl. When they had finished, though, he had lain back on the pillows feeling released for the first time in many months. Although he had never admitted it to himself he had felt a deep loyalty to Holly's memory and had kept himself celibate since her death.

Now he had become a free man again. He owed a debt of gratitude to Tania and he leaned over and kissed her breasts.

"What a beautiful man you are. I still want you madly."

"Not tonight, my sweet." He got up and pulled on his clothes, but while he was putting on his shoes she jumped out of bed and threw her arms around his neck. "Kiss me once more where I liked to be kissed."

"I'm leaving this minute." He pushed her off his lap but she pattered after him as he went toward the door. She was a beautiful little thing, he had to admit, a miniature Venus with a body designed for sex and a mind oriented in the same direction.

"I'll meet you tomorrow night at The Hawk Eye," she said.

"Forget it. I have another date."

"Then break it. I'll be at the bar waiting for you."

"Not a chance." He slammed the door behind him and went down the stairs.

He woke feeling totally renewed and refreshed. As he yawned and stretched, he wished for a minute that he had stayed with

Tania and could reach out and enjoy her body again. She had been good for him, he thought, but it would be foolish ever to see her again.

It was a sparkling September day, almost like the first days of summer, and everything seemed to go right for him. He and his news team had luncheon together in the UBC restaurant at the top of the building. They were beginning to know each other and be on easy terms. His producer, Oliver Prince, who had seemed distant at first, was starting to warm up and Sky could see that they had similar opinions of what makes news. The small, well-chosen bits to fill in the international and national stories would determine the success of a daily newscast.

He spent the afternoon going through the papers, but his mind kept wandering off to The Hawk Eye and Tania. He could still remember the scent of that heavy, golden-blond hair and its silky, sexy texture.

He had dinner alone in an uptown restaurant and went to a movie but when he came out he found himself hailing a taxi and giving the address of The Hawk Eye. I might be able to talk this kid out of the cocaine bit, he thought.

Tania was not at the bar. He stood at the edge of the dance floor, but there was no girl with long blond hair among the dancers, so he went back to the bar and ordered a drink.

"I was here with a girl named Tania last night. Was she here earlier tonight?" he asked the bartender.

"I know Tania, but I haven't seen her tonight."

"Does she come here often?"

"It seems like I see her every night. First she started coming alone, but now she comes mostly with that tall black boy. He's a painter with a fancy name."

Sky decided to wait around and after a while he ordered another drink. "Are lots of the kids around here into cocaine?" he asked.

"How do I know? When the kids get on coke, they don't care about drinks anymore."

He paid his check and went out. What a little bitch she is, he thought. She's probably high again and on cloud nine. He had every intention of going home, but when he got into the taxi, he suddenly decided to go to her apartment instead.

When they reached the place, he could see that the loft was dark, and he told the driver to wait. He went up the stairs and banged on the door, but there was no answer. Back in the cab, he said, "Look here, fellow, I've decided to sit this out. You can keep the meter going and I'll pay the tab, or I'll give you fifty dollars for the rest of the night."

"I'll take the fifty."

The time passed slowly. The driver slept and snored at the wheel; Sky, with his rage increasing every minute, alternated between sitting in the back of the taxi to striding up and down the block.

It was after two o'clock when he saw her coming down the street with her handbag swinging from her shoulder. He was trembling with rage as he got out of the taxi and grabbed her. The handbag went spinning across the sidewalk, spilling its contents as he shook her. "What a little bitch you are. Where have you been all night?"

"It's not all night, and what's it to you?"

"Nothing, thank God." He slapped her face so hard that she went staggering across the sidewalk.

"You bastard." She picked up her handbag quickly and hit him with it across the face. "Did you think I was going to sit there at The Hawk Eye waiting for you to make up your mind whether I was respectable enough to see again?"

"I came, didn't I?"

"Yes, but look what you've done. You've broken my cold-cream jar. I hate you."

"If you weren't such a miserable little tramp, you wouldn't be carrying your whole dressing table around with you. I'll take you up to the loft."

He pulled her half sobbing upstairs, but once inside the loft, she turned and pressed herself against him as she had done the night before.

"What a mess you are," he said, stroking her hair. "Go wash your face and take off your clothes. You're prettier that way."

While she was gone, he looked around the loft for the first time. It was all white, and the windows along the street were completely screened with tall plants. She had thrown down her big pouch handbag on the coffee table in front of the white slip-covered sofa, and spilling out of it were a thick roll of bills and a gold pillbox. He flipped it open to see if she was carrying cocaine, but the box was empty. He noticed the initials H.H. on the top.

Hanging on the walls were some good but not great contemporary paintings and when she came back, he asked her about them.

"They're the work of a friend of mine. He's Haitian and very talented. His name is Lucien Lavalle."

"He's pretty good."

"He has already had several shows."

"He's the boy you were dancing with at The Hawk Eye last night. Are you living with him?"

"We have been, off and on, but not just now. That's why I ran away from home. My mother didn't approve." She climbed into his lap, rested her head on one arm of his chair and let her legs dangle over the other. "I'd do anything to spite her."

"Does your mother live in New York?"

"Of course, but let's talk about me. I like being naked with you, Sky."

"How did you know my name? I was just thinking I had never told you."

"I guess I saw your picture somewhere or else somebody like the bartender at The Hawk Eye told me. Does it matter?" She spread her legs, gently reached for his hand and put it on the curly blond tuft of hair between them. "Do you like it?"

"As I remember, I was admiring it last night."

"Kiss my breasts again. I rather like the sensation."

"You've had quite a lot of men for your age, haven't you?"

"Not so many as you might think. It's just that I enjoy sex." She moved her hand over his leg. "That's natural, isn't it? I have an erotic imagination when I make love and most women don't. They just lie there and take what comes."

"You haunted me all day, Tania. I had to have you tonight."

She slid off his lap. "Then let's screw until we're dead tired. Nobody has ever screwed me like you."

He lay down on the bed and as she bent over him he saw that the red mark on her cheek where he had struck her was beginning to turn black and blue.

"I love that big, beautiful prick of yours and I'm going to keep it hard that way all night," she said, as she began to fondle him.

Luckily, the next day was Saturday. Sky left the loft before Tania woke. When he reached his hotel, he fell into bed and didn't open his eyes until late afternoon.

The whole episode had the elements of a fantasy dream, but he faced the fact that he was infatuated with a nineteen-year-old girl named Tania, about whom he knew nothing except that she lived in a loft in Soho, had a native Haitian boyfriend, and was a cocaine addict.

He was glad that he had made a date to spend Sunday with Oliver Prince and his family in New Jersey. He stayed as long as possible and felt normal when he returned. This is all madness. It has got to end, he told himself, but all the next week thoughts of Tania kept him from concentrating on work and he began to sympathize with the struggles of those who try to give up liquor, cigarettes or drugs.

It had been a Thursday when she had first spoken to him at The Hawk Eye and on the following Thursday he gave up and took a taxi to Soho.

She was not at The Hawk Eye. "I'd have seen her if she'd been in. She always comes and sits here and says a word or two to me," said the bartender. "She hasn't been here since you were here the last time and neither has her boyfriend. They probably found some new place." He shook his head. "Some folks are fickle. You might try a new place called Cerebrum."

He took another taxi to the street where she lived, but the loft was not only dark but also looked as if blinds had been pulled down over the windows. He told the driver to wait, went into the building and rang the superintendent's bell. "I'm wondering if Miss Tania Thomas still lives here," he said.

"No, sir. She moved out early this week. Monday, I think it was."

"And did she leave a forwarding address?"

"No, sir, she was in a hurry, and she just paid up her rent and said good-bye."

"Was anyone with her?"

"Yes, that black boy she was seeing a lot of, was helping her move."

He went back to the hotel and stopped at The Monkey Bar for a drink. He had been disappointed and angry at first, but now felt a great surge of relief that she had ended it quickly.

For a few days he suffered from wanting Tania, but as the pressure of his work increased and the date of his first newscast came nearer, he forgot.

He had long sessions with Oliver Prince about the format of the show. His four writers were assigned to different beats. One was international, the second was focused on Washington and the other two covered whatever else.

"For the opening identification," Prince said, "I've got an idea that may work. It has the globe of the earth in the background with a skyrocket going off diagonally as it goes up and bursts into a brilliant array of sparks."

Sky looked dubious. "I'm not sure."

"It may sound a little corny, but it could become a trademark that would help separate your evening newscast from all the others."

"O.K., it's different, so why don't we try it."

"It might end by becoming the name of the program: 'Sky-rocket: The Evening News with Schuyler Madison.'"

When the day for the launching of his newscast finally arrived, Sky woke early. He was already keyed up and, although he wasn't nervous, he could feel his adrenalin rising.

The setting for the program was to be a newsroom, and though Sky had seen enough newsrooms to realize this was a glorified version, it was highly photogenic. In the foreground was a horse-shoe-shaped table, at which he occupied the anchor spot. Oliver Prince sat next to him, and then the four writers were spread around the table before their typewriters. The background that occupied the camera during the beginning and the final fadeout of the program showed a couple of reporters converging on the desk, either with memos or wire copy.

The first evening newscast, as he and Oliver Prince went over their material in the early afternoon, would include the White House preparations for West German Chancellor Ludwig Erhard's visit, the brutal murder of Valerie Percy, daughter of the Illinois senator, and the merger of three New York dailies, after a settlement of a 140-day strike, to be called the *World Journal*

Tribune, and the opening of the new Metropolitan Opera House at Lincoln Center.

It was just a half an hour before the newscast went on the air that one of the young writers assigned to whatever else, came to Sky with a wire-service report. "There's an heiress missing. It's the kind of thing people enjoy hearing about."

Sky reached for the piece of wire copy that had just come from the Associated Press, and read:

> One of the best-kept secrets is the disappearance of Heather Hale, heiress to the Bradshaw Green newspaper chain. The nineteen-year-old heiress left the home of her mother, *Globe* publisher Indiana Green Hale, several months ago, and has been missing ever since. Interviewed this afternoon, Mrs. Hale says that since she has received no ransom notes, she does not believe her daughter has been kidnaped. "I believe," said Mrs. Hale, "that it is all a part of the unfortunate youth revolution and that she left of her own free will. Today I have engaged private detectives and notified the police."

"Good God," said Sky. "She's my second cousin. Scramble around fast, will you, and find out what else you can. I'll be able to fill in the necessary details." He turned to one of the other writers, and Sky's voice was urgent. "Hurry and get a picture of her from the AP. I'm sure she'll be pretty, and it will be a good light end to balance the heavy stuff on the program."

There was a quick reshuffling of program items to allow this one, which they hoped might be an exclusive. Oliver Prince didn't seem to mind the tension. "It always happens. The hottest items come in at the last minute," he said.

Sky smiled. "Last-minute changes tend to stimulate me." Then the red light flashed on and the newscast began. As always, Sky gave the impression of being totally engrossed in the news he was delivering and of adding some personal observation that was unavailable anywhere else. When he had finished telling the story of Heather Hale, he looked quickly at the monitor to see what kind of photograph they had been able to find.

The blond girl still on the screen had probably been photographed at one of the mass debutante parties. She was a beautiful blonde, wearing a white evening gown and gloves and carrying a bouquet of roses. My God, it's Tania, he realized.

He sat stunned, staring at the screen until he remembered suddenly that he had business in the closing scene of picking up his papers and turning to smile and talk to his team around the table.

When the red light went off, Oliver Prince got up and clapped him on the shoulder. "We made a good start and the Heather Hale bit was especially good, but let's not get overconfident. We'll all go upstairs to the restaurant for a postmortem."

By this time reports were coming in that the top brass was pleased, and that calls had started coming in too fast to handle. Sky, though, managed to send for his secretary. "I must have the address right away of a painter named Lucien Lavalle. He lives down in Soho and if you can't find him in the phone book call all the Soho galleries and try to get it. It's a must."

She brought it to him while he was still upstairs. He folded the paper, put it in his wallet and got away as soon as he could with the plea that he needed sleep.

It was after nine o'clock when he reached Lucien Lavalle's address. On the way down he had been able to put the pieces together: her instant recognition of him, the career mother, the gold snuff box with H.H. on the lid and the four-letter words delivered in a Foxcroft finishing-school voice. Of course she had grown up in a home where there had been pictures of him with her father and she knew who he was the minute she spotted him at The Hawk Eye.

Lucien Lavalle lived on a better street than Tania had and, though the apartment was still a loft, it was probably a large one. Sky went up the stairs, rang the bell and she opened the door.

"My God, Tania. I can't believe you're little Heather Hale."

"Not anymore. Lucien and I got married this morning in Connecticut. We were tipped off by a friend of his that the news was going to break. Lucien is out getting our tickets. We're leaving tonight and plan to live in Haiti for a while and paint. His father is something important in the government there."

"I can't believe it. This whole thing is unbelievable."

"Come in, won't you?"

"Just for a minute." He glanced around the spacious and well-arranged room. "Your husband has taste."

"He studied architecture in college. Do sit down. I have lots to say before Lucien gets back."

He sat down on the sofa. "Go ahead."

"I grew up hating you. I loved Daddy, but I resented mother, and I guess everything she liked I instinctively disliked. I remember she had your picture in some special kind of frame and Daddy's was just plain silver."

"He was my closest friend."

"Anyway, when you came into The Hawk Eye that night, looking so square, I told Lucien to get the hell out. I was going to have some fun."

"Well, you did."

"I was pretty sure I could make you and then I was going to tell mother. I couldn't think of anything that would make her more furious."

"What a little bitch you are."

"You're no Sir Galahad, yourself. I had to buy some make-up to cover that bruise on my face."

"It was quite a little act you put on."

"Not really. It started as a game, but it soon got real. It got terribly real, so real that I felt like taking sleeping pills when you didn't show up after the night we spent together. I waited a couple of days and then I went back to Lucien."

"Before you leave for Haiti why don't you call your mother and clear the whole score. Tell her about Lucien, tell her about me or whatever you want, but for heaven's sake tell her where you're going."

"I wrote her this afternoon and mailed it right away so she would get it in the morning. I told her I was married this morning to Lucien Lavalle and that we were going to live in Haiti."

"Good."

"I also told her I had met her darling dream prince and that you'd been screwing me." She laughed, "God, how I'd like to see her face when she reads my letter."

"You like to hurt people, don't you, Heather?"

"Only when I think they deserve it. Come on," she reached for his fly. "Let's go to bed again before Lucien gets back."

"No chance," he had said as he slammed the door and walked out.

CHAPTER TWENTY-EIGHT

Iris Peacock was in Indiana's office sorting her mail. Bradshaw Green had left Miss Peacock a substantial sum in his will and Indiana had offered her a liberal retirement pension, but she begged to stay on as Indiana's personal secretary. Though she was in her seventies, she had been with the Green family so long that she couldn't bear the thought of not being an inside spectator to their endless drama.

At first she was squeamish about working in the office that seemed to her to be haunted. Whenever she opened the door, she lived over again the shock of seeing Bradshaw Green on the floor with his eyes just glazing over, and when she went to close the window from which Gage had jumped, she couldn't bear to look down.

Indiana seemed to have no such qualms. She had quickly redecorated the room, had her father's desk lacquered white and sent the rest of the furniture to the Salvation Army. Miss Peacock admired what she thought of as Indiana's spunk, and little by little had become less nervous.

As Miss Peacock separated the bills from the personal correspondence, she realized that there were fewer bills than usual from the jewelers, the designers, and the department stores, and that they had been dwindling for some time. Indiana's not spending money on herself the way she used to, she thought. Iris Peacock always believed that the Green fortune was endless, but, of course, the will had left his two valuable homes plus two million dollars to his widow, and Indiana's largest share of the estate had been the newspapers.

In the personal pile, Miss Peacock's sharp eyes quickly detected the handwritten letter with a California postmark. She speculated on what Heather was up to now, whether it was a new husband or another plea for an advance on her trust-fund income. Miss Peacock hoped Indiana would confide in her, as she often did since they had been working together.

Just then Indiana walked in. She was wearing a red tweed Chanel suit and as she sat down at her desk, Miss Peacock was struck by how young and spirited she looked. She had kept her figure and there were no gray hairs yet in the thick, short mop of dark curls.

"That's a very becoming suit you're wearing."

"I've always liked red. It's an old suit, but for once I've got a lipstick that matches. Try to get Lincoln LaPorte, will you, and ask him if he can come up here for a minute."

Lincoln came in smiling. "I had a hunch, love, that I might be hearing from you this morning," he said as he sat down.

"Where on earth did you dig up the blind item in today's paper? The one about the certain TV personality?"

"I've had the Soho bit in my files for years. The bartender at The Hawk Eye told me. He's a good friend of mine, and said they were getting together in a big way right on the dance floor. Since she was your daughter I didn't write it then, but when I heard Mr. Goody Two Shoes was out for the White House I couldn't resist."

"Where did you hear that Schuyler Madison was going into politics?"

"Diana and her darling Harrison were silly enough to have their secret confabulation with Madison at 21. A pal of mine, Alan Adler, sitting near them with his girl friend, Taharanda, called me the moment they left."

"I can't believe that Sky is going to give up his TV evening newscast. I've watched all the other stations and his is far the best."

"I never watch TV," Lincoln said in a patronizing tone.

"He manages to be very real, and I'm sure that what he has to say becomes believable to people all across the country."

"I suppose he's quite a power, but all the more reason that he's beginning to itch for the ultimate. Don't all American mothers tell their sons that if they eat their breakfast cereal and come home from school with an A card, that they may grow up to be the President of the United States?" He waved his hands. "It's the big American dream."

"Perhaps at one time, but I doubt if anyone today still thinks the President has much more than moderate power."

"He's pretty well strangled among Congress, the unions and now the media, who pick at him for whatever he does," Lincoln said in his southern drawl.

"My own opinion is that a man in Sky Madison's position or in Tom Malone's as a labor leader have more power than anyone involved in politics."

"So how are you and Malone making out these days?" Lincoln tended to become bored as soon as a conversation became serious and impersonal.

"Every morning I pick up your column and expect to read that we're a twosome. We've just had a few dinners together."

"Quite a few, I hear through the underground, especially since his divorce. I'm not writing it, though, boss lady. I know better than to bite the hand that feeds me."

"You have acquired a lot of power, yourself, Lincoln." As she looked at him, she realized that his small frame was at least fifteen pounds heavier than when she had hired him. His small, delicate features seemed to have vanished into his round face and only the big horn-rimmed glasses were prominent.

"It's good for the paper and, oh God, do I ever love it," he said.

"Let's have luncheon soon, Lincoln. I need to get caught up on the things you don't dare write, and with all the difficulties around the paper, I need a good laugh."

Lincoln went back to the cubicle where he typed his column, feeling slightly depressed. When Indiana had invited him to luncheon the first time, he had been a young writer with stars in his eyes, and one novel and a few free-lance articles behind him. The idea of a gossip column sounded a little demeaning but she was young and good-looking with all of Bradshaw Green's power behind her, and he had decided to give it a try.

He had been surprised when the first bottles of champagne

and scotch arrived with thank-you cards from the men and women he had mentioned. The few had been followed by a torrent and they had ended by creating his lifestyle.

He had moved from his small Park Avenue apartment to a much larger one and had air conditioning installed even in the closet where he kept his wine supply. Gradually his column had become more caustic, but the nastier the stories were, the more prestige they seemed to bring him.

There was almost nothing except food and taxis that wasn't given to him freely or at a minimum cost. As far as food was concerned, he was invited out to dinner every night with sometimes a choice of three parties, and a car was usually sent for him.

He had always been badly dressed because standard sizes didn't fit him, but now his suits were all made to order. Though he regretted not having been able to select them himself, his apartment was filled with at least moderately good paintings, rare plants, silver cigarette boxes, and luxuries from all over the world that had come as Christmas presents.

Lincoln had heard rumors that the paper was in trouble, and now the first confirmation had come to him through Indiana. As he sat at his typewriter, the thought that his smooth-running, lovely life might be interrupted was so shattering that he was unable to start writing his column.

Here I am now, middle-aged virtually, and how can I get back to doing a novel? It's too late in life to get back to work in a garret. Escape thoughts began running through his mind like a squirrel in a cage. I can't be such a cad as to leave Indiana for another paper, when this one may survive. Perhaps I ought to try buttering up Schuyler Madison. He seemed like a friendly guy that afternoon when we were having drinks on the terrace of that hotel in Cannes. I think I'll just write a note telling him how brilliant his program is. Maybe if things go wrong here, he could find a spot somewhere for five minutes of gossip. Lincoln wrote the note, dropped it into the outgoing section of his wire tray and started his column.

As soon as Lincoln had left, Miss Peacock had returned to Indiana. "Your bills are all laid out for you to initial, and then I'll have them paid immediately."

"Thank you. I'll look at them right away."

"There's also a letter from Heather in the other pile. I know you were expecting it."

It was on top of the pile, and she tore it open. Miss Peacock stood in front of her desk, watching her expression. It didn't change until she looked up at the end and smiled. "She agrees to my terms if she can have the money. I'll write the answer in longhand tonight and you can type it tomorrow but in the meantime send her the documents that my lawyer drew up for her to sign."

"I'm glad for you." Miss Peacock smiled.

"I'll be happier when the papers are signed, but now please get me our director of advertising. If he's not in his office in the Advertising Department, try Bleeck's. Morgan spends too much time there."

Five minutes later Bill Morgan walked in. "I've been drowning my sorrows downstairs. I suppose you've heard that the Newspaper Guild is threatening a wildcat strike tonight, and the pressmen and teamsters will follow out of sympathy. The paper may be shut down tomorrow along with the other papers."

"I know, but it will hurt us the most."

"We lost one hundred thousand readers in the last general strike eight years ago because those one hundred thousand people had got used to getting their news every day by watching television instead of reading."

"And we've never been able to get them back." Indiana's voice sounded weary.

"Don't I know? We've had to cut our advertising rates again. Today many of the advertisers are using at least a part of their budget for TV."

"I don't see how it can possibly bring the advertisers the same results."

"It can't for the retailers but it's the national advertising that either breaks you or makes you rich."

"Is there anything I can possibly do?" Indiana asked.

"Well, you can try to work on Tom Malone, if you have any drag with him."

"I'll try to talk to him if I can reach him." Actually, she was expecting Tom Malone for dinner at the apartment that evening. She would have liked to go home early so that she could formulate what she wanted to say to him, but her calendar for the afternoon was full. It included a conference call to her editors across the country and a completely hopeless interview with the boy who headed the Newspaper Guild, and it was late before she was ready to leave.

As she gathered up Heather's letter and dropped it into her handbag, she remembered the shock of another of Heather's letters that had come to her seven years ago. She would never forget its contents:

> Dear Mother:
>
> I was married this morning to Lucien Lavalle, and by the time you read this letter we will be in Haiti, where his family lives, and we are going to paint. Lucien is a homosexual and I know you don't like him but he has been very kind, and he seems to be the only one who understands me. You don't, and I don't think you ever tried.
>
> I ran into your dream prince, Sky Madison, and we had a wonderful time in bed together. He's great at it. You ought to try him sometimes.
>
> When Lucien and I are settled, I'll write you my address so you can forward the income from my trust fund.
>
> > Love,
> > Heather

The letter had left Indiana in shock and she had sat at her desk for the next half hour in a trance. Heather has always hated me, she thought. Somewhere along the line I must have done something wrong, though I don't know quite what. The more she thought of Sky the more furious she became. What a bastard. He's gone through the family as if he were a shopper in a store, trying us both on for size and then rejecting us. It was even more humiliating to think that he and Heather might have been laughing at her when they were in bed together locked into each others arms. How could he have done this to me?

Her first impulse had been to tear the letter into bits, but fortunately she had put it into her desk drawer instead. The next day she had given it to Miss Peacock to file, in case she ever had to prove in court that Heather was wayward and incompetent.

The telephone on her desk rang, bringing her sharply back to the present. It was Tom Malone.

"Sorry, Indiana, but we're still negotiating and it looks like a long session, as they've just ordered sandwiches and coffee sent up."

"I'm sorry."

"I'm sorry to especially miss dinner with you tonight, but I must see this through. Don't worry, dear, I believe it's going to turn out O.K. for all concerned."

"Thanks for telling me, Tom, and I hope you are right." She sat back in her chair with a sigh of relief. Miss Peacock heard her and came to the door.

"Did you call me?"

"No, I thought you had gone home, but since you're here, let's go up to the cafeteria and see if they can give us something. There's not going to be a strike, at least not now, and I feel like celebrating."

"I suppose you remember that I've put three cocktail parties for this evening on your calendar, and you have a dinner date."

"The dinner date is off and the cocktail parties always seem to be full of the people whose telephone calls I haven't returned, because I can't do what they want me to do."

When they sat down at a little table in the cafeteria, Miss Peacock said, "I often think it's too bad, Indiana, that everyone wants something from you. It has kept you from finding the right man."

"It's not just a feeling. The first date is always good, but on the second go-round I always know what they're after, a job for themselves or somebody, a feature about some girlfriend's needlepoint or cooking."

"Or even just a mention in Lincoln's column. I screen a lot of those for you," Miss Peacock said quickly.

"I'm not being cynical but that's why Tom Malone has lasted. At least I want more from him than he wants from me."

"It's too bad your father ruined your young romance with Schuyler Madison. He's made such a success of his life and would have been the perfect husband for you."

Indiana was quiet for a moment, staring into space. "I wonder."

Miss Peacock sensed her mood and waited a moment before she spoke. "'The Skyrocket Evening News' is the best on the air. I never miss it."

"Neither do I."

"I thoroughly disliked destroying all the letters that Mr. Madison sent you, and it has been on my conscience ever since. I kept them in a file for a while, but I was afraid somehow Mr. Green would find them. He was so adamant on the subject, and I never disobeyed him."

For a moment Indiana thought how different her life might have been if she had received the letters, but it was foolish to think of that now. "How did you happen to meet Daddy and how did you manage to stay so loyal to him, Miss Peacock?"

"It happened soon after I came to New York. I was seventeen and rather pretty then, at least I was tall and skinny and wore the fashions of the time rather well. I got a job at Keeley's, a shop on Broadway, not to model clothes but shoes. I have narrow feet, small for my height and good ankles and legs."

"So Daddy came into the shop?"

"Oh yes. Keeley's was an exciting place in those days. All the Broadway stars like Marilyn Miller used to come in to buy their shoes." She sighed.

"I'll never forget the afternoon your father arrived with Irene Castle. I was modeling pumps with high-button spats and he asked for the same thing in her size." She looked down. "Her feet were larger than mine, but he bought them for her and in three different styles besides. As he left, he said to me, 'You have a fortune in those feet of yours.'"

"I've always noticed your elegant feet and ankles, Miss Peacock."

"I suppose they've spread a little, but almost to the day of his death he was fussy about the shoes I wore."

"That's just like him."

"After the first afternoon with Irene Castle, he came back with other actresses. I particularly remember Gaby De Lyn. He always asked me to model. Finally he said to me, 'You're a very bright girl and good at what you're doing, but if you ever feel like switching to an office job, I think I could use you at the *Globe.*'"

"I suppose he was very attractive then?"

"He was still in his early thirties and very dashing. I kept looking at the card he had given me and finally decided to go and ask for a job."

"Where did he start you?"

"I was lucky. It was at the time he was running for governor. At first I was one of several secretaries, but soon I could see that he preferred to work with me because I was trusted with his most confidential work. Of course I was fascinated and flattered, and I guess I had a few Cinderella dreams."

Indiana laughed. "It would have been much nicer to have you than Diana as my stepmother."

"I suppose it might have been if I hadn't discovered that I'm a totally frigid woman. One evening after I had been with him a couple of years, we were working late and he made what I suppose you would call a pass at me. I was sitting at my typewriter and he came up behind me and started stroking my hair and then his hands moved down toward my breasts. I sat there like a wooden Indian, hating every minute of it and wanting it to end. He never tried it again, but it was the beginning of a closer relationship that went on undisturbed through all his many love affairs."

"Why on earth should you have hated his touching you?"

"How do I know? I simply never felt any physical response to anyone. Everything comes naturally to you, Indiana, but to me the very idea of sex has always been too embarrassing even to contemplate."

As they left the cafeteria, the presses for the next morning's first edition were beginning to run. The sound always started slowly and tremulously and mounted to a busy, humming crescendo. Its tremor could be felt all through the building and it was like the heartbeat and breathing of a human being, Indiana had always felt. She had loved the sound of the giant presses running ever since she was a child.

CHAPTER TWENTY-NINE

As he sat in back of the town car Diana had sent for him and watched the East River, the Triborough Bridge and finally the still-green, rolling fields of Westchester flash past his window, Sky couldn't help thinking of the first weekend he and Gage had spent at South Wind. He remembered the falling snow, Miss Peacock in the corner of the car observing them minutely and the excitement of arriving at South Wind that looked as somber as houses in an old Victorian novel. He thought with a sudden pang of Indiana, how pretty and eager she had been, of Pinkie, the Indian servant who had materialized one morning in his bedroom and even of the old canoe with Kuckee painted on it, which had intrigued him so much in the indoor swimming pool.

He had been sure that Diana would have made some changes but he wasn't prepared for what he saw when the car passed through the gates and started the long drive to the house. It was completely landscaped with clusters of white birch trees, clumps of mountain laurel and rhododendrons that must be overwhelming in the spring when in full bloom. At the end, the old house, painted snow white, loomed up like a castle in the setting for an operetta.

The massive doors were opened by an English butler wearing white gloves, and the ugly old family chairs that had once furnished the big entrance hall had been replaced by some fine old English pieces.

Sky followed the butler to his room, which he believed was the one he had occupied before, close to Indiana's quarters. The butler told him he was to join the Kirbys on the east terrace by the pool, that there would be time for a swim before lunch and that a terry-cloth robe was hanging in his dressing room. Before going downstairs, though, he went to the window and looked out. Instead of the expanse of green lawn that he remembered, he was now looking at a small lake. There was even an island in the center of it and as he stared, two white swans scrambled down the bank and floated off in their stately way.

On the terrace, Diana came toward him with both hands outstretched. "Sky, darling, it's so wonderful to have you here at South Wind."

"Yes, Sky, we're glad you could afford the time," Harrison Kirby said as he shook his hand. "We've invited just one guest. Senator Berkeley is visiting friends nearby. He made a point of saying he's anxious to meet you and he's such a good friend of ours we can talk as freely as if we were alone."

"How nice. I've always admired him."

"You have plenty of time for a swim before the senator comes," Diana said. "Go ahead and dive in."

"I was just thinking of that. In California there's a pool wherever you go, and I miss that part of life in the East." He took off his terry-cloth robe.

"Look, Harrison, at how marvelous Sky looks. You certainly keep yourself in good form." Diana's eyes sparkled as they traveled up and down his slim, muscular body and stopped for a moment at the bulge in the brief swimming trunks.

"I try, but I think it's the tension that keeps my weight down." He dived in, swam from one end to the other twice with a leisurely stroke and came out feeling refreshed.

The butler was just serving drinks on a silver tray. Sky started to put on his terry robe. "As soon as I finish dripping, I'll run upstairs and change."

"Don't bother with your robe. You have plenty of time. Luncheon isn't until one-thirty."

Sky took an orange juice from the butler's tray. "Diana, I can't get over the changes you've made in this place."

"Isn't the lake picturesque? I suppose you've already spotted it?"

"Of course I have." He looked at Diana in her flowered print dress with the oval, ruffle-edged neckline, the big straw hat to protect her delicate blond skin, the lake and the white swans in the distance and realized they were all part of the English country house that she had managed to create from an American Victorian horror.

"You see, it was very fortunate. There had once been a lake there, so I knew that all we had to do was to excavate and the basin would be there."

"Wasn't that the lake in which Indiana's mother was drowned?"

"I didn't know until after we started digging and one of the servants said something about it, but of course it was long, long ago."

"I wanted Indiana to be here for luncheon today," Harrison said, "but Diana vetoed it."

"Darling, I only thought the memories might be too painful for her."

Harrison interrupted. "I doubt that Indiana is as fragile as you seem to think, my dear. She is the most powerful woman in the state today, and her papers across the country carry great weight for our future planning."

He turned to Sky. "It is absolutely necessary for us to have her on our side from the very beginning."

The butler returned to announce Senator Berkeley's arrival. "Meet us in the library," said Diana as Sky pulled on his robe and headed for his room.

If he had been startled by the white painted towers, the artificial lake and the swans, he was even more surprised by the transformation that had gone on inside. The rooms smelled delicious, and though the scent seemed to come from nowhere, Sky remembered from her flat in London that she always burned scented candles in the rooms for hours but snuffed them out and removed them just before her guests were due to arrive.

The long refectory table and the high-backed chairs in the dining room were gone and, instead, a round table for four had been set up with bamboo chairs that had needlepoint covers in flower designs. He supposed that Diana had a stack of such tables, and that she filled the room with them for her parties.

He was riveted by the large portrait of Diana that hung over a long, antique English buffet at one end of the room, and noted it was painted by Philippe Lord.

"What a really fine portrait of you, Diana. Philippe has captured you perfectly."

"I don't think Harrison likes it very much, but he does admit it's decorative."

"Philippe and I were war buddies in North Africa during the war. I remember he often said he'd like to paint Diana in the nude."

"Well, he has kept her as nude as possible," Harrison said. The painting showed Diana reclining on a chaise longue. She was wearing a lace-trimmed pink satin negligee that was just slipping off her shoulders to show part of her full breasts and followed the voluptuous curves of her body down to her feet, which were tucked under her. Beside her was a lace-covered table set with a pink-and-white English-china tea set. "I should have preferred to have him paint Diana in her hunting clothes. It would have been more appropriate for our dining room."

The cold watercress soup was being served and Senator Berkeley, who had taken no part in the subject of the painting, turned the conversation to more general subjects. "The other night I wanted to take the whole family to a nice movie that we could all enjoy, something with no four-letter words. The kids, though, said they wouldn't be caught dead in a G movie."

"How did you solve the problem, Senator?" Sky asked.

"That's the joke. We compromised on an old movie, no naked sex, no violence with a sentimental ending. The kids ate it up."

"How do you explain the contradiction?"

"I don't. I think the kids are terribly mixed up with all the pornography that's laid out for them, and mostly on TV. What's your opinion of the TV violence programs that come on one after another, Mr. Madison?"

"Obviously, I'm not responsible and see them only occasionally by chance."

"Do you think the government should step in and do something about it?"

"No, sir, I don't. I think it should be a matter of individual responsibility. I thoroughly dislike the sloppy way that so many people are trying to dump all their problems on the government.

They're like spoiled children, wanting to be kept in comfort, with Washington acting as God, parent and teacher. I think this country is losing its guts."

"It's just what I was going to say," Senator Berkeley said. "It's no longer the land of the free and the home of the brave."

"We are too mealy-mouthed," Sky replied. "We fear that the word 'capitalism' is unpopular. We talk about the 'free enterprise' system and run to cover in the folds of the flag and talk about the American way of life."

"Senator, Mr. Madison already knows that we have hopes of having him for our next governor and from there on to greater things," Harrison said.

"And how do you feel about it?" the senator asked.

"I feel that it is a momentous decision. My present position with all its daily excitement and variety suits my temperament very well, and I feel that my career in the medium of television has just begun."

"You are weighing your own personal power and the freedom that goes with it against political power, which can be a kind of balancing act but provides you with a place in American history."

"It's something like that. At times in one's life, it's difficult to think clearly, but I've never been averse to venturing into something new."

"All I can say to you, Schuyler, is that the country needs desperately a man who has a great deal of both charisma and honest guts. The country was charmed by President Kennedy, though the love affair might have cooled if he had lived. Now it is bitter after what it feels was the betrayal of Nixon, but it would not be too hard for you to re-establish its faith."

They had coffee on the terrace, and when the senator started to leave, Sky was half minded to say yes, yes he would run, but instead promised to be in touch with him by the end of the following week.

"He's been in politics a long time, Schuyler," Harrison Kirby said. "He knows all the ropes and he said to me at the car, 'Madison will be a winner.'"

"That's encouraging."

"Harrison usually takes a bit of a nap after luncheon, don't you, dear?" said Diana as she patted her husband's hand. "I thought Sky might like me to show him around the place."

"Yes, that's a good idea. Excuse me, Schuyler. You know, when you get to be my age, a little rest helps."

He started for the door. "I look forward to seeing you for cocktails around six."

"We'll take the golf cart and then be back in just a few minutes." Diana took Sky's hand and they sauntered toward the garage.

Harrison Kirby had turned part of the acreage of South Wind into a three-hole golf course. It provided him and the guests he invited for weekends just the right amount of exercise. It was amusing to guide the cart, with its scalloped white canvas top, over the rolling land, and Sky could see that the greens were in beautiful condition.

Diana snuggled close to him, holding his arm and squealing whenever the cart bumped. "Isn't this fun?" she said. "I just had to get away with you somewhere so you could tell me all about Soho."

"Soho?"

"Yes, Soho. The little bit in Lincoln's column that you promised to tell me about."

"It was nothing," Sky shrugged. "When I came to New York seven years ago, I had some time on my hands. I was curious about what the kids and Soho were all about, so I stopped in at a nightclub a couple of nights."

She smiled. "But you did have a big romance. I can tell by your voice."

"It was what you might call a brief encounter or just one of those things."

"What was she like?" Diana's lips were parted and she was drinking in every word.

"It's been so long ago I can hardly remember, but I think she was skinny, nineteen, and high on cocaine."

"Nineteen. So you've started robbing the cradle. What was her name?"

"Why are you so curious, Diana? I think her name was Tania."

"I don't believe you're telling me all the truth. This girl may turn up somehow to blemish your candidacy."

"Come now, Diana, don't be foolish. Let's take a ride around the lake." He turned the cart and they went bumping across a meadow to the edge of the water.

"Now you're cross with me because I'm overanxious for you to become the President of the United States." She squeezed his arm. "Besides, no matter who I marry I always have a place in my heart for you and a yearning to be in bed with you again sometime."

He leaned over and kissed her on the cheek. "You're a lovely flirt, Mrs. Harrison Kirby."

Diana didn't answer and was quiet as they drove around the lake, which had a miniature boathouse at one end with a small rowboat tied to it. As they returned the golf cart to the garage and walked back to the house, he decided he had liked South Wind better in its old ugly self. He supposed that Bradshaw Green's old canoe with "Kuckee" painted on the side had gone the way of all his other possessions, but just for old times' sake Sky would visit the indoor swimming pool before he left.

There were guests for dinner and while Diana and Harrison were saying good-bye to them, Sky wandered through the rooms that he remembered led to the pool. Diana had knocked down some of the walls to make larger rooms, and she had done a superb job of editing Bradshaw Green's collections. The indoor pool now had backgammon tables on one side and cafe tables and ice-cream-parlor chairs on the other. The pool, itself, had been covered with what looked like a removable dance floor and there was no canoe in sight.

When Sky had said good night to Diana and Harrison and went upstairs to his room, he thought of Diana's affectionate mood in the golf cart that afternoon and decided to bolt his bedroom door.

When he woke in the morning, Pinkie was standing beside his bed, smiling and holding out to him a crystal bud vase with a single rosebud. "For you," she said.

He sat up in bed. "Why, Pinkie, that's beautiful."

"You come back finally, and you remember my name."

"Of course I remember you, Pinkie. Remember we once had a long talk about the lake."

"The lake came back, too."

"I was startled to see it when I arrived yesterday. Is it just the way it was before?"

"Not so pretty as then. There were willow trees along the bank. Very beautiful. This was her room, so she could be close to her baby."

"Say, how did you get into this room, Pinkie? I had the door locked."

"Through the door in the big closet. That's the door she used to go in to see the baby."

"Did Mr. Green drown Indiana's mother, do you think?"

"Oh no. Couldn't have been. I was with him when we heard her scream. It was a hot summer night. She had walked down to the lake for some fresh air. There used to be a little dock alongside. It must have given way. We heard her scream. We all run fast and Mr. Green ran fastest, but it was too late."

"I think it was you, Pinkie, who told me she had bruises on her throat."

"Not so much but a little. They had a big fight that afternoon because he thought she liked the boy who took care of her horse."

"Of course she didn't?"

"No, she liked nobody but Mr. Green. When Mr. Green died Miss Indiana wanted to take me with her and I wanted to go, but Miss Diana said I was born here and was part of this place, so I had to stay." She grinned, "Miss Indiana always sending me presents, though."

"I'm sure you find Miss Diana very pleasant, too."

"Oh yes, she very proper lady, very nice, but not fun like Miss Indiana."

"What became of the old canoe that used to hang on the wall of the indoor swimming pool, Pinkie?"

"Miss Diana, how she hated that thing. She kept asking him for God's sake to take it down, but nothing would persuade him to. The minute he died, she said to take it down. One of the stable boys thought he could use it, but he didn't, and it is still down at the stable, up on the loft."

"If I get dressed right now, will you take me down and show it to me, Pinkie?" He hardly knew why he wanted to see "Kuckee" again but from the moment he first saw it hanging on the wall of the swimming pool, he had been fascinated by its incongruity in the setting. He remembered that when he and Sidney had discussed it they had both been certain it had some special meaning for Bradshaw Green.

He and Pinkie climbed to the loft of the stable. The canoe was the worse for having been taken down. Some of the boards were broken and it was certainly beyond repair. He felt the boards and even felt under the broken ones to see if there had been room to hide anything below them.

"All gone," said Pinkie, who was watching him.

"You mean there was something in the canoe when they took it down?"

"Old papers, very old. Fell apart."

"What papers? Do you remember?"

"No, but ask Randall. He helped take canoe down."

"Who is Randall?"

"He the chauffeur that drive you back to New York today."

"Was there anything else, Pinkie?"

"Yes, old purse but no money. No good."

"Do you still have it?"

"Yes." They went back to the house and Pinkie brought him an old leather wallet. A piece of paper was folded in it and as he took it out gingerly the edges began crumbling in his fingers. The communication was dated September 1, 1901. It was addressed to Bradshaw Green, editor, Buffalo *Globe*. It thanked him for his interest and monetary support of Project M, which was planned to take place at the Pan-American Exposition within the next few weeks.

Sky felt he had drawn a blank, but asked her if he could keep the letter.

She nodded. "No good to me."

He took out a twenty-dollar bill, put it in the old wallet and handed it back to her. "I want you to buy yourself a present, Pinkie, to remember me by."

She gave him her toothless smile. "I remember you anyway. In kitchen every night I see you on TV."

Harrison was waiting at the breakfast table on the terrace when he arrived. He was in the midst of a genuine English breakfast, complete with a soft-boiled egg, bacon and toast with orange marmalade. "Did you ever see a more perfect morning, Sky? Every time I wake up in this glorious setting, the wonderful fresh air and the sunshine make me feel at least ten years younger."

Sky was amused. Actually, Harrison looked ten years younger than he had when they lunched together at 21 the week before. Diana must have been using her old Chinese trick, Sky thought.

"Diana and I are both hoping you have slept on our idea and have come up with a favorable response."

"I'm seriously tempted."

"That's good news."

"What do you really think my chances of being elected governor would be?" Sky asked.

"Excellent and after that for President, too. However, we must have the Green papers on our side. I suggest that you talk with Indiana as soon as possible and make sure of her support." He shook his head. "If she were not with you, the campaign would be difficult, but not impossible."

"I'm afraid I haven't seen her for a long time, but I'll be glad to call her. There's a possibility she may not want to see me."

"We see very little of her, too. She and Diana are not unfriendly, but they seem to have very little in common. I admire Indiana. She has been a strong publisher and her father would have been very proud of her success."

Sky saw the chauffeur standing at the door and stood up. "It's time for me to leave, I see. Give my regards to Diana and thank you both for a pleasant weekend." He shook Harrison Kirby's hand. "I'll call you in Washington within ten days."

Once on the way to New York, Sky said, "Randall, I hear that you helped move the old canoe from the indoor swimming pool to the loft in the stable."

"Yes, sir, I never could understand why Mr. Green had it there, and it really went to pieces when we began to take it down."

"Pinkie said there were some old papers inside."

"Yes, sir, some old newspapers. They crumbled up quick. I just remember they were the biggest headlines I ever saw."

"What did they say?"

"All across the front of the paper it said, 'PRESIDENT SHOT.'

I thought it was going to be President Kennedy, but the date was 1901."

"That's very interesting. It must have been President McKinley, whose death made Teddy Roosevelt President."

"You can't prove it by me, sir. I don't know my American history that well, but I do remember when I started driving him, Mr. Green was always talking about Teddy Roosevelt. He liked him a lot."

So Green did have a hand in getting rid of one President and putting in another whom he liked better, Sky thought. The rumor that he knew beforehand that McKinley would be shot and that his papers were on the street almost as soon as the gun was fired was true after all. Sidney and I hung him for the wrong thing and managed to miss the big story.

CHAPTER THIRTY

Indiana returned from five days in California feeling tired but triumphant. She had accomplished her mission and drove straight from the airport to the office.

Miss Peacock had finished the mail, but was busy putting the latest books and magazines into neat piles and flicking dust off the top of her desk with a handkerchief.

Indiana opened her briefcase and took out a manila envelope full of papers. "Please give these to my lawyer to check over and then put them into the safe. There were no hitches and everything is settled."

"How did you find Heather?"

"She seemed more mature and much softer and we managed to talk civilly to each other for the first time I can remember."

"She's happy?"

"I don't know about that. She's married to another painter and he seems to have more talent and more stability than the first."

"You liked him?"

"Yes, I suppose so. They seem to get along together but the house is haphazard and she's very pregnant, expecting a baby in another month."

"I don't like to hurry you but it has been a hectic week and I have at least two pages of things to which you have to say yes or no."

"What's urgent?"

"The head of the Editorial Department needs to talk to you about suggestions for filling Rockefeller's place as governor."

"I'd like to talk to him around eleven tomorrow morning."

"Bill Morgan has a crisis in the Sunday magazine section. Both

Saks Fifth Avenue and Bloomingdale's claim they have been promised the fifth page, and he wants you to arbitrate."

"He must be crazy. Obviously, it goes to the better advertiser, but tell him to come up to my office late this afternoon."

"Gregg Gordon, the sports columnist, is resigning in a huff. He doesn't like the new logo, and thinks the column isn't well enough placed in the paper."

She picked up the phone. "I'll tell him to come up right away. He's good and now that it looks like the paper will go on, I want to keep him." After she finished the call she turned to Miss Peacock. "Maybe I can adjust both complaints, and a little praise always helps."

"Mr. LaPorte has had an offer from another paper, but he has turned it down. He wants you for luncheon next week."

"Tell him Friday."

"Schuyler Madison has called every day since Monday. He must see you if only for a few minutes."

"Tell him I have no time open for the next month. I wouldn't see him if he were bringing me a ton of gold bricks."

"What a pity. He's so pleasant and he's better-looking than ever, too."

"So you've seen him?"

"I kept telling him you were in California. Perhaps he didn't believe me, so he stopped in to see if I couldn't slip him in between two other people."

"Well, just get rid of him if he calls or comes here again. I'm not interested in seeing him."

"But what can I tell him?"

"Why not tell him the truth? Tell him that I couldn't stand the sight of him and to go straight to hell. Spice it up with a few four-letter words, too."

"Oh I couldn't do that."

Miss Peacock looked so doleful that Indiana burst out laughing. "I suppose he wants to tell me he's going to run for governor, then President, and save the world. I'll have to listen to that crapola sometime, I suppose, but please put it off as long as you can."

The next afternoon she was interviewing the head of the

Newspaper Guild, which included the stenographers, clerks and all the reporters who were below editorial status.

"You're Nathan Kresky, aren't you? Please sit down. I sent for you because I wanted to hear in your own words why your guild is so full of angry people."

He hesitated for a minute. She knew that he saw her as an expensively dressed woman surrounded by inherited status symbols, like the three-foot-tall bronze owl on the shelf behind her, that had appeared on the masthead of her grandfather's first newspaper. She was to him simply a selfish woman who stood between him and the benefits life owed him and his coworkers.

"We're not asking for higher wages this time," he finally said. "All we want is job security and more leisure time to enjoy life."

"How can anyone guarantee anyone else security? Everyone has to make his own security, and there's still no guarantee."

"Mrs. Hale, you have total security. How can you possibly understand?" He talked on and on and she tried to listen patiently.

Finally she said, "Let me tell you about my security. This newspaper has been losing two million dollars a year. If you go on strike, I may well close it once and for all, much as it breaks my heart. Even if you don't, I shall probably be obliged."

When the boy had left, she called Miss Peacock. "I'm tired. Could you have the cafeteria send me a glass of iced coffee with no cream?"

"Mr. Madison is here to see you."

"Tell him I'm not in." Her voice was hard.

"But I told him you were. If you refuse, he may think you're afraid of seeing him."

"Let him think what he wants."

"He's very determined. He'll keep coming, so why not get it over and done with?"

"Perhaps you're right, but give me just a minute to tidy my desk."

The top of her desk was completely clean, so Miss Peacock knew she would be reaching for her handbag, which held her comb and lipstick. She gave her plenty of time before she let Sky in.

He had never seen Indiana at work and it came as a slight shock to see her in Bradshaw Green's old office surrounded by secretaries to guard her and a line-up of people waiting outside.

She put down the pen she was scribbling with and held out her hand. "Why, Sky. It's nice to see you again."

Her voice was cool and the hand she held out was cold, but Sky pulled up a chair and sat down. "Harrison Kirby was singing your praises to me over Labor Day weekend."

"I suppose they had you at South Wind. How was darling Diana and didn't you find the house fascinating?"

She was smiling sweetly, but he realized he had made a clumsy beginning. "I didn't like it as much as I did the first weekend I saw it."

"Let's not look back, Sky. What do you want from me now?" She knew, but she was determined to make him say.

"I suppose that most of the people who try to make appointments want something from you, don't they?"

"Only about ninety-nine and seven-eighths per cent of them do."

"Harrison and a group of his party are anxious for me to be a candidate to replace Governor Rockefeller."

"And from then on to the White House, of course?"

"That's the way they talk, but it seems incredible."

"And they want to know if I'll support you?"

He nodded, "Yes."

"What makes you think I wouldn't?"

"Because I think that if I were you, I would hate my guts."

"I did, and perhaps I do, but my personal feelings have never influenced my editorial judgment. Frankly, I think your candidacy would make a great story, and if you want it, I think you could be a damn good governor or President."

"Thank you, Indi."

For a moment she almost lost control but managed to pull herself together. No one but Sky had ever called her Indi. She went on, "Unfortunately you've come at a bad time. I'm threatened with another strike and I have just told the president of the striking guild that I will close the paper immediately if they persist." She shrugged her shoulders. "I suppose it is only the question of a short time before I have to end it, anyway. The number of newspapers that have disappeared is frightening."

"I'm sorry, Indi. I know how much you have always loved the paper."

"Yes, I do love it. It has been like a live companion to me. I feel contented every night when I hear the presses starting and if I have to hear them stopping for the last time, it will be like listening to a person stop breathing."

"Isn't there any alternative?"

"I don't think so. I can't go on losing money forever. Daddy loved me and I suppose when he left the newspapers to me he thought they were the most valuable part of the estate, but as things have worked out, Diana, and Heather, when she gets her inheritance at thirty-five, will be wealthier than I am."

"Couldn't you have broken the will?"

"It would have been a long, ugly fight. I'm sure Daddy meant to change it himself. He had an appointment with the lawyer on the day he died, but he couldn't make it." She hesitated for a minute and then looked directly at him. "You killed him, you know."

He looked bewildered. "What do you mean?"

"We had a big to-do about whether or not to go to the big social preview of your film, *The Power and the Glory*. Diana went, but Daddy threw a tantrum and refused. The next morning, though, he went to an early screening. When he reached the office, he had a heart attack and died right here in this room. Later they found the ticket stub to the movie in his coat pocket."

"What can I say, Indi?"

"Why, nothing, of course."

He looked at the bronze bust of Teddy Roosevelt that she had set up on one of the book shelves and wished he could tell her the whole story.

"Never mind, Sky. My papers will support you as long as they can. The *Globe* can give you a big sendoff."

"That's very generous of you."

"And when you get to the President bit, the other Green papers can carry on. By that time I may have moved away and become active in running one of them. I haven't decided."

"Indi, I haven't made up my own mind, either. I like my job at UBC and I don't know whether I want to get into politics."

"You are very good at what you are doing."

"I'm glad you think so."

"There's always a certain amount of phoniness and playacting in politics, but you could take that in your stride, too. Nobody can advise you."

He stood up. "I know that, and I've taken a lot of your time. I suppose it's unfair to ask you for more but I desperately need a friend to talk to."

"I'll look at my calendar, and either I or Miss Peacock will call you. I'll be thinking about both sides of the situation, too."

As soon as Sky had left, Indiana rang for Miss Peacock, who came in quickly. "Are you glad you saw him?"

"Yes, I knew I had to, and it wasn't at all unpleasant. I think I made it clear to him that we were no longer close friends and never could be again."

"You didn't tell him why you went to California?"

"No, but as I think it over, I believe I will. It's only fair, I suppose, and besides, I want to see his face."

"I'll bring in your calendar, so you can see how you'll be able to fit it in."

"I don't think I want to see him here again. I'll invite him to the apartment. Let's say Sunday night, cocktails at seven."

"Very well."

"If he's not free I may not bother to try again."

CHAPTER THIRTY-ONE

Sky was surprised when Miss Peacock telephoned Indiana's invitation the next day. He had been sure she would keep her word, but she had been so cool and impersonal that he had expected nothing more than another brief talk at her office. After he had accepted, Miss Peacock added that there would be a guest whom Indiana believed he would enjoy meeting. Probably another senator, he decided.

It was a turbulent day for him and his team. Gerald Ford had just pardoned Richard Nixon. Sky and his team were collecting the pros and cons and weaving them into an editorial that would be used with a brief statement from the President, and a comment from the Washington correspondent.

At the same time, he had asked one of the writers to gather up facts and figures on the demise of the many American newspapers of the past few years. He had been deeply interested and touched by the situation at the *Globe* and in his mind he called this editorial "A World Without Newspapers." At one time, not long ago, there had been a lively rivalry between the press and television, but now he could plainly see that most of the newspapers were limping along while television zoomed ahead. The world had been glued to their TV sets ever since the moving presentation of President Kennedy's funeral. That had been the turning point. He decided to take the part of neither management nor the workers, but to talk about the power of some of the early newspapers and their publishers, like Horace Greeley, William Randolph Hearst, Joseph Pulitzer, Bradshaw Green, Roy Howard, William Allen White and Herbert Bayard Swope. He would end by eulogizing the pleasure of leisurely reading. At this point, UBC could afford to be gracious, he felt.

When he and his team were having their usual postmortem drink upstairs, Sky looked around the room and felt a sudden surge of contentment. This is the life I love, he thought. Why the hell have I been trying to make myself believe I want to be governor, let alone President, political jobs that I don't know a damn thing about? I must have been crazy to think seriously about it even for a minute. He was tempted to get up, go to the telephone and call the Kirbys with his decision but decided to play it out and see what Indiana and her senator had to say.

Sky decided to be a few minutes early for what he supposed was a small party at Indiana's apartment. He wanted to tell her what he had decided before her other guests appeared on the scene. Perhaps he should have simply regretted the invitation but, he told himself, he had found her interesting and would enjoy talking to her again.

A maid let him into the drawing room and he sat down and looked around. As Fifth Avenue apartments go it was a moderate size with tall windows that showed an expanse of Central Park. The sofas looked comfortable and the whole effect was colorful, provocative and very feminine. At one end the room opened into a dining room; at the other end, there was another room, which seemed to be a library.

In a few minutes, Indiana came in. She was wearing white silk evening pajamas and a heavy gold chain around her neck. She was no longer the cool, efficient editor of the *Globe* he had talked to earlier in the week, but the Indi he remembered with the wide smile and the big, sparkling eyes.

"Hello, Sky. So glad you could make it."

"No problem. My days are busy and I tend to hang around with my working team until quite late, but weekends are free. I don't have that many social dates."

"The maid should have put you in the library where there's a bar, but since you're here, how do you like my paintings?"

"The Matisse above your fireplace is a beauty."

"I adore it, and I planned the colors of this room around it."

"The Monet is a fine one, too."

"I love the water lilies and I suppose I could live on it for several years if I go broke and have to sell it."

"That's not like you, Indi. You have too much hell-fire in you to be downed by anything for very long."

Whenever he spoke her name, she could feel her heart beating a little faster, but she was determined not to show it. "I suppose you're right, Sky."

"You'll find your way out of this mess somehow, I'm sure."

They went into the library, where a butler's tray had been set up. "What shall I fix for you?" he asked.

"Just a glass of white wine on the rocks, please."

"New York is certainly into white wine. They don't seem to be serving anything else at cocktails."

"I drink it because it's easy, but now that I think of it, there's a bottle of champagne on the bar. Let's have that."

"Just as you say." He picked up the bottle and started to open it. "I never turn down a chance to drink good vintage champagne, especially Taittinger's Blanc de Blancs."

"I like mine on ice."

"So do I. I dislike the bubbles."

He fixed the two glasses and they sat down, one at each end of a leather sofa.

"By the way, Sky, I can't tell you how much I enjoyed your editorial about newspapers versus television last night. I thought it was very gallant of you and you expressed so beautifully what so many of us in the publishing business feel. It may even help."

"Everything you said to me in your office the other day struck a responsive chord."

She reached for a bowl of nuts on the table and passed them to him. "How have you solved your own problems, Sky, or have you made up your mind?"

"To tell the truth, Indi, I was sitting around with my editors and writers the other evening, and suddenly I wondered why the hell I had let myself get into such a stew. Why on earth should I leave something I do reasonably well and plunge into something that if I were elected I would have to be guided through like a blind man?"

"Of course, that might be quite advantageous for the guiders."

"I don't think that's why they came after me. It's just that I'm not about to bite. I feel that any reasonably successful commentator on TV has as much power if not more than officeholders, and to me they have a better chance at a good life." He paused. "You think I'm crazy, don't you?"

"Not at all, Sky. I've always thought you made sense. How about pouring some more champagne over my ice? I was thirsty and gulped down the first as if it were water."

As he stood at the bar filling the glasses the wall beyond, which had been in the shadows, was suddenly illuminated by the setting sun.

He set down the glasses and stood transfixed. "Good God, Indi, how did this get here?" Hanging against the wine-red wall of the library was the Picasso painting he had sold to put himself through college.

"I bought it a long time ago."

"But where the hell did you find it? When I first came to New York, I went the rounds of the smaller galleries looking for it and had no luck."

"You showed me a picture of it once. Remember, you used to carry it around in your wallet as if it were a picture of your best girl?"

"I remember." He turned from looking at the painting to her. "It brings back all kinds of memories of my father taking me to a little Left Bank gallery where I met Picasso."

"Your Picasso is really responsible for my starting to buy. I asked for it whenever I went to a gallery, whether in Europe or here, and I sometimes ended by buying something else."

"Where did you finally find it?"

"I had told so many people what I wanted that I finally got a letter and a color photograph from a gallery in Boston. I flew up there to make sure it was the right one."

"You must have paid a fantastic price for it even then."

"Not so bad as you might think, and it has at least tripled in value since then." She had meant to tell him she had found it when she went to his hotel after Gage's funeral but had forgotten in the emotion of the night. She could never forget the pain she had suffered when she had never heard from him again.

"I'm happy it fell into such good hands."

"I've become fond of it."

"Should you ever think of selling it, be sure to give me first crack."

She smiled, but she thought, he'll rot in hell before he gets that painting, and to think I had every intention of giving it to him when I first bought it.

They were still looking at the painting when a maid appeared at the doorway and Indiana left him to speak to her. "Excuse me, Sky. I told you I had someone here whom I wanted you to meet."

He was gearing himself for a senator or some other political figure when she came back holding a small boy by the hand. "Sky, this is Chance."

"It's nice to meet you, Chance," he said, holding out his hand.

The boy came forward and took it. "You're Mr. Skyrocket, aren't you?"

"I suppose I am." He was a good-looking kid, Sky thought, probably six or seven, blond, well-built, looking vaguely familiar.

The boy smiled. "I like that rocket. I watch it every evening before I go to bed."

"Chance is going to live with me," Indiana said. "He'll start school next week."

"Good for you, Chance. Which school will it be?"

"We thought quite a while about it, and then we decided on Trinity," Indiana said.

"I went there through the fourth grade and liked it." Sky had never been associated with young children. They had always seemed to be aloof, disinterested and off somewhere in their own world. They made him feel awkward and aware of his age, but this one seemed to be different. Sky still wondered, though, why Indiana was giving such importance to their meeting.

"How old are you, Chance?"

"I'm just six, but I'm tall for my age."

"I suppose you'll be going in for sports."

"Oh yes. I've traveled quite a lot and every place we went I had tennis lessons. I haven't had a go with team games yet."

"Chance, tell Mr. Madison what you'd like to be when you grow up," suggested Indiana.

"I want to be President of the United States."

Sky smiled. "Then I hope I'm around to help you get elected,

Chance." He thought of himself for a moment and the opportunity he was about to throw away. "Sometime while you're here, Chance, I'll take you down to UBC and show you behind the scenes."

"Oh boy."

"Chance would like that and we'll try to arrange it, but now his dinner is ready and I think he's going to have to leave us."

Chance said good night to both of them politely. He's very bright and gets along easily with adults, Sky thought, as he watched the navy-blue blazer and the towheaded boy disappear. He turned to Indiana. "Nice kid, but what's he doing here?"

"I've just adopted him legally. He's my son, and I'm very happy."

"That's a surprise." He was seeing Indiana in a new light. "You've become a proud parent already, and I must say he seems like an exceptional kid."

"He is."

"But do you know anything about the parents?"

"Of course I do. Do you think I'd be so stupid as to get into something like this if I didn't know all about him?"

He looked puzzled, but kept silent.

"Oh Sky, how can you be so blind?"

"What do you mean?"

"Doesn't that face, the way he walks and even the way he looks at you, make you think of somebody you know very well?"

"I thought there was something familiar about the little fellow, but I haven't been able to place it."

"I didn't think I'd have to tell you, Sky. Chance is your son."

He set down his glass, and Indiana could see that his hand was trembling. "For God's sake, Indi, let's stop this melodrama right here. I have no son."

"He is also my grandson. Does that make it any more clear?"

Sky stared into space. It was several moments before he spoke. "Indiana, I'm terribly shaken." He got up and began pacing up and down the room. It didn't seem possible that the frenetic two nights in a Soho loft had produced the mature little boy who had just left the room. He stopped in front of her. "Isn't it possible that there's a mistake? Tania was married to a Haitian boy."

"Tania?"

"That's the name she was using when she picked me up. I had no idea she was Heather Hale until the night I was broadcasting the item and they flashed her photograph on the screen."

"She didn't tell me that."

"For God's sake, Indi, do you really believe that I would have got involved with Gage's daughter and yours if I'd known who she was?"

"I guess I was too angry to think, but she wrote me a nasty little note in which she told me about her affair with you, and her marriage to a homosexual painter."

Sky sat down on the sofa and put his face in his hands. "Why didn't you think of telling me all this six years ago instead of waiting until now?"

"There was a great deal of confusion, as there always is with anything that concerns Heather. She came here to have the baby so it could be an American citizen, and after that started roaming around Europe. I was determined not to have the child brought up like a gypsy."

"How did you get him?"

"Heather is now in California. She has married another artist and is pregnant again. She was more than willing to let me have Chance, especially since the new husband disliked her having a memento of her former life."

"Goddamn it. You've thrown a bomb at me as if you were happily tossing a tennis ball. It has hit me hard."

At that moment the maid came to the door and announced dinner. "Will you stay and have a light Sunday supper with me, Sky?"

"I won't stay, if you don't mind. I've got to go somewhere and think this out."

"Just as you like, of course."

She got up and followed him to the door and then came back to the library. The evening had been a total failure, she thought. Though Chance had already charmed him, she was sure Sky would hate her forever.

As he left the apartment building Sky turned toward Madison Avenue, where he hoped to find a bar. He was breathing hard and walking as fast as if he were escaping from a major disaster with which he couldn't cope.

It was Sunday night and no corner bars were open. Then he thought of the Westbury Hotel and went into the restaurant and sat down with a sigh of relief on one of the stools at the bar and ordered a scotch.

The bartender beamed, "Why, Mr. Madison. It's an honor to have you here."

"Thank you." He tried to smile but couldn't. He was totally unable to think until he felt the straight scotch beginning to warm his body. What he had wanted more than anything else in life had just been handed to him, but in the strangest, most ironic way. From the night of their marriage, he and Holly had talked of having a child, but Holly, who had seemed to him to be the personification of life and youth, was unable to bear one. He remembered the tears that followed what might or might not have been a miscarriage, the trips to different doctors, all the suggested remedies. She had desperately wanted to have an operation, but her grandfather was afraid the risk was too great.

"Another scotch," Sky said to the bartender. As Sky picked up the glass he began to wonder whether if the war and Bradshaw Green hadn't interfered, he and Indiana would have married and had a family. Visions of Indiana began racing through his mind. He remembered the first time he saw the little six-year-old brat on the *Île de France* and later as the debutante of the year who had fallen in love with him, head over heels. He had loved her, too, but it had all been young and casual. He had taken her for granted, just as at that age he had expected everything good to fall in his lap. If she had only waited for me after the war, instead of marrying Gage, our first kid would be almost twenty-five by this time. My God, I'm going to be an old father, he thought.

It was the first time he had accepted the fact that the little boy he had met an hour ago was his own flesh and blood, who had something in him of his own mother and father, of Gage, Indiana, Heather and ironically even Bradshaw Green. He tried to recall the child's face but could only remember that Indiana had said that Chance looked like him.

What a hell of a name Chance is, he thought, but after all, it did happen by chance. His mad craving for Tania had been the most violent emotion in his life, but it had come and gone like a disease.

He was about to order another drink when he felt a tap on his shoulder, and he swung around.

"You don't know me, Mr. Madison, but my wife and I recognized you right away and she wondered if you would autograph this menu for her," said the man in a plaid sports jacket, who was holding out a card for him to sign.

"Of course I will." He looked across the room at the woman, who was smiling and waving to him. He waved back and reached for his pen.

"We listen to you religiously," went on the man as he watched Sky sign his name on the menu. "Even Leroy, our little dog, recognizes your voice and barks and wags his tail each night when he hears it."

"I've heard a lot, but that's a new one," said Sky, trying to manage a smile. He paid his check and left the bar.

After Sky had gone, Indiana sat down on the library sofa. She picked up a magazine and began to leaf through it without reading the type or even looking at the pictures.

The maid came to the door. "Will you have your dinner now, Mrs. Hale?"

"I'm not hungry, Candida. Please tell the cook to hold it for a half hour or so."

As she went on turning the pages of the magazine she thought of the candlelit table set for one in the dining room. She could see endless years of solitary, candlelit tables stretching ahead of her. Why did I set my heart on this man the minute I saw him at the World's Fair and go on loving him for all this time, when he obviously doesn't care for me? I was a fool to think he would go into ecstasies when I brought him and his son together and that some of it would spill over on me. He may even try to take the child away. It will be a nasty court battle if he does.

She picked up the last drink he had poured for her and began finishing it automatically. Plenty of men have loved me, but I've never been able to return their love. Gage loved me and I should have loved him. He deserved it, but I didn't. He was kind, gentle, intelligent, all the nice qualities, but they didn't make any difference. I suppose it was because he didn't have the drive to get somewhere that I guess I got from my father. I was angry when he gave up and killed himself. I resented it. I couldn't even shed a tear and here I am ready to cry my eyes out over this son-of-a-bitch who has just walked out on me again.

She got up and started walking around the room and paused in front of the Picasso painting. If I'm honest with myself, I can't blame Heather for not finding me the perfect mother. When she was a baby, I used to look at her and wish that Sky was her father instead of Gage, and she must have felt it. The one thing I'm certain is that I will never see Sky Madison again.

The maid appeared at the door. "Mr. Madison has returned, Mrs. Hale."

She stood motionless for a moment and then went quickly to a Chinese mirror hanging over her desk. She saw that she needed lipstick but there was nothing she could do. "Send him in, Candida, and please set another place." And as an afterthought, "And tell the cook I'm ready."

Sky came in looking white and tired. "I'm still bewildered." He sat down. "And I'm half drunk on a couple of drinks at the Westbury bar."

"I'm glad you came back. I was just about to start supper. Please join me."

"I'd like to. I'm hungry as hell, too."

They sat down in the dining room and stared at each other across the small table, which was lighted by votive candles.

When the maid had brought in the first course and left the room, Sky said, "Of course, you realize that I must have my son, if he really is my son, and he must have my name."

"Like hell, you'll never get him from me. The adoption papers have been signed and he's no longer my grandson but my son."

"Since you've managed to convince me that he belongs to me, he must be Chance Madison, and as long as you've been involved with this since the beginning, why such a ridiculous name as Chance? It would have been kind of you to consult me."

"The boy's name is legally Chance Hale, though as far as I'm concerned you can throw in Schuyler or Madison for a middle name."

They were quiet while the maid was serving the lamb chops, the corn soufflé and the green salad. When she had gone back to the kitchen, Sky asked, "What is he going to call me?"

"Why don't you let him call you Skyrocket? He seems to like the name."

"What does he call you?"

"We haven't settled that yet, but he's not going to call me Granny, if that's what's worrying you."

They stared angrily at each other across the table, and Sky suddenly had the curious feeling that they were behaving like a married couple who had thoroughly explored each other's faults and snapped at each other almost for the enjoyment of it.

"Indi, it's going to take me a while to think this out thoroughly," he said.

"Take your time. It's not going to be as complicated as you think."

"We'll tell him the truth when he's older, won't we?"

"Of course, but think what it would do to your chances of getting to the White House if we said anything right now."

"Luckily I told you earlier in the evening that I was going to say no to all that."

"I wasn't sure you meant it."

They were silent for a moment. Then he said, "I'll tell you what."

She looked up at him. He was smiling. It was the same fabulous smile that she had almost forgotten, the one that had originally captivated her at the World's Fair. For the first time that evening she felt herself relaxing. "What?" she asked.

He was still smiling. "What do you say we leave the White House to Chance."

A Note on the Authors

Eugenia Sheppard needs no introduction to the millions of readers of her nationally syndicated society/fashion column. Earl Blackwell is founder and owner of Celebrity Service, with offices all over the world. Both authors live in New York City, and between them know everyone who's Anyone.